Somewhere

in

Hollywood

SOMEWHERE IN HOLLYWOOD

a novel

lisa czarina michaud

Barre Chord Press
Copyright © 2024 Lisa Czarina Michaud O'Rourke
Copyright © 2026 Barre Chord Press

Lyrics for "While I Have You" and "Swimming Pool Eyes"
written by Lisa Czarina Michaud O'Rourke
Copyright © 2024 Lisa Czarina Michaud O'Rourke

Library in Congress Control Number 2024908849

Cataloging-in-Publication data
Names: Michaud, Lisa Czarina, author.
Title: Somewhere in Hollywood / Lisa Czarina Michaud.
Description: Barre Chord Press, 2024-2025.
Identifiers: LCCN: 2024908849

ISBN [Daydream Edition Paperback] 978-1-7369445-6-1 [Daydream Edition eBook] 978-1-7369445-7-8 ASIN B0DKKNFDML [Daydream Edition Hardcover] 978-1-7369445-5-4 ISBN [Sunset Edition Paperback] 978-1-7369445-8-5 [Sunset Edition eBook] ASIN B0DKKNFDML ISBN [Hollywood Hotel Edition Paperback] 979-8-9951862-2-9 [Hollywood Hotel Edition eBook] 978-1-7369445-4-7 [Hollywood Hotel Edition Hardcover] 979-8-9951862-1-2

Subjects: LCSH Coming of age--Fiction. | Friendship--Fiction. | Hollywood (Los Angeles, Calif.)--Fiction. | Queer fiction. | BISAC FICTION / Coming of age | FICTION / LGBTQ+ / Bisexual | FICTION / Women | FICTION / Friendship | Classification: LCC PS3611 .I34 S66 2024 | DDC 813.6--dc23

Somewhere in Hollywood is a work of fiction. All characters, names, places, and events presented in this novel are products of the author's imagination and are used fictitiously. Any resemblance to events, places, or persons, living or dead, is purely coincidental.

*Daydream Edition Cover Art by Rita Lighthouse Illustrations and Layout by Michelle Trask
Sunset and Hollywood Hotel Edition Art by Lattice Rose Studios Paris*

Acclaim for Somewhere in Hollywood

"I loved every minute. A powerhouse. Blissfully character-driven. This is an author that deserves to be read." - *A Book Wanderer*

"Touching, fierce, romantic in a good way, sharp-witted [from] a very talented author. I loved everything about this." - *Book Mark!*

"A slow-burn queer coming-of-age story with a badass soundtrack. Written so vividly I could hear !!! [Chk Chk Chk] and smell the Pabst Blue Ribbon dripping off the page." - *Livre Le Rock* zine

"Characters [with] quirks…so well-developed."- *Redhead Reads*

"Cool world building [of L.A.] and music references." - *Abby Reads*

"Navigates the complexities of growth and connection [with] a poignant blend of humor and melancholy." - *The Bookish Hermit*

"Vivid and realistic, it played out like a movie." - *Titles with Tyler*

"Lyrically written. A beautiful story." – *Reads in the Wild*

"Illuminating prose…one for music lovers." - *TB Honest Book Reviews*

"I didn't want to punch these characters in the face, which is always a feature when reading fiction." - *Someone on the internet*

This is for my L.A. parents Terri and the late Dean Chaplin

I wouldn't have survived the jungle without you.

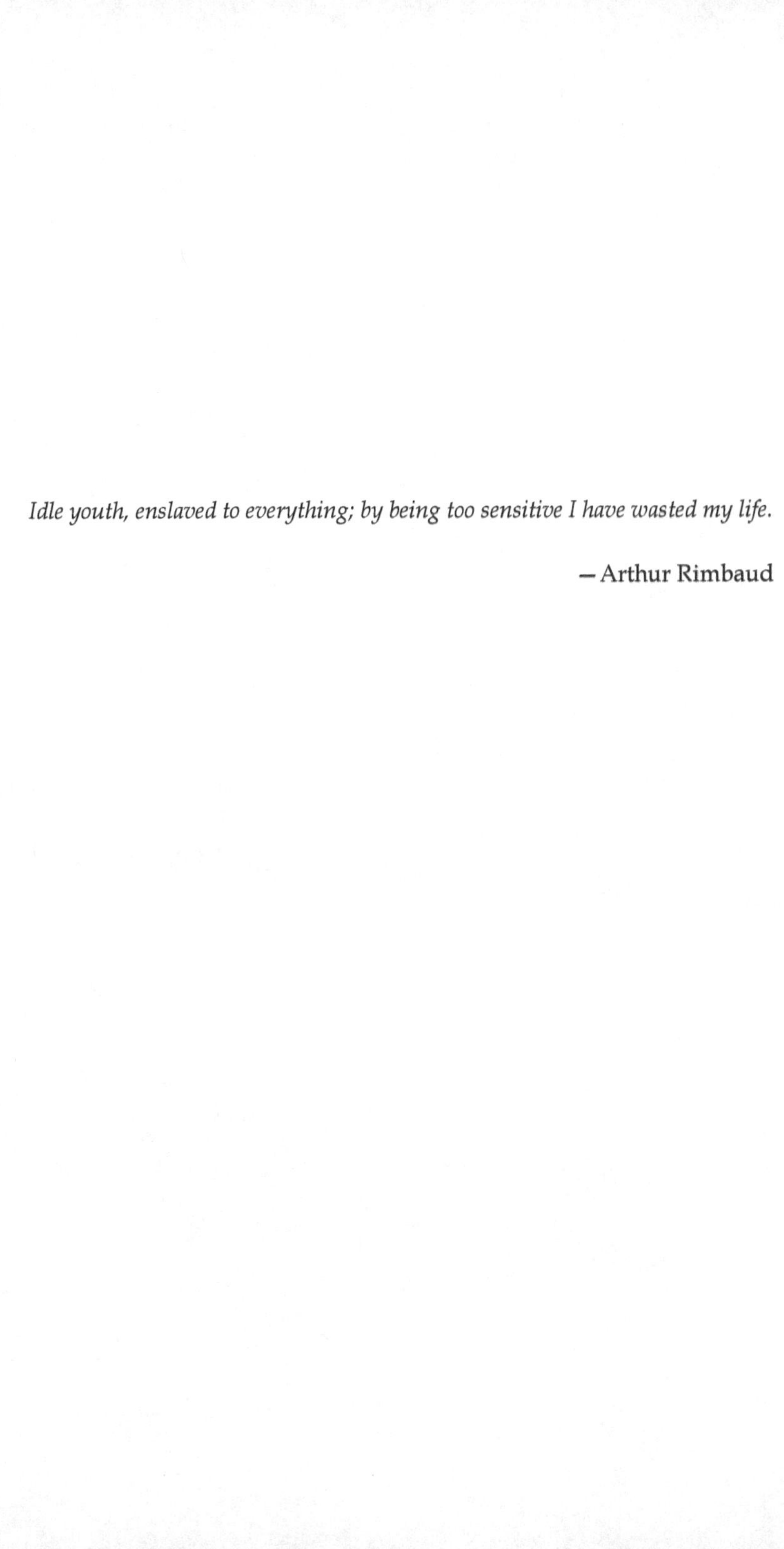

Idle youth, enslaved to everything; by being too sensitive I have wasted my life.

— Arthur Rimbaud

CHAPTER 1

Pete

I had to stop doing it. That thing where I measured my life in two columns: a *before* and an *after*. Yet, as I stood in the break room at work, which smelled like microwaved compost that morning, watching my espresso drip into the chipped mug, I found myself doing it again. The before column, though, was easy, filled with rite-of-passage moments like my first job, teenage sex back when I wondered why people weren't fucking all the time, and realizing my parents were actual people. Those moments moved forward in blocks of time and emotion that made sense. Then, a life-defining cross-country road trip with my best friend followed by a sudden move here, to a strange, new land, promised continuous forward motion where each year was supposed to outdo the previous. It was exciting and mysterious, and the weather wasn't half bad.

But now, two years later, I was festering in my *after*, like an idiot waiting for something to happen.

With my coffee, I left the breakroom, heading towards music you'd hear at Walgreen's, stoned at ten o'clock at night to get shaving cream and strawberry Mentos. The music and the scent of the celebrity-branded perfume that got stronger with each step meant our temp Victoria was in. She sat across from me and exclusively listened to music I could only describe as unreasonable. Top 40 hits, with her argument being that if it played on the radio, it was obviously good. I'd trained myself to tune out both her music and opinions, but when she played songs with titles like, "Your Body is a Wonderland" and looked at me with the sinister eyes of a little sister, I knew she took delicious pleasure in my sonic misery. I got to my desk and as predicted, I found her eyes peeking over the computer, salivating for a reaction. With every cringey lyric using words like bubble gum and candy to describe parts of a woman's body, her eyes said, *I can wait.* But I remained indifferent as I pulled my chair out only to find her stuff bleeding over to my side of the desk. Bright magazines with unflattering candid shots of famous faces, and flashy headlines celebrating their misfortune, all while abusing exclamations points. Divorce shocker! DUI scandal! Scary Skinny! Cocaine!

"Here," I said, handing her the magazines over our computers. "Take your porn."

"Porn," she balked. "You might actually learn something."

"Learn something?" I curled my lip at the idea.

She momentarily lost interest in me as she looked at her computer before gasping at something. I chose to ignore it as I focused on the digital hourglass making tiny somersaults on my screen, knowing her distraction was only short-lived.

"Well, Mr. Know-It-All," she said, her eyes popping back over our computers. "I bet you didn't know that Britney Spears got married this weekend. It literally just dropped on Perez Hilton."

Literally.

I placed my eyes on her. "You know I hate the internet, Victoria," I stated plainly, "so you know you are correct in saying I didn't know that."

As I tuned out the details of Madame Spears's nuptials, I pulled out a biography of French punk poet Arthur Rimbaud from my backpack to root myself to my interests, as well as to protect myself from the pop culture satire that was hemorrhaging into my life.

"Don't you want to know who she married?" she asked, reminding me that I was still participating in the conversation.

"I really don't."

"Peter!"

"What?" I shuddered, jolted by her burst of emotion.

"You have no interest," she accused.

"I don't," I confirmed.

"Well, you have to have *some* sort of comment," she said in muffled outrage. "Britney Spears is a national treasure. Like, what's wrong with you?"

I closed my eyes for a few seconds in a futile attempt to make the conversation go away.

"Well?" she pressed.

"Fine." I let out a sigh as I opened my eyes. "My official statement is 'Who cares?'."

"*Everyone* cares, Peter."

"Everyone," I scoffed. "Meanwhile our country invaded Iraq and is run by unelected war criminals, but, you know, Britney Spears eloped this weekend."

"Oh, God." Her expression twisted in agony. "You're not going to make me listen to "War Pigs" again, are you?"

"No," I grumbled, even if I thought the lyrics to the Sabbath song were eerily fitting for the times.

"Good." She perked up. "Besides, you know I don't follow politics."

"Politics?" I said incredulously. "It's just what's happening beyond Beverly Hills."

"So is this!" she declared. "She married Jason Alexander in *Vegas*."

My eyebrows furrowed for a second. "She married George from *Seinfeld*?"

"Huh?"

"Never mind," I muttered, dropping my head in resignation until I heard the familiar clicks and cracks of my computer, which meant it was ready for me.

Since the office was reopening after a two-week Christmas break, a hundred and sixty-seven emails were waiting in my inbox, and I figured anything was better than talking tabloids with Victoria. Let's see who missed me. I scanned the list, quickly deleting any debris that cluttered my inbox.

An LVMH winter sample sale, which I dragged to my personal folder. *Merci*, Agnes from HR.

I was copied on a conference call about the budget with the Paris office who, as a side note, thought the L.A. office was lazy and incompetent. Nope. Not for me. Delete.

The Paris office approved the basic winter events calendars that I designed on PowerPoint, and they were ready to print and go out by the end of the week. Noted.

A proud announcement of the school's new website that I knew included the embarrassing staff photos we were all required to pose for. As I clicked on the provided link, I recalled that day when the school hired a photographer to take "staff candids". I managed to avoid him before the fucker ambushed me at my desk, wearing the headset I sometimes wore to avoid craning my neck. With dead eyes, I looked at the photo of myself captioned by full name and job title. A part of me, I suppose, had to feel proud that I had made it to 2004 without leaving a trace on the Internet while also wincing that my debut was a photo of me looking like a 1-800-MATTRESS customer service representative.

I clicked out and moved on to the next e-mail.

The toilets overflowing with fecal matter in the fourth-floor bathroom. Finally. An email for me.

As I added calling the plumber to my mental to-do list, the phone rang.

"First call of the new year," Victoria announced, like this was exciting news.

I forced my office administrator smile that my business card boasted I was and took a deep breath to start an exciting new year.

"Bonjour, Institut Français?"

Carla

It stopped. Oh, thank God, it stopped.

The *thud, thud, thud,* or was it the *untz, untz, untz?* It went back and forth. Either way, they were both awful and pounded against my skull like that morning's hangover, making me question why I was still putting myself through this. After hearing the terrible song for the tenth time, which implicated women as whores with some sampling melody that sounded vaguely familiar, I'd had enough. Songs like this made me feel old because I didn't get it. Feeling way outside of my age demographic, I looked at a girl who had been mouthing the lyrics, happy in her sideways trucker cap. Next to her was another girl, also pleased with the music wearing a pair of low-rise Frankie B. jeans so low my Italian-girl origins would require a full-on bikini wax to wear.

In a fingerprint-spotted mirror, I regretfully caught my reflection. My voucher stated my role as GIRL IN CLUB, while the give-it-to-me-baby red cocktail dress provided by Wardrobe was more MAIL ORDER BRIDE. My boobs weighed the fabric down, which forced the rhinestone straps to dig into my shoulder and chafed my pale skin into a shade of pinkish violet. The flickering neon lights cast an odd glow, reflecting the strangeness of the moment. The prop manager completed the oddity, walking around with a pitcher to fill empty martini glasses with a drink the same color as my rash. The wardrobe people snapped digital photos and fixed clothing details that no one would ever notice.

Just then, all went silent as the crew scurried to the sides when the director yelled, "Rolling!" signaling the start of filming. Then came "Playback!" to start the music for the scene, and finally "Background!" which was my cue to start dancing until the director was satisfied we were all in sync. The music would then stop to leave audio space for the actors' lines, while the extras continued to dance without sound, which felt like some kind of sick social experiment. The director then shouted "Action!" where the actors sprang to life, many of them looking relieved to not be dancing without music. It was always at this moment that I felt it the most, the undeniable realization that I was an extra in someone else's dream, the background to someone else's story.

Welcome to Hollywood. What's your dream?

Not this.

CHAPTER 2

Carla

I stood on line at the wardrobe trailer with the red cocktail dress draped over my arm. I inched forward wearing my street clothes, ready to exchange the dress for my paycheck voucher.

"Long day," the girl in front of me said.

"Yeah," I agreed, offering a noncommittal nod.

"At least the music was good."

I forced a smile.

The wardrobe assistant took my dress with two fingers as if it were a biohazard and dropped it in a canvas laundry basket. She handed me my voucher, concluding my day of fake dancing at a closed-down strip club on Pico called Wiggles 2 for a whopping 54 bucks.

I walked back to my used Volvo, which I imagined was once a luxury car since it had fancy things like seat heaters. As I pulled out of the lot and joined the city's famed traffic, I popped X's *Los Angeles* album into my Discman just in case I'd forgotten where I was. I crawled forward, knowing I had miles of taillights before turning into my neighborhood. The high pitch of my tired brake pads announced every inch of the route home while reminding me I was too broke to fix them.

Eventually, I turned onto Sanborn Avenue, located on the bohemian end of Sunset Boulevard, and began my search for a parking spot. I passed bungalows and small apartment complexes, cautious of neighborhood cats as the street's overgrown tropical flora swept across my windshield like a car wash brush. I pulled into a spot just as a car was leaving, right in front of my four-story building. Growing up watching TV shows based in California, I had a preconceived idea of what apartment buildings here should look like, and this wasn't it. For one, we didn't have a pool in the middle, like the one in *Melrose Place*, so no pushing boyfriend-stealers into it. There wasn't a gym. No outdoor hallways. No air conditioning. But, we had Barbie, our building manager. Barbie was a former Zeppelin groupie with hair as red as a White Stripes album and as high as Courtney Love in the 90s. Despite Barbie growing up in L.A, her alabaster skin hinted that it had never seen the sun, thanks to the black beekeeper's veil she had worn for most of her 20s and 30s.

"There she is," she sang out from behind her desk in the building's management office. "She's a native New Yorker!"

"I'm from Long Island," I reminded her as I did every time she sang the disco song I only knew from her singing it to me. "It's not the same thing. Trust me."

"Close enough for me."

I slumped down into the seat facing her desk, letting my work duffle bag plop onto my lap. Through her cat-eyed glasses, she gave me a once-over before gesturing to the tiger print sweater I had on.

"That top looks good on you," she said. "Keep it."

"Thanks." I looked down at it. "I tried to get them to let me wear it for the scene, but I ended up wearing a piece of fabric they called a dress."

"Welcome to Hollywood, baby." She lightly shimmied her shoulders, causing her stacked jewelry to jingle. "But you should wear more stuff like that."

"More animal print?" I crossed my arms over my chest.

Noticing my guarded stance, she said, "You know, women in this town pay big money for those." She pointed her pen at me. "They're so perfect, they actually look expensive."

"I don't look like I make enough money to afford fake boobs. Good thing I don't mind being invisible."

She cocked her head to the side. "Says the Movie Extra."

"Yeah," I said, sounding like the wise ass teen I never got a chance to be. "Like I said, invisible."

"You know, I saw you on T.V. last week, and your hair took up half the goddamn scene, so you can't be that invisible."

"That's not why I have the job." I rolled my eyes, noticing her lips pursed to show she wasn't buying it. "Seriously," I laughed nervously, "I couldn't get any other job here. You need, like, ten years of experience, plus references and a master's in hospitality just to serve coffee."

I thought back on all the restaurants, cafés, and bakeries I went to only to have the managers place my résumé onto a pile of others that had headshots attached. "And you know I don't give a toot about acting."

"You give a toot about music." She shot me an accusatory look. "At least you used to."

"I don't have time for music." I sighed, which blew my bangs up.

"Well, all I'm saying is no one moves to L.A. for fun. That's for damn sure." Her office chair then let out a loud squeak as she leaned back to look out the window. With the pen, she moved the vertical blinds to the side as a blue pickup truck passed. "I thought that'd be Kurt. What time is it?"

I consulted her digital clock radio. "Six twenty-eight."

"He should be home any second now," she mumbled.

"Parking *was* a little tight," I informed her with a regretful face. "Why don't you guys use the garage? The truck will fit."

"You know Kurt's tools take up half the damn space, but he'll find a spot," she said with confidence. "He manages to get home every night and then I wish he would go back to work already!" She laughed to herself before taking on a more deliberate tone. "Do me a favor, honey, and don't get married."

"Married?" I tried to imagine something so permanently in my favor. "I'm flattered that my cat likes me."

"Speaking of…" she tapped her pen against the desk in a matronly way, "your little girl dug up all of Salvador's zucchini seeds out back. Kicked up dirt all over the damn place and I had to replant them all myself!"

"Sorry," I said tightly on behalf of my sassy cat.

Then, with a tired smile that indicated she'd reached her chitchat threshold, Barbie collected the papers from her desk to close out her day.

"See you tomorrow?" I said, standing up.

"I'll be here."

Letting myself into my apartment, I hit the lights, bringing life to the walls painted a color called A MIDSUMMER NIGHT'S GREEN. I relaxed my shoulders, feeling at home surrounded by my found objects, thrift-store scores, and framed reprints of images that provided me with a false sense of sophistication: an old *New Yorker* cover in a bent gold frame, early 1960s fashion illustrations of dresses that I wished were still in style, a vintage ad for Campari. The smell of second-hand books and used record sleeves comforted me, giving the space a lived-in warmth I was proud to call my own. A candle on its last burn, my unmade bed, a 20-dollar folk guitar that never stayed in tune, a pink rotary phone with a mismatched red cord — artifacts of a quiet life. At first, living on my own made me feel like a baby tossed into the deep end of a pool. Unexpected lessons came up, like buying things that seemed like they came with the house I grew up in like toilet paper, Windex, salt, *spoons*. Through my window, I could hear my neighbor, whom I'd heard having sex the night before, now on the phone with her mom. As I let out a sigh to dispel the day, there was a knock at the door.

"It's open!" I called out.

The door opened and my eyes fell on him. Wearing his office attire that I admit made me smile, he held my black cat.

"Hi, honey, I'm home," he said, smiling like he meant it.

"Hi, Pete."

Pete

Los Angeles. Where do I begin?

Living inside a Red Hot Chili Pepper lyric would *not* have been my first choice. From having to get around in a car to the bagels that crumbled like sand in my mouth, it seemed like an unlikely fit for me. My family back home, of course, didn't help matters. My French grandmother feared I would join a cult. My buddy Tony left messages asking how Paris Hilton was, which triggered my PTSD from the time she opened her car door on Robertson, and I almost flipped over it on my bike. (To be honest, I thought it was Angelyne.) My dad worried about the bread situation, in which I told him there was no situation since the entire city was "no carb." My mom asked about getting "punk'd" by Ashton, a sentence, I needed Victoria to translate for me.

Carla and I found ourselves at the epicenter of reality-TV culture but might as well have lived on an entirely different planet. In a city of superstars and serial killers, where glamor met grime, and poverty rubbed elbows with exaggerated prosperity seen in douche-mobiles like the Hummer Limo, we found ourselves somewhere in between. With two studio apartments facing each other, we had space to think. Perhaps too much space.

Before taking a seat on the lumpy side of her couch, I handed her Joni before reaching for the folk guitar, wondering why she even bothered with it. She had a gorgeous vintage Telecaster guitar, but she kept it stashed away in her kitchen as a relic of her past—*our past*. As I twisted the pegs on the guitar, knowing it was only a matter of minutes before it would go back to its nightmare tuning, I avoided the real issue, pretending the cheap guitar was the problem here. In between us the cat rolled onto her back, as Carla fawned over her, oohing and ahhing as she did cat things.

"Do cats know they're cute?" Carla inquired, scratching under Joni's arms raised like a winning gold medalist. "Like, are they aware of their power over us?"

"They just might," I answered, recognizing it as a typical Carla question.

My eyes lowered in a deep appreciation of her. Looking at her, this dear ethereal being whose curiosity I knew kept her up at night and felt things deeper than most people I knew.

"How was work?" I asked, with one ear angled towards the guitar, testing the sound of the strings.

She pointed to her dolled-up face. "Like this." She glanced at my work attire. "You?"

I shrugged my shoulders. "Like this."

I looked at the guitar, satisfied I had tuned it to its full potential and began to pluck a simple arpeggio. As the gentle notes came to life, my thoughts drifted to how life had crept up on us. With every rent check signed and grocery schlep home, we didn't seem any wiser. I wondered if we'd ever have anything to show for it other than thrift store art, jobs we sleepwalked through and the glory of saying we had moved cross-country. My French half saw no purpose in seeking intangible concepts like happiness, while my American side craved for conclusions and happy endings.

I glanced at her, my best friend, before quickly looking away. Carla and I went to high school together but found each other after. We spent the first year of our friendship wondering why weren't friends as teenagers, knowing the answer was social politics. She was seen as "weird", and I was the "cool" stoner kid who spoke French. Our paths never crossed except for a random class we were in together where I never had the courage to tell her that I thought she was cooler than any of the assholes in our school. But we eventually found each other and moved here from our hometown on Long Island for music, not realizing that was a pretext for something. What exactly? I wasn't sure but at least we had our adult lives to make up for the lost teenage years.

My eyes then wandered to her unmade bed.

Then there was that. The constant reminder that we weren't in it. But a physical exploration of our friendship would've meant defining it, which was too tricky. Well, at least for a Monday night. I didn't know where we stood but I did know that over the course of these past few years, if we'd have gone anywhere near that island of uncertainty, then I was pretty sure we would be sitting there as each other's exes.

Or worse, not sitting next to each other at all.

CHAPTER 3

Carla

I felt wetness on the tip of my nose. My senses then felt the weight of her paws, feeling like tiny black ink pads pressing into my chest. There was the thundering of short purrs as I breathed in particles of fur, my nostrils toying with the idea of sneezing. With a mouth that felt like I had eaten cotton balls for dinner, I opened my eyes to see it was only 7:05 a.m.; two hours before my scheduled alarm. "Thanks a lot," I muttered as I patted the top of her head.

Dragging myself out of bed, Joni followed eagerly, nearly tripping me as I stepped over my inside-out jeans on the floor. In the kitchen, I avoided eye contact with the empty bottle of wine on the counter and sprinkled the cat's dish with dry food. As Joni crunched her fish-flavored kibble, I leaned against the tiled counter with a glass of water, listening to the upstairs neighbor's *Morning Becomes Eclectic* clashing with the beeps from garbage truck out front and the neighbor above Pete who we were pretty sure only listened to Wilco.

While my coffee maker slowly dripped into the pot, I slid over to my kitchen table where I kept the laptop Pete had lent me from his office. I stared out the window, as the modem screeched like nails on a chalkboard before AOL loudly announced that I had mail. Clicking on the icon, I began my habit of deleting most of the messages in the inbox, starting with a chain letter from one of my brother's friends threatening bad luck if I didn't forward it to ten people I didn't even know. Next was an e-mail from MAILER-DAEMON bouncing back the application for a barista job at Studio City Coffee Shop due to a misspelled email address. When I saw that I typed *Sudio* instead of *Studio*, I laughed, thinking about the Phil Collins song before opening the next from my best friend, Alex.

"Check it out!" were the only words she wrote, which included a link directing me to a website called *Flash Harper*. Clicking on it, the site featured Manhattan party photos, but not the glitzy Tribeca Film Festival kind but dirty, overexposed snapshots of young faces wearing bright colors. In the pictures people were seen making out, sucking on cans of backyard-brand beer, seeming unburdened by their inner dialogue I was beginning to think only I had. With spun-out eyes, the guys wore close-fitting T-shirts with ironic sayings, and girls wore neon plastic hoop earrings and colored eyeshadow. I scanned the pops of color until I found my best friend with her blonde eyelashes tinted turquoise, wearing a matching leotard I recognized as her mom's from the '80s. I admired the way Alex settled into her twenties with a job she could grow into and new friends she posed with in pictures. I turned to my fridge that contained the photo documentation of my life. Four Polaroids that Pete and I took using Barbie's old camera we didn't think had film, which explained the first photo: a close-up of Pete in a relaxed state with soft eyes and ever softer lips. Even in the unflattering flash, his eyes resisted the perils of an unexpected photo ambush and instead, remained true to their natural honey color like the wings of a monarch butterfly. They invited me in but only to a point. In spite of this — or perhaps because of it — it was his most beautiful picture. I moved onto the others: the one of him in his beloved Mets cap holding his hand out for me to wait before taking the picture; one we tried to get the two of us in with half of his face cut off; and one of just me in my kitchen wearing a sweater he had knit for me that I always lingered on. Discovering that he knitted was how I learned that he had this secretive side. After walking in on him in the act — a real sting operation — of making what he explained was a popcorn stitch beanie, I couldn't shake the feeling that it was an odd thing to keep from me. If he was secretive about something as meditative and sweet as knitting, it made me wonder what else he was hiding.

My hangover then conjured up unwanted thoughts, reminding me of my expectations when we moved here. In the walk-in pantry was where I stored my electric guitar. The orange Telecaster, once a symbol of our synergy when we'd get lost in the music, lost in each other, now felt heavy with broken promises. I avoided it fearing the smooth orange lacquer would feel like holding onto the past. Its bright, sharp tone would be a representation of my faded optimism, the sustain would remind me of lingering glances and the guitar's signature twang, a conversation when I told him I thought the word was ugly.

We came out here to give our band a shot, and after one show, I let the weeks stretch into months and then years, with neither the band nor *us* happening. I thought we would, at worst, be best friends, or at best, be in love. But we had plateaued, suspended in this weird space of no longer bandmates, more than friends but hardly lovers and I could never tell whose fault it was. My default was to blame myself and as easy as that would have been, I couldn't because he had changed. Things were different. And I knew I could never bring it up because how could I blame someone for not loving me?

Pete

Ten minutes before my alarm was due to go off, I found myself awake. It was Tuesday, garbage day. Through the cracked-open window, I could hear the truck backing up, its mechanics hissing and roaring like a beast. The night before, I had stayed up working on music, smoked a spliff, and even managed to mend a moth hole in a sweater before exhaustion took hold.

Outside, Barbie's voice resonated upward as she conversed with the garbage men, while my upstairs neighbor indulged in his favorite band Wilco. He went through phases of the band's catalog, hinting at his emotional discord with last week's "I Am Trying to Break Your Heart" playing on loop, making me wonder if I should have knocked on his door to see if he was okay.

That morning, however, he was enjoying the rest of *Yankee Hotel Foxtrot*, letting the album play through which I silently cheered for. Lingering in bed longer, I absorbed the familiar sounds of the neighborhood as my focus became distant while mindlessly playing with my half-erection. Out my window, the Greater Los Angeles area greeted me with yet another sunny day. Endless blue skies slashed with cloud formations that a dude with a beard braid on Venice Beach once told me was part of a top-secret government project to control the minds of the

American people. He cautioned me to remember our conversation twenty years from now, which I couldn't help but chuckle at as I could barely remember the week before. But that guy and whatever else I feared happening to all of us was the last thing I wanted occupying my thoughts with as I woke up. So, I listened to the birds. They seemed to have had it all figured it out, I thought as my mind's focus blurred into oblivion.

I took a few long deep breaths to exhale negative thinking before fully reaching down to let my mind drift, searching for the right person to…*spend time with*. My inner eye saw the tatted-up blonde with the side-swept bangs at the Coffee Bean on Hillhurst. There was our UPS guy in the summer when he wore those tight shorts. The banker at WaMu who was way too hot to work at a bank. And of course, Carla. They all worked as distractions to my celibate California life — two words that felt in opposition to each other. As I felt myself getting firm in my hands thinking of Carla without a shirt on, a mystery figure joined the mental tableau to complete the fantasy that always brought me home. I closed my eyes, thinking of this person I had never met. He was muscular, which was something I didn't find myself attracted to in real life. He was also suntanned, which I think was this place rubbing off on me. He had hair long enough to pull, and I liked picturing him behind me while I had Carla under me. I imagined our three bodies moving in one wave as I took on both passive and active sexual roles. The imagery of our three-person tango became more vivid, as I mumbled obscenities and my focus alternated between her and him until I released, feeling the warmth fill my hands and my heart pounding from the exertion. I lay there for several long moments, feeling satisfied but still grumpy. As I regained my breath, I wondered how long I could go on like this.

Back in my work clothes, I descended the building stairs, passing two feline commuters making their way to the backyard. I admit to actually saying hello to them as their collar bells jingled in response. After unlocking my bike from the building's rack, I dipped my head into Barbie's office.

"Oh, hey Peter," she muttered in her usual hurried and exhausted voice as she shifted a pile of papers from one side of her desk to another. "Do you want today's paper? I have it here somewhere."

"Sure, but don't you want to read it first?" I stepped into her office. "I can just grab it tonight."

"I can't take any more bad news." She shook her head, as if rejecting both the information and probably the *Times* for delivering it. "Also, I have a letter for you. What's-her-face up in 202 got it." She continued shuffling the papers around. "Now where is the darn thing? I just had it."

I watched as she opened and closed drawers, getting more flustered by the second. "Here it is!" she announced, holding it up triumphantly. "And it's from Par-ee!" Her regard became fanciful and a little impressed, like it always did when I got something from France. "Must be from a certain cousin Guy and," she snapped a painted fingernail on it, "it feels like a card. It's not your birthday yet." She thought for a second. "Or is it?"

"Not until July." I reached over her desk for it. "It must be a New Years card."

"A New Years card?" She pressed her eyebrows together. "I've never heard of that."

"A *carte des voeux*, they're sent out after the holiday just wishing you a happy new year," I explained. "Same concept as a Christmas card but sent after the holidays."

"Well, that's different." She seemed to appreciate learning something new. "But I just think it's wonderful that you and your cousin write each other letters. It's so old-world European."

"Yeah." I slapped the letter against my palm, as I took note of my cousin's Parisian private school penmanship. "I don't always want to know what's in these letters," I mumbled before regulating to a friendlier tone. "But thanks, Barbie."

"You got it," she said. "Also, I have some tomatoes from the back for you. Nice and ripe too. I know you'll put them to good use, so I'll leave them in a bag on your doorknob."

"Thanks." I slipped the letter into my backpack. "Seriously, what would any of us do without you here?"

"You'd buy your own goddamn tomatoes!"

I chuckled in appreciation of her directness I felt the town didn't provide me with enough of. I looked around her office for a moment, as the morning light poured through the window, illuminating her hair that stood up like cotton candy. An early Stones song — "Get Off of My Cloud", I believe — puttered out from the dusty digital clock radio. The air smelled like a mix of a freshly lit Pall Mall and her hazelnut coffee as she took a long sip from a mug that said NO ONE ASKED YOU.

Over her long cigarette, curls of smoke circled as she studied me. "Long night?"

"Long life." I circled my neck, hearing the snaps and cracks.

"Already?" She raised an eyebrow. "You know you have a few more years to go, right?"

"God willing."

"But even in your morning malaise, you're still cute as a button."

"Thank you," I replied, starting to get embarrassed. "I guess that solves everything, right?"

"Your dimples seem to agree," she said, which probably deepened them as her eyes dripped down to my sleeveless sweater. "How many of those do you have?"

"As many as Goodwill can supply me with." I lightly pulled at it. "They're good for riding my bike. My underarms get too hot with long-sleeved sweaters."

"Those dress pants aren't Goodwill," she stated, appraising them. "Or that dress shirt. They fit your trim figure too perfectly."

Blushing at the attention, I slid my hand through my hair before sheepishly admitting that they were not from Goodwill. Far from it, in fact. The pants were Céline and the white dress shirt, Dior Homme, which made me feel like a total tool.

"Access to fashion sample sales is one of my work benefits," I explained, feeling the guilt on my face as if I had stolen the clothes. "And even with the cost of the tailor, the price is still less than wholesale, so I stock up on work clothes… it's embarrassing though when you think of the retail cost of a piece of fabric."

"Well, you look sharp," she asserted as if fact before returning focus to her paperwork. "Like Howard Hughes, but let's hope you're not as crazy as he was." Her eyes popped as if she seemed to have remembered something. "Oh, my sister wanted me to tell you that she and Mike took the van out for a drive. It needs that every few months, you know."

"Right." I felt the guilt of her sister in the Valley maintaining our defunct band's van. "We should probably get it out of their garage soon." Sell it, I wanted to add.

"Oh, she's fine with you kids keeping it in there. After all, you are letting her husband use that beautiful drum kit of yours, so I say it's an even exchange." She thought about it for a second. "Well, maybe not so much for my sister. Mike can't play for shit."

I thought about my tangerine sparkle Gretsch and mourned for something that used to be a part of my creative identity. My drums were my everything but were now relics of my yesteryear. Just as I was about to wish Barbie a good day, her cordless phone stopped me. As it rang, she looked at it wearily like the inconvenience it was, before picking it up.

"Sanborn Management," she answered in her smoke-stained voice. "No." Barbie's shoulders dropped with fatigue. "Let me stop you right there." She held a hand up as if the caller could see her. "You're looking for the Deepak Chopra Enlightenment Center, aren't you? You've called the wrong number. I know… our numbers are very similar, but it's not us. Good day now… bye bye."

After hanging up, she found my eyes begging for an explanation. "I get at least two of those a week," she explained. "Our numbers are just one digit apart from the spiritual guru."

"Take advantage. Tell them Deepak is no longer taking disciples and then start your own shit."

"I don't think they'd want my brand of enlightenment."

"It would probably be better than the hocus pocus shit that sells around here," I huffed, thinking about all the gurus and meditation centers that promised inner peace at premium prices.

"That's L.A. for you. Everyone's trying to find themselves, usually on the big screen, and when that doesn't happen, they settle for enlightenment in drawstring pants. It's what makes us unique here. But you know, back in my day, I preferred the drugs. At least they were honest about ripping you off to feel good."

"Good point," I replied, sharing a chuckle with her. "But you know, I think I'm too broke for enlightenment. I find confusion and emotional distress more in my budget."

"Confusion?" She gave me a sideway glance. "What do you have to be confused about?"

"Everything?" I said. "But maybe I'm just spending too much time in my daydreams. It gets comfortable in there."

"Well, now you sound like Miss Bangs." Her eyes flitted to the ceiling as I smiled at her nickname for Carla. "But you're still young," she continued, "and I don't worry so much about you. I know you'll figure it out." Her eyes brightened. "And if you don't, there's always the—"

"Deepak Chopra Enlightenment Center?"

"I have the number if you need it."

CHAPTER 4

Pete

Outside the apartment building, standing with my bike balancing between my legs, I slipped on my headphones and flipped my tape to side A.

So. Okay. It was 2004, why the fuck was I still listening to cassettes? Because I was ironic and hip, with my reasons steeped in pure aesthetics.

I'm totally kidding.

No, because CDs skipped every time the bike rolled over uneven pavement, or a pothole and I couldn't afford an iPod. So, instead, I made compilation tapes pieced together from my vinyl collection, which would always feel more satisfying than a digital playlist.

I took a whiff of the carbon-fueled air, noticing a low layer of smog haunting the horizon and pressed play. My morning commute kicked off with the reggae-inspired syncopation of "Estimated Prophet" by The Grateful Dead. The song's themes addressed ideas of grandeur while grappling with isolation and skepticism in a sunny setting. "California," the chorus sang, sounding like both a warning and a promise. As I reached Vermont Avenue, the distant and deranged opening notes of "This Town Ain't Big Enough for the Both of Us" by legendary L.A. band Sparks took over. I passed gated storefronts and doctor's clinics, when my gaze landed on a new street art mural, the wet paint still glistening. This one depicted a crazed, balding politician with dollar signs for eyes perched atop an army tank. Stenciled beneath were the words HOMELAND SECURITY, portraying the brewing sense of unease so many of us felt, wondering where exactly we were heading with all of this. The anxiety mixed with the song's theatrical urgency propelled me forward, cranking my commute into high gear. I stayed mindful of cars inching past as I then breezed through Bukowski's Hollywood. I rode past the liquor stores, and lower-rent apartment buildings, coasting under the skinny, thirsty-looking palm trees that lined this side of town. With their dried-out husks hanging like burnt hula skirts, they loomed like a cautionary tale of how this city could leave you out to dry. Short buildings displayed billboards in Spanish for auto insurance and dance radio stations. I noticed a new one for the indie dance-punk band Click Track, surely targeting hipster assholes like me who were responsible for the neighborhood's gentrification and rent hikes.

If I was making good time, TV on the Radio's "Young Liars" owned the stretch between Normandie and Vine. I always raised the volume on this song that somehow made loneliness and fear sound sexy. New music didn't easily move me, but it still happened, with this band's debut EP sending chills down my arm the first time I heard it. It gave me hope for the future of music I knew I should have been contributing to.

Crossing into the acidic belly of Hollywood, with its dead-eyed billboards made "Hungry Freaks, Daddy" by The Mothers of Invention a fitting choice. But if this song kicked in on, say, Seward Street, that meant I had to pick up the pace to make sure Captain Beefheart's "Electricity" contrasted the listless, hungover end of East Hollywood. I passed the steam-dripped windows of donut shops and unlit neon cocktail signs that probably saw a thing or two the night before.

The cassette auto-flipped to Radiohead as I entered the bright colors and clean sidewalks of West Hollywood. I cut across the intersection at La Cienega, coasting under the waving rainbow flags, as I tightened my grip on the curled handlebars. Here, surrounded by symbols of acceptance and freedom, I felt like an impostor as I questioned my place in this world of pride, wondering if I deserved to claim it. I admired figures like Jack Kerouac, Arthur Rimbaud, James Dean, and Mick Jagger, all rumored to be bisexual, depending on which biography you read. Yet, in more modern times, I found myself with no contemporary heroes, and fearing rejection from both sides for accusing me of being indecisive, promiscuous, not gay enough, not straight enough, or worse, simply *dabbling*. Even music, my refuge, my safe space, seemed to betray me as the lyrics of "In Limbo," both challenged and comforted me. Thank you, Mr. Thom Yorke, for singing about being on my side while also accusing me of living in a fantasy. But was it really a fantasy if it was purely avoidance?

At Doheny, the calypso jaunt of Ween's "Bananas and Blow" saved the day with some comedic relief as I entered the toned arms of Beverly Hills. The song bounced along in its steel drum and flamenco guitar glory as I cruised under healthy, lush, palm trees, manicured lawns, and shops that sold, like, two things. The existentialism of "Ego Tripping at the Gates of Hell" by the Flaming Lips made me reflective again until the scrappy acoustic minimalism of Animal Collective's "Two Corvettes" cleansed my emotional palate, polishing off the commute.

Taking my headphones off and approaching my office, I let out a sigh, feeling like I had already lived the most interesting part of my day.

Carla

If my job as a movie extra consisted of doing nothing, then that day I was exploring my role to its theatrical capacity by playing PERSON IN COMA. I sat up in the hospital bed in a loose-fitting gown as the crew set up the shot around me. The prop department taped a long, skinny tube to my forearm and then debated whether to place a bouquet on my nightstand. The question was if people in comas actually received flowers, and would the bright colors take attention away from the speaking roles in the next bed? The makeup people dusted white powder on my cheeks, while the hair people complained about my bangs—did people in comas have them? The question lingered with long stares before they decided not to risk it by pinning them to the side.

"For the scene," the assistant director coached me, "just keep your eyes closed, okay?"

"Okay," I replied.

At lunch, I picked at soggy vegetables but decent chicken, sitting with the other extras at our assigned table. As I moved my food around, I listened as they talked about which shows were booking for the following day while gossiping about the famous actors some liked to claim they were working *with*. Over by the catering trays, I caught an older woman, also an extra, filling Tupperware bins with leftover food before stashing them into a suitcase. After clearing my dish, I wandered around the set, which was an abandoned hospital until I found a vacant doctor's office to hang out in for the remainder of the break. Settling into a squeaky office chair, I read a few lines from the book I brought when my phone vibrated. Seeing who the caller was, I hesitated, wondering if I had the emotional strength.

"Hi Mom," I answered to get it over with.

"I just called your apartment," she said, which made my face tighten from forgetting to unplug the rotary phone that drove my neighbors insane.

"You didn't pick up," she informed me.

"I know," I said, thinking it was a joke.

"Why didn't you pick up?"

I glanced at my cell phone as if answering her question.

"You there?" she snapped.

"Yes, I'm here," I answered gently. "I'm at work, mom." I waited for her interest but knew better by now. "How's Dad?" I then asked to fill space even though I had called him at his shoe repair shop the week before to check in.

"He's fine," she answered, sounding almost suspicious that I'd ask about my own father. "Why?"

"No reason."

"So, you'll never guess who I bumped into at Waldbaum's."

"Who?" I asked, hoping it wasn't Pete's mom again who also shopped at that supermarket. Since our parents didn't really know what their kids were doing in California, bump-ins between the two families were always a little awkward.

"You'll never guess," she pressed.

"Do I have to?"

"Fine, if you're going to be testy about it: Judith Nelson."

"Who?"

"Jackie Nelson's mother?"

"Oh."

I paused to quickly flip through my mental rolodex. Who was this person? It was obviously someone I had gone to high school with. Hearing the name in my head, I wondered if it was the mean cheerleader that Alex and I thought looked like Willow from the fantasy film. I chuckled to myself, not having thought about it since the '90s. As I tuned out my mom talking about the deli counter or whatever, my mind wandered back to this person before realizing I was thinking of another Nelson altogether. Jamie! The one who used to call me and Alex psycho-whores with no self-awareness that in grade school, she and her friends made signs to protest the kids in Special Ed.

But, yeah, not that one.

"Anyway, long story short," my mother's voice barreled through the memory. "She's engaged." She announced it as if it were somehow my fault. "How do you like that?"

I didn't understand the question.

"Well?" she insisted.

"How do I like that?" I asked, feeling like it was a trap.

"You don't have anything to say?"

I searched my mind for a second. "I guess that's exciting," I felt forced to say before pointing out, "but, I don't know, isn't she a little young?"

"Don't be jealous now."

"Jealous?"

"I know how you get."

How I get?

I decided against defending myself and instead bit my lower lip to deny her the gift of upsetting me. It took moving across the country and living on my own to realize that my mother, in the plainest terms, liked to fuck with me and took sick pleasure in pushing my buttons. Whoever said that parents coddled the children of my generation had obviously never met an Italian family.

"*Tanti auguri* to her," I said, hoping the family expression would remind her that I was her daughter.

"I guess, but you know," she trailed off where I could sense the disappointment in her voice since I wasn't giving her the desired reaction, "I debated on even telling you since... oh, never mind."

"Okay, never mind then." I refused the bait. "So, how was your day?" I adopted a cheerful tone designed to irritate her.

"What I wanted to say before you cut me off was that I know you're chasing that boy around and I knew this news would hit you hard." Mentioning Pete, she knew she was going for the jugular as I felt my nostrils flare. "Don't you know that if a boy likes you, he'll let you know?"

I wanted to remind her that Pete followed *me*, but that was an inconvenient truth that she selectively forgot. She could remember a look I gave in, like, 1998, but details about her daughter's move to California always seemed to be a source of confusion.

"But he's French," she continued, "and you know how closed off they are. Not to mention they're all cheaters. You really shouldn't marry him anyway."

"I'm not looking to get married."

"All girls are and those who say they aren't, are lying."

"That's not true," I dared to say.

"It *is* true," she asserted as if it were the final word. "There are nice boys here who could offer you a much simpler life." She then went down the list of Long Island's most eligible bachelors. From so-and-so's grandson of the salumeria in Glen Cove to the nephew of the fish store in Syosset. She ignored me when I said I wasn't attracted to these people, not to mention, I didn't want a husband who came home smelling like fish.

"I don't think I'd have anything in common with these people," I opted with.

"That's still important to you?" I could feel her eyes rolling from three thousand miles away. "Now you're just being extravagant."

I wanted to ask her if she thought Angelo, whom I referred to as my mean brother, was being extravagant when he said he wouldn't marry a girl with a big ass. Or what about my other brother Claudio, the nicer one, who wouldn't even date a Sicilian girl? No, because they were being *selective*.

"Carla, you can't afford to be so picky."

"Why not?" I said, allowing myself to feel *and* sound insulted because what the hell.

"Your eggs for one. They're going to dry out like beef jerky." I squeezed my eyes shut like I always did when she mentioned my *eggs*. "Your cycle is a reminder of what you're here to do. Don't let those Tampax commercials fool you into thinking it's one big party now that the wrappers are in those flashy colors and can fit in those tiny pocketbooks for the nightclubs you all go to."

Nightclubs. Pocketbooks. Flashy colors. My mother had no idea who I was.

"You're not gaining weight out there, are you?" she asked, making sure to get to all my pressure points.

Some. "No."

"Well, at least there's that because you know, when I was your age, I was back to a size 2 after having three kids," she said in a way as if I wasn't one of them, "and you can always get a divorce, but you can't always have kids."

"So just have kids? That's the solution?" I waited a second for a response that never came. "Mom, I don't even have health insurance." My mother replied with a deep exhale that attacked my ear, forcing me to pull the phone away. "And as for my *eggs*," I continued, now in a hushed tone as I could see the crew returning from lunch, "I'm more worried about making my rent."

"Well, no one told you to move to California and I don't feel one drop sorry for you."

Pete

I spent the afternoon sequestered in a windowless copy room. On the walls were these faded travel posters of the South of France that, quite incredibly, made vacation look depressing. As my mix tape played in a boombox the school used for the oral placement exams, I breathed in fumes from the copy machine that I was certain wouldn't pass a city smog test. The machine was not only a threat to the environment but also had it out for me. It usually chose the day I had a time-sensitive project with the higher-ups breathing down my neck, to give me vague reasons why it couldn't complete the task. That day, I had to print out two hundred double-sided pamphlets for the upcoming spring semester, but the machine kept insisting I CHECK TRAY. I checked and nothing stood out, so I pressed cancel hoping to trick it into starting over, which sometimes worked. But no, I had to once again, CHECK TRAY. I rolled up my sleeves and got down on my knees to dismantle the entire thing. As suspected, I found nothing noteworthy of tray checking as I looked around like a total idiot desperate for a clue. The machine beeped then with a new message flashing on the display. SIDE DOOR OPEN, it informed me. Well, no fucking shit.

As I contemplated stepping out a smoke, Victoria barged in. Returning from lunch, she wore a North Face puffy coat and in her hand was the day's mail.

"Brrr." She bristled her lips as she pushed away her swath of extensions that looked sticks of dry spaghetti.

"Brrr?" I watched her unzip her coat.

"It's January."

"It's also sixty-five degrees out." When she refused to see my logic, I added, "And aren't you from, like, Michigan?"

"Minnesota." She gave me the evil eye before noticing the machine's guts spewed out on the floor. "Stuck again, huh?"

"Yup. Just checking the tray." I framed the words in air quotes.

"Here." She tossed the mail on a nearby table. "Maybe the new Staples catalog will brighten your day." She then noticed the boombox playing my music as I watched the displeasure cancel out her usual pep.

"Peter," she said, looking at me with hopelessness in her eyes. "I'm not trying to be rude or anything, but this music is, like, not good."

"What?" I feigned shock. "It's just my California mix."

"What, 'California Dreamin' was too long of a download?"

"Download," I sneered. "As if I'd ever."

I took a second to savor her distaste for my music, which I interpreted as an endorsement. The defeated look on her face paired with the sour milk curl of her lips quickly dissolved when the phone in her hand began to buzz. She snapped it open with military obedience and attended it, as I returned to inspecting the machine. Behind me, I could hear her grunts of frustration as I imagined her manicured thumbs jabbing into the mini keypad.

"You okay over there?" I asked over my shoulder.

"Sorry, I'll help you in a second," she replied absently. "I'm just trying to send this text and it's taking forever."

"Why don't you just call them?" I gestured to the phone on the wall. "Go ahead."

"Calling would be weird since we already started to text, you know?"

"No. I don't know." I pulled out the final tray from the machine. "Calling, I think, would be more efficient."

"Call?" Her face twisted with confusion, and then a look of pity like I was out of touch. "I forgot, you're, like, old school."

"Old school," I repeated with a dismissive tone, while locating the culprit of the machine's paper jam. "If that means saving time, then you might be right." My voice became laborious as I yanked out a piece of paper wrapped around one of the mechanisms.

"I'll have you know that in Europe, they only text," she said, clearly missing my point. "And the problem here is that I just need a better phone."

"Need?" I slammed the machine door shut, listening for the click that allowed it to finally birth my copies.

"Yes," she asserted. "Need."

"If you only knew just how little we need to get by on –" I then cut myself off, knowing that my lecture on the evils of consumer culture would be lost on someone who hosted a viewing party for the premiere of *The Simple Life*.

"I'm not riding my bike to work if that's what you're getting at," she said with pure distain in her voice.

"For the safety of yourself and others, I'd actually advise you not to."

I thought I'd insulted her, but instead her eyes, done-up in hues of brown and gold that day, lit up as she took a step closer to me.

I took note of our proximity. "What."

"Speaking of," she said in a new-sounding voice that made me uncomfortable.

"Speaking of ecologically responsible transportation?"

"No." Her expression became worryingly coquettish. "Speaking of *others*." She blinked to the side for effect. "My roommate asked about you again."

"Did she?" I turned to the copy machine to pull out the stack of warm copies in the delivery tray. "Here." I handed her the pile. "Fold these in three parts, please."

"Oh, come on, Peter," she whined, taking the copies. "You told me yourself that you were single."

"I did," I confirmed while regretting our conversation at the Christmas luncheon when we split a bottle of champagne.

"So?" She held her hands out like it was all so simple. "She's indie like you!"

Oh, God, I thought in horror, wondering what the hell that even meant.

"She likes Coldplay!"

"In that case…" I shook my head at what the post-9/11 definition of indie had become. "But seriously, though," I relaxed my shoulders and turned to her, "I'm really not all that interesting."

"Well, I know that, but she doesn't… yet." She made a pleading face. "Oh, come on!"

"Fine." I decided to humor her. "What's she like?"

"You've seen her. Her hair is like mine but less blonde and shorter and wavy." When she could see me drawing a blank she added, "Remember, before the break she stopped in?"

"I'm sorry, I don't," I said, feeling sort of bad. "But look, I'm not asking what she looks like. I'm asking what she's *like*?"

"No, you're asking what she *likes*, you snob."

I shrugged. "Having things in common is important."

"Peter," she stretched my name out into more syllables than necessary. "She's super cute and she thinks you're, like, crazy hot, so what's the problem?"

"Super cute and crazy hot," I mused. "A romance for the ages."

"Oh, don't worry, I told her your hotness wears off once you open your mouth."

"How insightful."

"So, come on, what do you say?"

"No."

"Wow." She pulled her face back. "Tell me how you really feel."

"It's not personal, I just have a lot going on right now."

"Does *a lot going on* have anything to do with that girl you moved out here with that you *literally* refuse to tell me about?"

"Literally." I smirked at the performative and overused word.

"It *is* her," she stated as fact. "Cara."

"Carla."

"Right." Her eyes became dreamy. "Carla."

She batted her eyelashes, seeming to script out some made-for-reality-TV scene as she tried to study my face for some kind of tip-off.

"Are you done?" I asked, unable to hold back my smirk.

"I see that look on your face," she said, misreading my amused expression like she had me all figured out. "And don't think I didn't notice that fourth cup of coffee you had this morning. You never have a fourth cup, so I figured someone had been keeping you up all night." She bounced her eyebrows up and down suggestively as I sputtered out a laugh at how wrong she was. "I'll believe it unless you tell me otherwise."

"Look." I let out a deep breath not quite sure what to say. "It's just... complicated."

"Peter, if it's complicated then you're not exactly single now, are you?"

Carla

I tried not to let my phone call with my mother get to me, but spending an entire day in a hospital bed pantomiming near-death gave me nothing but time to think. On the way home, I stopped at Trader Joe's for a medicinal bottle of their finest Two-Buck Chuck, ready to erase the day. As I walked down the hallway to my apartment, I bumped into Joni wandering in from the backyard. With one hand, I scooped her up, curling her body over my shoulder. As I tried to pinch open my purse's kiss lock, I balanced clumsily, careful not to drop the cat. Or the wine.

"Need help?" Pete asked, turning the corner.

"No, I got it." I then reconsidered it, since I didn't want him peeking inside my grocery bag. "On second thought," I said. "Take her."

He carefully took the cat, allowing me to reach for my keys with more ease.

"How's it going?" I asked.

"It's going," he said as my peripheral vision could see Joni rubbing her cheek against his. "You?"

"I got paid to sleep all day."

"Yeah? I fought with a copy machine. And Victoria drove me insane," he said in a baby voice reserved for the cat before returning to his normal voice to say, "So, I think you win today."

I couldn't help but smirk. "Winning. Is that what I'm doing?"

"Something like that," he said, echoing my cynicism as he put Joni down.

When he came back up, I could see him noticing the orange scarf he had knitted for me. He purposefully chose the color of my guitar and his drum kit, feeling like it was some kind of fuck-you scarf aimed at me for dismissing our band.

"It was chilly today," I felt the need to explain.

"That's why I made it." He looked at me with soft eyes. "I'm glad you're wearing it."

I looked away to avoid melting when he looked at me that way. He caught me off guard, though, when he reached for the scarf, giving it a teasing tug as if he might pull me closer. As I watched him wrap the tangerine-colored yarn around his hand, his natural woodsy scent wandered into my personal space, making me wonder if it was laced with some kind of pheromone that made me powerless. Slowly, I lifted my eyes, stepping back as the scarf stretched between us. With my back against the door, I gave him a challenging look.

"What's up, Pete?"

"Nothing," he replied, letting the scarf drop.

I looked at him like we both knew that wasn't true and waited for him to say what was on his mind.

"Okay," he surrendered with a playful glint in his eye. "I wanted to know if you'd like to have dinner with me tonight?"

He asked in a way that could've been interpreted as both friendly and romantic. But we had been here before and frankly I was tired of getting high on hope, knowing with him, it would always be just dinner. He hoped for music. I hoped for sex. We were at an emotional impasse.

"I'm just going to make some tomato soup." He pointed to the bag of tomatoes hanging on his doorknob. "I'll put the crème fraîche on the side, if you want."

"Alright," I said, feeling an awkward mix of defeat and arousal.

"But," he continued as if attaching a caveat. "I might insist on dessert." He shot me a sneaky look, which meant he had snagged something expensive from work. "Choux à la crème." His eyes lit up. "It really would be a crime to not have one."

I looked at him, giving in like I always did. "Let me just drop this stuff off and I'll be right over."

"The door will be open." He then looked at Joni, who began circling eights around his ankles. "You coming with me, *ma belle*?" I looked at her, smiling at how much my cat loved him. "It's only because she knows I keep food for her," he said, as if responding to my inside voice. A look was exchanged between us before we turned our backs on each other to face our respective doors.

Before returning to his place, I brushed my teeth and fluffed my hair, like the latter was the problem here. In my socks, I walked in, hearing his answering machine playing back a message in the kitchen. It was from his flight attendant mom who had a similar New York accent to my mom's, with them both pronouncing words like *fathah* and my personal favorite, *speakah*. But his mom mixed in the odd French word as the official language in the Albrecht house was *Frenglish*. As I half-listened to her message about her canceled layover in L.A. that I knew Pete was looking forward to, I breathed in his air. A combination of notes I knew I'd be familiar with for the rest of my life, it was a combination of smoked tobacco, ground espresso, used paperbacks, and his sandalwood bar soap. His apartment mirrored mine, but on the wall where I had my couch and framed pictures, Pete had cubby shelves that he and Barbie's husband Kurt built one weekend in the garage. Lined neatly inside them were his records classified by season. Mind you, it wasn't necessarily the season of the album's release, but the season the album had the most impact on Pete. If you didn't know him, looking for a record could be absolutely maddening but I did know him, so I knew that *Kind of Blue* was late winter while *At Folsom Prison* meant summertime "fun". Music equipment took up the rest of his space, from the electric drum kit to the upright piano the apartment actually came with. Next to it was his wicker basket of yarn. In it, I recognized leftover scraps from the scarves and berets he'd made over the years, as well as loose ends of his works-in-progress like the socks I knew he was making for his mom. Joni passed the basket and, out of principle, snatched the strands spilling off the side before moving on.

"I'm going to change," he said emerging from the kitchen as he unbuttoned his sleeves. "Help yourself." He pointed to the dreaded record shelves. "Put whatever you want on. I think you're an expert on the order by now."

If only he knew how much saying something like this hurt me. The acknowledgement of our closeness while rejecting me daily came out in well-intended sentences like this and made me wonder if he was being deliberately obtuse.

"It's okay." I angled my shoulders away from the shelves to distance myself. "Whatever you already have on the turntable, I'm sure is fine."

"Godspeed You! Black Emperor?" He squinted with doubt, knowing they weren't one of my favorites.

"It's fine, Pete," I said, forcing indifference.

It's fine. I knew he hated it when I said that, and he reacted accordingly, letting out a deep groan while heading to his changing area, or cove as he called it. Our apartments featured this unique alcove, serving as both a spacious walk-in closet and a passageway to the bathroom. To close off the area, my place had a removable pivot wall, something that I had never seen in an apartment before, but Barbie told me was typical for these post-war buildings. Pete, on the other hand, had to install a curtain that, with the light on, you could see through.

I sat on his bed that directly faced him. Through the curtain, I could see him peeling off his dress shirt, exposing the lean muscles that ran down his back. Not wanting to feel like a bored housewife stealing glimpses of the topless guy, I forced my attention to his nightstand. Grabbing the book on it, I saw it was in French. As I fanned through it, delighting in the smell rising from the yellowed pages, I tried to make out the words, noticing the different shapes of the accents. What were vague symbols to me were very much a part of Pete's reading experience and I wondered what it was like to see the world in two different languages.

The thought stayed with me until he reemerged, sporting his Pete Albrecht after-work aesthetic. Running his hands through his hair, he possessed the laid-back air of a movie star on their day off. He wore low-slung, faded work pants paired with a fitted white tee that he bought in packs of three at the Army Surplus store on Hyperion. I caught a glimpse of his inner bicep tattoo as he slipped on the black-rimmed glasses he'd worn since 5th grade. He walked through adulthood with the same stoner gait he had as a teenager, but he had acquired maturity and a deepened sense of self. As he crossed the room, he stopped to examine something on my face. Looking at him, looking at me, I began to feel self-aware and touched my face, feeling around for dried toothpaste.

"What?" I asked.

He read my face for another second. "You talked to your mom today, didn't you?"

"I did." I knew I sounded a bit defensive.

"And?"

"And nothing. Not everyone has a cool relationship with their parents, Pete."

He tilted his head like that was far from the point here. "Do you want to talk about it?"

"I don't, actually."

"Okay." He tapped his socked foot against mine. "How about we go in the kitchen and *not* talk about it while I make dinner." He reached his hand out to help me up, springing me back onto my feet.

"So," I said, changing my tone to a friendlier one. "I have some back home gossip for you."

"Oh?" He appeared intrigued as we made our way towards the kitchen.

"Jackie Nelson is engaged."

"Engaged?" he said in a tone that suggested that he also thought we were a little young.

"Wait." He stopped mid-step. "Who was she again?" He turned towards me with small eyes, giving the subject some thought. "Was she that mean girl who protested the Special Ed kids?" His face appeared to sting at the awful memory.

"No, you're thinking of Jamie," I replied, feeling relieved that I wasn't the only one to remember something that seriously no one was ever held accountable for.

"That's right." He looked off, imagining it before turning back at me. "You know Tony and I always thought she looked like Vigo from *Ghostbusters* 2." He clenched his jaw in guilt. "That's sort of mean, right?"

"*She* was sort of mean." I held back giggling at *their* childhood movie comparison, thinking it also worked.

"Yeah, I guess she was," he concurred, shaking his head. "But seriously, what the fuck was wrong with our school?" He looked at me for an answer, which I didn't have. "These people were brutal and precisely why I kept my shit to myself."

I agreed but as I followed him into the kitchen I couldn't help but wonder, what shit was he talking about?

CHAPTER 5

Pete

I remember when I turned eighteen, this older hippie dude told me that time speeds up as we age. It wasn't a perception, he said, but an actual scientifically proven theory. Looking back, I call bullshit because the week dripped by like sap from a maple tree, answering endless calls from new students nervous about spring registration. But it was already February, so time must have been going somewhere. I just wish I knew where. On my desk sat another letter from my cousin Guy, which I was avoiding like his unanswered New Year card and next to it, the phone that hadn't stopped ringing that week.

"Bonjour Institut Français," I said into the receiver as my attention momentarily shifted to Victoria walking in, her heels rattling the track lighting.

"The placement test," I answered the caller's question, "is just that... to place you in the right class. No, we don't have grades here. Or give school credit. We're a French cultural center. Yes... no... that's fine... no problem. *Merci, au revoir.*"

"Busy morning, I see." Victoria scooched forward in her chair, stretching her arm around to the back of her computer to boot it up. "Spring semester. In like a lion, out like a lamb."

"Something like that," I replied in a faraway voice as I read a new email from my boss Etienne, adding to my already overloaded to-do list. "Like I have nothing else to do," I mumbled to myself.

"What's that?" Victoria's eyes met mine over our monitors.

"Upstairs wants us to start the preparations for the Spring Party."

"Already? We're still in spring reg."

"Reg? Really?" I retorted. "It takes too much time to say the whole word?"

"It does when you make a point to ask."

"Anyway," I said, returning my focus to the e-mail. "I told them that *registration* was a priority, but to get started on this, just grab the spreadsheet from last year's party where you'll find all the sponsor info and use it as a template to create a Spring '04 document."

"So, we have that, on top of answering phones and showing faculty, once again, how to use the coffee machine. Not to mention assisting visitors at the front desk?"

"You got it," I replied, eyeing another email pop into my inbox. "And that's why we get paid the big bucks."

"Big bucks. Yeah, right. I'm still a temp."

A feeling of guilt overcame me. "I know," I said with regret. "I'll follow up with them about hiring you full time."

We worked through the morning with me skipping my mid-morning smoke in the back alley. The phone calls continued, with us answering them with "Please hold." Eventually, there was a lull, a stillness that felt almost louder than the ringing phone. I'd done a decent job that morning tuning out Victoria's music until one came on that felt like an actual affront. A made-for-Starbucks-compilation bossa nova guitar riff strummed softly, accompanied falsetto lyrics repeating the dumbest lyrics since "Mambo No. 5". When I couldn't take it anymore, feeling held against my will every time the singer cooed *she will be loved*, I dropped my head into my arms in surrender.

"Make him stop," I pleaded, my voice muffled in the sleeves of my shirt.

"Make who stop?" I could hear her chair squeak, which meant she was leaning back presumably looking at the waiting area. "Who are you talking about?"

"This guy." I waved my hand wildly over my head. "Whoever is singing. Just make him stop."

"What's wrong with him?" she actually asked.

"What's wrong with him?" I repeated as I yanked my head up. "I don't know. Everything?"

"It's just 'She Will Be Loved.'"

"You don't say."

"Everyone knows this song."

"Everyone. Well, in that case." I leaned back, letting the chair bend to the shape of my back before springing forward with a point to make. "Seriously. What's wrong with music today?"

"Oh, my God, Peter." Her eyes narrowed like I had finally lost it. "Can you be any more dramatic? It's just a song."

I looked at her like she was on the outside of some great conspiracy. "It's never just a song," I declared. "It all means something."

"Right and the meaning of this song is that the singer wants the girl to be loved. How can you, like, not see the beauty?"

"The beauty?" I couldn't believe what I was hearing.

"Yes, Peter. The beauty. But I'm convinced that you don't see the beauty in anything."

I wanted to protest that, of course, I saw beauty in plenty of things. But I knew I had never given her any reason to believe otherwise as she looked at me like I was an old grouch.

"I'm just trying to realign my romantic juju," she explained.

"With this song?" My eyes must have looked spun out from how weary her logic made me. "I'm pretty sure you have access to better resources."

"Do you even know what tomorrow is?"

"Yes," I answered. "Saturday."

"No." She squinted her eyes at me. "Tomorrow is Valentine's Day and I'm in desperation mode."

I drew a blank, not *quite* making the connection.

"And if you must know," she continued in her accusatory tone, "I don't have plans."

"Should you have plans?"

"I didn't think I did until I saw these!" She held up a box of conversation candy hearts as if it were raw evidence. "They're making a mockery of my singledom!"

I didn't mean it—ah, fuck, maybe I did— but I couldn't help but look amused.

"It's not funny, Peter!" she howled.

"It's not?" I allowed myself to laugh, because surely she was joking. When I realized she wasn't, I composed myself. "Okay, okay." I held my hands up in truce, as I fought off the lingering laughs. "I'm sorry."

"Yeah, right," she sneered. "But here." She handed me the candies. "Take these self-esteem stealers away from me."

"Oh, come on," I pleaded with her, as I took the box. "Do you really think these little hearts, or this song, hold the prophecy to self-fulfillment on the most useless day of the year?"

"Self-fulfillment?" She looked at me like a calculus problem. "Prophecy? It's like you can't help yourself from being weird." I shrugged at my harmless comment before she added, "But let me ask you something, does your *girlfriend* think Valentine's Day is the most useless day of the year?"

When I didn't immediately respond, Victoria clarified, "You know, the one that things are so *complicated* with?"

I chose not to answer and tried to refocus on my work emails.

"I thought so," she said, sounding satisfied with herself.

My brain suddenly felt crowded, wondering what Carla thought of the day. We had never talked about it because it always fell on a weekday where overtime at work and rush hour traffic sort of hijacked the whole thing. But that year it fell on a Saturday, a day I usually spent with her.

"Tell me you have something planned for Valentine's Day," Victoria's voice returned.

I let her see my eyes slide to the side, signaling her intrusion into my emotional space.

"Oh, my God, you don't," she decided while clearly ignoring my discomfort.

"Victoria." I tilted my head. "That's personal."

"Peter. How do you not have anything planned for Valentine's Day?"

"I didn't say that."

"You don't have to. I know you don't have anything planned for Valentine's Day."

"Oh, my God. Can you please stop saying it?"

"Not until you tell me why you haven't planned anything for Valentine's Day."

I let out a full sigh. "Because we're not like that."

"I know, because it's … *complicated.*" She framed the word with finger quotes. "But whatever your situation with her is, which I'm sure involves some kind of no-strings-attached-sex deal that you guys manage to talk us into…" She shot me a dirty look, which said more about her situation than mine. "Don't ignore the day completely. It's mean."

"Mean?" I did nothing to disguise my contempt. "No, Valentine's Day is mean and excludes a huge part of the population. Present company included. You should be outraged."

"I am," she said rather unconvincingly. "But let's talk about you."

"Must we?" I stared at my inbox, mentally willing another email to come in.

"Just don't make it worse by pretending the day doesn't exist," she said in a tone that I knew was meant to be kind. "Seriously, I know it sounds dumb, but at least think about it if you care for her at all."

"Okay, I will," I said earnestly while still wrestling with the importance of it. "But thank you, Victoria. I do appreciate your concern."

"You're welcome," she said sweetly.

We then sat there for a few moments both freaked out by the sudden tender conversation. We sort of shifted and bobbed our heads in agreement, while not feeling totally comfortable in this space.

"We can, like, go back to being mean to each other now," she suggested.

Snapping out of it, I said, "I think we most definitely should." I leaned over to reach for my bag. "I'll put music on."

"Yup, that'll do it. But please, Peter, not your California mix again. I'm too fragile today."

Ignoring the jab, I pulled out the small CD binder I kept at work, containing the one album we could both agree on. I tactfully skipped the song "Happy Valentine's Day," out of fear of reprising that entire conversation and went straight to "Hey Ya!"

We bobbed our heads, letting the bounce of the pop song with its clever lyrics distract us from the concerns on both our minds. It worked as I admired the production quality of the song, and over my computer, could hear Victoria singing along.

"Peter?" she said, her voice cutting through the song.

I looked up from my screen. "Yes, Victoria?"

"Am I a Beyoncé or a Lucy Liu?" she asked, referencing the lyrics.

"Neither," I said flatly.

"Why?"

"Because the song isn't about you."

"Ew. You're *so* rude."

I grinned. "Thank you."

And just like that, we were back to our regularly scheduled programming.

Carla

"Argh," I yelled when I opened the lid of the washing machine to see my neighbor's clothes still inside.

It was the third time I'd trudged downstairs with my bulky sack of laundry only to see the same clothes in the building's two machines. I considered taking the clothes out and leaving them on top of the dryer like I'd seen other tenants do, but that seemed impolite. It was also impolite to take up two machines.

On my rare weekday off because there was no work for my type that day, I spent way too much of it staring at my neighbor's wet clothes. As I pondered laundry etiquette, I heard my rotary phone ring from two stories down reminding me that I was also not a perfect neighbor. Racing past the washing machines and mailboxes, I hurried up the stairs.

"Your phone is ringing," Paul, the assistant key grip who lived on the third floor grumbled as we passed each other on the stairs.

"I know, getting it now," I huffed, noticing his socked feet. "Is that your laundry that's been in the machines since lunch?"

"Yeah, sorry. Grabbing it now."

Rounding the corner, feeling like a cartoon character, I passed another tenant with a basket of laundry and let out a groan, knowing she was going to get the newly available machine. I barged into my apartment, almost tripping over my coffee table to make the phone stop.

"Hello?" I panted into the receiver, hoping it wasn't my mom.

"Ooh to the Car la, la," my best friend's voice cooed into the phone. "Bad time?"

"Hardly," I replied, falling back on my couch, as I closed the door with my foot.

"Your cell went straight to voicemail," she said as I could hear the sound of New York City whirring behind her.

"It's charging in a dead spot where I don't get service." I eyed the kitchen doorway.

"Well, I got you here," she said. "Did you get my email?"

"No, I haven't checked it today. Why?"

"I sent you my latest article."

"Oh, great. I'll read it tonight," I said, twirling the telephone cord around my finger as I looked at my clock to calculate the East Coast time. "You heading home early?"

"No, I'm getting coffee for my office," she said, her voice unable to contain her resentment. "Two assholes were hired after me, yet I'm still getting coffee."

"Still?" I sympathized. "Say something."

"Oh, my God, I have but they tell me some bullshit about how the office is a collective and everyone helps out. Somehow they always need coffee when they know I'm not working on something, like right after I hand in work to my editor. The blatant sexism is, like, timed with this creeping undertone that I should be grateful to be working there."

"You're writing reviews now," I reminded her in an upbeat tone.

"I am but they're all so predictable, pandering to the same audience. You should have seen my boss's face when I offered to write up the Kelis album. He acted like I was being ironic, which you know how much I hate hipster irony."

I smiled that she and Pete had that in common.

"Sorry," she interrupted herself. "Can you hold on a sec?"

Thinking now of the song "Milkshake" that we both obsessed over the year before, I listened to her read off the list of coffee orders. I smiled, knowing the medium Americano with two pumps of vanilla was for her.

"K," her voice returned. "That order will eat up at least forty minutes of my day. But enough about my glamorous life. How's yours?"

"Out of control," I said evenly. "Yesterday I played GIRL IN COURTROOM on some legal show I've never heard of."

"You should do *Friends*," she offered as if it were the easiest thing ever.

"I should," I replied diplomatically, deciding to spare her the inner workings of extra work and how that show was like the holy grail of extra gigs. "So, what do you have going on this weekend?"

"Claire and I are going out tonight, but we're debating between going to Union Pool because there will be bands playing or, being honest about tonight's objective and just going downstairs to Clem's to get shitfaced at the bar."

"Decisions, decisions." I didn't stop myself from rolling my eyes at the mention of her *amazing* rockabilly roommate Claire.

"It's a tough one, right?" she deadpanned. "Claire's thinking is that we need to be just hungover enough to not realize what tomorrow is."

"What's tomorrow? Her birthday or something?"

"No, my Lala, it's Valentine's Day."

"Is it?" My eyes flitted around the apartment, as if that would clarify anything.

"Yup. Smack on a Saturday for all to see." She let out a moan like she was in physical pain. "We're trying to get ahead of it with a solid plan."

"We're?" I crooked an eyebrow.

"Me and Claire."

I know.

"It's just Valentine's Day."

"Easy for you to say, you have, like, a live-in boyfriend." When I tried to interrupt to offer a more accurate description, she barreled over me. "When I told Claire that Pete knits and is kind of jacked –"

"I never said jacked," I pushed my voice through hers.

"Fine," she placated. "Your exact words were 'toned, long, lean muscles.'" Her voice then took on a sassy tone as she laughed into the phone like it was the funniest thing she had ever heard.

I let out a regretful moan. "I really need to stop drunk dialing you."

"Don't. Drunk Carla is the best."

I didn't respond.

"La? You still there?"

"Still here."

"Oh, come on," she groused, accurately interpreting my silence. "It's funny…" When I still didn't respond, she said, "You know we're just jealous of your buff guy who knits, like some kind of pumpkin spice erotica, or like, Anthropologie porn."

"Oh geez," I said, laughing at the descriptions wondering how many bottles of wine it took for her and Claire to come up with them. "I assure you ladies, there is nothing to be jealous of."

"At least you have someone to hang out with on Valentine's Day."

"Since when do you care about things like that?"

"I don't, but I guess I just thought at 23, I'd at least have someone to at least make fun of it with."

"Stop sleeping with non-committal guys who either have bed bugs or say gross things like their ex-girlfriends' vaginas smell like Big Mac sauce," I reminded her, cringing at her Williamsburg dates that made me wonder why she bothered at all.

"I know," she said through gritted teeth. "It's just hard sometimes."

"Is it though? Because these guys sound like total assholes," I pointed out. "And I don't care if they're a spitting image of Sufjan Stevens." I then remembered the description of the last guy she told me about and added, "Or Paul Giamatti for that matter." I made a face because I didn't understand that one.

"I just wish you were here so we can just be weird together," she said in a voice that made her sound sixteen again.

I smiled as I pressed my ear to the phone as if it were her shoulder. "We are weird, aren't we?"

"The weirdest," she confirmed. "But here's to another Valentine's Day spent hungover with legs spread under the faucet while thinking about all sorts of dirty deeds done dirt cheap."

"I'm going to the 99 Cent Store tomorrow," I offered cheerfully. "And then I'll have the day to myself, so my Valentine's Day probably won't look much different than yours. I'll probably check Craigslist to see if any cafés are hiring."

"You're going to job search on Valentine's Day?"

"It's not a national holiday, you know? And it's not like I have so many options."

"Maybe it's time you did something about it."

"I'm not going down on him in his sleep," I asserted, remembering last year's suggestion. "Or wearing a lace teddy." The one from the year before.

"Why not?" she pleaded. "You have keys to his place! What guy would object to a little deep-throat wake-up call with you in something latex from Frederick's?"

"You're still in the coffee shop, right?"

"Yes. Don't change the subject."

"There is no subject."

"Ugh. You don't deserve to live in L.A. is all I'm going to say. You, like, get a free pass to be tacky *and* slutty and you're just letting it pass you by." She waited for a reaction I didn't have. "You're going to regret it."

"I'll take the risk."

A muffling sound suggested she had the phone balanced under her chin and I could hear her strain, presumably to open the coffee shop door.

"All I'm saying," she continued like I knew she would, "is that you two are obviously into each other and he's being respectful by not coming on to you after everything you've been through with your mom and the eating stuff," I squeezed my eyes shut at the reminder of my issues while half-smiling that only my best friend could get away with the oversimplification of it all.

"My point is, maybe it's time *you* seduced *him*."

"Seduce?" I cringed at the word that I didn't think people our age used.

"I think it's time and so does Claire."

"Does she now?"

"She does," Alex confirmed in a no-bullshit tone. "But La, look, I can't talk and carry all of this shit at the same time, so I'm going to go. I expect a full report the next time we speak."

"Prepare yourself for tales of the 99 Cent Store."

"But it's Valentine's Day!"

"So, you keep telling me."

CHAPTER 6

Carla

I planned on having a quiet night in. But tell that to the marching band pounding across my head the next morning. On my coffee table was the bottle of wine I had felt noble about not finishing before collapsing, face-down into bed. Even if only a few drops remained, it still meant I hadn't drunk an entire bottle. Alone.

Pulling myself up, my tired bones lumbered out of bed as I stepped over the *Sea Change* and *Songs of Leonard Cohen* album sleeves; a reminder I had been in good heartbreak company the night before. With Joni leading the way, we walked into the kitchen when a knock on the door startled me more than it should've. Hearing the rattle of keys and jewelry, I knew it was Barbie and before answering it, I hid the bottle of wine beside the couch.

"Morning," I said, forcing a friendly tone as Joni zoomed past my ankles.

"And she's off," Barbie said, watching the cat race down the hallway to the backyard door. Decked that morning in a Pucci knock-off caftan with one of Kurt's fleeces over it, she turned back to me. "I just put some food out for the little kiddles, so she'll be all set this morning." Her eyes then traced the angles of my face as if looking for something. "What'd you do last night?"

Got drunk and masturbated.

"Laid low," I decided was a better response, as I gestured to the folksy records as proof of my wholesome and sober night. Instinctively, I swallowed and licked my lips, worried about red wine residue crusting in the corners of my mouth.

She leaned into the apartment and twitched her nose as if sniffing for a clue. "Did you sauté onions last night?"

"I did," I replied, just remembering I had made some food. "I tossed them in my scrambled eggs."

She frowned. "That's not much of a dinner, but it explains why it looks like you'd been crying last night."

I rubbed my eyes as if erasing her observations. To avoid any more remarks my hangover didn't want to deal with, I quickly suggested we water the plants out back, gently ushering her out the door.

"While we're out there," she said, clearly picking up on my urgency as she picked up her pace, "why don't I trim those bangs of yours. How can you see anything with those curtains in your eyes?"

"Good idea."

"The gardening shears are out back," she joked.

I followed her down the hall to the building's backyard as we stepped into Saturday morning. Since the building was situated on a hill, the slanted outdoor space was only accessible from the second floor. Closed in by a spray-painted pink lattice fence, the place crawled with overgrown tropical flowers and had faded green striped patio furniture owing to Barbie's pastoral punk description. The punk rock Beverly Hills Hotel as she often referred to it, served as an escape for the tenants when they wanted to forget they lived in L.A. That was if, of course, they didn't look over the fence at the view of Downtown haloed by a layer of smog. I held onto the banister to help myself down the stone steps, taking in a deep breath of the air perfumed with star jasmine. I listened to the birds taunting each other in the citrus trees and smiled at the building's cats jumping in and out of the tenant's vegetable patch like a surprise party.

"It's chilly out this morning," Barbie remarked, rubbing her hands up and down her arms as she walked over to the thermometer nailed to the shed. "It's forty-four degrees, that's why."

I grinned at Barbie's version of winter as I walked over to the hose. Mounted on a reel under Pete's open window, I began to unravel it. From above, I could hear him move about as the smell of his tar-like coffee and toasted bread for his morning tartine wafted from his kitchen.

"That should be long enough." Barbie stopped me, holding her arm out to collect the hose. "We have to get these tomatoes before the sun moves over this way."

I handed it to her, feeling the dry dirt coat my hands as Pete began to play his Saturday morning piano. That morning, we got a little jazz as we listened to his fingers dance across the keys, improvising a loose melody.

"Ah, there it is." Barbie gazed at his window proudly. "A little morning entertainment. It doesn't get much better than this, now does it?"

I smiled in agreement as I turned the rusty faucet when his upstairs neighbor suddenly put on Wilco. Instead of Pete pounding harder on his keys at his neighbor for sonically cutting the line, he worked with the moody ballad with some soft atmospheric playing to accompany the song.

"He's really good," Barbie said with awe. "Remember when he played 'River' that day?" Her face softened with nostalgia, as she began watering the tomatoes, which activated a rich, earthy scent.

"What happened that day?" I asked, seeing she was in the mood to retell one of her favorite stories.

"Well, you two had just moved in. Buddy Holly and Bangs, over here." I chuckled, as I always did when she called us this. "And I'll never forget, you came down the stairs with that worried little face of yours and asked if you could help out in the garden." I held my breath, hoping this time she'd leave out her imitation of me, which always came out sounding confused and starry-eyed like I was calling into the Psychic Friends Network.

"Meanwhile Peter," she continued, thankfully, sparing us the imitation, "was at his place like he is now, and he started playing 'River' by Joni Mitchell."

My eyebrows raised in acknowledgement of the song he played every December 1st.

"And that was when we heard them. Right behind that tree," she pointed to it, "is where we heard their tiny cries." I leaned forward in anticipation of the big reveal of a story I already knew the ending to. "That was when we found the litter of tiny black kittens so small you could hold two of them in the palm of your hand."

I nodded along, remembering how tiny they were.

"That's when we got my Darby, Lisa on the third floor got Charlie, and you found your little Joni, naming her in honor of the song." She sighed wistfully at the memory as the overgrown bush behind her began to rustle from the cats playing hide n' seek with each other. "Now these black kitties run the damn place!"

From the top of the stairs, the backyard door creaked open with Kurt walking down, balancing a giant bag of gardening soil on his shoulder.

"Oh, there you are," Barbie said to him. "Are we going to Costco today or what?" Kurt always took a second to respond, which drove her visibly insane. I watched her red hair grow brighter in aggravation watching him mindfully place the bag of dirt on a stone bench. "Well?" she insisted, this time raising her voice an octave.

"I'm thinking," he replied.

"Well, think quicker, we don't have all day."

"Oh, hey Carla," he said when he noticed me. "Got anything planned for today?"

"Kurt!" Barbie snapped.

"What?" He held his hands out in confusion.

"You can't ask a girl what she's doing on Valentine's Day," she said under her breath like I wasn't standing right there before turning back to face me. "Like I said, don't get married."

"Don't worry," Kurt said in a tone reserved for teasing the shit out of Barbie. "You'll get your little roses today."

"Roses?" she recoiled. "After twenty-something years, I don't need goddamn roses, just take me to Costco and then the bank after."

After she released what always seemed like steam from a pressure cooker, I could see her face relax. The sides of her mouth then curled as she walked over to give him a kiss on the cheek. "You sleep okay last night, my dear?"

"I did." He smiled, like he always did even when she was screaming her head off about this or that. "Thanks for letting me sleep in."

"You only get one Saturday morning," she reasoned, not wanting him to make a big fuss about it.

I left them to have their moment just as Pete's playing stopped. When I heard the piano bench scrape across his floor, I walked over to his window.

"Hey, Chopin!" I called out.

I could hear his footsteps approach before pushing open the window entirely, fitting himself into its frame. With a hand-rolled cigarette between his lips, he took it out of his mouth and looked out the window to assess the day.

"Top o' the mornin'," he then said, giving a nod to Barbie and Kurt, who had gone back to talking about Costco.

"Morning to you, too," I responded as his eyes settled on mine which felt like an unfair advantage as I squinted from the sun bouncing off the building's stucco.

"Have a nice night?" he asked before taking a long drag.

"It was quiet. How about you?"

"Less quiet. I worked on some music." He raised his eyebrows suggesting I could have joined him.

Over my head he surveyed the day again, giving it an approving nod, before returning his focus to me. "What do you have going on today?"

"Barbie's going to trim these." I pointed to my hair. "And after I'm running some errands like going to the bank if you want to come along. I can give you the car insurance money today." I frowned. "Sorry, it's so late."

"Don't worry about it," he said with sweet eyes as if I didn't owe him a hundred bucks.

He then blew out another steam of smoke, which I interpreted as too casual and unaware that it was Valentine's Day. I then begrudged Alex for planting this dumb seed in the first place. I never cared about the day before and now it was the only thing I could think of.

Pete

Maybe she didn't know it was Valentine's Day. Maybe we could let the day sneak by unscathed, which felt more our style. Not that I was trying to avoid the are-we-more-than-friends Valentine's Day extravaganza. I just didn't know what to do, especially since I found faults in what should have been decent ideas. Going out to dinner, complicated. A bar, she didn't really drink. Roses, cliché. Music, uneventful, even if Courtney Love's solo album had just come out. One idea was to take her to The New Beverly, a landmark theater that ran double-features of old movies. Hoping they'd do something dark like *Harold and Maude* or even defiant like *Evil Dead* 2, I frowned when the monthly calendar informed me of an Audrey Hepburn double feature running that weekend. For some reason, it felt a little too-on-the-nose for the day. But also, I really couldn't picture Carla sitting through *Sabrina* since she didn't exactly do Cinderella-style romance. Stumped on any meaningful ideas, I decided to let the day unfold the way it was meant to.

Joining her on errands later that morning, we left the building with her bangs so freshly cut that would make her look like a 5th grader for about a week. As we headed to the car, we encountered other neighbors, exchanging greetings that barely registered as words, more like a series of polite sound effects. Together we walked down the curves and bends of our long street, as I took in the details of our idle morning: the way the late-morning sun revealed dark cherry highlights in her hair and a dark blue sweater I had never seen on her before. I realized I must have been smiling at her when she chuckled nervously.

"What?" she asked.

"That sweater matches your eyes." I was incapable of hiding my appreciation for it. "Almost, but not quite, sailor stripe blue."

"Like your dad's T-shirts," she completed my thought.

"Summers in France will do that to you." I tapped my elbow against hers in reference to an old conversation as she slipped on a pair of oversized sunglasses. "But today you're less nautical and more Italian movie star now with the shades."

"Oh yeah? Which one?"

"I don't know," I had to admit. "An Italian one."

Smiling, she pointed ahead of her. "We're parked right up here, Fellini."

"Chopin *and* Fellini on the same day," I bragged. "I feel like I won something."

She handed me the keys. "You did. You get to drive today."

"As if I wasn't going to anyway."

We got to the car, parting to our respective sides, our eyes meeting briefly over the roof. Then, like an awful sitcom, we slid into the car at the same time, with our shoulders tapping against each other. As I unlocked and released the Club—a Christmas present from her brothers— from the steering wheel, she opened the glove compartment to take out our CD binder. Placing the anti-theft bar in the back seat, I noticed the frosted windows.

"Let's give the car a few minutes to warm up," I suggested.

"Alright," she said with indifference, turning the vinyl pages of the book before landing on one she liked. "Belle and Sebastian?" She looked at me before sliding it out.

"Belle and Sebastian," I agreed.

She popped the CD into the discman where the triumphant tempo of the album's first song filled the car with a marching band beat. The sound was full and cinematic, but she quickly pressed the button to advance to another song.

"It's too early for big drums," she grumbled, reaching for the skip button. "Here, you'll like this one," she said. "It's about your dear Mets." She looked at the CD booklet. "Piazza, to be exact."

"A song about the Mike Piazza?" I replied, intrigued about how a song about one of the greatest catchers in Major League Baseball could make its way into an indie rock song. But I guess stranger songs had been written.

"Let's hear it," I said, turning the key in the ignition. "Because I can't even imagine."

In comfortable silence, we sat in the car, letting it warm up as the engine tinkered and sputtered to life. The song seemed to transport us with its romantic themes about eloping and sailing around the world. I couldn't help but smile, knowing why the song resonated with her even if I wasn't sure what it had to do with the baseball player. Then, unexpectedly, the lyrics shifted to ponder his sexual identity. My chest tightened with the memory of the media circus that had erupted years before, dissecting the catcher's private life. While the papers debated if he *was* or *wasn't*, I remember thinking they were all missing the point that it was no one's business while wondering why he couldn't be both. It appeared it hadn't occurred to anyone that we're not all just one fucking thing. I sat in the car, lost for a moment in these reflections and frustrations. The song's direct line of questioning felt suffocatingly personal, as if demanding where I stood. As the haunting feelings of isolation resurfaced, I felt starkly exposed, forcing me to open the window for air while questioning if she had chosen this track on purpose.

"Are you okay?" she asked, picking up on the sudden shift of energy in the car.

I didn't answer immediately, turning my head away to shield my expression from her curious gaze. I considered opening up about myself, but the idea was abandoned when a neighbor walked by, reaching under her skirt to pull at a wedgie—a visual I most certainly didn't want to associate with my coming out to her.

I snapped back to reality, wrestling with the seatbelt, pulling it over me. "Yeah," I responded, forcing a brighter tone. "I'm fine."

And we left it at that even though I knew I was doing to her what I hated she did to me. Nothing was fine but pretending it was, seemed easier. I suddenly understood the appeal of an otherwise irritating coping mechanism.

While driving, my thoughts drifted to my cousin and how my internal conflict drove him mad, suggesting I was complicit in my own misery, an architect, if you will, of my own distress. In a way, he was probably right. If I were an observer of my own life, I'd also think this miscommunication was indulgent. But there were songs written about how words didn't come easy, so I knew I wasn't complicating things for the fun of it. I needed my feelings to make sense to me before I could expect them to make sense to anyone else.

Our first stop was the bank, where we tended to the business end of our relationship. After she paid me her portion of the car insurance I managed from my account, I was eager to move on from the prickly subject of finances. As we headed out, the receptionist at the front with a veneer smile, noticed the parking ticket in my hand.

"Do you guys need to be validated?" she asked without a stitch of irony.

Carla and I looked at each other blankly, as I shook my head, thinking some days I really wasn't in the mood for this town.

CHAPTER 7

Carla

I thought he'd like the song, but he seemed anxious over it. And I couldn't figure out why. I was also pretty hungover and could barely piece together my shopping list. After the bank, we went to the 99 Cent Store, which only made things more tense with the stuffed bears that held creepy signs that said I WUV YOU. There were also heart balloons on plastic sticks, and chocolate that stared at us as we did what felt like a perp walk down the aisle. We usually liked this aisle that on any other Saturday housed the Jesus candles and miniature silk flowers poking out of glass tubes that Barbie once told us were crack smoking devices fronting as gifts. But that day, we didn't talk much as we bought canned food and cheap shampoo.

Our errands continued in this weighted silence until the tension broke when we were inching out of the Trader Joe's parking lot. Pete gently pressed the brake to let the topless tan man us locals referred to as the Silver Lake Walker rush by. Our eyes followed him, furiously powerwalking with his head down while reading the newspaper. This reestablished conversation, easing us back into each other's comfort zone as we took guesses on his story.

When we returned to the building, he invited me over for some winter's stew he'd made during the week. Joni followed us, and after we all ate, the three of us stretched out on his bed. I read a novel that I probably shouldn't have enjoyed as much as I did, while he worked on his mom's socks he worried wouldn't be the same size, and Joni took turns napping and stalking his loose tails of yarn.

I lay beside him, my scuffed sneakers tossed next to his checkered Vans like old friends. On his turntable, Nick Drake's *Pink Moon* spun, the needle tracing the warped vinyl's grooves like a tipsy tightrope walker. The album's sparse guitar work and distant vocals stirred what felt like inherited nostalgia, borrowing a memory we didn't own, from an era before ours. I thought back on an old conversation we had about how this album was a commercial miss upon its 1972 release, only to fast forward to the present day with the titular track now featured in a popular Volkswagen commercial. Yet, in that moment, its placement in pop culture faded with only the sounds that we let guide our emotions, creating a shared introspection—or as I liked to think of as a soundtrack of us.

From the corner of my eye, I watched him knit. I marveled at his fingers' light choreography that made it look so easy, reminding me of the time he had tried to teach me. The needles, though, felt cumbersome, and the stitching fell apart in my hands. As his hands moved, so did the tattoo on his inner bicep. Just like his dad, he had the Alsatian coat of arms. Instead of the clean lines of his dad's with a red shield slashed with a gold band of crowns, Pete's was a rough sketch with outside-the-line coloring and crowns in a similar style to a Jean-Michel Basquiat painting. I liked his artistic interpretation of the French region's otherwise noble symbol. It also got me thinking that I'd probably never get a tattoo honoring my parents.

"How's your dad?" I asked, still watching his fingers work like it was the easiest thing they had ever done.

"Busy," he replied, his eyes locked on his moving hands. "He's still working on the interiors of that McMansion I was telling you about with people who don't know what they want. They keep saying they want *Mediterranean*, but they keep saying that word and I do not think it means what they think it means." He smirked, knowing I'd appreciate the reference before taking note of my book. "How's that going?"

"You warned me," I answered, closing it on my finger to use as temporary bookmark.

I looked at the cover of *Women,* by Charles Bukowski. A book set not too far from where we lived about a drunk writer with back acne and dysfunctional relationships with women. "It's completely offensive," I stated, thinking back on some of the novel's raunchier lines. "And definitely a perspective I know nothing about, but it's been keeping me company in a sick way."

Appearing amused, he said, "From *The Last Unicorn* to *Notes of a Dirty Old Man.* What has this city done to you?"

"I *have* gotten cynical, haven't I?"

"I think we both have." He turned to me, holding a significant gaze before breaking it to think about something I knew I wasn't a part of. The afternoon sun streamed like golden threads through his window where I could see the green in his eyes bleed perfectly into the gold, making them the tie-dyed color I'd always admired. I knew if he had turned his head slightly, taking in direct sunlight, they'd go completely gold like a tiger's stone. I remembered telling him this when I sat across from him as a kid in homeroom; a time so long ago it was starting to feel like a rerun to an old TV show.

I knew he could feel me looking at him, but his self-confidence allowed him to accept things like this, whereas I'd get uncomfortable assuming something was wrong with me. I placed the book beside me and looked down at my fingers. Appraising them, I noticed the cracked cuticles and bitten-down nails spotted in chipped light blue nail polish.

Noticing me checking my hands out, he set his yarn down and held his hand out. "Can I see?"

I looked at his hands beckoning mine and then back at him, confused.

He lightly tapped my hand. "I just want to see the left one."

"Oh," I said, understanding why he was asking, as I tucked my fingers into my palm to rob him of making a point.

"Come on," he continued to playfully insist. "I'm just curious."

He walked his fingers across the comforter like two tiny feet. When they got to my hand, his finger tapped my knuckle.

"Knock, knock," he teased.

"No one's home." I clenched my fist tighter.

"That bad, huh?"

"No," I defended myself.

"Then let me see."

With faux reluctance I placed my hand in his. Taking it, he opened my fingers, slowly one by one with the intimacy of undressing me. When he had my opened palm in his hands, he ran his thumb across the tips where the scarred skin used to be.

"Just as I suspected," he said softly. "When was the last time you touched your guitar?"

"This year?"

"Oh, shit." He let out a deep laugh.

"I know." I evaluated my fingertips that used to remind me of my hard work, but now were pampered princesses. "I need to practice my scales, but I just don't feel like it."

He shook his head like I had it all wrong. "Fuck scales. That's a part of music, but it's not everything. Music comes from a need to communicate. Scales and all of that is the technical side." I watched as his thumb continued its caresses across my fingertips. "You've got some great pedals, too."

"I think I forgot how to use them," I replied, looking for something, *anything*, to contest.

"You forgot how to use them," he said plainly, as a smirk slipped the corner of his mouth. "You step on them."

"Fine," I surrendered. "Then how's I haven't written a good song in ages for a response?"

"I don't know," he said, his voice getting quieter. "A wise woman once told me to write the worst rock song ever written and see where it goes from there." His eyes met mine. "Have you ever heard of such a crazy idea?"

"Trust me when I say she might not know everything."

"I disagree," he said. "I'd say she's pretty intuitive."

I blew off his compliment knowing nothing could be further from the truth before looking at his hand still holding mine. I could feel my body get warm the way it always did when we got close like this. I dared to let my thumb play a little with his, feeling my pulse quicken at the contact. I breathed deeply through my nose, my eyes then moving up to his lips that I would always describe as kissable and hating myself for wanting him, hating myself for getting wet from just being with him. Damn him. I remembered every single one of these close moments that I would revisit in my quiet moments, wishing he would touch me, kiss me, fuck me already. But he never did, so I began to classify these instances by color rather than detail to protect my unsatisfied heart. I softened my gaze to envision the black and white shadows of the movie we saw last summer at the Hollywood Forever Cemetery. Then there were the sun-faded blues of our life jackets when we rented paddle boats in Echo Park. The overcast grays mixed with the Christmas tree greens of a trip up to Northern California. The whiskey browns of the wood-paneled walls of an East Side dive like Little Joy for cheap beer and The Cramps and Gang of Four on the jukebox. On this day, the memory would be tie-dyed in shades of gold and green. His eyes locked onto mine where I swear I could sense a flicker of something deeper between us. But I knew better to analyze it and quickly stowed the memory in a safe place in my mind. He gave my hand a light squeeze as if gently sending it off. I always sat there stunned because didn't he know how his politeness was slowly killing me?

I suppressed a deep sigh, frustrated, once again, by his measured reactions. So, I did what I did best: I changed the subject.

"You know who I was thinking about the other day?" I said, aiming for casual.

"Who?"

"The Weekend Warriors."

"Oh, God. I wonder whatever happened to them."

"Same thing as us," I guessed. "They probably got day jobs and no longer had time to play."

"Probably, but in their case that would be a good thing because they really weren't a very good band." He shook his head in recollection. "That was a fun night though, even though I had to tune the drums because their drummer was actually a keyboardist, and the lead singer was so drunk he pissed himself."

My eyes glazed over thinking back on the night that already felt sepia-toned. Our first *and* last show in Los Angeles, played at an empty dive bar with another band whose lead singer called our band Tits and Sticks, which I never told Pete about.

"The drummer guy was nice though," I offered a bright side.

"He was," Pete agreed.

And we left it at that as I looked out his window, allowing my thoughts to drift into nothing. A moment or fifty passed as we lingered in the afternoon. The record had long ago finished, leaving us with our long inhalations competing with Joni's purrs, a passing car, and the steady syncopation of the clock ticking away in his kitchen.

"I know I've asked you this before," I said, turning to him to break the lull, "but what made you start knitting?"

I caught a glint of appreciation in his eyes. "My grandmother wanted me to do something with my hands other than smoke."

I nodded my head in recollection of a memory I didn't own. "Because you didn't have your drums, right?"

"Uh, yeah," he said, his voice laced with hesitation before holding up his work to appraise it. "This seems like a good place to stop. I could use a smoke." He turned to me, his eyes seeking affirmation. "You down?"

I went back and forth on smoking weed. I couldn't tell if I liked it or not. Sometimes it made me feel dreamy, this sort of heavy euphoria, but other times, it plunged me into a deep introspection that took forever to claw out of. His stuff was strong too, homegrown in Humboldt, so a mix of all of these feelings were within the realm of possibility.

He reached over to his nightstand drawer, pulling out his rolling papers and a repurposed baby food jar that housed his stash. Even sealed in glass, I could smell how potent it was. Herbal, woodsy, skunky, and rich with earth that I figured a hit or two would probably be good for me. Beside his bed he kept a large coffee table book that he placed on his lap to use as an even surface. As he began to assemble the joint, I noticed there was something ceremonial about the process with movements deliberate and precise. As he deepened the crease of the rolling paper, I stretched back on his bed. With my head on his pillow that smelled like him, I stared at the ceiling as I instinctively reached for Joni.

"When did you start smoking?" I asked, burying my hand in the warmth of her fur.

"Sixteen."

"But why?" I gently pressed, thinking our generation grew up with enough PSAs against smoking. "Because you were in France and that's what you do there?"

This made him chuckle and when he could see my question wasn't rhetorical, he answered, "I just had a lot going on that summer. I arrived and then my grandfather died shortly after."

I rolled my head towards him, my eyes softening with understanding.

"I mean, we knew he was sick, but I guess it's never the right time for someone you love to die…" he trailed off for a second as he thought back on the painful memory. "I blamed myself for it, too."

"For the death of your grandfather?" I pressed my eyebrows in, thinking it was out-of-character for him.

"I did," he replied with a directness that startled me.

Taken aback, I thought about it for a few seconds. I was someone who was capable of blaming myself for the death of a family member, but Pete, who saw everything with a certain logic? It didn't quite add up.

"How could you possibly blame yourself?" I suddenly felt protective of him.

"Like I said, there was a lot going on that summer."

He popped off the metal top of the baby food jar that made the entire apartment smell like the Redwood Forest. I looked at

Joni whose nose twitched at the odor's pungency before abandoning her suspicion to curl into a tighter ball.

Out of the jar, he pulled out what could have been the world's tiniest tree. Coated in crystals, it picked up flecks of light as he delicately broke off small stems to sprinkle down the seam of the rolling paper. I continued looking at him like he'd have to give me a little more than that even if I could tell he was getting uncomfortable.

"I guess we thought we had more time," he said, seeming pressured by me to explain. "But the messed-up part was we had to spend the entire day with his corpse."

"What do you mean?"

"It was a mess and *so* painfully French," he said, stifling a laugh. "So, what happened was the funeral home couldn't take the body until his doctor signed the death certificate, but he was away for the weekend and since it wasn't technically an emergency because, you know, my grandfather was already dead, he took his time getting back to the region."

I shook my head. "No way. You're making that up."

"I really wish I was," he said. "My grandfather died at seven in the morning and the doctor didn't get there until at least eight o'clock that night and, mind you, my grandmother's house is small. As we waited for the family to fly in and drive in from Paris, it was just the two of us having full meals with grandpa's body just lying in the other room." His fingers stopped moving for a second to think about it.

"It was definitely a bonding experience with my grandmother," he said absently as I flinched at the thought, imagining my family and dead relative in the room. With certainty, I knew the body would have ended up face down on the floor with my family fighting over it about something completely unrelated.

He brought the joint to his lips, running his tongue along the length of it. After some final twists and rolls, he inspected it with satisfaction before reaching for his lighter to fire it up.

"Here you go," he said, blowing the flame out on the tip. "That should be good."

I smiled, appreciating his gesture in offering me the first hit, his smoker's etiquette unwavering as I took the lit joint.

"So, what about your family?" he asked, as I tried not to cough too hard on the first hit. "No one does funerals like Italians. Didn't your grandmother take pictures of the open caskets to send to Italy?"

"My great-grandmother," I corrected him with a pinched voice. "She took pictures of the flowers too." I exhaled thinking of the doubles of all of those pictures of dead Italians my parents still had in the attic. "But at my grandmother's funeral," I grinned at the memory that really was not funny at all, "a brawl ensued."

"Over money?" His eyes filled with excitement. "Or something that went down at the fish market. A deal gone wrong?"

"Pete." I turned to him. "I told you my family is not in the Mafia."

He looked at me doubtfully, presumably thinking back on the time I told him about the famous mob boss that used to go into my dad's shoe repair store.

"The brawl," I said, ignoring his organized crime fantasies, "happened because my cousin placed a mini orange juice carton he got from the deli on the top of some random tombstone to pursue a fight with one of my brothers after he didn't like the way he said, 'Hi.' Apparently, there was a *tone*."

Handing him the joint, I starting to laugh, thinking about the story that hadn't crossed my mind in years.

"My family loves accusing other family members of *tones*," I continued. "But my other brother got pissed about the orange juice on the random tomb, fast forward and they're all calling each other guidos. Meanwhile, my grandmother wasn't even in the ground yet. The priest, who had called her by the wrong name during the entire Mass, waited to start the sermon until the brawl finished. And then out of nowhere, a distant aunt added to the chaos by asking if the guests were getting a luncheon afterward since they drove out to Queens and all."

Pete laughed as he seemed to picture it perfectly.

"Anyone end up in the ground?" he asked, his voice slightly choked as a mushroom cloud of smoke hovered over us.

"We weren't far from it." I rolled my eyes at my family's addiction to drama.

"And the orange juice container?" he asked, smiling as he rolled the edge of the joint along his charred copper dish to evenly ash it. "What happened to it?"

I smirked. "I knew you were going to ask that."

"You know me so well." His now-glassy eyes smiled, taking it as a compliment.

"Well, you know what happened."

"You ended up taking it and throwing it away for them," he guessed.

"You know *me* so well."

Pete

Within minutes she drifted off to sleep. Curled on her side, she formed the same shape as Joni as I watched the two dark beauties sleep. Her lowered eyelashes were soft and full like an artist had painted them on with a feather, and her cheeks flushed a peony pink. Below her left eye was a pinpoint beauty mark that I had watched form under the California sun. I used to think we were born with our imperfections, but watching this one deepen from golden brown to milk chocolate, I learned they were also environmental. She once pointed to the first star at nightfall, saying it felt personal, like it belonged to her. I'd always feel that way about her beauty mark. She'd inevitably get a boyfriend, and rightfully so, but I'd have this one thing the poor shmuck wouldn't have any reference to.

Looking at her, I knew this person, my best friend. Sometimes I wondered if she was my other half. Well, my nicer, more discerning, calmer other half. But I knew her. I knew she cried whenever she heard "Für Elise". Or as a child, she was afraid of the "rhythm" sung about in Gloria Estefan's "Rhythm is Gonna Get You." And that she referred to her mind as a dangerous neighborhood that she avoided walking through, especially at night. She trusted me with these parts of herself, and I wanted to reciprocate. I wanted to tell her so many things, like why that teenage summer was so painful for me because it was the first time I had felt the cruelty of contrast: a summer of love followed by a summer of indifference, and then, my grandfather died. It was the perfect opportunity to tell her the whole story, but I chose instead to get us both high and listen to records. The music would always connect us, our breathing aligned in 4/4 time — the steady rhythm, classic and reliable, defining the stillness that was us.

As she slept, I listened to the cars outside drive leisurely on the lazy end of a Saturday afternoon. The smell of the backyard's desert brush filtered in through the window, until her nose twitched, and her eyes slowly blinked open, as she reoriented herself.

"How long was I asleep for?" she asked, swallowing as she glanced out the window to gauge the time.

"About an hour."

She stretched her arms over her head, releasing a few deep yawns as Joni covered her eyes with her paws. "Your stuff is strong," she said, turning her body to face me, her eyes still heavy with sleep as she appeared to still be dreaming.

"Pete," she eventually said. "Do you have anything sweet?"

"Sweet," I echoed back.

"Yeah, I'm craving something sweet."

I grinned at her drowsy eyes. "Someone's got the munchies."

She lightly pushed my shoulder. "I do not."

"Oh, I think you do," I teased.

"Alright, whatever," she said, somewhat owning up to it. "Well, do you or don't you?"

When she saw my eyes trail towards the kitchen, she said, "And I don't mean the rest of the stew or something annoying like the three-bean salad that I know is in your fridge."

"How is three-bean salad annoying?" I asked, clearly amused. "Or sweet for that matter?"

"When you're craving something satisfying, I swear, it's like the Gilbert Godfried of items you could find in the refrigerator."

"Because you're always confronted with three-bean salads that resemble '80s comedians when you're stoned?" She didn't answer as I could see she was still waiting for the sweet verdict.

"I actually have something that just might interest you."

"Really?" She jutted her chin out, remaining skeptical.

"Really." I chuckled to myself, noting the deep concern on her face. "But in order to get it, you're going to have to close your eyes."

Too stoned to argue, she complied as I padded to my front door where I hung my backpack. Inside, I took out the small box, hoping it wouldn't trigger the same reaction it did with Victoria. Hearing the candies rattle in the box, Joni's head popped up with hopeful eyes.

"Are you giving me cat treats?" she asked, smiling with her eyes still closed.

"No," I replied, grinning at her building impatience. "And again, those aren't sweet."

I opened the box in search of the perfect expression, sprinkling a few into my palm. I sorted through YOU'RE HOT, BE MINE and E-MAIL ME, setting them on the piano as rejects, before shaking out another batch. A light blue MARRY ME fell out, which I then popped into my mouth to avoid an all-out crisis.

"What are you doing?" she said with a laugh, trying to make sense of the sounds.

"Just another second," I said as the sound of my back molars chomping into the candy filled the room. There was AS IF and IN DA MOOD, followed by CHARM ME, which I also threw in my mouth because what the fuck? Charm yourself. I shook out a few more until I found one that worked in its simplicity. Well, that one, and a bonus one.

"Alright," I said, shaking the two chosen hearts in my hand like a pair of dice as I walked over to the bed. "You said you wanted something sweet, now hold both hands out." I had to chuckle at how sleazy it all sounded. I was expecting a comment because I certainly would have had one, but instead she sat up to follow my instructions. With her palms out, I placed a heart in each hand before closing it.

"You can look now but open this one first," I instructed, tapping on the suggested hand.

She opened her eyes and in her palm was a periwinkle blue heart that said MAKE MAGIC. It was such a small thing, but witnessing her skepticism melt into a smile made it feel more authentic than any forced dinner.

"Now this one." I tapped on the other one.

She opened her hand and in it was the completion of my thought with a yellow heart that simply said HAPPY VALENTINE'S DAY.

CHAPTER 8

Carla

Something about stepping on stars just felt wrong. But there I was on Hollywood Boulevard doing just that. I rarely ventured to this side of town, only sometimes to pick up medication for Barbie when Kurt was working late. With her blood pressure pills shaking in my bag, I hummed an old song by the Kinks about this very street. I *could* see all the stars as I walked down Hollywood Boulevard as the lyrics went. I also saw souvenir shops selling dreams in the form of plastic Academy Awards, the blue button-down Mafia promoting personality tests, and tourists who looked sorry for choosing Los Angeles as their vacation destination. At Cahuenga, I maneuvered around a lady taking a picture of Marlene Dietrich's star and headed toward my car when I saw the parking ticket tucked under my windshield wiper. Bright and glowing in its signature convict-jumpsuit orange, it felt like a big ha-ha in my face. The joke was on me. If the gift shops wanted to sell the real experience, then they'd sell plastic versions of these, because it didn't get any more Hollywood than a parking ticket.

"Damn it!" I cried out as my phone rang. Opening my purse, I pushed aside the pharmacy bag to reach my phone. "Hello." I knew how unwelcoming my voice sounded.

"You okay?" asked Alex's voice at the other end.

"No, thank you," I said impatiently to a man waving pamphlets in my face as I marched towards my car.

"Who are you talking to?"

"This man trying to sell me a map to stars' homes."

"Those really exist?"

"Yes," I said under my breath, not meaning to sound impatient as I yanked the envelope out from under my windshield wiper. "Sorry, I just got a parking ticket for…" My eyes scanned the printed text, "Expired registration?" I walked around to my back license plate. "But it expires next month!"

"Which is next week," she noted.

"Right," I agreed. "*Next week.*"

"So, you got a ticket because they assumed you wouldn't get the registration in time?" Alex sounded amazed. "That's fucked up."

"Seriously." I reached into my bag for the keys. "I must really suck at being an adult if even LADOT assumed I wouldn't take care of this next week."

"LADOT," Alex said with a bounce in her voice. "They make it sound so cute."

"Sure, sixty bucks cute."

"You may have unbeatable weather, but I'm just happy I don't have to deal with all that car shit."

I silently agreed as I opened the door to let myself in, chucking my bag with the parking ticket onto the passenger's seat.

"Sorry I didn't call last week," she said. "I got caught up but want to know how it went."

"How what went?"

"Valentine's Day. Did you seduce him like I told you to?"

"No," I answered without a second thought, "I didn't." I held my finger up to stop an impending comment I knew was coming. "However," I said with emphasis. "It wasn't a total bust, and it actually turned out to be pretty nice despite the fact that I never cared about the day before."

"I'm liking where this is going."

"Don't, because nothing, you know, *happened*. There were just some… nice moments." I smiled to myself, thinking about the heart candies and the close talking. "And you?" I said in a teasing tone. "Did you and Claire get *blackout drunk*?"

"Something like that," she said as a matter of fact. "We went to see this band the Weekend Warriors."

"That's so funny." My eyes stretched in amazement. "Pete and I were *just* talking about them."

"You were?" She also sounded stunned. "Sleaze neo-garage rock coated in Dorito dust isn't exactly either of your thing."

"No," I said, chuckling. "It's definitely not, but when we first got here, we played a show with them."

"Wait. That one show you guys played was with them?" She didn't have to wait for me to respond before adding, "How come you never told me that?"

"Because I didn't think it was a big deal," I said, shrugging. "We never really heard much about them after."

"Well, they're, like, getting big –at least according to the New York blogger girls and their Myspace pages. They're also Glasshouse Records' newest pet project."

"Glasshouse," I repeated. "That's Click Track, right?"

"It's their label where pretty much everything they put out turns to fucking gold. They also represent Rocktoya," Alex said, followed by a dramatic pause. "Need I say more." I smiled at her obsession with the singer she often described as horny electroclash trashier than Peaches, which I didn't think was even possible.

"You went to her show a few weeks ago, right?"

"Yeah, at Mercury Lounge," she replied. "You saw the pictures, right?"

"I don't think so. Did you send me a link?"

"No, they're on my Myspace," she said before realizing, "Oh, right, you still haven't set up your account."

"I haven't," I confirmed in a righteous tone. "Because I'm sorry, but didn't we already do this with Friendster?"

"Sweetie, no one's on Friendster anymore." I could see her shaking her blonde bob as if I didn't get it. "Myspace is where you need to be. Plus, it's great for new bands…"

"I don't have a band," I reminded her as I slipped my keys in the ignition.

"Then move back to New York already! That place sucks."

Glancing at the parking ticket, I could see her point more than I wanted to.

"Because seriously, La," she insisted, "if you guys aren't doing the band, then why are you even out there?"

Pete

Overnight, someone had changed the ringtone at work to a digital version of the song, "It's My Life." At first, it was sort of funny in that make-it-stop kind of way, but by the hundredth time, it felt like a meat grinder churning out my nerves.

Over my desk, I glanced at Victoria who remained on hold with the IT department to figure out how to change what she called the No Doubt song. I didn't have the mental capacity to tell her it was actually an '80s new wave song because she would've just accused me *again* of being anti-Gwen Stefani. Like that was the only thing I had on my mind.

I signaled for her attention. "IT must be busy," I told her. "Why don't you take your lunch, and we'll just try them again this afternoon."

"You sure?" She hesitantly pulled the phone away from her ear. "You're not going to have a meltdown?"

"Too late."

The phone rang again, as if testing my patience that had already left the building. I recognized the number coming from upstairs, prompting me to reinstate my professional voice.

« Bonjour, c'est Peter. »

« Oui, Peter, c'est Etienne. »

I relaxed my shoulders since it was the easy-going boss whose family also came from the Alsace region. This gave us common ground, and therefore authorizing our exchange in the informal *tu*.

« Salut Etienne, ça va ? »

« Oui, oui, merci, écoute, je voulais savoir si tu peux me rendre un service aujourd'hui ? »

« Oui ? » I answered, even if his request for a favor was more of a rhetorical question. He didn't wait for my response but instead informed me I would be conducting placement tests for new students during my lunch break.

« D'accord, » I stretched the word out to convey my reluctance.

« Je sais, » he replied, acknowledging the inconvenience before explaining why he was asking as my eyes glazed over with disinterest.

"You've done them before," he said cheerfully, switching to English, adopting the user-friendly tone he reserved for meetings with Americans. "So, you should remember, they're easy and you're going to be really great."

I winced at the appropriated motivational tone, which sounded more like he was training a small pet. As I let him over explain the exam procedure, figuring I'd waste some of his time, I let out strategically placed sighs to underscore the inconvenience of it all.

« *Des questions ?* » he asked, deliberately ignoring my unwillingness.

"Yeah, just one."

« *Vas-y.* »

"Are they going to get all pissed off at me if I assign them a level they feel is beneath them?" Etienne laughed, recalling the time when a girl flipped out on me because, apparently, she had studied the year before at the American University in Paris. She didn't like it when I told her that they must have forgotten to teach her the subjunctive because she wasn't fucking using it.

"Study-abroad know-it-alls are the absolute worst," I caught myself complaining.

With a chuckle, Etienne said, "I wish I could control that, but it'll be fine. Just follow the guidelines in the binders and if they don't like it, explain that it's for their benefit and the classes should be challenging but also fun." I made a face because I didn't see anything fun about learning French as a second language, in which I had my mom as proof. "Don't let them bully you," he said, which came out more like *boolie* with his accent.

"And Peter," he continued, "you're to speak in the formal *vous.*"

"Even if they're my age?"

Oui, of course was his answer, his voice carrying a hint of flirtation, which I admit I found appealing. "And," he added, his words smoother than the smile I knew he had on his face, "you're to introduce yourself as Monsieur Albrecht."

« *Serieux ?* » I said, thinking it was beyond absurd.

« *Serieux,* » he confirmed, slightly teasing me. "Your generation is too *à la cool.*"

"Really, now." I rolled my eyes. "You know it's cliché to complain about the younger generation, *n'est-ce pas?*"

"Is that right? Well…" his words tapered off in light-hearted dismissal, as we sat on the line for a few silent beats, once again, making me wonder about him. I knew he lived with his trust-fund Parisian *bobo riche* girlfriend in Venice whose job was simply "artist." Over time, I learned that "artist" was code for someone who nourished themselves on fifty-dollar smoothies containing, like, ghost whispers and rose quartz shards and frequented workshops for things like vagina yoga. They'd been together forever, he once told me, but I always wondered if there was ever a Monsieur bobo riche in his romantic family tree. In short, were we the same?

"I just sent you an e-mail with the roster for today," his words sliced into my mental musings. "Your first appointment is with a Misha Taylor. She noted that she learned some French in school, but if she can't answer past the third question, just recommend the Introduction to French class."

"Yeah, she might not like that."

"Probably not *mais tant pis* and after that, you have a Brian Kurtz, a new hire at Nestlé who needs Business French and also has some school-level French. This test is a little more involved, but the same rules apply." He then bristled his lips making the little horse brush noise that the French do to signal a conclusion to an exchange.

« *Bon,* » he added as a final touch.

« *Bon,* » I returned the sentiment even though I didn't think any of this sounded particularly *bon*.

Having been tasked to wait for Misha Taylor meant eating in the break room. I forwent my usual spot in the back alley we shared with an Italian restaurant and sat by myself at the lunch table looking like the punchline to an office comic strip. The plot thickened though when Misha never showed. Disgruntled for wasted time in a room that smelled of warm egg salad that day, I flicked on the espresso machine, rupturing the silence of the empty office by banging the espresso grounds from the portafilter into the knock box. This was when I heard the ring of the hotel bellhop bell we had out front. I looked at the clock to see the business French student was twenty minutes early.

"You're just going to have to wait," I said as I continued with my coffee routine.

I firmly pressed down the metal tamper to pack in the fresh coffee grounds and just as I was about to click the portafilter into place, the bell rang again.

"You've got to be kidding me." I aimed a tired look at the break room door like it was its fault. "Impatient French Business fuck."

Then it hit me.

"Ramón!" I burst out of the breakroom, knowing the only person who would dare ring the bell twice was our UPS guy who ran on a tighter schedule than his shorts in the summer. I jogged down the corridor to reception, but when I got there, I didn't see Ramón. Instead, I saw my one o'clock whom I couldn't picture taking Business French. With sun-kissed, chin-length hair flipped to the side and well-built arms he probably spent way too much time on, he could have walked out of a beach perfume ad. Cute, but he had pressed the bellhop bell twice, so therefore he was an asshole.

"May I help you?" I asked, placing my hand on the bell.

"Oh hey, what's going on?" he responded in a cool California timbre that made me turn my nose up. "I'm here to take an exam?" He extended a piece of paper like he was handing me a summons.

"Business, right?"

"I guess this is business," he said breezily. "Sure."

"Well, is it or isn't it? I have to provide the right materials." I realized then that I probably should have taken the paper he tried to hand me, but it was too late to backpedal. "What time is your appointment?"

"That's the thing, I'm actually a little late," he explained. "My appointment was earlier."

"Earlier?" I glimpsed over his shoulder at the clock on the wall. "It's not at one?"

"No, noon." He offered the paper again that this time I decided to take. Quickly scanning down the document, I looked up at him with curious eyes. "You're Misha Taylor?"

He made a face as if this happened all the time. "You were expecting a girl, weren't you?"

"No," I white lied as I placed my hands on the partition and leaned forward to take a position of authority. "I was expecting someone on time."

Just as he was about to launch into an excuse, he stopped himself as our eyes momentarily locked. It was probably a split second but felt as long as a minute as I noticed how striking his blue eyes were. Not like Carla's outer-space blues where it was always midnight, his were the daytime version. Practically Californian, they reminded me of a swimming pool and the way the ripples quietly move, as if breathing in rhythm with the sun.

"I was going to say," he stumbled, "I got caught in an –"

"Audition?" I completed the regional cliché with bored eyes.

"Well, yeah." He made a guilty face. "But if you want, we can reschedule."

"Why? So, you can be late for that too?"

We gave each other the once-over as I noted the rest of his attire. The fitted T-shirt, the laidback cargo pants, the flipflops I imagined were on his sand-weathered feet. I must have been sneering at the informality because he appraised himself before looking up to say, "What?"

"This is what you wear to an office?"

"What's wrong with it?" he asked earnestly, which made me laugh, because clearly he was joking. "No, really, tell me." He grinned seeming to find humor in my comment.

"I would," I said, borrowing a drop of his good nature with my own smile, "but I don't have time."

Bing! The elevator announced its arrival, followed by the sound of Victoria's heels. She was already back from lunch, and it made me flinch as if she was about to catch me doing something I shouldn't have been. "Shall we?" I tapped the binder.

"I'm all yours." He let his regard linger a second longer than necessary.

I wanted to ask him if that look worked with all the boys, but I forced a professional composure, quickly turning on my heels to not let him see me blush.

As I led the way down the hall with him behind me, I could hear the sound of his flipflops slap against the bottom of his heels, as my leather shoes seemed to click in protest at the inappropriate office attire.

"I'm not exactly starting on the right foot, am I?" he said, which made me wonder if he could read my thoughts.

I couldn't help but grin to myself. "That remains to be seen."

"Yeah?" He sounded intrigued. "On what?"

At the conference room, as I reached for the door handle, I turned to him. "Well," I answered. "Have you studied abroad in Paris?"

CHAPTER 9

Carla

It was half past five when I left the apartment. The city was so quiet, it felt like I could hear it breathing peacefully in the early hour. With my trusty duffel bag containing various outfits, I headed to my 6 a.m. cattle call. I usually avoided these big jobs that cast hundreds of extras that were herded like, well, cattle. Something about walking into a job that metaphorically compared me to a farm animal wasn't exactly the stuff self-esteem was made of. But with rent looming, I didn't have the luxury to ponder my dignity.

The day should have been easy enough, since I was playing GIRL IN ROCK CLUB. I arrived on set confident I could do the job without needing clothes from Wardrobe. But once again, I was wrong and forgot how Hollywood liked to overcomplicate everything. So, instead of wearing a plain tee and jeans, I wore an off-the-shoulder leopard print top with shiny pleather appliqués spelling ROCK in that pointed AC/DC font.

Walking through the set, I made my way over to the extras' holding area; an open space of folding chairs and nearby, a table of sugary snacks that we'd call home for the next ten hours. I found a seat next to a girl I recognized from other shows I'd worked on. She sat on a canvas camping chair with a fleece blanket placed over her lap while she read a magazine.

"You're well-equipped today," I noted as I sat down on the folding chair beside her, the plastic squeaking in response.

"I did this show last week," she said with a glazed-over look in her eyes. "The actresses can't act, which means it'll be a long day with lots of takes." She glanced at my folding chair. "I figured I might as well get comfortable."

"I've been trying not to." I let my bag drop beside me, noticing her sheepskin slippers.

"That's what I said too. And that was seven years ago."

"Oh," was all I could think to say as I reassessed the space, mentally sketching out the long hours ahead. I had my Discman and Barbie's worn Pepto-pink copy of *Valley of the Dolls*, as I noticed her advanced operation of snacks and magazines.

"Did you want to read one?" She glared at me.

I looked at the cover of one of them featuring a squeaky-clean actress busted for drug possession.

"Alright," I said in a conspiratorial tone. "Maybe that one."

She handed it to me and just as I was about to take it, she snapped her wrist back. "One thing, though." Her expression suddenly became grave. "I haven't read it yet, so don't tell me what's in it."

"Okay," I agreed, while wondering if she was kidding or not. "I won't."

"I'm serious. Like, don't even gasp in surprise because that'll make me want to know." I didn't know what the big deal was until she said, "Don't rob me of my one pleasure."

And then I got it. Knowing how few of these we got in life, I assured her that I understood. Her interest in my sincerity, though, waned as I watched her eyes follow the principal actresses passing by in full make-up, holding Starbucks cups.

"These strawberry cupcakes can't act for shit," she mumbled, "and I'm going to need something to fill the time."

"I won't tell you what's in the magazine," I promised.

She seemed appeased, allowing me to slowly take the magazine from her. Before digging in, I waited a moment for her to settle back into her own reading material when I felt a hand on my shoulder. I didn't know anyone on these sets intimately enough to warrant this kind of greeting, so I flinched, which made the magazine slip from my lap. As if in slow motion, I watched it land in front of her feet, open to an item about Jessica Simpson.

"Nooooo!" she shrieked as I tried to kick the magazine closed.

Before I could take hold of it, her arm swooped down like an eagle, snatching and then stuffing it back into her bag. "Offer rescinded!" she snapped before returning to her own magazine, turning the page hastily to emphasize her irritation.

"Sorry," I meekly offered before whipping around to the person who had obviously mistook me for someone else.

"Hi," I said with impatience. "Do we know each other?"

I really wanted to tell him thanks for nothing, but upon closer inspection without tabloids flying around, he did seem familiar.

"Carla, right?" He said my name as he pushed aside his side-swept bangs.

"That's me," I replied as I examined his face, still trying to place him.

"Jay." He pointed to himself, but it wasn't enough of a clue. "You haven't gone all Hollywood on me, have you?"

I gestured to my surroundings. "I wouldn't exactly say that."

When he could see I was still drawing a blank, he pointed to his chest again. "Jay," he repeated. "Drummer from Weekend Warriors?"

I tossed my head back in sudden recognition before standing up to officially greet him. "I'm sorry. It's just been forever." I looked at his hair. "And you got a new haircut."

"Yeah, they just cut it." He pointed in a general direction over his shoulder. "I guess I'm supposed to be a hipster."

It was unclear what he was referring to, so I landed on a subject I did know about. "I hear the band is taking off."

"Yeah, we got this TV show thing so maybe that'll give us a boost or something. You never know with these things." He shrugged. "Are you guys doing the show too?"

"Us guys?" I turned around to see what he was talking about only to find the extra had moved on from her tabloids and was now holding up a compact mirror to pluck her eyebrows. "What guys?"

His eyes searched for a moment. "The Disentanglement?"

"The Disenchanted," I corrected him on the name of my band.

"Yeah!" He clapped his hands together. "The Disenchanted. You guys doing a fake performance today, too?" When I didn't immediately respond, he tacked on, "Or whatever."

Completely lost, I looked at him waiting for him to complete his thought.

"Bez, you know our lead singer?" he asked, in which I vaguely nodded. "His dad is Petra's agent," he pointed in the direction of the actresses, "so they thought we should do this show even though our record company is against teen shows, calling it gimmicky." He seemed unbothered by the word I would never want associated with my band. "And so here we are. Bez's dad said the timing will be perfect with our album coming out the week the episode airs. So, we'll see."

"What about you?" he asked, still not connecting why I was there.

"I'm actually background today." I angled myself in the direction of the other extras as if presenting them. "Gotta pay the bills somehow."

"Totally." He scanned the others, the fear visible in his eyes. "But you guys are still doing the band, right?"

"We are," I fibbed just to get him to stop looking at me like a wounded animal.

"Oh, thank God." He placed a hand on his chest in relief. "You guys are, like, the real deal. Especially your drummer. I bet he's doing, like, symphonies and soundtracks and shit. That dude is on another planet."

"Yeah," I couldn't contest. "Pete's really talented."

From there we didn't know what else to say to each other as we had exhausted our common ground. This was evidenced as I balanced back and forth on my heels, and he scratched his forearm. I pressed my lips together as his eyes darted around the room, perhaps looking for a rescue.

"So …" we said at the same time.

"Oh, you go," he offered.

"No, no, you go."

"Hey!" the extra cut in, which felt directed towards me as I turned around almost obediently. Looking only at me, she announced, "I gotta pee."

I didn't respond, unsure what she wanted me to do with the information.

"Well, will you watch my stuff while I take a leak?"

"Yeah, sure," I said, my mortification of my association to her now complete.

"And don't let anyone touch my magazines!"

"I won't," I said, rolling my eyes back to Jay who I could see was still plotting a tactful exit. I wanted to tell him that he should just go. It really was fine. He didn't owe me anything. But he stayed, reaching for other body parts to scratch and more hair to brush out of his face. Thankfully, a production assistant interrupted us and acknowledging only Jay, he said, "Hey man, breakfast for principles is being served outside in the catering tent."

"Oh, I already ate." He pointed to the extra's table, an offering of blackened bananas, rock-hard bagels, and a tin foil tray of tootsie rolls.

"Tell me you didn't eat any of that." The PA's face dripped with concern so fake he could've have run for office, placing a fraternal hand on Jay's shoulder. "Dude, that's for background. For cast and crew, we have human food."

They both slowly turned to me where I fought off every ounce in me not to say, moo.

Pete

The large metal door felt heavier that day as I strained to push it open. Once it gave way, the back-alley stench did its job by assaulting my senses of fresh-squeezed dumpster juice; an overheated car transmission that smelled like burnt maple syrup; garlic-stained restaurant grease, all cooked *à point* in the late-morning sun. At a padded card table where the waitstaff counted their tips, I set down the letter from my cousin I'd been avoiding. His New Year card didn't exactly wish me a happy one but rather asked me how I was going to make that year different than the last. Although he meant well, his straightforward manner struck me as too French, making me start to wonder if Southern California was making me soft.

I opened the envelope, surprised to see he had included an old photo of us. Dating back to 1995, it was us on the streets of Paris. With our summer hair grown out, tanned cheeks, Guy in his Germs Circle One tee and me in a striped rugby polo, we squinted into the camera like asshole teenagers who couldn't be bothered with making memories. I remember my aunt telling us that one day we'd love this photo and, of course, we didn't believe her and laughed in her face like she knew jack shit. *Like I said, asshole teenagers.* But seeing the photo a decade later, I smiled at the two of us, realizing she was right. The memories came racing back from our newfound independence of being allowed to walk the streets of Paris alone the year Guy and I had come out to each other.

After spending the summer with my grandparents in Alsace, I took the train to Paris to spend a week with his family before returning to the States for sophomore year. Fueled with teenage urgency, the two of us were in no mood for family snapshots and were heading to the one *tabac* that sold us cigarettes – Gauloises – to choke on in a back booth. "Joe Le Taxi" or whatever semi-out-of-style French pop song would play behind the bar run by an old man who the regulars called Lulu. There, Guy and I would pretend to smoke, sip on Cokes, and talk about boys. Since Guy was a year older and lived in a city, his stories were wild and exciting with hand jobs in the boys' room at his private school. My stories felt more innocent, taking place in the Vosges Mountains and involving one person. They held up to Guy's lavish tales, but I managed the impossible by one-upping him by having actually fallen in love with someone.

I reached for the letter, first, taking a long drag to brace myself for his criticism. Reading it, however, he was less sharp, choosing to focus on the old punk song "Ever Fallen in Love (With Someone You Shouldn't've)," by The Buzzcocks. He told me it was rumored to be about a guy, while also informing me that I shared the same first name as the lead singer. I couldn't fault Guy's exuberance that practically jumped off the page, thinking he had gifted me with my very own bisexual icon who he thought would serve as the catalyst for my coming out. He used to argue that I was lucky because I had "cool parents," unlike his Jean-Marie Le Pen-supporting dad whose response to Guy's coming out was calling him an attention whore. Sometimes I wished I could blame my parents, but I genuinely liked them and made the deal with myself that I'd tell them once I met someone.

"*Quel luxe*," my cousin would snort, which I couldn't disagree with because it *was* a luxury to have supportive parents.

After crushing my cigarette out, I picked up the picture and zeroed in on myself. I felt judged by my own teenage eyes, who surely would have called bullshit on the adult me, who frankly sucked. He was weak, a coward and irritatingly inarticulate. How did I seem to know more when I was younger? Wasn't it supposed to be the reverse? I looked at teenage me wondering how I could make him proud, but I knew he had long given up on me.

CHAPTER 10

Carla

On Monday, I had 1960s girl group hair and a rockin' mini dress for the show *American Dreams*. Tuesday, it was combed out for jury duty on a courtroom drama. Wednesday, my car got fired for having squeaky brakes, making me lose out on the additional twenty-five bucks for casting it. But at least I got to keep my "role" as SHOPPER IN MALL PARKING LOT. And by Thursday, I had disco fever with Farrah Fawcett winged hair and purple eyeshadow for *That 70s Show*. When Barbie saw me walking into the building, she shot up from her desk, waving excitedly.

"I knew you'd like it." I gestured to my wildly made-up face. "Even if you say you don't remember the '70s."

"I don't," she said without a second thought. "But close the door." Her excitement returned with bursting energy that seemed to make her hair a brighter shade of brass. "I have something to tell you!"

"Okay…" She watched me shut the door like I wasn't going to do it properly.

As I sat down, I kept a skeptical eye on her, fearing the buildup was going to end up being gossip about the cats.

"You'll never believe what I have." She opened her drawer and pulled out a folded piece of paper with my name on it.

With intrigue, I leaned forward. "What is that?"

"Tyler gave it to me."

My eyes flicked up, trying to make the connection, which only made my false eyelashes tickle my eyebrows. "Who's Tyler?"

"In 301," she said, looking at me like that should mean something. "He's on the other side of the building!" she loud whispered, waving around the paper.

"I don't know the people on the other side of the building."

"Oh, you don't know the people on your side of the building either, but anyway, he's been asking about you."

"Why?"

"Because he's *interested*." The excitement in her eyes couldn't be understated.

"Interested in what?"

"Oh, do I hate when you do this, when you play obstinate." She exhaled from her nostrils to show mild irritation before exclaiming, "You! He's interested in you!"

"I don't even know this person. Why would he be interested in me?"

"Beats the hell out of me," she teased. "Now open the damn thing. I've been dying to read it since this morning!"

My eyes met hers. "You know you could have opened it."

"I know," she admitted, "but I wanted to wait for you."

I took it and as I began to open it, she tried to accelerate things with hand movements and huffs. I pulled apart the origami-like fold of the paper, the elaborate design hinting that this guy might be a psychopath.

"Now I know why you didn't open it," I said, straining to get the damn thing open. "It's because you couldn't."

"That too," she admitted, focusing intently on my fingers. "Now what does it say?"

Holding the letter up, I cleared my throat and began reading it to her:

Hey Carla,

So, I hope this isn't totally weird, but I've noticed you around the building, mostly talking with Barbie, and wanted to know if you'd like to get a coffee with me sometime. A little about me: I'm 24, and work in graphic design. Mostly promotional work for "Must-See" (hint, hint!) TV shows.

Additional fun facts include: I'm from Connecticut. I've been in L.A. for over a year, and I like Thai food, going to Spaceland on Mondays and tacos at El Siete Mares. Your turn?

Tyler, 301

I placed the letter on my lap and waited, giving her the opportunity to react first. She looked at me in amazement as if I had invented something as she plucked a Pall Mall from the soft pack on her desk.

"What do you think about that?" Her tone was airy as if there was a mystical meaning to it all.

I glanced at the letter again. "I don't really know what I think of it."

"He's certainly good on paper. Great job, right age, from the East Coast like you."

Seeing the disinterest on my face made her frown. "Well, you can't hide in your apartment forever."

I shot her a challenging look. "Wanna bet?"

"No," she said, detecting the seriousness in my voice. "No, I don't."

"My apartment is my safety nest. Nothing bad can happen there because I won't let it," I explained as she leaned back in her chair, tapping the end of the unlit cigarette against the desk and assessing me like a mob boss.

"But let's get back to Tyler," she said. "I know you already don't like him."

"Why do you immediately assume that?"

"I'll tell you why. Because he likes you, so there *must* be something wrong with him. The old Groucho Marx defense strikes again."

"Who?"

"Groucho Marx who famously said, "I don't want to belong to any club that would accept me as a member."

"And that's me? I'm Groucho Marx?" I blinked at the lost reference. "Whoever that is."

"Oh, young people," she grumbled as she finally lit her cigarette. "You know, I had a feeling he was going to make some kind of gesture because he'd been asking me about you."

"What has he been asking exactly?" I pressed back, feeling spied on.

"Oh, would you stop it?" she said to the assaulted look on my face. "He just wanted to know what was going on with you and that greaser guy you're always with." Her eyelashes fluttered. "His words."

"Greaser?" I said, not seeing it. "And you told him …?"

"That you two are just friends." She narrowed her eyes in search of new information. "Unless there's something I don't know?"

"Nope." I smacked my lips, realizing our Valentine's Day closeness was just another moment I had made up in my head. "We're just friends."

"Alright," she said in a cloud of smoke. "Then why not grab a coffee with him then?"

"Because?" I said, briefly thinking about Alex's dating horror stories.

As she lectured me on wasting my youth, my eyes glazed over on her cigarette in the ashtray, watching the smoke belly-dance from the tip. With my car keys in hand, I ran my thumb up and down the smooth surface of my keychains as I thought back to the day Pete and I bought them. At the Santa Monica Pier, it was right after we bought our car from a family on that side of town.

"But alright, Miss Bangs," she said, hitting the table for my attention. "It's time."

"Time for what?" I snapped into focus.

"Time for a little Barbie registered trademark tough love."

I dropped my head back. "Can we do it tomorrow?"

"No," she quickly replied. "We can't. Now listen up."

I yanked my head forward and took a deep breath, preparing myself for words I knew I wouldn't want to hear.

"You and Peter can't keep waiting for or avoiding each other because you know what I think?"

"You're going to tell me anyway."

"Damn straight," she confirmed. "What I think is that you two aren't mature enough right now for the kind of relationship I think one day you *might* have."

"Why *might*?"

"Because things don't always pan out the way we think they will."

I could feel my face fall in response to what felt like the cruelest thing she could have ever said to me.

"I know," she said, reading me accurately. "Hearing that feels like the end of the world. You're still young, a time when everything still feels like life or death but ..." She let her words hang between us until I realized she was planning on keeping them there.

"But what?" I eventually asked.

"With you and Peter, I sometimes wonder if what you two have is deeper and possibly more special than traditional romantic love." She paused to register my response. "Oh, don't make that face. Good, *real* friends are hard to come by."

"I feel like I made my friends at the age of ten."

"My point exactly."

"Not that I'm exactly trying," I forced myself to admit. "I just don't have anything in common with other people."

"That's how I felt too," she said, accepting it as fact. "I have Mary-Beth whose been my road dog since we were kids. But you'll meet people in passing along the way and that's life, that's how we grow."

"Just in passing?"

"Sure, and that's okay. You'll make mostly acquaintances or party friends. And remember," she said, setting her palm against the desk to make her point. "It's not who's there for you when you're down, but rather whose there for your when you're up."

"That makes absolutely no sense." I tightened up in resistance to what she was saying.

"It will one day," she chuckled to herself. "Get ready to come across some real assholes in your time."

"This has got to be one of your worst pep talks."

"I know." She brought her cigarette to her lips to take a drag. "The point is people will come and go as footnotes you'll sometimes revisit when you get old like me wondering whatever happened to so-and-so. God, when I think back on all the people that I used to know." She looked off as if she could see them. "Some proved to be terrible friends, and the good ones, well, they're mostly dead." She let out a sigh. "But Peter," she said with certainty, "is a good friend to you."

"Yeah?"

"Yeah," she affirmed, not accepting any navel gazing. "And speaking of ride or die friends, how's Miss New York City?"

I smiled at the name she had for Alex, who was my emergency contact on my lease. "She's too far away."

"Hopefully you can get her out here one of these days. But in the meantime," she said in a sneaky voice, gesturing at Tyler's letter. "Why not write a few footnotes?"

Pete

The afternoon slump kicked in with the option of either getting more coffee or consuming sugar that would make me sleepy right after. This was usually the time when Victoria filled me in on celebrity gossip. That day, she wanted to know why she couldn't find me on Myspace, which felt like my cue to step out for a smoke. But when I returned, it was as if someone had turned the office upside down with everything happening all at once. I checked the clock to make sure it had only been ten minutes because the phones were ringing on multiple lines while she tried to help a student and sign Ramón's clipboard. Kicking into high gear, I raced towards my desk to forward the calls to voicemail and tended to the delivery boxes. As I unloaded the final one, freeing Ramón's hand truck, the side of my face felt warm, like someone had been observing me. A prickling sensation crawled up my neck with the unmistakable feeling that I was not entirely alone with my thoughts. When I turned, my suspicions were confirmed when I saw that Misha guy smiling as if charmed by my administrative concerns. My stomach dropped as I imagined the color draining from my face in a puddle of embarrassment before me. I took a deep breath to regain my composure and approached the partition with the professionalism of a federal agent.

"May I help you?"

"Mr. Albrecht, right?"

"Yes," I replied, as if we hadn't spent twenty minutes alone in a windowless room, half-flirting with each other.

"Hey there," he said, effortlessly, placing his hands on the counter. "I forgot my workbook and was wondering if you had maybe a master copy so I could Xerox the three pages I'll need for class today since I'll be coming straight from an…" he let his voice trail off before concluding his sentence, "I just won't be stopping home first."

Before I could answer with a buttoned-up response, Victoria jumped in. "I can take care of that." Her tone suddenly chipper. "Which book is it?"

"It's *Salut!* The blue one." Misha turned to her sounding indifferent to who helped him. "Pages three to five."

"No problem." Victoria smiled at him, which made me seethe, filling my body with what felt like warm resentment.

"Victoria," I asserted, feeling the need to demonstrate some authority she had just hijacked from me. "The publisher updated the books at the end of last year, so just grab a new one in the supply closet and mark it as the new master."

She glanced to the side. "I know, I did that in January."

"Right," I said, launching into recovery mode by coolly slipping my hands into my pockets. "Then, I guess, I'll leave you to it." I turned to Misha. "She'll take care of you."

"Okay, great." He held his gaze for a second, his blue eyes pressing into mine.

"Great," I needlessly replied.

With the grace of a robot, I turned on my heels toward my desk in fear that my eyes would give something away, like the fact that I had been waking up to him every morning since the day of the placement exam. I had a choice of opening the deliveries stacked in the corner or pretending to work at my desk. But both options involved Misha's visual proximity to me, which both excited and scared me.

"Um," I said, hating how inarticulate I had suddenly become. "It could be a few minutes, so if you'd like, you can take a seat over in our waiting area."

He didn't acknowledge my pointed finger, and with the confidence of someone used to attention, he said, "If you don't mind, I'd like to stay here. I've been sitting in my car all day, so it feels kinda good to stand."

"Um, sure." I was going for nonchalance but all the ums that leaked out of my mouth negated the attempt at cool.

At my desk, I could see him in my side view, which made me feel awkward in my own body. My limbs felt cumbersome;

I feared my lips were in a frown, and my hands felt large and disconnected from my body. As I read and reread the same line in an email from Etienne, I could feel my underarms sweating, making me thankful for wearing short sleeves that day.

"The machine is jammed," Victoria announced, making me nearly jump. "I need you to work your magic."

"Alright." I got up and turned to Misha. "Um, it'll just be a few more minutes."

"No problem. But I was actually wondering… could I make the copies with you? I know I said pages three to five, but I just want to be sure. I'll know the pages if I see them." He blinked. "I'd hate to have to come back."

"Sure," I said, maintaining my aloofness. "Follow me." Victoria turned on her heels like she too was coming. "Actually," I said, stopping her. "I'm going to need you back on phones."

Looking at her, I remained impartial to her disappointment and proceeded to the copy room with Misha in tow, focusing on keeping my gait steady.

"You run a tight ship here," he said to my back, which made me smile. "I made sure to dress properly this time." The sound of his sneakers padded down the hardwood floors as I secretly lavished in the attention. "I don't own any sleeveless sweaters though," he referred to what I had worn the last time. "Or vintage Lacoste."

I allowed myself a quick glance over my shoulder as I watched him take note of my dad's pink and maroon striped polo from the '80s.

"I thought I would avoid a summons from the fashion police," he then added.

"Is that me?" I chuckled as I pushed open the copy room door, letting him in before me.

"Yeah." His voice was smooth as he walked past me, leaving just enough space between us. "That would be you."

"Do you always think of language school staff when you get dressed in the morning?"

"So, he does have a sense of humor." He appeared amazed. "And here I thought…" he stopped himself. "You know what, never mind what I thought."

"As you want," I replied, feigning disinterest while secretly dying to know what he thought.

Under any other circumstance I would have asked, knowing I'd have the tools to respond with composure, but he was just so observant that it made me doubt the way I functioned as a human. Was I using the right tone or was I talking a little higher than usual? Could he see my hands shake as I turned the pages of the textbook? Now add a jammed copy machine and I was a nervous wreck. As I lowered to the floor to yank out the lodged piece of paper, I was careful of the positioning of my body –which usually involved me getting on all fours in order to see inside the machine. But with him standing right behind me, I refused to provide a visual of what having me could look like, so I balanced on my feet. Misha leaned against the machine, angling his body in a way that framed his pelvic region in my eyesight. It would have been too easy to unbuckle his belt right there and reenact one of my morning daydreams that wasn't too far off from this exact scene.

I knew I wanted to take the entire length of him in my mouth and the more I tried to push the thoughts away, the more flustered I became.

"It's turned on, right?" he asked, interrupting my salacious thoughts.

Making sure he could see my eyes tossed up at the stupid question, I rose to my feet. "Of course it is."

"You sure?" He pointed to the dim display screen. "Because it doesn't seem like it is."

I didn't answer as my eyes followed the thick cord along the floorboards of the room to see that he was right. Feeling mildly embarrassed, I avoided the satisfied look I was certain was on his face and walked to the corner of the room to plug it back into the socket.

"Machines generally work better when they're powered up," he quipped.

"I guess they do." I took the workbook from him and proceeded to make the copies, amplifying my interest in the task as I could feel his eyes on me.

"Here you go." I handed him the warm sheets of paper and turned towards the door to show him out. "Try not to forget your book, we're understaffed as is and if every student forgot their book, I'd be in here all day."

It was meant to come out as a joke, but my nervousness made it sound off-putting and kind of mean. The truth was photocopying these pages for him was the best thing that had happened to me in weeks. But the look on his face told me it was too late.

"God," he said, his voice heavy with irritation. "I know you take your job really seriously and that's great. We should all be so lucky to love what we do for a living, but you don't have to be so uptight, it's just a language school."

I stood there, utterly dumbfounded. It was the first time anyone had described me as uptight, and it felt like a punch to the gut, anathema to my entire ethos. *I'm not uptight!* I wanted to declare, which I was sure would somehow make me sound even more uptight. Before I could shoot off a sassy retort or explain that I actually hated my job, he walked out, leaving me standing there speechless, and looking exactly like the high-strung asshole he had every right in thinking I was.

CHAPTER 11

Carla

Something was off. Way off. Pete had been acting weird and detached. Or maybe distracted was a better word. But something was definitely off. He was foggy and not in his usual stoner way where he just needed a day to reset. It had been going on for over two weeks and I couldn't help but take it personally. Of course, asking if everything was alright got me absolutely nowhere, and forcing normalcy by doing things together only created more strain between us. Take Easter Sunday: we went to a matinee of *Eternal Sunshine of the Spotless Mind* at The Vista. We sat next to each other in the quiet theater, and when his elbow touched mine on the shared armrest, he apologized. Then, on the walk home, I knew to keep the movie analysis on the safe side by avoiding the film's central themes about the suffering of falling in love. I also avoided the plot where the characters agreed to brain procedures to erase memories of their past relationships. Instead, I mentioned the movie's soundtrack, which included a new Beck song, which didn't get much of response. But when I expressed my amazement that the movie took place on Long Island, especially since it didn't have sharks, the Mafia, or haunted houses in it, the perplexity on his face suggested that maybe it was *his* mind that had actually been erased when he replied, "It took place on Long Island?"

After two weeks of this kind of staccato communication, I did what any girl who felt rejected would do: I agreed to a date with a guy I had absolutely no interest in.

That night, I got ready for my first real date that I tried not to think too much about. However, the hot rollers Barbie had lent me, along with the Holly Golightly record spinning pretty much screamed *date*! Well, a date in 1964 even if this album had come out the year before. At the end of my bed Joni sat, her body tucked in tight like a loaf of bread, watching me with curious eyes.

As "Without You Here," played, the lyrics feeling painfully autobiographical, I leaned as close as I could to the mirror to apply my eyeliner. Feeling the liquid coolness as I dragged it across my eye crease, I tried to remember Barbie's perfect cat-eye tutorial. "Go bold like Bardot!" she advised me. But what was effortless for her was a project for me with the bunches of blackened toilet paper piled in the garbage as proof. After many tries, I got it, and stepped back to look, satisfied that both sides were even—*ish*. For the occasion, I wore a skirt with black opaque drugstore tights and a loose-fitting sweater. As I locked up on my way to meet Tyler in the lobby, a part of me hoped to bump into Pete. *A part?* Okay, all of me wanted to bump into him, where for once, he would be the one asking the questions. But looking at his door, I could tell he wasn't home. At seven o'clock, I couldn't imagine where he was. But then again, I hadn't known where he was for weeks.

Pete

My day went by in a scurry of obscenities, such as eating lunch at my desk and answering the phone with my mouth full, as the office whirred in the mayhem of the spring party. The interns who worked for our sponsors were in for the day, buzzing about and taking the party prep to absurd levels of seriousness. By the time evening rolled around, I was absolutely drained from the secondhand enthusiasm and in no mood for a work party. It was better than being home, though, where I knew I was making things beyond weird with Carla. After changing and a freshen-up in the upstairs executive bathroom, I headed up one flight to Le Ciel, the school's rooftop banquet hall.

In my hand, I held the compilation CD Etienne had asked me to personally prepare. A mix of French bands I liked — Phoenix, M, Bertrand Burgalat— so we wouldn't listen to the Edith Piaf *Greatest Hits* on loop like we did at the Christmas party. I walked into the place glowing in pink and gold from the sunset seeping through the glass roof and noted the tropical greenery that lent the room the Côte d'Azur chic promised in the school's brochure. The sound of clinking glasses and silverware filled the room as the sponsors took their respective corners. The French Air people churned the handle of the raffle sphere to mix up the tickets. The caterers made indiscernible adjustments to their trays of food that the Fashion people scurried away from in their high heels that resembled bear traps.

« *Bonsoir,* » I greeted Etienne, handing him the CD.

« *Ah, bonsoir,*" he replied, giving me an approving once over. « *Chic, comme d'hab.* »

My cheeks felt suddenly warm since I didn't really think I was chic *as usual* but thanked him, nonetheless.

"You look like Yves Saint Laurent on vacation," he tacked on.

"Do I?" I smiled and tucked my hands in my pockets, pretty sure I had the answer to my long-time question about him. As I was about to blow off his comment, explaining the fashionable sweater was a sample sale find that wasn't exactly my style, one of the interns I'd recognized from the day presented herself.

"Good evening," Etienne and I greeted her in unison.

"I think you mean *bonsoir,*" she countered with the same enthusiasm she had been harassing the office with all day. In her hand was a small basket, and with the pep of a car commercial, she announced, "Everyone has to wear one."

Motivated by his own curiosity, Etienne tipped toward the basket to find a collection of multi-colored metal pins and without skipping a beat said, "I'm in Givenchy." He took his Blackberry out of his breast pocket and walked away, leaving just me.

"You have to pick one," she said, appearing to try and trick me into her manufactured joy. "Come on." She shook the basket seeming to get off on my unwillingness, as she pulled out a yellow one that said: MAIS OUI! JE PARLE FRANÇAIS!

"*Parfait,*" she announced, her American accent unmistakable. "Now wear it."

"Aren't they for the students though?"

"Not at all!" She rattled the thing again. "It's for faculty and staff."

I pretended to consider it. "You know what, I'm good." I smiled tightly. "But thank you."

"Umm," she began to say where I could see her preparing a passive-aggressive answer. "It's kinda, sorta mandatory?"

Sensing her doubt, I raised an eyebrow. "You sure about that?"

"Yes, I'm sure," her voice began to falter. "Everyone has to wear one." I could see her straining to stay chipper as she pawed around for another one. "What about this one?" She handed me a red one that said JE T'AIME.

"You're kidding," I snorted, refusing to take it.

I could see her patience thinning as her fingers worked overtime to pull out another pin. "Well, then what about this one?" This time, she held up a blue one that said: C'EST LA FÊTE!

I looked squarely at her. "No."

"What's wrong with this one, doesn't it mean 'It's Party Time'?"

"I really don't want to poke my sweater with a pin." I tilted my head sympathetically like she had to at least understand that. "What's even the point of them?"

"Everyone working tonight has to wear one because *the point* is to encourage French culture."

"And how is a pin going to ensure that?"

"The pin lets our guests and students know who speaks French, so the party will be entirely *en français*." Her shoulders bounced at the last part.

"That's not as exciting as you think it is. Trust me."

"But there's more!" she exclaimed, shooting a finger up like an infomercial. "Your job as an ambassador of Institut Français is to be on the lookout for students speaking English so you can gently guide the conversation back to French!"

"On the lookout?" I blinked. "You mean spy?"

"Surveille," she corrected me.

"No. Spy, as in eavesdrop and then interrupt perfectly functioning conversations and impose an entirely different language on them. Seems a little fascist, no?"

It reminded me of the history of my ancestral region of Alsace when the Germans took it over the second time, making French a forbidden language that only the wealthy elite had access to with their connections and travel abilities to Paris.

"So, I don't know what that means," she said.

I decided to spare her the historical lecture. "Won't that just make people feel really uncomfortable?"

"It shouldn't." I noticed she began tapping her foot.

Before I could make my final point on how creepy the idea of lurking staff and faculty was, she straightened her back and pressed a pin into my hand almost stabbing me with it. And in a completely flat voice, abandoning the chipper Disneyland tone of the last few minutes, she said, "Just wear the pin, asshole."

And it made the entire exchange worth it as I watched her storm off, the sound of her pins shuffling off with her. I turned my hand over, curious what the new pin said, and let out a low chuckle when I read the words C'EST LA VIE. *Touché.*

By eight o'clock, no one gave a fuck what language we were speaking, as the interns took shots of Lillet and the bosses loosened their ties while MC Solaar played, indicating the end of the CD. I sipped on a beer as I engaged in a conversation with a student telling me about her recent trip to Paris. When the conversation came to its natural close, I decided it was a respectable time to leave.

I cut through the kitchen, dodging servers carrying trays of salmon mousse *verrines* that made your breath smell like cat food and the fig and goat cheese canapes that were the focus of way too many emails. I grabbed my bag from the staff locker room and padded down the freight stairwell as quickly as I could before someone could stop me to give me something to do.

In the cool night air, after bumming an American Spirit from one of the caterers outside, I walked to the bus stop. Since it was after eight, I could have ordered a company car to take me home, but I enjoyed walking the quiet streets of Beverly Hills. The streetlights bathed the sidewalk in a soft amber light, giving the manicured palm trees an expensive glow. I checked out the windows of closed boutiques that didn't have anything exceptional enough to justify the insane prices. In the reflection, I caught sight of myself, wondering what Etienne was talking about when suddenly, I felt a car idling behind me. *Shit,* I thought, as I looked around for a place to put out my cigarette, feeling like smoking might've been prohibited in the ritzy part of town. I took a last drag and turned around ready to apologize just to avoid a ticket. But I didn't see the black and white security sedan and instead, saw a mushroom brown Mercedes-Benz station wagon. Its presence was almost ghostly, the soft purr of its engine barely disturbing the silence as if manifesting from out of nowhere. In a town known for serial killers as much as celebrities, I admit to feeling a bit uneasy. The car's tinted windows offered zero explanation, only my own reflection looking back at me until it lowered. Inside wasn't the second coming of Manson but Misha.

Looking at me with his mix of intrigue and amusement, he said, "Can I offer you a lift, Monsieur Albrecht?"

Carla

If I get drunker, maybe this guy will get cuter, I thought to myself, as I reached for my glass.

But no matter how many sips I took, the wine was just not getting me there fast enough. I realized almost immediately that I didn't like Tyler, as I watched him swirl his wine as he talked about himself. He did things like ask the server questions about the harvest in a way that I suspected he knew nothing about winegrowing. He also looked at me in this smug way like *I* had left the origami note with Barbie. This was all before he told me that he thought his mother was a complete moron. I was far from an expert on dating, but I was pretty sure these were the signs of a bad date. My careful attention to eyeliner suddenly seemed silly because this guy was so not worth the perfect cat-eye.

I reached for my glass again.

"So," I said, taking Barbie's advice and not going into this like a total bitch. "How do you like living in L.A.?"

He appeared to love the question. "Oh, it's great here," he responded passionately. "The weather, the girls, what's not to like?"

I was pretty sure I curled my lip at the second point, but he didn't seem to notice.

"And my favorite," he went on, "being from the East Coast by default, you're, like, the smartest person in the room." He waited for a reaction that I didn't have because I was waiting for him to tell me he was kidding.

He wasn't.

I grabbed my wine glass again, seeing I was creating some kind of drinking game.

"So, where'd you go to school?" he asked.

"I didn't."

"Funny." He pointed to me like a slapstick comedian. "That's a good one."

Wine.

As he talked about someone from work, I glanced out the large window. Tyler had chosen the French restaurant located at the foot of our street saying that we could pretend we were in Europe. He had also suggested we walk, in which he said we could pretend like we were in New York. As I watched him and all his wine swirling, I realized he was also pretending to be an adult, just like I was trying not to look like a little kid, feeling like at any second my tights were going to slide me right off the vinyl banquette.

I set my glass down feeling like my sip wasn't big enough, but I had to wait at least another few minutes before reaching for it again so I wouldn't look like a drunk. I distracted myself with the menu where the prices nearly slapped me across the face. As I calculated how much I had in my checking account, plus the two checks coming in the mail, minus the rent, I gave myself an extravagant thirty-five-dollar budget, imagining all of the 99 Cent Store goodies I could've piled up for that much.

"I was thinking," he said, looking up from his menu, "we could order a bunch of things and share?"

I was too embarrassed to tell him I couldn't afford much on the menu, so I agreed, hoping he wasn't in the mood for the hundred-dollar rib eye steak and frites. When he focused back on his menu, I reached for the glass, taking a fishbowl sized gulp to accelerate my buzz.

"Do you like charcuterie?" he asked, barely waiting for my response before translating, "that means a plate of cured meats in French."

Wine.

He raised an eyebrow in anticipation of my admiration but before I could offer *any* response, he was already speaking again.

Wine.

"I'd recommend a cheese plate because I hear they're amazing, but lactose makes me a little gassy." As he said this, he pressed his hand on the lower pouch of his stomach and twisted his face suggesting past complications. I gave Tyler credit for his ability to one-up himself since I thought calling his mother a moron would have been the most shocking thing he'd say. Tyler, however, didn't seem bothered by his assertion, which made me wonder what it must have been like to be so self-assured that you could reference your own flatulence on a first date. When it came time to order, Tyler peppered it with words in French to the server who could have very well been from Monrovia since he wasn't exactly moved by Tyler's *s'il vous plaits* or *je voudrais*.

"I studied abroad in Paris two years ago," he volunteered, handing the server our menus.

He and I exchanged glances, wondering if I blinked twice would he recognize it as some kind of code that would disassociate me somehow from my date.

My eyes returned to Tyler knowing the polite thing to do would be to ask follow-up questions about his study abroad escapades but instead, I looked out the window and thought of Pete. I imagined him racing around the corner on his bike and whisking me away. I hated myself for missing him, which I decided was Tyler's fault.

Wine.

"So," he said, seeming to look at me for the first time that night. He leaned back, almost haughtily, holding the wine glass in his hand like an expert of fine things. "Tell me what one of your pet peeves is? I love this game."

"Game?" I knew how confused I must have looked.

"I feel like the best way to get to know someone is to not find out what they love but find out what ticks them off."

"Oh, I see," I said, nodding along. "Okay, give me a second."

I looked off, biting my lower lip as a few came to mind: the sound of candy wrappers or popcorn shuffling in a bag at the movies, when someone talks to me in a fake Italian accent that sounds more like a bad actor in a string cheese commercial when they learn of my origins, or when someone I don't know calls me sweetie, or worse, baby. Across from me, I noticed Tyler shifting with impatience, which made it clear he was only asking me in order to volunteer his. Another pet peeve of mine.

"Alright," I said, knowing I didn't pick a great one but figured it would do. "One of my pet peeves, I guess, could be when I don't rinse my frying pan well enough and the next time I make eggs they taste like dish soap."

Tyler placed his wine glass on the table. "You don't have a dishwasher?"

"No." I looked at his wine glass, wondering why he had to set it down. "Why? Do you?"

"I think my dishwasher moved in before I did," he remarked with a clap, throwing his head back with a hearty laugh.

"I actually don't have enough dishes to fill one."

"So not the point," he said, looking at like I was quaint or something. "You're so quirky. I figured you would be, too."

"Oh," I think I said.

"But okay, my turn," he announced, leaning forward as if preparing me for greatness. "You're from the East Coast, so I know you'll get it," he paused for a buildup, "don't you hate it when people don't pronounce the *t* in the word mountains?"

When I didn't immediately jump up in agreement, he said, "Maybe I'm not explaining it right. Wine makes me inarticulate."

Me too. Wine.

"So, you've never noticed some people when they say the word 'mountains' they sort of jump over the *t* in the word mountains and say *mow-ints*?" His nose scrunched up with distaste.

"Maybe?" I looked off, trying to remember the way I said it and honestly couldn't since both ways sounded fine to me. "I'm not sure, actually." I then looked at him. "And why does that bother you so much?"

"It just sounds so uneducated, you know?"

I recognized a theme knowing it would never work between us. I could imagine his reaction when I told him I was an aimless college dropout who did extra work and was merely scraping by. I wasn't proud of it either, but I didn't need his face to articulate what I already knew. As we sat there, it was clear that this wasn't a match for either of us, which felt like almost a relief since we did live in the same building. But we still had food coming and had to endure each other at least until then.

I looked at him. "Want to talk about music?"

"Yes." He looked relieved. "Yes, I do."

"Awesome," I said. "What do you like?"

He placed a hand on his chest. "I'm a hipster, so you can probably guess my taste."

"I can?" I shuddered because who actually labeled themselves a hipster? *This guy*, I answered my own question. *This guy described himself as a hipster*, I thought as I breathed hard out of my nostrils. Tyler then proceeded to *explain* bands to me, the *Garden State* soundtrack, and in general, how music worked, seeming to forget I was even there. I knew it was useless to say that I played guitar or that I owned vinyl. So, I let him talk, pouring the rest of the wine down my throat, once again reminding myself that he was so *not* worth the perfect cat-eye.

Pete

I slid into the passenger's seat of Misha's station wagon. I was hoping to play it cool but whoever sat in the seat before me must have been half my size. I looked caricatured, like a giant in a fairy tale, with my knees pressed against the dashboard. Misha noticed, letting out a small laugh.

"The seat adjustment is just to your right." He pointed to the mini control pad on my arm rest.

I pressed one of the buttons that illuminated into a burnt orange color.

"That's the seat warmer," he said, reaching over me to point to the right button. "It's this one." He pressed it and my chair began to glide back, giving my knees some much needed relief.

"You got it from here?" His eyes smiled at mine in the dark.

"I think I can manage." I returned his gaze.

After stretching my legs out and buckling in, it was then I felt something crunch under my foot. Looking down I could see it was the spiral binding of his Thomas Guide that I leaned over to reach for.

"Oh, you can toss that in the back," he instructed me. Along with my bag, I placed them both in the back where I saw his black and white 8x10s scattered along the seat.

When I repositioned myself in the passenger's seat, he looked at me. "So, where to?"

"Silver Lake?" I turned to him, letting our eyes meet again in the dark. "Is that out of the way?"

He gently bit back a laugh. "Everywhere in this town is out of the way," he said before his eyes grew soft and dare I say, affectionate. "But I'll make an exception tonight."

I returned the gentle look, hoping to start over with him. "I appreciate it."

He pulled away from the curb as his luxury car glided with ease down the vacant boulevard. With one hand on the wheel, he used the other to maneuver the stick shift, just inches away from my leg. Sitting in his car, I was careful not to move in a way that would make the leather seats make compromising sounds as we passed the sights I had seen every day. With him, they somehow felt different, new even, making me appreciate the city like a visitor.

He momentarily took his eyes off the road, shooting a glance my way. "You weren't walking to Silver Lake, were you?"

I smiled at the question. "No, the bus stop."

"Do you not have a car?" he asked without judgment.

"I do but I usually take my bike or in some cases, the bus."

"From Silver Lake?" I liked the way he sounded impressed.

"I guess it's my cheap way around a gym membership."

He laughed, and the sound was rich and genuine, immediately captivating me. I found myself wanting to hear it again. To coax out another laugh, I could've asked about his classes with Monsieur Fontanet, our toughest instructor but something made me want to earn it like the arrival of a warm season after a long winter.

"So, what brings you to L.A.?" he asked.

I looked at him, his cheeks glowing red from the brake lights of the car in front of us. "How do you know I'm not from here?"

The red hue disappeared from his face as he pushed the gear into first, propelling the car forward. "Because we would have known each other by now."

"Oh, really?"

Looking straight ahead, he smirked. "Really."

Chuckling at what I interpreted as a provocative comment, I continued looking at him, waiting for him to continue his thought.

"You also have that East Coast assholery."

This time I let out a full laugh. "I'm sorry, what?"

"You heard me," he replied. "I bet you talk loud in restaurants and ask if there's anyone else working when the service seems too slow."

"I guess you have me all figured out." I looked out the window, smiling to myself that he was even trying.

"And what about you?" I asked. "Where are you from?"

"Born and raised in WeHo," he said as if guilty as charged.

I looked at him. "Do people from West Hollywood really call it that?"

"Not really," he admitted with a wry twist of the mouth. "I was trying to be hip."

"We're in a station wagon," I pointed out.

"That we are."

Our conversation for the entirety of the drive remained light while speaking in circles, both of us seeming hyper aware of each other. I could feel my disappointment when I watched the scenery transition into my neighborhood as we passed familiar haunts like the cover of the Elliot Smith album, El Cid and the 4100 Bar. My street came too soon, and I felt a sense of loss as if I were now inside an actual Elliot Smith song — perhaps the song "L.A." but hopefully not "Someone That I Used to Know" — as I instructed him to the painted red curb across the street from my building. He slid into the spot where I felt my heart hiccup when he turned off the engine. I had never wanted to make out with someone in a car more than I did at that moment but wasn't sure if I was ready for it because surely I needed to obsess more to make the kisses taste even sweeter than I'd imagine them to be. Or was I writing more fiction in my head? Forcing a casual disposition, I twisted my body towards the back seat to grab my bag where I couldn't resist the headshots.

I picked one up, admiring his commercial-ready smile. "Nice picture."

"No, they're not," he said, establishing his right to call me out on bullshit. "They're terrible."

With my body still contorted toward the backseat, putting me in awkward proximity with him, I looked at the picture again. I tried to extract details, but there weren't any. Everything from the plain shirt to his nice smile was nondescript.

"They're not bad." I smiled at the polished version of him. "Maybe a little boring," I gently critiqued. "But they sort of have to be, don't they?"

"No, they're versatile," he said in a mocking voice. "But grab the black binder back there if you want a little more personality."

I moved the pile of pictures to reach for the book. Taking it, my hand suddenly became limp from not expecting it to be made out of metal. I took its weight more seriously by gripping it firmer and mindfully passing it over the seat careful not to hit his head with the sharp edges. With it in my lap, I looked at him for authorization.

"Go ahead," he said, almost like it was a dare.

Opening it, the first image stretched across both pages was him in jeans and a dress shirt strategically left open to showcase a very sculpted torso. Stretched out on a grassy field, his husky eyes pierced the camera with a regard that had nothing to do with clothing.

"What a natural looking photo," I said, my delight increasing as my eyes lingered down the trail of undone buttons.

"What?" he murmured as if following my line of vision. "You don't lounge in an isolated field wearing nothing but unbuttoned clothing and a fuck-me look on your face?"

"Only on bank holidays," I said as I studied the picture, trying not to blush at the image of him fucking. "This looks like an Abercrombie and Fitch ad."

"It *is* an Abercrombie and Fitch ad."

"Oh, come on." I looked at him like he was putting me on before he pointed to the small print I couldn't make out in the dark car.

"What do you think paid for this car?" He patted the steering wheel. "There's also Levi's, Calvin Klein, Robinsons-May."

"So, you're a model?"

"Don't look so horrified."

"No, I'm… I'm… just surprised."

"Geez, thanks."

"That's not what I mean." I let out a small laugh while holding my hand out to backpedal. "I guess it's – I've never met an actual model, so I'm surprised, that's all. I didn't think you were actual –"

"People?"

My eyes flicked to the side. "Well, yeah."

I suddenly felt unoriginal and cliché for crushing on a model. I felt culturally airbrushed, wanting to blame the town for brainwashing me into a new standard of beauty. But looking at his picture, I knew I was it was all over for me and that my East Coast *assholery* wasn't going get me out of the fact that I wanted to be naked with this person.

"I model here and there between roles to pay the bills," he explained. "I don't like doing it though. The vibes are weird."

"Really?" I said, looking at him to elaborate.

"Yeah, a little predatory," was all he said as he looked at the page I had inadvertently turned to. "This was a funny shoot though."

In the photo, he wore a fur-trimmed parka with a chunky knit scarf I could have made myself. In his hand was a Christmas tree that he dragged through the snow. Next to him was a girl who was also winter-perfect wearing earmuffs and puffy coat with the tips of their noses dusted with snowflakes.

"In this one," he explained, "my snow partner here was doing bumps of coke in the bathroom, I guess taking the snow analogy literally."

"She looks so New England proper," I said, haughtily.

"Far from it."

We smiled at each other before focusing back on the book, which served as a terrible buffer since he was half-naked in most of the photos. I noticed an ad in Russian and used that as a jumping point away from chocolate-bar-cut abs and cokehead models.

"So, with a name like that, I'm guessing you're Russian?" I glanced at him.

"Half."

"What's the other half?"

"Hungarian," he said with a shrug.

"Do you speak both languages?"

He appeared amused by the question. "I do."

"So, then French should be easy in comparison."

"It's still another language to learn and, with the others, I grew up with them. They're a part of me, if that makes any sense."

I smiled. "It does."

His expression lightened as we unearthed common ground. "And you're French, right?"

"French American," I specified. "Or rather, French-New Yorker since my mother identifies as that." I rolled my eyes at my brazen Queens-born mom.

He smiled. "Could be worse."

"I guess." I blew off the impressed look on his face. "By default, people think I'm an asshole since most people dislike the French and New Yorkers." He laughed, seeming to get it.

Wanting to continue the small connection we established, I asked, "So, tell me, growing up, did your friends think your house was weird and foreign?"

"Oh, God, yes." He leaned his head back against the headrest appearing to imagine it before rolling his head towards mine. "It also didn't help that our house smelled like meat pies and cabbage, and our groceries had Russian labels on them from the market over on Santa Monica." I tipped my head in recognition of West Hollywood's Russian community that I admit surprised me when I first moved to town.

"But that's my story," he said modestly. "Not much to it."

"I'm sure that's not true."

We exchanged quick smiles before I turned the page to a shaving cream ad. I immediately recognized it from a coupon I had actually used. Knowing I had held his picture in my hand months before meeting him felt too abstract for me, like living in some kind of simulation, forcing me to close the book. Even though I wanted to know more, I bit my tongue, not wanting to collect anymore memories I wasn't sure I would get to own. I knew he liked me, but I was certain a guy of his stature liked a lot of people and would easily be into someone new the following week. I couldn't waste my time flattering myself that this meant anything. Sitting there, I accepted the moment for what it was as we took turns half-smiling at each other and pretending to be interested in something out the window. I knew I was supposed to begin the parting rituals with words like *so* or *anyway*, but I couldn't bring myself to do it, as if I was daring myself to steal more time with him.

"Anyway," he then said, which I felt in my gut. "I should probably let you go."

"Uh, yeah," I said, forcing my voice to sound laidback. "It's getting late."

He reached for the keys dangling in the ignition, the powering up of the car sounding louder than usual, as if drawing attention to what felt like a rejection. I didn't know what I expected from him, which made me feel exposed. Maybe it was the topless ads or his cool demeanor that made me feel like I had my inexperience etched across my face. He was so self-possessed in a way I was also capable of, but with him, my powers weakened. The way he looked at me hinted that he knew about the things I let him do to me in my dreams.

"You think a lot, don't you?" he said, his voice low and intimate.

"It happens."

"Thinking is good," he pondered. "Not enough people do it."

I let out a small laugh. "That is definitely true."

I sat there, buying a few more seconds with the air between us feeling charged with anticipation. Anticipation of what exactly? It was hard to say, but it was something. It had to be or else I should've looked into a fiction writing class from how detailed our intimacy was in my mind. We looked through the windshield, sitting in a comfortable silence reserved for people who knew each other much better than we did.

I listened to his deep breaths syncing with mine, and in that moment, I realized I wanted to do more than have him undress me. I longed to unravel the layers of his past, like, did he wear Sergio Tacchini track suits in junior high? Did his class pictures have that pink and blue laser backdrop? Did he pass his driver's test on the first try? But maybe I'd never find out, so I absorbed this memory for as long as I could to take ownership of it. Even if he never drove me home again, this moment would be mine to mold it into any shape I wanted.

"Well," I said, choosing another parting word as I fought off the feeling of loss for someone I never had. "Thanks for the ride."

"Anytime," he said in a breezy tone, reminding me it was meaningless, laidback California banter. "Thanks for being nice tonight."

"You caught me on an off night."

CHAPTER 12

Carla

The morning after my date, I woke up feeling like a rag doll. And the way Joni's green eyes blinked at me meant I probably looked like one too. Just as I was accepting my cat's judgmental glare while tracing back events from the night before, a loud knock on the door revealed that I also had a skull-slicing headache.

"You home?" Barbie's voice barreled through the door.

"Hold on," I grumbled, not even trying to give the impression that I'd been up.

Trudging to the door, Joni padded alongside me, nearly tripping me as I opened it. The hallway breeze felt cool on my cheeks as I admired Barbie, a vision in purple polka dots with a matching silk scarf in her hair. Noticing the mail in her hand had me asking what time it was.

"Too late for you to just be getting up on a weekday." She poked her head around me to see my unmade bed. "I came to see how your date went."

"Came to see how it went or if I was still on it?" I pulled the door entirely open for her to see. "It's just me in here."

She didn't express much of an opinion as she walked in, beelining straight to my kitchen.

"No job today?" she asked, the sound of her heels clacking against the hardwood floors.

"No," I answered as I followed her. "I couldn't get through the lines yesterday. I kept getting a busy signal."

In the kitchen, she tossed her mail on the table and pulled out one of the chairs for me. "I'll make some coffee." She shot a look over her shoulder. "You look like you could use some."

I sat down, feeling the chair cool against the back of my legs. Out my kitchen window, a neighbor listened to NPR as Barbie began dumping heaps of coffee into the filter. Next to her was the bottle of wine I had opened when I got home, which she didn't seem to notice.

"So, how'd it go?" she asked, keeping one eye on the coffee measurements.

"He's not my type."

"He's not Peter, you mean."

"Well, that," I owned up, feeling too tired to deny it.

"At least you didn't revenge-fuck him," she said before glaring at me. "Or did you?"

I stared at her with intent. "No," I replied. "I didn't."

Unmoved by the seriousness on my face, she said, "Well, good because you know that'll never work if you're trying to get back at Peter."

I made a knowing face she didn't see, thinking back on the one time I had tested him with a stunt like that. It didn't work and resulted in us not speaking over breakfast burritos in the middle of New Mexico.

"So, you came home and got drunk by yourself," she said, not needing to look at the half-empty bottle.

Shit.

"I didn't get drunk," I lied.

"Well, then what happened?" she insisted. "Something had to have happened."

"We just have nothing in common."

She tossed me a look that I was going to have to do better than that.

"Okay, fine," I obliged. "He's just so uppity." I stuck my tongue out to signify that it grossed me out.

Considering it, she seemed to agree. "He does come from a rich family. You know, his mom mails me the rent every month."

The mom he called a moron, I thought, shaking my head.

"I'm too working class for him," I concluded. "And we'll leave it at that."

"Alright, alright," she resigned. "I won't bring it up again, but at least you went."

"That I did."

Once the coffee was made, I took a long sip, feeling the night distance itself from my mind. Sitting across from me, Barbie began opening her mail, as I absently looked at the envelopes; the water bills and takeout menus that I knew were waiting in my own mailbox. There was one, however, that caught my attention.

"What is this?" I asked, reaching across the table to grab the envelope. In my hand, I looked at the red heart that replaced the O in the word LOVE. "How cute."

She looked up, her eyes squinting to read the small print. "Oh, Locks of Love?" she said. "That's an organization that makes wigs from donated hair for sick children."

I looked at the envelope and back at her.

"I donated mine a few years before I started dying it." She ran a hand through her thick hair. "It's too treated now otherwise I'd do it again." She looked at my long locks cascading over my shoulder, her eyes noting the generous donation as I grabbed it protectively. "Why? You're interested?"

"No," I said almost sheepishly, knowing I could never be so bold. "Just curious, I guess."

"That's your security blanket," she said with a warm smile. "And that's okay. Charity comes in all shapes and forms. Contributing to society could mean simply taking care of yourself. It's all connected, my dear."

I looked at her wondering how she figured that, but she was back to reading her mail.

"Oh, this one's for you," she perked up, reading the envelope. "It's from Central Casting. Looks like Ms. Carla A. Bucchio got paid."

"Oh, great."

She eyed it as she handed it across the table. "What's the A stand for again?"

"You know what it stands for." I placed the envelope beside my mug, roughly knowing how much the check was for. "And you know I hate it. It's ugly."

"You cut that out," she mumbled as she grabbed another bill. "It is not."

"It's a prostitute's name."

Peering at me over her bifocals, she asked, "And how many prostitutes have you met?"

"None."

"Didn't think so." She went back to opening her mail.

"I used to like my middle name back when I thought there was some mystical meaning behind it, like my mom was pregnant with me while sitting under the Aurora Borealis."

Her eyebrows shot up. "But?"

"But it was the name of her high school yearbook," I explained as if I had all the proof in the world to hate my name. "She was popular, unlike her freak of a daughter."

"You are not a freak, and the name is beautiful. I don't care where it comes from." A whimsical expression then swept across her face. "Carla Aurora," she said, looking off in the distance as if seeing my name in lights. "Can't you just see it?"

"No." I remained expressionless. "I can't."

"You know," she said, "back in my post-glitter critter days, I went by Barbie Barbiturates."

I grinned at the new piece of information. "You did?"

"It was after a bad break-up, I said fuck it and chopped all my hair off," she tapped the pamphlet, "this wasn't around yet otherwise I'd have donated it, but nothing says breakup like a new haircut and…. a hot new band."

"You had a band?" I leaned forward, wondering why I was just hearing about it.

"Damn straight." She nodded. "We went by Trashy Lingerie, and we were pretty good."

"How come I don't know this?"

"I've lived many lives, my dear." Her eyes became wondrous like a fortune teller's. "I could write a book."

"A good one, too," I added. "So, what happened?"

"Well, I was terrified."

"You?" I shook my head in disbelief. "You're not afraid of anything."

"Oh, sure I was. I was about your age, too, and I thought I was such an imposter."

"You?" I repeated, starting to sound like a freaking backup singer. "Come on!"

"Yeah, like who did this former Sunset Strip party girl think she was fronting her own punk band? I was also a little older than most of the kids in the scene my little sister was more a part of, but then I realized who gives a motherfucking shit what other people think?" She paused to let it sink in before poking herself with her long finger. "I'm the one I have to answer to." She tapped her chest a few times to drive the point home. "No one else."

"Easier said than done."

"True," she agreed. "It's one of life's big challenges, really because if you can't convince yourself you're something great then who can you convince?"

I took a sip of my coffee, thinking, well, then I'm screwed.

Pete

Distracted. Dishonest. Disoriented.

My three Ds of emotion.

Distracted because all I could think about was Misha. I wrote out different adaptations of that night in his car, replaying them in my head. Since I was the creative director of my own thoughts, I embellished it with new details. I analyzed the lingering looks, the side comments to find their hidden meanings. I played with alternate endings, some involving steamed-up Mercedes-Benz windows or tripping over ourselves in my dark apartment. It was harmless daydreaming until I almost got hit by a car.

But it wasn't exactly emotionally harmless, which led to my second emotion.

Dishonesty. Because I was avoiding Carla, who wasn't a moron and knew something was up.

And finally, Disoriented, because what did any of this mean?

To cleanse myself of it all, I decided it was time for a trip to my house of worship. My house of the holy... my house of the rising sun….my Carnival Cruise where everything would be okay. Some found self-prophecy with Dianetics on Sunset. Others sought it through a plastic surgeon, also on Sunset. But as for me, I found mine at Amoeba, which, you guessed it… was on fucking Sunset.

I locked my bike on the rack before walking around to the main entrance where the mere act of opening the glass doors put my mind at ease. The moving meditation continued as I glided past the check-out counters, the celestial whispers of Air's *Talkie Walkie* playing in the store, feeling like a voyage shooting through starry skies. The ambient introspection held its own over the sounds of plastic CD jewel boxes slamming forward from frantic fingers on the hunt for out-of-print Sub Pop 100 comps or *Amnesiac* B-sides. I walked past the New Release display, preferring instead the Staff's Picks that always spoke more to my tastes. As usual, I was not disappointed when I saw that an employee named Sam highly recommended the new Deerhoof. A handwritten, laminated blurb tacked onto the metal display described the album as, "Prog meets punk on three hits of good acid." I grabbed the CD. He also recommended the "hushed acoustic soundscapes," of the new Iron and Wine that I grabbed for Carla.

In an age where the iPod or CDs reigned supreme, the vinyl room was as quiet as a library, as serious as an office, and sparsely populated by long-haired, beer-bellied vinyl dudes who knew their Camel from their CAN, their Faust from their Feist. I parked myself in Pop and Rock, knowing I'd make it over to Jazz when a vacancy opened. Settling into position with knees bent and relaxed shoulders like at a high school track meet, I took a deep breath before putting my fingers to work.

"No, no, have, have, no, hold up," I mumbled to myself as I pulled out a beat-up copy of *St. Louis to Liverpool*. I continued to race through the alphabet, stopping when something caught my eye like the mint-looking *Exile on Main Street* for $9.99. Next to the price tag was a sticker that read: SEE CLERK, meaning they kept the high-priced disc behind the counter.

As I continued pawing my fingers in forward motion, building a small pile, I felt a sudden hand on my shoulder. I immediately froze, wondering if I had somehow breached vinyl room etiquette. I slowly turned around expecting to find a big burly dude holding Rosemary Clooney LPs. Instead, it was that pseudo-drummer from Weekend Warriors smiling at me.

"Sorry, I didn't mean to scare you there," he said.

"No, it's me," I admitted. "I'm a little jumpy these days."

He stepped back to give me a once-over. "Look at you," he said. "You look like you're about to crack Watergate."

I brushed off the comparison with a hand gesture. "I'm just getting off from work."

His face twisted in what looked like pity. "Rough, man."

"It's life," I said to his slacked jaw before asking the rest of his face, "So, how's it going?"

"Can't complain, man." He held his arms out before folding them across his chest with satisfaction. "The band is taking off, so you can't really ask for much more."

"Oh, wow," I said, aiming for an exclamation point but getting its limp-dicked cousin instead. I really hoped the look of shock on my face didn't offend him, but I couldn't help it, because the last time I'd checked, no one in his band knew how to play instruments. But details, I suppose.

"What's going on?" I asked, almost carefully, wondering if I really wanted to know.

"Well, let's see, we signed with Glasshouse," he informed me, scratching his smooth cheek. "Not sure if you knew that."

I didn't.

"And we're hitting the European summer festival tour. You know, Glastonbury, Rock en *Seen*—

Seine, I silently corrected him, feeling a gust of air exit my nostrils.

"Then off to Denmark," he continued, "but before that we're playing a bunch of local shows, hitting up San Fran, just sorta biding time before the album drops in May because, Ted, you know from Click Track who runs Glasshouse," he added unnecessarily, "thinks we should probably…"

I stopped paying attention at this point, hoping my face didn't look as bitter as I really did hate myself for feeling. I didn't normally do bitter. But I also didn't do distracted, dishonest, or disoriented. But alas, there I was, living in my own alternate version, my own B-side, if you will.

"And that's about it," Jay concluded.

"That's great." I looked to the side hoping everything he said was, in fact, great since I wasn't paying attention. But my expression must have given away how I was feeling because Jay suddenly looked uncomfortable. He tried to stuff his hands into his jean pockets but could only get his fingernails in from how tight they were.

"Oh, I wanted to say," he said, giving up on the pocket idea and letting his arms drop, "tell Carla that I'm sorry about the last time I saw her. I still feel really bad about it."

Fighting the urge to look confused, I calmly asked, "When?"

"On that stupid show." When he could see that I still wasn't following, he said, "She didn't tell you?"

I suddenly felt territorial and wanted to lie and say that she did tell me, and I too was outraged, damn it. But it was too late, and he was already filling me in on the gory details about Carla pantomiming being a fan of his band. Knowing what her job entailed, I took a deep breath, my eyes slightly fluttering back, imagining the horror.

"Yeah," he said in response to my face. "I was pretty mortified for her because she has so much more talent than that." I nodded in agreement. "And it's just so weird because we all started out playing that shitty dive bar and now –"

"It's not your fault," I interjected. "It's just the way the machine works sometimes."

"I guess," he replied when something immediately alerted him, making him reach into his back pocket.

"Hold on." I watched as he pulled out a fancy-looking phone that I was sure I wouldn't have known how to answer. With a flick of his wrist, I watched as the screen swiveled on what looked like an axis, revealing a teeny tiny keyboard. Jay noticed me noticing it.

"It was a gift," he felt compelled to say.

I looked at him with indifference to its origins and returned to my pile of records.

Pig Lib by Stephen Malkmus and the Jicks. *Musik von Harmonia* by Harmonia, *The Lemon of Pink* by The Books, the aforementioned Chuck Berry album, *Spirit Stereo Frequency* by local band All Night Radio (another staff rec), and of course the Iron and Wine and Deerhoof CDs. In my head I calculated my monthly music budget, thinking I might be going over with the pile I still wanted to add to when Jay pulled me out of the numbers and album covers floating in my head.

"Holy shit," he exclaimed, the excitement momentarily derailing me. "Today might be your fucking lucky day, brother."

I didn't immediately respond, as it wasn't entirely clear that he was even talking to me.

"Dude, what are you doing next week?" he asked, now looking directly at me.

"Next week?"

"I mean, what is The Disenchanted doing next week?"

I admit I was impressed he even remembered our band name. However, I didn't have the courage to tell him we didn't have a band.

"The thing is—" I started to say.

"How would you guys like to open for us at The Trop?"

"The Trop," I repeated to make sure I'd heard him correctly.

"Yeah, The Trop," he confirmed the two-thousand capacity venue, holding up his phone as some kind of evidence. "The opening band scheduled, I guess, has a conflict so that shit is up for grabs. The other guys are reaching out to the bands they know, but if I tell them you guys are in now, it's fucking yours."

I glanced at the phone, partly resenting its participation in this transaction as I imagined the satisfied look on Victoria's face. I had to admit to myself right there that without it, his offer would not have been a possibility. One disgruntled point for technology.

"So," he pressed, "you in or you out?"

I signaled that I needed a second as I weighed out my options. Obviously, I had to talk to Carla who I was on such weird terms with. But I also knew that my sanity depended on doing something other than obsessing over my personal life. I needed to breathe. I needed to feel free from thinking and just beat the shit out of my drums; the most primal form of therapy if there ever was one.

"So…?" Jay said as if dangling a carrot before me. "You in?"

Without thinking anything through like having new songs, remembering old ones, or, I don't know, having *willing band members*, I said yes. I said yes to opening a sold-out show at an iconic music venue.

Now all I needed was a band.

Carla

By late afternoon, I felt like myself again. As I walked back from the 99 Cent Store, the bag of cat litter knocking against the side of my leg, I watched the sun begin its descent. The long shadows stretched across the boulevard, painting it a golden hue that I'd only seen in California. It stirred a feeling of nostalgia in me that felt vague yet profound, like stumbling upon an old photograph of people I didn't know. I felt inexplicably mournful in my quiet contemplation feeling like I'd always remember this day. The colors, the cars, the weight of my heart, not knowing if it was about to get broken. Maybe I'd look back on it as either a time of freedom that I'd long for or with relief that time had distanced me from the emotional uncertainty I felt.

I passed Rag Mopp Vintage, its pistachio green signage always catching my eye. In the window, a navy blue and red Mary Quant-style mini dress was on display. Inside I could see the pretty things I knew I could never afford on an extra's earnings, teaching me to turn away from things I couldn't have. But then, as if the universe was showing off its quirky sense of humor, it presented yet another thing I could look at but not have. In the distance was Pete, approaching in the bike lane.

As soon as we made contact, I walked over to meet him at the curb. His cheeks were flush like they always were after his long commute but as he dismounted his bike, I noticed his clenched jaw, hinting at some kind of internal struggle. Our eyes met and locked, and for a moment it felt like everything around us was holding its breath waiting for one of us to speak. For someone whose bed I had napped in and whose parents I knew by first name, he now felt like a stranger.

"Just getting back from work?" I asked, a useless inquiry.

"I am," he replied as we both looked at his bike as if searching for confirmation. "You heading home?"

I nodded that I was.

He looked off for a moment, as if processing the information before looking back at me. "Do you think we can go somewhere and talk?"

Silently startled by the suggestion because we didn't do things like *talk*, I hid my surprise by merely looking back at him.

"I was thinking coffee?" He pointed to the turquoise façade of the Casbah Café. "We haven't gone there in a while."

We walked to the corner café with him balancing the bag of cat litter on one of his handlebars. At a small table outside, I watched his bike and my groceries while he ordered inside. Feeling my heart against my chest in fear of what he wanted to talk about, I listened to our order being prepared. The raucous shuffle of scooped ice for my mint iced tea and the thunder of the espresso machine for his Americano. Eventually he returned, balancing our drinks along with a small plate of honey-glazed Moroccan pastries that felt like more of a consolation than a casual snack.

"These looked good," he said, setting down the chipped porcelain dish. "Just something to pick on, I guess."

He sat beside me, and after settling into the tight space, he reached into his bag for his rolling paper and tobacco. While he built his cigarette, I sipped my iced tea, listening to the sounds of the city, the faint music playing in the café, and finally the flick of his lighter.

"Alright," he said, blowing a stream of smoke over our heads. "Are you ready for what I'm going to tell you?"

I had prepared myself for the absolute worst so when he told me what had happened at Amoeba with Jay, all I could say was, "That's it?"

"What do you mean that's it?" He searched my eyes. "What did you think I was going—" he then cut himself off, which pretty much told me everything as a sinking feeling hollowed out my stomach.

"You know we barely have a band, right, Pete?" I said, ignoring the guilty look on his face.

"I'm aware."

"Yet you still said yes."

"I did."

I stared at him for a few long seconds. "Have you completely lost your mind?"

I watched him consider my question, thinking long and hard about it. He then planted his eyes on me where for the first time in our friendship, he looked defeated.

"It's quite possible," he responded.

I watched him transition from the self-assured Pete I'd known since we were kids into someone looking at me for the answer.

"I just don't know what the fuck to do anymore."

"Okay, well, whatever is going on, I'm not sure opening for the Weekend Warriors is going to fix it." He didn't say anything. "You're not afraid we're going to make complete fools of ourselves?"

He thought about it for a moment, looking out onto the street with a distant gaze. "At least I'd feel something else," he said with a dimness that I didn't recognize in him.

Confused, I looked to the side for a second and back at him. "Why would you need to feel something else?"

I waited another several long minutes as I watched his eyes blur like a watercolor. Frustrated by these long pauses, I folded my arms in protest and turned my head in the opposite direction. A car then stopped at the red light in front of us. From the passenger window, the driver did a double take with a look of familiarity on his face, as if he'd been in our situation before. I looked down at my folded arms and then at Pete's faraway gaze and thought, of course this guy had been where we were. We looked like we were breaking up. And if we were, boy did I get the shit end of the stick, I thought as I marveled at the irony. I didn't get the benefits of a relationship but now had to endure the humiliation of the break-up, but even that wasn't panning out because the guy pseudo-dumping me was barely speaking.

"I think I'm going to go," I said, pressing my palms against the edge of the table, threatening to stand up. "This is too confusing for me."

"Please," he said, looking at me with desperation. "Just stay."

I ignored his pleading look, not allowing his boyish charm to fool me any more than it had. "I'm not going to guide you through whatever messed up thing you want to tell me. If it's this hard, it means it's obviously going to hurt me." I looked at him sharply, as if daring him to contest me.

"I just want to be honest with you."

I closed my eyes for a few moments, knowing this was the worst thing he could have said to me since I knew honesty didn't protect feelings. No, it plowed down its victims for the sake of virtue. Knowing I couldn't disappear no matter how hard I squeezed my eyes shut, I forced them open.

"You want to be honest with me?" I let the question sit for a second. "Because, what? You haven't been?"

"I don't know," he said in a faraway voice.

"You don't know?"

"It's a long story, I guess."

We then sat there, which was starting to feel like a face-off. Waiting for this long story, I wasn't sure he was about to share with me, I noticed his emotional state had drained his eyes of color, denying them the gold glints I usually cherished. I thought back on all the times I wondered what his eyes would look like above mine, as the weight of his body locked me into security. But not these eyes. These ones were dark and humorless. It was then that I knew with certainty that they were about to break my heart.

"Pete," I said with the reluctance of ripping off a band-aid. "Just say it."

"Okay," he agreed as he crushed his cigarette. "I will." He swallowed and took a deep breath before saying, "This has nothing to do with you, or us…. but… I met someone…I think."

Hearing these words, there was no playing it cool as the tears pooled in my eyes threatening to drop. I tried to keep them from falling by leaning my head back, but they were smarter than me. They found the smallest canyon in the corner of my eyes and worked their way down the side of my face.

"I don't want to hurt you," he said, reaching out to catch a tear with his thumb, "but I can't keep arguing with myself about this."

I flinched, rejecting his soft gesture, not wanting to be misled by him any more than I had been.

"But there's more to this, and I really need you to listen to this part, because it's important."

"Pete." I let out a deep exhale, feeling like I'd heard enough. "I get it, okay?"

"You don't though," he said, his eyes practically begging mine to listen. "Like I said, there's more."

Even with my vivid imagination, I couldn't imagine what more he had to tell me. Or better yet, I didn't *want* to know. Toughening up my resolve, I shot up from the table and looked at him like he was truly a cruel person.

"I really think you should let me tell you the whole thing," he said, now looking frustrated.

"Well, excuse me if I don't want to hear it."

Pete

I chased after her, nearly overturning the café table from my leg and then my bike bashing into it. She stormed off with not even the bulk of her groceries or the cat litter anchoring her fury. Out of breath and out of options, I finally caught up to her in front of the Vice store that had more people working than they had things to sell.

"I'm sorry," I said, catching my breath.

"Sorry?" she said, letting her bags drop on the sidewalk. "Sorry for what exactly, Pete?"

Her question hit me like a wave crashing against a cliff, heavy with sediment of our unresolved past. She, of course, wasn't asking about that moment. No, she was summoning me to finally acknowledge my inability to express my feelings to her all these years.

"I'm sorry for everything," I stupidly replied.

"Like what exactly?" Her eyes showed no sign of retreat as they bore into me. "I mean, we're just friends, right?"

I looked at her like she knew that wasn't true.

"I'm lost here, Pete. You're one of the most opinionated people I know, so surely if we were supposed to be anything more, I would have known by now."

I looked down, accepting her sharp words about the inadequacies of our relationship because she was right. How could I expect an intimate moment with her, revealing my longest kept secret if I had been denying her closeness this entire time?

"I know," was all I could say.

"I'm glad you know." She grabbed her groceries. "Are we done here?"

"I don't want to be," I replied, not knowing what to say, because this was clearly not the moment to tell her everything. She was too pissed.

"You don't get to decide everything, Pete."

"Car," I pleaded, reaching my hand out that she looked at with disdain.

"Don't Car me." Her eyes smoldered, turning her dark blues into jet black. "Seriously, can you be any more selfish?"

"Selfish?" I bristled, the word visibly offending me. "You have no idea how vulnerable I am right now and how fucked up I've been feeling about hurting you."

"*You're* feeling vulnerable?" She pointed at me as she stepped closer, which I admit frightened me a little. "You?" She briefly looked away in awe and began laughing as if now she'd heard everything. "I'm so sorry, Pete, that *you're* feeling vulnerable. How could I be so insensitive? What other cliché do you want to throw in my face? What? It's not what you think? It's not you, it's me?"

"Yes!" My head bounced vigorously. "Yes to both of them, especially that it's not what you think, because I'm *certain* it's not what you think."

"Well, here, I have one for you: I don't have to sit here and take this!"

Before she could take off, I blurted, "I'm just so confused!" My voice began to crack, as I felt like I was losing control of the situation. "It's just that when Misha came in for the—"

"What," she cut me off as she lowered her eyes into what looked like a death stare. "Did you say *Misha*?"

"Yes, Misha," I confessed. "But you *have* to let me explain."

"I don't have to do anything right now." She looked at me like I had just stolen something from her, which hurt me to admit that I had. I had stolen her time.

"Please," I begged again. "Let's just sit somewhere and talk this out."

"No!" she said in fierce resistance. "No. You owe it to me to spare the details because now you're just being an asshole. It's like you *want* me to know everything. You're, like, getting off on it"

"I *do* want you to know everything." I held my hands out, pleading with her to be reasonable. "You deserve to know everything."

"Deserve," she hissed. "But you know what Pete, I'm not stupid." She cocked her head. "I know what this is all about."

"You do?" I employed a hopeful tone.

"Yes. You want my blessing. You want everything to be cool, right?" My eyes flicked to the side because, well, of course I did. "Fine, Pete. We're cool." She choked back a bitter laugh. "But hey, there was nothing between us anyway, right?"

"You know that's not true."

"I don't know what's true anymore. But look, you're off the hook, you don't owe me anything, so go ahead, Pete, be with her. It's your life. I'm just an extra in it."

The light tremble in her voice told me to back off, knowing the conversation was fucked from the start. The betrayal she felt, looked back at me, making me wonder if disclosing Misha's identity would have even made a difference. Deep down, I knew it wouldn't because it didn't change the fact that I was interested in someone else.

And with that, I let her walk away.

CHAPTER 13

Carla

I always found it dramatic when people claimed they couldn't believe something. Like, when a very famous person wins an award and in their speech they go on about how they can't believe it. It's like, the award is in your hand, and you're wearing Versace, so believe it and spare us the rehearsed modesty. But there I was contradicting myself because the only thing I could think to say was, "I can't believe it." Where was I while Pete was falling in love with someone else?

"Did he actually say he fell in love?" Barbie asked, pulling out a container of hummus from her fridge.

"Well, no," I admitted, leaning against the counter, nursing a glass of wine. "But he may as well have."

"But he didn't say it, so don't be a drama queen." She picked up the platter of snacks and nudged me towards the living room. "Come on, let's go inside."

Wearing a floor-length caftan that she once told me she bought at a thrift store with Gram Parsons – or was it Frank Zappa? – I followed her into the living room on that 94-degree day.

"Shit. It's hotter than herpes in here," she griped, setting the platter down. "It's still April for crying out loud! I hope you worked inside today."

"Yeah, we were on set where it was almost too cold."

Sitting beside her on the couch, I took a cool, satisfying sip of my Pinot Grigio. My eyes ticked back and forth with the tail of her Felix the Cat clock before looking around her and Kurt's apartment. On the cranberry-colored walls were paintings gifted to her by former tenants. There was a hand-painted Day of the Dead skull, a ceramic bust of The King, and scented candles. On the floor sleeping was Joni's brother Darby who Barbie described as emotional. More full-figured than Joni's athletic build, he covered his eyes with his paws as if hiding from the heat. And blaring over it all, including my thoughts was an episode of Nancy Grace at the highest volume that held Barbie's attention captive.

"They're going to get that Scott Peterson," she said, lighting a cigarette. "They've already selected the jury for trial." She pulled in a long inhale as the curls of smoke circled the air. "Sick son of a bitch is going down." She turned to me and with a hand slapped on my knee, she said, "You see, honey, things could be worse."

I thought about it for a second. "Because Pete didn't kill me, I should be grateful?"

"Yes," she said matter-of-factly. "Yes, you should be."

Knowing she was serious, I shifted my viewpoint to see things from that perspective, but my emotions pulled at my skirt hem like a stubborn child. But her eyes were waiting for a satisfying response from me because she knew she was right.

"I am grateful," I said to her. "I am."

"That's my girl." Barbie saw me reach for my wine. "But now I want you to eat!" She pushed the bowl of chips towards me. "It's too hot for a real dinner, but at least have some of this."

"I'm not hungry."

"Well, you sure are thirsty." She glared at the glass. "Take it easy with that stuff."

It was then that I realized that I really *was* only thinking about myself because I was drinking a bottle of wine in the home of a recovering addict.

"Oh, my God." I pressed my hand over my mouth. "I'm so sorry."

"For what, honey?" she replied absently with her eyes glued to the screen.

"The wine." I held up the glass as if she needed evidence. "Is it tempting you?"

From the back of her head, I could see her considering my question before she slowly turned towards me. Looking like it was the most absurd thing she'd heard, she responded, "No. I'm not tempted. I wouldn't waste twenty-four years of sobriety on Two-Buck Chuck. But thank you for asking." She seemed amused with my hopelessness as she exhaled a puff. "Besides, back in my day, I was more of a cocaine and champagne kinda gal."

"Fancy."

"Yeah, right. Fancy," she muttered, "until it wasn't."

At a commercial break, she grabbed the remote to mute the TV and turned to me.

"But what I want to know is what you kids are going to do about this show on Friday?" She leaned back to look at the calendar hanging in the kitchen. "It's already Monday, and you two wasted the entire weekend moping like a pack of puppies."

"Pete was moping?"

"Not the point," she snapped. "Stay focused because we need to figure out what you're going to do."

"I have no idea," I said, not wanting to think about it. "We don't even have new songs and the old ones I barely remember."

"You'll remember. Besides you're opening, so you won't need that many tunes. How many minutes are they giving you?"

"We didn't get that far in the conversation."

"It can't be more than twenty-five minutes, which is like five or six songs. You can dust off some of the old ones and maybe even throw in a cover for fun. We used to do a punk rock version of 'These Boots are Made for Walkin'."

"I can't stand the thought of even being in the same room as him, so I don't see how we're going to make it on stage, not to mention rehearsing." The hair on my arms spiked up just thinking about it. "I don't think I can do it."

"You sure you're not just sabotaging yourself?"

"No," I replied wearily. "I just don't see how it's going to be possible with everything stacked against us."

"Everything stacked against you?" She rolled her eyes. "I forgot, your 20s are your drama queen years."

As the wine began to work its way through my body, my senses getting soft and fuzzy, I couldn't help but wonder what

Pete was up to. Things had gotten out of hand at the café where it seemed the more we tried to talk, the less we understood each other. We had done a good job avoiding each other that weekend, which didn't feel like much of a win. I leaned back on Barbie's couch, staring out her window that shared the same view as Pete's. The houses in the hills seemed to bake in the oppressive heat. Meanwhile, the scattered palm trees leaned more to the side than usual, as if they too were surprised by the sudden heatwave. That was when a brilliant idea popped into my head.

"Barbie," I said, a mix of curiosity and mischief creeping into my voice. "You know what I want to do?"

She eyed me with suspicion. "Go home and practice?"

"Not exactly."

"Well, that's what I think you *should* do." She continued studying my face, a look of concern now making her eyes smaller. "Alright," she said, turning completely toward me with her hand out like she was collecting money. "Out with it."

"I want to look her up."

"Look who up?" she asked.

I paused, not wanting to say her name again because I hated how cute it was.

"Who?" she urged, her voice edging with impatience.

"Misha," I finally said, which felt like curdled milk in my mouth.

She grumbled and nodded her head in disapproval. "I think I like my idea better."

Pete

What the hell were we going to do? I asked myself for the hundredth time since our dreadful talk at the café. I walked into my apartment with the echoes of Victoria's newfound love for the Black Eyed Peas still ringing from the day as I flicked my ceiling fan on. As the hot air circulated in my apartment, I removed my pit-stained work shirt, tossing it in the hamper. Walking to the window, I pushed it open to air the place out, not feeling much of a difference. Besides the shower, the coolest spot was in my windowsill where I smoked a cigarette. Dazing off, I looked at my view of the hills, seeing the houses cling to them like barnacles. I noticed the skylights that looked like tiny mirrors bouncing back the harsh light, probably turning those million-dollar properties into greenhouses. I shuddered, imagining the obscene amount of energy used to keep those glass boxes cool.

The unexpected heat had made everything more desperate with my emotions feeling deep-fried, as I wallowed in my personal hell of indecision. All I had to tell Carla was that I was also attracted to guys and that I struggled to manage those feelings. Boom. Let the healthy conversation and healing begin. But no. I fanned the flames by being vague, making me question my own readiness.

Without her, though, I felt alone. I needed my friend. It had been a weekend of not knowing what to do about each other and, more urgently, what to do about the show on Friday.

But it was too hot to think, so I sat in my hotbox apartment and lit another cigarette.

Carla

"I've heard of that MySpace thing!" Barbie waved her hands around excitedly. She then gave me a long look. "But are you sure you want to go poking around the Internet for this girl?" She didn't wait for my answer. "If you ask me, this sounds like the vino talking here."

"No, no," I denied that the wine could be altering my perception. "I'm not even buzzed."

"If you say so."

"No, really," I insisted with forced confidence. "I think it'll be good for me. I *should* see her."

"I'm going to have to disagree with you on this, honey." She gave me a crooked smile. "Do you really need to see what Pete's new flame looks like?"

"New flame," I mumbled, truly hating everything that was happening. "Oh, I don't know."

"Well, I do," she reiterated. "And it's a bad idea."

"I just think I should prepare myself since I'll probably see her at some point, and I might as well get the initial shock out of the way."

"You know," Barbie said, looking off as if considering the whole thing. "I was afraid of something like this happening." She glanced at me. "You're sure you don't want to give Tyler another shot?"

I narrowed my eyes at her. "I'm sure."

"Well, if you're going to self-destruct, I may as well chaperone." She stood up, brushing tortilla chip crumbs off her dress. "But leave the hooch here. I don't want anything spilling on my computer."

I followed her as she sashayed down the hallway of her apartment, her dress catching the warm breezes. Before reaching the end, she turned into the walk-in closet that she and Kurt had converted into a tiny office. Standing in front of an armoire with the doors removed, she pointed to a folded chair in the hallway.

"Drag that over here," she instructed as she lowered into her own seat, rolling it closer to her PC.

I grabbed the chair, positioning it as close to the computer as I could from out in the hallway. Leaning in, I stared at the screen as she typed in the website address using only two manicured fingers.

When confronted with the sign-in page, she turned to me. "Do you have an account?"

"No," I answered with a dumb stare. "Do you?"

She shook her head. "No."

We reflected on it, our eyes darting back and forth from each other and the screen as if we were about to embark on the biggest decision of our lives.

"I don't think we can snoop without one," she said quietly as if the machine could hear us.

"I don't think we can," I echoed the severity in her voice. "So, why don't we make an account?"

"Let's make an account," she agreed, continuing her conspiratorial tone before dropping the insider trading act. "I might as well, I hear my old glitter gals are on this thing, so what the hell, right?"

The sign-up process with Barbie dragged on slower than the hot day with her stressing out over every detail including the personal quote option. After *much* deliberation, she eventually went with: "If you want the girl next door, go next door," by Joan Crawford that we both agreed was perfect for her.

When we signed her in, we saw she already had a friend. She turned to me for an answer I didn't have as we both leaned closer, trying to make out this alleged friend of hers.

"Who the hell is Tom?" She squinted at the tiny picture, her confusion reflecting my own. "The only Tom I know OD'd in 1994."

I looked at her like she never ran out of anecdotes like these before shrugging, unsure who this Tom fella was.

"He's cute," she added as if that solved the mystery before moving on. "But alright, Missy, let's get this over with." She shot me a look, still sounding like she didn't like the idea while I tried to remain firm in my resolve.

On the screen, I watched her drag the cursor to the site's search bar where she entered the name and the city, announcing each letter as she pressed the key. When the search populated seven pages of hits, my eyes widened in surprise.

"How common is this name?" I looked in awe at the thumbnail pictures, unprepared for the mix of girls *and* guys named Misha. "And what's with all these guys?"

"Misha is also a boy's name." She scrolled down the page. "I went to high school with two Mishas."

"Oh," I said, distracted as my eyes skimmed over the male profiles to focus on the girls. "What about her?" I pointed to a girl wearing a green polka dot tankini. "Click on her."

"Her? But she's not Peter's type at all."

I glanced at her. "You never saw his high school girlfriend, Allison."

"Yeah? What was she like?"

"Like this." I pointed to Misha, 22-years-old from Huntington Beach.

But Barbie wasn't buying it as we clicked through photos of her at nightclubs with friends who looked just like her. All wearing variations of the same strapless top that would make my boobs hang like sad pineapples, they huddled together holding cocktails with skinny red straws poking out the top.

Barbie shook her head, not buying it. "Honey, this can't be her."

"If it's not her, it's someone like her," I said, knowing it didn't matter. "Pete can be very superficial. Don't be fooled by his whole tortured beatnik trip. He has a history of dating girls like this." I couldn't help but let out a woeful sigh. "He likes easy-going girls from normal families," I said, mostly to myself. "I think I'm just too complicated, too aware."

"Yeah, and that's a good thing," she said as she flipped through this girl's album at a Maroon 5 concert. "And if Pete wants easy peasy here at the House of Blues, then that's his problem." She then turned to me. "You have something more than her."

"An eating disorder in remission, mommy issues and a lack of self-worth turning into self-destruction?"

"You *are* drunk," she stated with a concerned look. "But let's focus on one problem at a time. What I was going to say is that you have an innate attention to detail that most people don't have."

"I wish I didn't notice as much as I did." I glanced at the picture of Misha, who didn't seem aware of, well, anything.

"But what you also have is the ability to bounce back and now's the time."

"I've bounced back," I fibbed. "Really."

"No, you haven't," she asserted. "I gave you all weekend to wallow, and yes, we're all surprised by the news." She stopped herself to consider it for a second. "Well, Kurt was."

"I thought you said he was oblivious."

"He is," she said in amazement. "He thought you and Peter were together this whole time, so imagine his surprise."

I dulled my eyes at her like this wasn't making me feel better.

"You know what also helps though?"

I gave her a jaded look hoping her solution wasn't another set-up with a tenant.

Reading my thoughts, she said, "Well, that helps, too. But you don't need to sleep with someone right now." She dismissed the idea with a wave of her hand. "No, what I was going to say was that writing helps."

"I guess."

"I got into journaling when I was in rehab, and it really did get to the source of my addictions because it's never about the substance, or the food or the weight, but you'll turn over those stones when you're good and ready."

"I'm not interested in group therapy or The Twelve-Steps." I returned her gaze. "Or church basements."

"Okay," she said, chuckling at the last one as her face softened. "There's no one-size approach to healing, but writing is always a good start."

"You know I used to write." I looked off, thinking about how much I used to love it. "Before I moved out here I used to write, mostly about the world I imagined waiting for me. The great unknown, I suppose, but now I realize it was only my imagination playing tricks on me, because no place can fix the stuff in your head." I looked at her. "There's no escape from your mind and it sort of sucks finding that out."

"Well, there you go," she said, as if receiving good news. "Write about the disappointment of unmet expectations!"

"You don't have to sound so happy about it."

"I'm not," she said before looking back at the computer screen. "But it sure as hell beats looking at pictures of this chick."

I had to laugh because she was right.

"Come on, honey, we're done here," she concluded, pulling open a drawer. "What I want you to do is take this notebook here and write about what's going on in there." She pointed to the top of my head. "Anything that comes to mind. The muddier the better."

Her words echoed the advice I had once given to Pete when he shied away from writing. I encouraged him to write the worst rock song ever written to rescue him from the traps of perfection. At the time, it seemed like sound advice, but now sitting on the receiving end, it didn't feel so simple.

Before I could negotiate another glass of wine or another day of sulking, she waved her hands as if shooing me away.

"Now go home and write," she demanded, "and leave that bottle of wine here! Doctor's orders!"

Complying, I took the notebook and went back to my place with an ear bent in the direction of Pete's door as I passed it. I could hear the shower running, which somehow I interpreted as his indifference. Stepping into my apartment, I found Joni stretched out on her back with her arms reaching skyward, sleeping off the heat. I settled in next to her as she lazily rolled onto her side looking at me like *now what?*

"We're going to write," I said, in which she blinked before abruptly looking at the window at some imaginary thing that momentarily caught her attention.

To the rhythm of her purring, I began Barbie's assignment seeing that once I started, I couldn't stop. As if cleaning out a garage, I took out all of my thoughts and organized them into imaginary piles. From there, I packaged them into songs. Six of them. Six emotional time capsules shaped into verse, chorus, verse.

Now all they needed was some music to go with them.

Pete

When I heard the knock at the door, it was already dark outside. On my end table, I reached for my glasses and turned on the light. I fastened the top button of my pants before stumbling out of bed to fish my work shirt out of the hamper. I was still buttoning it when I reached for the doorknob. Upon opening the door, the shock of the hallway light burned my eyes before allowing Carla to come into focus. Standing in front of me, she appeared depleted but wired with some kind of nervous energy.

"Hey," she said, looking at me blankly.

"Hey," I replied.

In her hand, I noticed she clutched a notebook as we stood there for a few moments in dreadful silence.

"Do you want to come in?" I reached my hand up higher on the door, opening it wider to make her feel welcome. "I can make us some coffee."

I tried to convey a warmth that told her I was still her friend, but her eyes had deepened into that dead-of-night blue that warned me to back off.

"That's actually not why I'm here."

I glanced at the notebook, taking a half-step back like it was a weapon.

"Look, if we're going to play this show on Friday, we need new material." She cleared her throat. "I've wrote some songs and was wondering if you could put music to them."

"So, you want to do the show?" I couldn't hold back my surprise.

"We sort of have to, don't we?"

"We don't *have* to do anything."

She raised an eyebrow, clearly not in the mood for what she'd describe as "my self-certainty." Without a word, she handed me the notebook to redirect my attention.

"So, they're not, like, life-changing or anything, but it's something to get us through this one show."

I fanned through the notebook pages to find them filled with lyrics. The messy musings of the mind with words crossed out for better ones, verses X'd out, and full choruses rewritten, reminding me how fragmented the songwriting process was. I looked at them, knowing they would probably go through another round of editing once paired with a melody.

"When did you work on these?" I asked, impressed.

"This evening." Her eyes returned to mine where I could sense frustration coming from her. "So, do you think you could write some music or not?"

Almost offended by the question, I replied, "Yeah, I think I can manage."

"Great, so let me know."

Surprised by the phrasing, I looked at her like I wasn't following.

"What?" she said.

I held up the notebook. "Shouldn't we work on this together?"

"I already contributed my part." Her eyes met mine in the coldest I'd ever seen them.

"I see." I surrendered, knowing logic wasn't going to win this battle. I looked at the notebook again, slapping the back of it against my palm and said, "I guess I'll let you know."

"Great."

She didn't wait for my response and simply turned around, leaving me in the wake of an unfamiliar distance between us.

"Great," I said as I closed the door, feeling like a stranger, yet holding her deepest secrets in my hand.

I settled back into bed with the notebook, preparing myself to read about what a piece of shit I was. But as I turned the pages, the lyrics weren't at all what I expected. I imagined sharp edges, her words hitting me in the face as if tossing the pointed edges of photographs at me. But what she gave me instead were insightful observations on life. Societal burdens, family expectations, perfectionism, self-worth, self-destruction and searching for purpose with only hints of unrequited love.

I read the lyrics a second time, now tuning into the melodies that practically sang off the pages. I scanned the room, taking inventory of my gear: electronic drums, keyboard, a folk acoustic, and headphones (to contain the noise) feeling like it was more than enough to get a musical point across. I shaped the lyrics into a melodic structure, noting chord progressions, time measures, and of course, drum patterns. The rat-tat-tat returned like an old friend, welcoming me back into the fold.

Knowing she didn't read sheet music, I made a makeshift demo without disturbing my neighbors. Due to the sound limitations as well as time constraints, I aimed for an atmospheric yet simple folk sound. By blending her introspective lyrics with my melodic structure, I crafted songs that were reminiscent of a spring day, but you know, tripped out on a tab of LSD. Despite its rawness, the music conveyed our connection packaged in a collection of simple and sweet songs I titled, *Homeroom.*

As I approached seven o'clock, the following morning, my body buzzed from lack of sleep. I walked across the hall with the completed work and on her doorknob proudly hung a canvas bag. Inside, it contained the demo cassette and her notebook with her lyrics reshaped into the respective melodies and the accompanying guitar tablature.

As I walked away from our collaboration that required separate rooms to create, I felt forlorn that it took hurt feelings, misunderstandings, and secrets for us to create music again. But despite the circumstances, I caught myself smiling because it felt good to be back in each other's musical graces.

CHAPTER 14

Carla

Some of my favorite artists claim to have written their big, breakthrough records in, like, no time at all. They're usually written in their bedroom with a rickety four-track, and on an acoustic guitar with, say, a missing E string. I found myself struggling to fully buy into these grassroots backstories because the works were just too good and so impactful that I figured a team of professionals were in the background somewhere fluffing musical pillows. But after listening to *Homeroom*, the pairing of my words with his musical prowess, I realized you didn't need the fancy record industry to write good songs; you just needed to feel like complete and total shit.

Listening to the demo with headphones on, the songs took on a shadowy quality, mostly because of his whispered lyrics from having to record in the middle of the night. But it worked with the melodies floating in like fog, making their presence known while creating an airiness to the sound. Mournful yet magical, unpolished yet unpretentious, they evoked images of a haunted countryside in another time period. His percussions that served as the heartbeat of the songs were steady handed yet distant employing his beloved ghost-notes, reminding me that what we can't see, or touch can still be deeply felt.

We practiced for the show but not together, which I convinced myself wasn't at *all* weird. From across the hall, I could hear the light taps of his electronic drum kit while my ears tried to guess the songs in our dysfunctional band practice.

As the week wore on, I found myself increasingly satisfied at the reintroduction of doing something I once loved. The scales and dexterity returned like it had never left, with memories of old licks and songs resurfacing as if no time had passed. By Thursday, I felt as ready as I would ever be. While Pete and Kurt picked up the van and his drums at Barbie's sister's place in the Valley, I treated myself to a date with Mister Carlo Rossi. As I listened to the first pour gurgling out of the jug of Chablis (which I chose only because it sounded fancy), I heard a pounding at my door.

Not recognizing the knock's cadence, as it was too aggressive to be Pete, and not enough jingle-jangles for it to be Barbie, I tiptoed closer. The knocking continued as I proceeded with caution. When I got to the door, I tried to look through the peephole only to find it blurred out by someone's thumb pressed over it.

"Who is it?" I said weakly.

"Honey," I could hear Barbie's voice on the other side. "Don't be scared. Open up."

Relieved but still confused by the chaotic pound, I opened the door to find Barbie, and next to her was none other than my best friend.

"Surprise, bitch," Alex said with her hands out. "You missed me?"

"OH, MY GOD!" I screamed, flinging my arms out to pull her into a fierce hug, feeling like it was the most animated thing I had done in years. "What are you doing here?"

"You think I'd miss your big show?" she said, our bodies swaying side to side, nearly toppling over in excitement.

I looked over her shoulder at Barbie beaming at the two of us. "Did you do this?"

"She sure did," Alex confirmed, stepping back from my embrace. "How were you *not* going to tell me about it?"

"It all happened so fast," I explained, ushering them inside. "I've barely had time to think."

I shut the door as Barbie walked over to my bed, placing a large bowling bag on it that she began to rummage through. Turning to Alex, I took in her appearance. It had been three years since we'd last seen each other and looking at her, she remained as beautiful as our fifteen-year friendship. Her blonde hair was the longest I'd ever seen it, keeping its natural wave giving her this Bob Dylan/Greenwich Village in the '60s look I appreciated. Despite the weathered look of her skin after a New York winter, it still possessed that ethereal, translucent quality reminiscent of a water-nymph. And her green cat eyes whose superpower was to see through bullshit could rival those of Joni's.

"How'd you even get here? To my apartment, I mean." My eyes flicked momentarily to Barbie who didn't drive.

"A taxi," Alex replied like a true New Yorker.

"Isn't that expensive?" My jaw tightened at the thought of cabs in L.A.

"It's a work expense because while I'm here I have to interview the Weekend Warriors." She raised her eyebrows impressed with her own resourcefulness.

"So, it's my first time in L.A.," she said, rolling her suitcase off to the side, "and I have to say, for a place obsessed with weight, there seems to be an awful lot of hot dog and burger joints. I think I passed, like, seven on the way here."

Her nose crinkled at the contradiction, looking at both Barbie and me for an explanation in which Barbie let out a deep laugh. "Welcome to Hollywood, baby."

Alex then took stock of my apartment. I watched as her sharp writer's eye took in the details from the pictures, the painted walls to the cat licking her paw.

"Very you," she admired the place. "It's like I just walked inside of your head." She inhaled deeply. "It even smells like you…like dried flowers and candle wax."

"More like dead flowers," I joked, which prompted Barbie to break into the chorus of the Stones' song.

Smiling, I turned back to Alex who seemed pleased by my healthier appearance since we had last seen each other until she got to my eyes. "You look sad."

I knew it was no use pretending otherwise as I could never hide my emotions from her. "I know I do."

Her eyes then blinked in the direction of the door, knowing where Pete lived. "And what's going on with him?"

I planted my eyes on her. "How long are you here for?"

"Oh, boy." She pulled me in for another hug. "We'll talk it out this weekend."

I wrapped my arms around her and as if filling my soul, I inhaled her natural scent that would always smell sweet to me — a blend of black current with a hint of dark chocolate. It had been years since someone had embraced me so deeply with each squeeze laden with meaning that I allowed myself to linger in a few more gentle sways.

"Alright, you two," Barbie interjected. "There will be plenty of time for hugging. We have a rock show tomorrow night, and we need to get you," she pointed at me, "Hollywood ready with costumes, makeup, hair, the works."

I looked down at my corduroy pants and second-hand sweater. "I was just going to play in something like this."

She made a face that told me to cut the crap.

"You always wear that," Barbie bemoaned as Alex frowned, seeming to share the disapproval.

"Or something *like* this," I stressed with a tinge of impatience at having to be so precise.

Barbie's eyes shot to the top of my head. "And your hair?"

"What's wrong with my hair?"

"Honey," Barbie said with a strained voice. "You need to make an impression, give them something to talk about and, unfortunately in this town, it's not just the music that's gonna do it."

"Well, it should be only about the music." I looked at her, appalled that she'd even suggest otherwise.

"Well, it's not," she said firmly, dismissing my naiveté. "I hate to break it to you." Her eyes then lowered to my seams held up by safety pins. "Oh, for Pete's sake."

"Is it for Pete's sake?" Alex chuckled but when she saw the expressionless looks on our faces, she recanted, "Sorry." She held her hands up apologetically. "I thought it was funny."

Barbie turned back to me. "Alright, we'll talk clothes later because we're not getting anywhere. But for now, let's do something about that hair."

I reached for it wondering what was wrong with it as I watched Barbie line up scissors, bottles, and mixing bowls on my bed. "What exactly are we doing with my hair?"

"We're going to wake it up a little," she replied, tossing me a black towel. "Starting with some color."

"What's wrong with the color?" I glanced in my mirror for a clue.

"The problem with the color is that there is no color." She looked at the top of my head like I had lice. "Have you ever dyed it?"

"No," I said, reaching for a few strands, safeguarding it from her predatory eyes.

"Ooooh, virgin hair." Barbie rubbed her palms together like a cartoon villain. "And I have the perfect color too." In her bag, she pulled out a metal tube, bringing it closer to her face to read the label. "They call it Film Noir." Her eyes sparkled through her bifocals. "How perfect."

I turned to Alex, noticing her blonde locks looking lighter than her natural color, which she once described as being the shade of sweaty gym socks.

Past my shoulder, Alex noticed the opened jug of wine. "Looks like the party's already started." She walked past me and into the kitchen where she announced, "You have hardwood floors in here!"

I smiled in her direction before turning to Barbie, who was shaking out a plastic tablecloth stained with paint droppings.

"Let's do this in the kitchen," she decided, stuffing the tablecloth into my hands. "Come on."

Inside I found Alex completing the tour, eyeing my turquoise tea kettle, the photos of Pete on my fridge, my shelf of second-hand mugs and etched wine glasses, taking one down for herself.

"Your kitchen is seriously so cute," she said, walking towards the jug of wine. "I bet you don't have a roach problem like Claire, and I do."

"Not in my building!" Barbie exclaimed. "And you better not have brought any with you in your suitcase. That's the last thing I need!"

As Barbie prepared my kitchen table, she mumbled to herself that she'd call the exterminator on Monday just to be on the safe side. I laughed to myself, loving that Alex was getting the true experience Barbie, who had just accused her of traveling across the country with cockroaches.

Alex carefully tipped the bulbous jug towards the glasses, filling them to the brim.

"Cheers," she announced, handing me a glass. "To makeovers and weekend madness."

"Hopefully not too much madness," Barbie intervened, watching us both gulp down the sugary wine. "Will you girls please be careful with that stuff?" Barbie shot us both with an imploring look. "Things can spiral out of control so fast you won't know what hit you. That stuff is pure poison." Alex and I looked at each other with eyes agape over the exaggeration.

"I just don't want something to happen to either of you girls." When she could see us brushing off her warning, she said, "You laugh now, but terrible things can happen under the influence and I'm not talking about the embarrassing stuff like farting and forgetting you're in bed with a guy."

I almost spit out my wine from the specific example, as Alex raised her hand guiltily.

"Been there," she confessed.

I looked at her, horrified. "The Missed Connections guy?"

"No, the Other Music guy," she said, cringing at the memory of the record store guy we had spent way too many phone calls analyzing.

"He doesn't deserve your embarrassment," I sneered, hating a guy I'd never met.

"No, he doesn't," she agreed, "but he got his share when he got fired for stealing Yoko Ono CDs at work."

The two of us snorted with laughter, reeling over the misfortune of someone who had treated Alex terribly.

"Will you two pay attention?" Barbie tapped the table to rein in our attention. "This is important. And I'm not talking about no Yoko Ono CD either!" Alex and I bit our lower lip like we did in grade school to stop ourselves from laughing. "I'm talking about something fatal—"

"Like becoming our parents?" Alex interjected.

Barbie's eyes trickled over to mine. "Well, there's that," she said, holding her gaze a second longer as I looked away, knowing I was nothing like my mother. "But I was thinking more like crossing the street drunk without looking or passing out with a lit cigarette and burning to death. Serious stuff like that."

"We'll be careful," we both said. "We promise."

"Alright, my public service announcement is over. Now, let's make this a real girl's night." She turned to Alex. "How about some music?"

Agreeing, she left the kitchen as I put my almost empty wine glass down, turning my attention to Barbie. As I watched her measure a creamy solution into a marked beaker, her eyes bounced to the top of my head, appearing to calculate the correct measurements.

"You know what," she said under her breath, "for your mound of hair, we're going to need two tubes. Good thing I thought ahead. I'll go get it in my bag."

"Hold on." I stopped her.

She turned to me. "What now?"

"You said I had virgin hair, right?"

"The purest," she answered, walking over to me to reach for a few strands. "It's a little dry but all in all it's in good shape." Her eyes became small. "Why?"

Ignoring her inquisition, I asked, "Do you remember the length requirements for that Locks of Love thing you told me about?"

"I do," she answered, her now voice trailing off in skepticism. "But it's longer than you'd be willing to give, meaning you can't just send them a bag of bang trimmings."

I nodded my head. "I figured as much."

"Why do you ask?"

I paused for a moment, reflecting on our conversation about haircuts and breakups, and the idea of transforming pain into purpose, a de facto theme for the week. I wasn't certain that cutting off all my hair would make me feel whole again, but it felt like a step towards something. A change in appearance, a shift in mindset, a way to stop obsessing over myself? My motivations were still murky, but I knew I had to decide soon, otherwise I'd lose my courage— my courage to change. So, straightening my back, mustering as much conviction as I could, I declared, "Because I want you to cut it."

Just then, Alex barged into the room holding two CDs that weren't mine.

"Are we *No Panties* or *Under Construction*?" She weighed the albums in each hand like an old-fashioned scale. "Which are we tonight?" She read the room with a discerning eye before deciding, "You're *definitely* under construction right now." She held up the Missy Elliot CD, declaring it the winner, before adding, "and we'll work you up to the no panties this weekend."

Pete

It had been a while since I'd driven a van, so I drove back from the Valley like I was transporting someone's grandmother. Gripping the steering wheel, I headed south on the 101, remembering the last time I was in it. The closed doors had sealed in scents of the past, activating vivid memories of simpler times. There was the cedar shelving my dad had installed, the vinyl-covered seats that when baked in the sun smelled like an old taxi, and Carla's vanilla hand cream that used to make her smell like a cupcake. In the back were relics of our road trip, like her worn-out purple flipflops tossed in a dusty corner and the Rand-McNally map with the ragged line connecting New York to California. I thought about the day we were supposed to drive back east. Instead, we called our parents from a payphone outside a Von's Supermarket to tell them we were staying in Los Angeles for no other reason than, why not?

As I trailed Kurt's pick-up truck, I thought of our songs we co-created that week, satisfied with how they came out. The rustic eeriness, like the creak of the floorboards in an abandoned house, felt fitting to us and would sound absolutely ridiculous before a Weekend Warriors cock rock show. I had also written a little song about Misha that I, of course, ripped out of the notebook to keep for myself. It was the second love song I had ever written, and my mind naturally compared the two songs. "Buttons," a song I wrote for Carla while we lived with our parents, had lyrics that still held up because I still wanted all of those things I wrote for her. But I also wanted what I wrote for Misha in "Swimming Pool Eyes," a nocturnal song alternating between sensuality and desperation. Neither song was right for our band, but they were mine, and I chuckled to myself at the idea of one day making a pretentious solo album with me middle-aged with a beard and looking pseudo-deep in thought on the cover. I knew I wouldn't do anything with the lyrics, but they gave me a sense of control, making me think I had resolved my conflict while feeling closer to both of them: a girl who wanted nothing to do with me and a guy I didn't know how to talk to.

After parking in Kurt and Barbie's spot they had generously cleared out for us, I tapped on Carla's door, hearing more activity on the other side than usual.

"Coming!" called out the voice of someone who was neither Barbie nor Carla. I looked at the door number to make sure I had, in fact, knocked on the right one. The mystery concluded when the door flew open to reveal Alex.

"Hello, Albrecht," she greeted me with a mischievous lilt as if insinuating something.

"Oh, hey," I said, stunned for a moment as I mentally cut and pasted her, taking her out of Long Island and placing her in L.A.

"You look like you forgot your lines." She peered at me like the idiot I must have looked like.

"Oh, sorry." I quickly snapped out of my disoriented state and extended my arm out to give an old classmate a hug. "I just didn't expect to see you here."

"Well, here I am," she sang in my ear, before parting from our quick embrace.

Breaking from it, she straightened her shirt out to convey a playful disturbance from the unscripted moment of affection. I tipped my head into the apartment that smelled of chemicals that pinched my nose before returning my focus back to her.

"Is she here?"

She tossed a thumb over her shoulder. "In the shower."

"Oh, hey Peter!" Barbie's voice then called out from the kitchen where I detected a trace of cigarette smoke.

Alex raised an eyebrow. "Peter?"

I slightly shrugged. "I go by my full name out here."

"Yeah, I am so *not* calling you that."

"Ah," I said, clicking my tongue. "And there she is: Carla's annoying best friend. You know, I was worried for a second that you'd gone soft on me. You can imagine my relief right now."

"Yeah, well I'm about to get even more annoying because best friend here has some questions."

I bobbed my head not doubting it. "I'm sure she does." She continued to dig her eyes into me. "And I have answers," I told her, holding my hand out for her to back off for the time being. "I promise, but before any of that, we need to do a little housekeeping."

I dangled a set of keys in one hand and the garage opener in the other before handing them off. "I'm getting out of work early tomorrow, so I'll meet you guys in time for set-up."

On the couch I saw Carla's folk guitar with still no signs of her electric. I had hoped our return to music would have sparked her desire to want to play the instrument that first bonded us. But seeing the folk felt like a silent declaration that she wanted a clean break from whatever it was we once had. I couldn't exactly blame her but that didn't stop me from lamenting our past, since the future was so uncertain.

"Earth to Albrecht." She waved her hand in front of my face.

I flinched, breaking away from my trance. "Right," I said. "I'm here." I then pointed to the guitar. "If you want, I can bring that down."

She pressed her eyebrows in. "But it's an acoustic."

"That's what we're using tomorrow night." I kept my reaction neutral as her eyes shifted, sensing a bigger story.

"An acoustic set before the Weekend Warriors," she said, thinking about it. "How antiestablishment."

"That's us," I said absently, scanning the rest of the place for anything else we might need. "So, I'll just take the guitar and if there's anything else, like bags or whatever, give them to me now."

"Pete." She shifted her weight to one hip. "I can't be mad at you for whatever's going on if you keep being so nice."

"Then don't be mad at me." I held my hands out like it was really that simple.

"I kinda, sorta have to." She presented her palm as if taking an oath. "Best friend on duty here."

"Whatever you want," I said, not willing to dispute her.

Behind her, I noticed Carla's keys dangling from the hook. "I'm going to need the keys," I said, pointing over her shoulder, "the ones with the letter keychains."

She turned around to unhook them, noticing the C and P keychains.

"How cute," she noted, running her thumb over them.

"I remember the day we got those," I recalled as she handed them to me. "The day we bought our car."

"Yeah?" She looked at me as if she was catching me in a lie.

"Yes," I replied with an edge of defiance. "We *have* made some memories here. Nice ones, too."

"We'll see about that."

I did my best not to grin at the overdramatization. Just as I was about to wish her a nice evening, she stopped me. "But I don't get it." Her eyes roamed, as if trying to piece the bits together, clearly sensing the strange vibe. "You two seem like you're high, or are you guys totally California'd out now?"

I looked at her like I didn't know what she was talking about.

"I mean, is this whole thing between you two even worse than I thought?"

"It really depends," I responded, knowing it wouldn't make a difference.

"Depends on what?"

"Depends on what your definition of what worse is."

CHAPTER 15

Carla

The next morning, I dragged my heels into the kitchen to feed Joni, stepping over evidence of our night – the empty jug of Carlo Rossi, scattered album covers, an ashtray piled with her cigarettes. My eyes softened on my best friend sleeping with my cat curled up next to her like they'd known each other forever. The night before, we talked about everything: the Pete saga, her neighbor I told her to stop sleeping with, her literature-themed Bat Mitzvah where I got to light candle number two after her parents, and classic high school stories that you just had to be there to see the comedic gold. Then there were things we didn't need to talk about—her doubts, my demons and whatever lurked between. Our bond allowed us to understand the inner workings of each other without always having to verbalize them. These corners of our past, which made up our present, would always be on standby, ready to discuss when necessary, and stowed away when not. As I filled the coffee carafe with water, a sudden jolt hit me, remembering the night before.

"Did we prank call Tyler?" I said under my breath.

Just as the memory resurfaced, I could hear Alex stirring in the other room.

"What time is it?" her cigarette-burned voice croaked.

"Around noon," I called out.

"What time is sound check again?"

"Five."

"Oh," Alex said with some pep in her voice. "We're good then."

On my way back to bed, I cracked open the window as Alex stretched her arms over her head with my cat following her lead.

"Hi, baby girl," she said, turning towards her to give her a few scratches. Joni rolled onto her back, lavishing Alex's attention as she twisted and turned reminding me of Madonna on the beach in the "Cherish" video.

"La," Alex said, grinning at my cat's theatrics. "Did you, like, give birth to your cat?"

"No, Alex," came my measured response as I slipped under the covers to join them. "I did not give birth to my cat."

"Then why the hell does she look just like you?" She leaned closer, inspecting Joni who looked at her from the side. "She even makes the same bitch face as you."

I reached for Joni, petting her fur to reassure her that she didn't make mean faces just as Alex's ankle brushed against mine.

"Damn, girl," she said. "When was the last time you shaved?"

"I was just going to ask you that." I reached down to scratch my ankle.

"Yeah, but I live in New York, so I have an excuse."

"It gets cold here, too, you know."

"It does *not* get cold here." She looked at me like I had missing brain cells. "I check your weather every now and then and honey, it's not cold."

"Okay," I said, placating her. "You're right. And we also drive to work in bikinis, go to the beach every day, and we're also all dumb out here, too, right?"

"You said it, not me." She tapped the tip of my nose as if proving her point.

"What. Ever," I gently pushed her hand away. "I'd rather be dumb and warm than…. " I thought about it for a second before landing on, "than be an asshole in wool."

"An asshole in wool, you say?" Alex looked at me like she was impressed.

"Registered trademark."

She looked off as if visualizing it. "Now *that's* a band name."

We burst into lazy laughter, agreeing on the name that, if I knew my best friend, she'd manage to work into her writing somehow. She then reached for a lock of my hair. "I can't believe you did it."

Registering the marveled look of awe on her face, I said, "Did what?"

"La?" Her eyes clouded with worry. "Please tell me you remember."

I offered a hallow gaze. "Remember what?"

"Okay..." she said, propping up on her elbow, "you're scaring me now." She braced herself as if she were about to break news to me, but I started to laugh because, of course, I remembered. I ran my hands through my hair, feeling it drop at my chin. I gave the messy bob a few tosses, feeling the freedom of having less of it.

"You dumb bitch," she said, falling on her back. "You scared the shit out of me." She whipped her head toward me. "But thank you for not making me be the one to inform you that you drunkenly hacked your hair off last night."

"I wasn't drunk."

"Yeah, neither was I," she said with a sly curl of the lips. "But I've never seen you with short hair." She moved a strand away from my eyes. "You're like a whole different person."

I shrugged. "That's sort of the idea."

"And I love that you're donating it." Her eyes twinkled at me. "You're going to make some little girl very happy."

"That's also the idea."

"So, I know you don't want to hear the superficial side of your *makeover*," she said, "but you can go fuck yourself because I'm allowed to tell you that it looks great." She pressed a finger to my lips to stop me from denying the compliment. "And before you respond, I'm going to tell you that looking pretty doesn't mean you're, like, selling out, or whatever '90s bullshit was sold to us."

"Alright, alright," I taunted her, biting my lip to try to appear serious. "You can lavish me in compliments. Carla Aurora authorizes it, so go ahead."

"Oh, does she?" Alex said, looking skyward. "Thank God, because I was actually worried there."

"I know you were." I stretched back on my pillow, laughing with my best friend and feeling my stomach burn like I had done a thousand crunches.

I rolled my head toward her. "Do you laugh like this with Claire?"

"Sweetie," she said, looking at me from the corner of her eye. "Are you jealous of Claire?"

"Please," I scoffed at the very thought of it. "You just talk about her all the time, so—"

"Yeah, and I talk to her all the time about you."

"Really?"

"Why are you so surprised?" She turned onto her side to face me. "Of course, I talk about you, my best friend who just moved across the country and made a life for herself because the one back home didn't suit her. That takes courage. I couldn't have done it without some financial support from my family."

I made a face that financial support would never be an option for me.

"And now," she continued, "you're playing this show with brand new songs you guys came up with in a week." Her eyes shone with awe. "Don't be the last to know how badass you are. I know it, Barbie obviously knows it, even Claire knows it. Now it's your turn."

"Okay," I swore. "I'll work on it."

"Good." She appeared satisfied. "So, when do I get a sneak peek of the new songs? Or do I have to ask that bitch Carla Aurora?"

I lightly smacked her hand in fake vexation. "Just for that, you'll hear them tonight."

"With everyone else?" She looked at me in horror. "Then what the fuck is the point of being friends with the band?"

I laughed in support of her argument.

"Come on," she insisted. "I want to hear all the juicy, revenge songs about Pete."

"There are none actually."

"What?" She did nothing to mask her disappointment.

"There are none," I repeated. "The songs are about… I don't know, life. Finding or really, not finding myself and wondering if I'm doing the right thing by not having a plan. Stuff like that."

"Really now?" She leveled her gaze at me.

"I mean, I hint at Pete stuff, but no, there's not a song titled Go Fuck Yourself, Pete."

"Well, there should be."

"Next time he breaks my heart, I promise," I half-joked, hating what felt like the inevitable. "But no, these songs are simple and imperfect. You know how inventive Pete can be with a melody, the ins and outs of the pentatonic scale and all that." I took another beat to organize my thoughts before adding, "But I'd say the soundscape is sort of grainy, raw yet ornate in emotion, you know?"

She looked at me with still eyes, turning them from their usual ocean green into a murky shade of polluted waters. "The soundscape is grainy? The pentatonic scale? Ornate in emotion? You know, you sound like him now."

"No way."

"Yes, way. You guys are even starting to look the same, so you're going to have to do better. I want to hear the songs, and none of this convoluted rock talk, because trust me, I get enough of that crap at work."

I hesitated, knowing I had one song I could play for her, but since Pete took the acoustic, that left only the Telecaster.

"Well?" she interrupted my thoughts.

"Well, I wrote one song about him that I decided to keep for myself."

"Oooooh, secret songs," she announced, bouncing her shoulders like she was getting the prize money. "Now we're talking."

"But since Pete took the acoustic, I'm just going to sing it to you a cappella."

"A cappella?" She looked offended. "What the fuck is this? La, where's the Telecaster?"

"In the pantry." I averted my gaze and paused a second or two before explaining, "I don't know. I feel like I'm scared of it or something."

"You're scared of my dad's guitar." She didn't hide her impatience. "Oh, my God, will you please go get it?"

"Okay, maybe not scared of it but what it represents."

"The past," she stated bluntly, seeming ready to move on. "Now please go get it because I am not listening to some weirdo Barbershop Quartet version of what is obviously going to be an amazing song."

One of the gifts of knowing someone your entire life is knowing when they won't relent. One look at her determined face told me this was going to be one of those times. I had to silence my inner voice that thrived on fear like a toxic friend as I walked to the pantry. Inside, the aroma of spices from residents past filled my senses as I reached for the padded guitar case. I used to think I was a decent guitarist, but the memories only embarrassed me. Images of my younger self flashed by, like awkward yearbook photos with me shaming myself for thinking that I was special.

"I can hear you in there trying to talk yourself out of it," Alex called out. "Cut the shit and get out here already."

A smile tugged at my lips, knowing that my inner voice had nothing on my best friend. On the couch, I sat next to her with the case on my lap and slowly unzipped the fabric flecked with cat hair. When I opened it, it felt like reuniting with an old friend who didn't notice I had been avoiding them. More vivid than I remembered, the orange popped like a vintage Italian postcard. What was once a symbol of our creative vow to each other, now felt heavy with unresolved emotions, which I wasn't convinced a simple strum would remedy. I thought back to our first gig, romanticized over time as part of a gilded age. In my hand wasn't just the orange guitar her dad handed down to me when we were teens, but a lifeline back to myself that I wasn't sure I wanted to see. Alex gave me a few moments to reacquaint myself with the past before looking at me like it was time for the future.

Handing me my pick, she said, "Let's start easy. First, what's the name of the secret song?"

"While I Have You."

"While I Have You"

We moved out here to start over
Picking the last place that felt like home
Billboards, big dreams and hangovers
Little failures are my to disown

You were my friend when I didn't know
How to be one to my self anymore
Lost ambitions or could it be the weather?
That's making me feel weighed down, so slow

My eyes you describe as sailor stripes
In your dad's t-shirt that lines stretch dark blue
I laugh and ask you how you thought of it
You say summers in France tried and true

But that's now long gone I guess it's over
You're in the parts of my mind that hurt
From mistakes to heartaches I'm not sober
As I write this three-part little rhyme

If only I knew how to read you
Words between us not making a sound
Tossed off and discarded like I'm seasonal
Stepped on leaves, corners curled and brown

But winters and summers here look the same
Glassy-eyed as I'm watching you change
From crushes to kiss-offs, how dare you?
Fall in love in my fucking face

But how did we get here?
My thoughts undress you
Ticking time mind that I overuse
Look at me now, exposed are my issues
Hallowed and hungry what a terrible muse
Sleep with me now it's the least you can do
Or give me something more...

While I have you...

While I have you...

While I have you...

Pete

The way the day was going, it didn't seem likely that I'd be getting out early. Even though Etienne had already approved my written request, tell that to the Paris office who pillaged the office like Stormtroopers in Vuitton. The day was muted chaos with the flashing dots on my switchboard and a frazzled Victoria who looked like she'd had just about enough of French people. Needing a break and to relieve the pressure on my face, I removed my glasses. As I dug the heels of my palms into my eye sockets, I mourned for the naïve version of myself at eight o'clock that morning who thought I'd be walking into an easy Friday.

"Peter," Victoria said, walking toward me with a stack of copies. "You have to review everything before I bring it upstairs."

"I know," I said, sliding my glasses back on before looking at each other in regard to Etienne's frantic email. I took the pile from her and turned each page, verifying the sequence while looking out for anything that might disrupt the flow of a presentation.

"Alright," I said, signing my initials at the bottom corner of the cover page, "these look good. You can bring them up." I offered her an apologetic look at the absurdity.

"You're supposed to leave early today, aren't you?" She looked at me as she gnawed her lower lip.

"That was the idea," I replied, unable to give her the reassurance I could tell she was after. "But hey," I affected an optimistic tone, "let's hope they're still on Paris time and will leave soon." She still looked nervous. "It'll be okay, alright?" I promised her. "This is just work bullshit."

"Alright," she said, not seeming entirely convinced.

"And how about on Monday we go out for designer cupcakes." I searched for a smile on her face. "On me."

The idea of seeing me in that milieu seemed to please her.

"Even if the paps are outside waiting for reality stars?"

"Wait, is that what happens there?" I asked, the look of horror apparent on my face.

"Why do you think I go?" She looked at me like I'll never get it.

I swiveled back to face my computer, the sound of her heels disappearing down the hall when my phone rang. Looking at the Caller ID, I could see it was coming from upstairs. With my hand hovering the receiver, I took a deep breath, assuming they wanted another round of espressos, in which I was prepared to tell them to go fuck themselves.

No, but I wasn't far off.

« *Allô, oui ?* » I said somewhat casually, knowing it would be Etienne.

« *Il faut virer Victoria aujourd'hui.* »

I'm sorry what? I pulled the phone away from my face, looking at it for an answer before asking Etienne to repeat himself.

« *Oui, il faut virer Victoria aujourd'hui.* »

Unfortunately, it didn't soften the blow the second time around because he was still asking me to fire Victoria. My eyes spaced out for a moment, thinking about this awful request based on literally nothing. *Literally*, I sighed to myself. I knew I was having an emotional crisis when I found myself exaggerating with hyperbole.

"I think you all have been closed in that conference room for too long," I responded, adding that perhaps they needed some fresh air or, to put it bluntly, fucking go home already.

"It's what they want," Etienne said, sounding wiped out himself.

I fell silent for a few moments, leaving room for him to reconsider.

« *Allô ?* »

"Yeah," I replied, flatly. "I'm here. I'm sorry, but I don't agree."

I needed to stand my ground, because as much as she drove me nuts with her PhD in Perez Hilton, she didn't deserve to get fired. I suggested we could talk about it on Monday because his nerves sounded as frayed as mine, but it seemed there was nothing more I could say. He assured me that her temp agency would find her something by the following week and that it was just business.

"Fire me then," I tried one last resort and meant it. "If someone's head has to roll then let it be mine."

Etienne let out a loud sigh. "We're not prepared to do that," he said, his tone formal. "And if you quit, which is what you'd be doing, they'd still let Victoria go."

Feeling backed into a corner, I rivaled his sigh with a louder one. "So, now what?"

"You let the temp go."

I squinted my eyes in resentment of the deductive wording since she was obviously more than that. « *D'accord,* » I finally agreed as I could hear her voice on his end, dropping off their latest pile of crap.

When I informed him I would handle it as soon as she came back, he suggested I wait until the end of the day, as if offering severance. But no. I wasn't going to make her care about this job any longer than she was mandated to. I reaffirmed that I would be taking care of it as soon as she came down and wished him a good meeting. *Click.*

I took off my glasses to pinch the bridge of my nose, thinking again that this was not at *all* the kind of day I anticipated.

I missed 8 a.m. Pete, that naïve fuck, more than ever.

Carla

I strummed the final chord of the song, letting the melody dissolve into silence. Like how certain perfumes transport you back in time, holding and hearing the Telecaster had the same effect.

"I think you should play it tonight," Alex said, looking at me like a proud best friend. "I really love it."

"He doesn't know it." I took the guitar off my lap, leaning it carefully against the couch.

"And?" She looked at me like I was going to have to do better than that since Pete would have had no problem improvising a drumbeat. "Why wouldn't you play a song you wrote and composed yourself?"

"Because this one is really personal."

"Which is precisely why you should play it."

She picked up my notebook, her eyes scanning the lyrics with her sharp, critical eye. "*How dare you fall in love in my fucking face*," she read the lyric. "It's just so real."

"A little too real," I grumbled. "It's just not like me. You know I'm not expressive like that."

"Well, maybe it's time you were because if that's not a fuck-you song, I don't know what is."

She flipped through the notebook with practiced ease, her fingers moving quickly but precisely as I got a glimpse of what she must have looked like at work. She nodded her head as she read the other song lyrics, her New York journalistic edge evident in the way I could practically see her thoughts move.

"This is good shit," she said, running her finger down the page. "Direct, poetic, relatable."

She continued turning the pages when she appeared to notice something.

"Wait a hot second," she said, narrowing her eyes as she brought the book closer to her face.

"What is it?" I leaned in to see what she was looking at, but all I saw was a blank sheet of paper.

"I think I see something here." She began tracing her fingertips over the flat surface. "I feel something too."

"Where?" I followed her fingers but still saw nothing.

"Here." She pointed to the paper, which made me wonder if she needed water or maybe some food at this point.

"Sweetie," I said, my eyes beginning to strain. "What am I looking at?"

Her fingers then ran down the spiral binding. "It looks like a page has been ripped out."

"Yes," I said carefully, looking at her like she was starting to worry me. "The notebook was Kurt's, whose a glazer, so, I imagine a page has been ripped out at one time or another."

"You don't see that?" She held the book so close to my face I couldn't see anything. I gently pushed it back but still saw nothing but lined white paper.

"There are imprints of words here!" She brought the notebook once again closer to her eyes. "This looks like longform." Her cat eyes then comically shot up over the book, aimed at me. "Do you have a pencil?"

"I do," I said, appeasing her.

"Well, go get it!"

With one eye on her, I tiptoed over to my dresser and reached into my makeup bag. In it, I pulled out a golf pencil from a country club scene I did on a TV show about rich kids.

"Here," I handed it to her, "knock yourself out."

"Perfecto."

From the back of the notebook, she ripped out a clean sheet of paper. Placing it over the one in question, she began to lightly run the pencil over it.

"I knew it," she chirped. "I'm getting something!"

"It's probably Kurt," I said, dismissing anything sinister going on with his notebook. "Although I do find this detective act very entertaining."

On the couch, I sat back and sipped my coffee while she continued dragging the pencil across the paper. My mind drifted off, wondering what I would wear that night and other loose ends until she interrupted my thoughts.

"So, I guess it was Kurt who wrote a glass measurement titled 'Swimming Pool Eyes'?" she said sanctimoniously.

I tilted forward. "Huh?"

"Huh is right."

Alex held up the decoded page and I leaned closer, still hoping it was Kurt's. Looking at it, though, there was no denying Pete's unmistakable half-cursive handwriting.

"Swimming Pool Eyes," I repeated involuntarily, resenting that I'd collected another clue about the girl who was making such a mess out of him.

I turned to Alex whose eyes were waiting patiently for mine. "I guess you're not the only one whose been writing secret songs."

Swimming Pool Eyes

You see through me, Your gaze is still
So self-aware I'm thinking you know
What happens when...

i'm all alone, safe in my thoughts
my mind likes to write stories of us
affectionate...

...are these ones when, i don't act weird
i want to know about what you do
i'm interested

you say you like my sweater vest
the one with the hole
my grandmother sewed
winter solstice...

...falls on this place, but that can't be real
my mind likes to revise
the things that we do when i fall asleep
moving clockwise
I'm bracing myself to float or to drown
in those swimming pool eyes

would we be friend who kiss at night?
daytime uptight
i know i want more...
like witnesses
is this in my head?
lost in daydreams
wondering what your tongue tastes like
the sweetest when...
...i'm on my back, breathing us in
waiting with your hands pressing down
on my wrists...

...stretto coffee like i'm overseas
drinking like it's fine
i'm complicating, self-medicating
so i don't recognize, i'm diving into a world
will i be cast out or baptized?
pretending to be above vanity
immune to those swimming pool eyes...

CHAPTER 16

Pete

The elevator dinged open, making my stomach clench in a fist as Victoria's heels approached.

"Sheesh," she said once she rounded the corner. "They have no sense of humor up there." On my desk, she dropped a pile of papers for me to review. "I thought the French didn't work."

I had to then laugh, because she was right that we were definitely not benefiting from the stereotype. As she walked to her desk, she stopped mid-step, her eyes squinting in an effort to read my face.

"What's wrong? You look like you just heard a John Mayer song."

I looked at the ceiling for a moment. "I wish it was that."

"Okay, now you're scaring me."

This comment deserved one of my hand-crafted, snarky replies but instead, I looked at her with eyes glazed over like she was about to die.

"Seriously, is everything okay?" she probed again, slowly lowering into her seat.

"You know what?" I said, stopping her. "Why don't we grab a coffee in the breakroom?"

"I'd love to, but we can't both leave reception. They'll lose their shit upstairs."

"They'll live." I grabbed the phone to forward calls to voicemail.

"Peter," she said through gritted teeth as if they were listening. "I don't want to get in trouble."

"I wouldn't be too concerned with that."

In the break room, she sat nervously at the lunch table while I made her a cappuccino. As I frothed her 2% milk, I thought about how it was all my fault. I had failed her by assuming that my bosses understood my repeated requests to hire her officially (plus benefits) implied satisfaction with her job performance. But clearly, I was being too vague. Behind me, I could feel the weight of her suspicion pressed against my back as I mentally outlined what I was going to say, while trying to predict her response. As I tapped the bottom of the cinnamon jar, spotting the foamed milk with dark red flecks, she interrupted my thoughts.

"They want you to fire me, don't they?"

I froze with the jar in my hand hovering over the mug.

"It's alright," she said. "Just tell me. The suspense is killing me."

I turned slowly to find her glaring at me, arms folded, her crossed leg wagging. "How'd you know?"

She fixed a penetrating stare. "Peter, you're putting cinnamon on my coffee." She switched her crossed legs. "When do you ever put cinnamon on my coffee? I'm lucky to get a splash of milk."

I carefully placed the mug in front of her, as if extending an olive branch.

"I'm sorry," I offered, the words feeling trite. "I should have done more for you."

She shook her head. "It's not your fault, Peter."

I bit back the urge to contradict her, knowing she would feel obligated to absolve me of blame, so we settled on silence. We sat in the somber mood as I looked around the space, imagining it through her eyes. *Her* before and after. Would she miss any of this? God, I hoped not. But this was the bookend of one phase of her life that included me, a strong cappuccino, and a stuffy breakroom that she had to at least be relieved to never sit in again.

Back at our desks, we went through the motions of her returning the office keys and packing her things into a cardboard box like they did in the movies. I listened to the shallow thuds as she dropped into a box her tabloids, loose burned CDs, and her Jennifer Lopez hand cream. After she put on her floor-length cardigan she once told me was called a duster, I walked her to the elevators. She held her box as we stood there, neither of us wanting to say goodbye like this.

"I still want my cupcake on Monday," she demanded.

I smiled for the first time that day. "And you'll get it."

"And even though you just fired me, I still want to say thank you. You were a pretty cool first boss to have."

"If you need a recommendation, or anything, please let me know."

"Don't worry," she said. "I'm not shy."

The elevator doors opened, and I let my arms drop to my sides in response to the finality of it.

"I guess this is it," I said predictably as she stepped into the elevator.

"Oh, Peter, one last thing," she said as I placed my foot to block the motion sensor. "Monsieur Fontanet sometimes calls down for a projector for his Friday night class."

"Alright," I said with a dismissive wave to show she didn't have to care about this shit anymore.

"I thought I'd also tell you…" she said, sliding her eyes to the side evasively, "that was the class I transferred Misha Taylor into the other day."

My stomach dropped when I heard his name. A wave of regret then washed over me upon learning he'd come back to the office after the sexiest ride home I'd ever been given.

"You were out back smoking," she explained to what I imagined was a wistful look on my face, retrospectively wishing I had been there. "And I think he was looking for you, too."

She then pressed her gaze into me, where I caught a fleeting glint of understanding, as if she was silently saying, *I know, Peter.* I inhaled deeply, marshaling every ounce of composure, stiffening the muscles in my face to remain neutral, all while thinking, well, son of a gun. The girl didn't know who The Strokes were, but she somehow sniffed out my interest in Misha.

"I see," was all I could think of to say as I tried to organize my thoughts, wondering how obvious I'd been. I realized it was time to officially relinquish my role as her boss and simply said, "Thank you.".

"No problem." She took a step back into the elevator. "I don't know, maybe things don't have to be so complicated all the time." With my hands in my pocket, I bobbed my head, acknowledging the simplicity of her words. "I mean, aren't we supposed to be young or something?"

I stifled a laugh. "That's certainly the rumor."

Carla

I didn't want Pete's song to haunt the day of our show, but it left me with more questions than before. Having discovered something so secret and personal, I wanted to know what he meant when he wrote about a world he feared being cast out of. What world? Just as I tried to mentally dissect it, Alex barreled through my mind chatter with a comment I knew was designed to distract me.

"Can we please talk about how we prank called your dorky neighbor last night?" she called out from my closet. "And how we could hear his phone ringing from this side of the building."

The distraction worked as I laughed at her retelling of us calling Tyler. Under the ruse that Alex was a journalist for *L.A. Weekly*, she told him she was covering an in-depth investigation into Silver Lake's hipster culture. But before featuring him and possibly considering his face for the cover, he would have to take a mandatory hipster test. After he enthusiastically agreed, she conducted one on the fly, asking ludicrous questions that even included multiple choice, which required him to use his phone's keypad to answer.

"We are *such* assholes," she said, cackling at him frantically pressing the pound sign to answer a *crucial* question about Death Cab.

"We so are," I agreed mid-snort, the sound of the pound key replaying in my mind like a punchline I couldn't get enough of. "But I'd say he and I are even now."

We walked out of the building, looking like hungover gypsies. Both donning dark sunglasses, my hair flailed about, its new length making it impossible to twist into a neat bun, and Alex, in her boho chic phase, draped in multiple silk scarves and chunky beaded necklaces. Lugging bags of clothing with stray cables spilling out, we piled into the van looking like we were about to run away with the circus.

Once settled in, I gripped onto the steering wheel, feeling its grooves for the first time in years. Sitting in it after so much time had passed, the memories of travel and long-distance thoughts came rushing back, realizing just then how young I was when I drove it across the country.

I started the engine, twisting my body around unable to see anything out of the gated back window. Relying on my side mirror and Alex, I crept the van out of the tight garage. As I inched out onto the street Alex was less than helpful as she called out, "Don't run over Tyler!"

I slammed the break, thinking he was actually there as Alex burst into laughter.

"You scared me!" I said, trying to stop myself from laughing because it really wasn't funny.

"Hold up a second." She placed a hand on my wrist to stop me from maneuvering the car for a second.

I looked at it, still holding back laughter. "Now what?"

"No, really, serious question." She swallowed. "If you had to choose," she said in a lowered tone as if this were a sacred initiation.

I leaned forward in anticipation. "Between?"

She looked left and then right. "Between running over one of the cats," she said, blinking her eyes in total seriousness, "or running over Tyler. Who would you choose?"

I eyed her like we didn't have time for silly questions, especially when she already knew the answer.

"Tyler," I whispered hastily. "I would obviously run over Tyler." I looked into the rearview mirror. "Now tell me if anyone's coming!"

On Hollywood Boulevard, we cruised with the windows down, the oldies station cranking out the Supremes, as we passed legendary locales—Jumbo's Clown Room Strip Club, the Thai restaurants featuring nightly Elvis impersonators, 1960s dingbat apartments, and the Hollywood Downtowner motel. I loved acting like a tourist with my best friend who fawned over the quirky charm of my acquired town. As we continued west, I'd like to say the wind was whipping our hair to add to the insouciance of two friends driving through Hollywood. But with traffic backed up between Western and Bronson, it was more of a limp breeze that kept our hair exactly in place. Observing the empty sidewalks, Alex commented, "I guess the song was right and nobody walks in L.A."

After we crossed Gower, I realized I hadn't pointed out the Hollywood sign to her. I considered a detour but then reminded myself she had seen the strip club where Courtney Love once danced, which for us, *was* the iconic Hollywood landmark. The sidewalks then transitioned from the regular plain concrete to the black terrazzo embedded with the famous pink stars.

"Oh, my God! The stars!" Alex called out, her neck practically craning out the window to see. "The famous stars!"

I drove slower, giving her time to soak in the faux glitz of the famed boulevard. The sense of adventure that felt palpable before was about to burst like confetti as we approached the Trop Theatre. Seeing our band's name on the art deco marquee struck us silent, sending a wave of goosebumps down my arm. I pulled over to the marked curb in front, as we both leaned forward to get a better look at our name. The large letters gave the impression that we were as important as the headliner, like we had things like managers and merch. Alex and I exchanged knowing looks, the air feeling alive with change that both excited and scared me.

"Do we have a camera?" Alex turned to me.

"Shit." I nodded my head that we didn't.

She stared at the marquee, as if imprinting it into her psyche. "We're going to have to rely on memory tonight," she said, squeezing her eyes shut. "Remember this moment because it's awesome."

I agreed, fixing my gaze on our name encased in unlit neon. My eyes then drifted over to the closed gates of the will-call booth and the shadowy entrance of the club, where gold script over the glass doors promised cocktails and dancing from another era. The walk-of-fame stars embedded in the sidewalk contributed to the eerie, old-world glamour of the place that I got chill knowing I was a fleeting part of.

"Before we go in," Alex said, turning to me. "I think we need to talk about something."

"What is it?"

"What if Pete invites this Misha girl tonight?" A guilty look crossed her face for even thinking about it.

"He wouldn't do that," I quickly said, before reconsidering it. "Or would he?"

"I don't think so, but we also didn't think he'd, like, get a girlfriend all of a sudden either."

"She's not his girlfriend." I glanced at her. "Right?"

"La, I don't know what's up with him, but I think at the very least we should be prepared in the event he turns out to be an insensitive asshole." She stated all of this pragmatically, as if reading from an instruction manual. "Most guys are."

"Alex." I wrinkled my nose, letting the worry show on my face. "I really don't know what I'll do. I mean, am I supposed to act like it's cool and that he and I have always been just friends?"

"You two never were and never will be just friends."

While her words confirmed I wasn't imagining things, they didn't exactly reassure me because it didn't alter the existence of Misha.

"What will you do?" she said to herself, chewing on the question as she drummed her fingers on the top of her thighs. "What will you do?" A sly look crept onto her face. "I'll tell you what you're going to do."

"I'm not going down on him on stage," I said, anticipating her thoughts.

"That wasn't what I was going to say, you dirty, bird. But if you wanted to upstage the headliners, that's one way." She paused for a few long seconds, clearly envisioning it.

"Okay, okay!" I waved my hands to dispel the thought cloud I could practically see floating over her head. "Stop thinking about it!"

"Why not? It's hot!" She laughed as she ducked her head in surrender. "What I was *going* to say before you got all dirty, is what you're going to do tonight is you're going to look fucking fabulous. I grabbed some of your cute tops and I have tons of makeup in my bag, so let's do it up. Eyeliner, mascara, the full *ill na na* to give this sexy haircut the treatment it deserves."

I fixed her with a penetrating stare. "That's it?" I said. "That's the big plan?"

"Well, we can't exactly go with *your* idea."

Pete

After Victoria left, the office felt as quiet as the last day of school. Never did I think I would grieve celebrity gossip and Top 40 hits, but there I was wishing I knew her thoughts on the last season of *Friends*. *What was happening to me?* I thought as I scrambled through my bag to regain some semblance of myself. In it, I pulled out the CD I bought at Amoeba and the knitting project I brought, thinking I was going to have all sorts of downtime backstage.

The upstairs execs, I could tell, were avoiding calling downstairs, so I used to the down time to my advantage. Stretching back in my office chair, I knitted as I bobbed my head along to the experimental, neo-prog album that was love-at-first note. I then imagined Victoria coming back for whatever reason, and how she'd perceive the scene: me knitting and seriously rocking out to Deerhoof. For me, this was soul-soothing, but to her, it could have been misinterpreted as glee, or rather, a celebration of my newfound sonic freedom. Plus, the knitting would have completely thrown her off. So, I turned off the music, returning the office to its morbid state, and prepared myself for what I was really avoiding. I had disappointed one girl that day, and reaching for the phone, I was about to disappoint the other.

"Are you here?" Carla's voice snapped upon first ring.

"That's actually why I'm calling."

"Okay, I'm starting to feel left at the altar here, Pete."

"You're not," I replied, taken aback by her uncharacteristic comment. "I'll be there but I have to stay here until six."

"Pete!"

"I know."

"Sound check is in ten minutes!"

I squeezed my eyes shut in agony. "I know."

"And I set your drums up!"

I opened my eyes. "You did?"

"I had to!" she said wildly before flattening her tone. "And yes, I placed the mics around your kit to ensure optimal sound the best I could since we're only getting four channels on the PA, and the Warriors barely made room for our stuff on stage."

"Seriously?" I sighed, afraid something like this would happen. "Well, ask for more… everything."

"Their management scares me a little. It's pretty intense. You'd think the Stones were playing tonight."

I dropped my head, imagining how they were all pushing her around and felt even more guilty for not being there. She let out a deep breath that sounded like a wind tunnel in my ear.

"Do I even want to know why you're not here?" she asked, her voice dripping with accusation.

My eyes went dead at the idea that I'd jeopardize our show for whatever romantic entanglements she was currently imagining. "You're kidding, right?"

"You know what? Never mind," she said, the chill in her voice unmistakable. "I told you. I don't want the details."

"It's not because of… *that*," I said, daring to even address *it*.

"It's none of my business, Pete."

It's none of her business, I said to myself, exaggerating an eyeroll in regard to the oversimplification. If it wasn't her business then why were we barely speaking? I felt an overwhelming temptation to point out but stopped myself thinking the day was complicated enough.

"I had to fire Victoria today," I explained. "That's why I'm stuck here."

"Oh," was all she could say as I sat for a second in mild satisfaction of proving her wrong. "That's terrible, Pete." Her voice returned to the friend I knew. "Is she okay?"

"She is, actually," I said, reflecting for a moment on what a good sport she had been. "But seriously, what the fuck are we going to do?"

"Alright," she said, now using her thinking voice. "Just give me a sec."

I pressed the phone to my ear and literally sat on the edge of my seat waiting for her wisdom that I knew she had more than I did at the moment.

"I still need to do a soundcheck," her voice returned, "so I'll see if I can get Jay to fill in for you."

I closed my eyes, imagining Jay at my kit.

"I know," she replied as if she could see my face. "But he's the only nice one here, and we'll just do, I don't know, a few Nirvana covers or whatever just to hear our equipment on stage."

"Okay," I agreed as if there were a choice.

"Okay," she replied, making me feel like we were in this together.

Not wanting to get off quite yet, I asked, "So, what's the vibe like over there?"

"The vibe is we're opening, and no one cares."

CHAPTER 17

Carla

When I told Jay he could pick the Nirvana song as a thank you for filling in for Pete, I didn't think he'd go so on-the-nose with the band's biggest hit. It also didn't help that the sound guy was only interested in hearing one song from us. As I embarrassed myself with an acoustic version of "Smells Like Teen Spirit", I noticed he'd turn the knob a quarter inch here and there only when the huffy stage manager hurried by. The fake sound-mixing made absolutely no difference as I tried to get through the sound check from hell.

"Sounds good," he said from the booth. "You guys are on at eight sharp." He then pressed a button and turned a knob before reaching for his phone in his back pocket. If Pete were there, he would have pushed back on this guy's indifference with concise technical instructions and improvements to the sound. But he wasn't there. I was. As I watched him dig his thumbs into his phone, I remembered Barbie's advice.

"I actually couldn't hear anything," I said into the mic, playing the role of an assertive person.

"What?" he mouthed, looking up from his phone, his face twisted by the inconvenience.

"I said, I couldn't hear myself," I repeated, but this time louder. "Especially, the guitar."

He pressed a button and leaned into the mic. "I don't know what to tell you," he replied. "You're all mic'd up."

"Do you think we could run through another song, but this time, turned up because again, I couldn't hear it, and I was strumming really hard."

He looked at me like my question was taking up too much space. "That's normal," he said in a breathy tone, designed to convey impatience. "You're not supposed to hear yourself."

Engaging in an argument in stereo like this, with my words echoing back at me felt like my own personal hell. I may as well have been stark naked standing up there, making the urge to retreat strong. My hands sweated in the discomfort of projecting myself as I encouraged myself to keep going.

"Um, I actually do think it's important that I hear myself."

"You need to calm down," he then responded, which spiked my temperature from warm under the heavy lights to now a simmer.

"I *am* calm," I retorted. "I just don't think I'm asking too much to be able to hear myself play."

"Sweetie," he then said, which took my blood from a simmer to boiling because there was no *way* Pete would have gotten the sweetie treatment. "You got your little sound check," he said as if I were playing make believe. "What else do you want?"

And with that, he flicked a switch, and my mic went silent. I tapped it twice to confirm it was indeed dead. I stood there in awe of the lack of professionalism, thinking, because this guy didn't like what I'd said, he'd silenced me in the most childish way imaginable. He might as well have stuck his fingers in his ears to block out my voice. I turned to Jay in seek of support, but he meekly shrugged, seeming embarrassed for me.

Off to the side of the stage, I could see Alex chatting with the Weekend Warriors management team to organize their interview. Seeing the look on her face, I could tell she was enduring her own share of patronizing nicknames as they looked at her like she was a little girl. Feeling defeated, I placed my acoustic on the stand and walked across to the other end of the stage. I pushed aside the velvet curtains that coughed dust in my face, and through a padded door. Assuming it would take me backstage, it instead brought me to a rounded stairwell. I walked up threadbare green carpeted stairs, the walls lined with chipped candelabra sconces and torn palm tree wallpaper that led to a pocket balcony overlooking the stage. I pushed down the seat of one of the velvet auditorium chairs and slumped into it. The discomfort of the deadened springs dug into my back, as I took my phone out of my pocket. From the elevated view, I could see the stage where Pete's tangerine sparkle drumkit stood beside my acoustic that purposefully held no specific memory. Staring at the stage, my fear for our show crept in like mold. I knew being in good graces with the sound guy was crucial and I felt like I had failed. As I rewound scenes from the soundcheck, wondering how I could have handled it differently, my phone vibrated in my hand.

I flipped it open. "Hi," I said with haste, wondering where he was.

"You sneaky little devil." But it wasn't Pete.

"Oh," I said, dropping my head in disappointment. "Hi, mom."

"I'm really proud of you," she said, her voice sounding sincere.

"What?" I briefly pulled the phone away from my face, looking at it like a foreign object. "It's Carla," I reminded her.

"I know," she said humorously. "You don't think I know when I'm calling my own daughter?"

I looked around feeling like I was being set up.

"Of course," I said tentatively. "How are you?"

"Good," she responded with actual color in her voice that I admit worried me. "Claudio told me all about it."

"He did," I said, my eyes still darting side to side in what was starting to feel like a dream sequence.

"Yes and I think it's really great."

Trying to get a few steps ahead of the conversation, the only conclusion I could quickly come to was that my brother had bumped into Pete's parents somewhere who must have told him about the show.

"Thanks, but it was really Pete who got us the show," I explained, "but we put our minds together and came up with some cool songs, so..." I trailed off, thinking I had laid down enough breadcrumbs for her.

"Songs?" Her tone sharpened. "What are you talking about songs?"

Confused now as if it actually *were* a dream sequence, I said, "You're not calling about our show tonight?"

"No," she replied with a sting. "I'm calling about Angela."

"Angela?" I leaned back. "Claudio's girlfriend?"

"Yes, she got the job you helped her with."

At this point, I stopped talking, no longer feeling like I was in a dream but had entered the Red Room in *Twin Peaks*. I braced myself for my mom to start speaking in reverse, which in a way she was doing, because nothing was making sense. I did know that it was eight o'clock on the East Coast, which meant I was talking to bottle of wine. But still, even in her drunkest moments, she wouldn't have completely fabricated a story making me the hero.

"Carla," she said with a strain in her voice. "The dental hygienist job?"

I could feel my eyebrows pinching in, thinking the more she spoke the more confused I became.

"Claudio told me one of your old classmates works in the office and that you called all the way from Hollywood to put in a good word for Angela."

I took a second to trace back through my own wine nights, none of which included a bicoastal phone call to a dentist's office to reach a classmate I didn't even know. It didn't add up. I stayed quiet, though, letting the pieces fall into place.

Then it hit me.

Like he'd been doing since we were kids, my nice brother lied to my mom to get her to like me. I paused, the realization sinking in wondering what was worse: that she didn't like me, or my family was well aware of it and had to lie on my behalf.

"The poor thing was so nervous too," my mom continued as if it were the best news ever, "but you know how modest she is." There was a deliberate pause, which meant she tailored this comment for me and that I was supposed to learn humility from my brother's girlfriend who had a hole-punched loyalty card for the tanning salon.

"She's so modest," I placated, knowing there was no use in arguing.

"She is," my mother replied, followed by another deliberate pause designed for me to reflect on.

"Anyway," she segued, "we celebrated at Trattoria di Meo. I got the sole Francese, and your father got the eggplant."

I nodded in recognition because, of course they did, before saying, "I'm glad she got the job. I'm sure her parents are very proud."

"They are, but I'm also proud of you, because I know how you let your little resentments get in the way of being the good person I know you are."

I exhaled sharply through my nostrils, my eyes narrowing in irritation. I knew defending myself or denying jealousy would only strengthen her conviction, so I decided to cash in on her good mood with my own good news.

"I don't know if you heard me before, but I'm playing a show tonight." I glanced at the stage, using the sight of our equipment as both a shield and proof of my endeavor.

"I heard you," she said, now sounding bored. "I didn't think you were still doing that."

"I am, or at least trying to," I replied, reminding myself not to take her disinterest personally. "Anyway, just thought I'd add that to the family's good news."

"It *is* good news."

"You think so?" I hated the sound of hope in my voice.

"I do and maybe after tonight, you'll finally get it all out of your system." The line went quiet for a moment. "This whole band business," she added.

That was as good as it was going to get. It seemed we had touched on every emotion but anger. Knowing we were only a sentence away from wrath, I tactfully ended the call.

After hanging up, I sat for a moment, her parting words repeating on loop like a one-hit wonder I wanted to forget. I surveyed the theatre, observing the bar staff setting up and the club's calm before the storm, wondering if I could find a home in this life. As I wrestled with redefining what family meant to me, Alex's voice boomed through my thoughts as if providing an answer.

"There you are," she said from below. I peered over the balustrade to find her on the empty dance floor. "You look like a princess up there."

I managed a weak smile. "Yeah?"

"Uh-oh. What's wrong?"

"I just spoke to my mom." I held my phone up as proof.

"What the hell possessed you to do that?"

"She called, I picked up, the rest is insanity."

"La, you know it's wine o'clock on Long Island. I won't even talk to my parents, and they like me."

I looked down at her in stunned silence, the open secret that my mom simply hated me hitting me like a bad joke that I was the butt of. I had no recourse but to laugh, finding the sick humor that everyone knew before me. She joined in the laughter because what else could she do? She then looked at me with eyes that told me she got it but also ones that promised to be my buoy in the emotional storm.

"So, what do you say we catch up with them?" she proposed. "There's a bottle of warm vodka in your dressing room and I'm sure we can scrounge up a cheap bottle of wine somewhere in this place."

I returned her smile. "I'll be right down."

Pete

After delivering the final project upstairs, I raced down the freight stairs, heading to the parking lot to get to the show. But as I passed the third floor, a tingle in my gut stopped me, knowing it led to Misha's classroom. The right side of my brain told me to keep moving, because I didn't have time, while the left side pushed me to go for it. *But go for what?* Before I could answer, as if having an out-of-body experience, I saw my arm reach for the door.

As I marched down the hall toward his classroom, I could hear my heartbeat thundering, the low and heavy bass reminding me I had no plan. *I was going to knock on his classroom door and then what?* But I didn't have the courage to answer myself as I kept walking with borrowed confidence that I knew I'd have to return once Monsieur Fontanet asked me what the fuck I was doing there.

I got to the door where more doubt washed over me, but I knocked anyway, feeling like it was now or never. Monsieur Fontanet's steps approached as I put off my game plan until the very last second. The turn of the doorknob made for a dramatic lead-in as he opened it, appearing both confused and inconvenienced.

« *Oui Peter ?* »

« *Oui, bonsoir, Monsieur,* » I replied before stumbling over words, forcing him to ask me how he could help me. Remembering the projector, I asked if he would be needing it. Naturally, he leaned forward, looking down the hall in search of the offered piece of equipment that wasn't there.

« *Il est où ?* » he asked, his confusion evident.

I explained that it was still in the office in which he glanced at his watch before looking at me as if I were a Jehovah's Witness at his doorstep. Past his shoulder, I caught Misha appearing entertained by the scene, as I once again tried to convince Monsieur Fontanet into needing the projector I didn't even have.

« *Non, merci,* » he concluded, before advising me to get some rest over the weekend.

I stood with the door closed in my face, unwilling to let my embarrassment deter me after coming this far. *I'd done the hard part*, I reminded myself. I knocked again, this time sparing the now irritated Monsieur Fontanet the long-winded fable and simply asked if I could please speak to Misha Taylor.

« *D'accord,* » he said drearily, as if we were finally getting to the crux of this senseless exchange.

With a clear disinterest in the entire thing, he summoned Misha who looked pleased, collecting his books like he got to leave school early. At the door, Monsieur Fontanet's gaze tossed back and forth between us, looking at us like schoolboys who'd been caught smoking.

"Make it brief, *les enfants*," he said. "I'm running an adult class here, not *un lycée*."

We nodded like dutiful students as he shut the door. Once the silence was ours, my pulse seemed to drown out any organized thoughts. A part of me hoped he'd rescue me by initiating conversation with some emotion, animation even. After all, he was an actor, wasn't that what they did? But he just looked at me expectantly, making me work for it.

Yes? He didn't have to say, but it was louder than if he had.

Bear with me for a second, I pleaded with my eyes.

I hadn't written and rewritten this moment a thousand times in my head, so the transition from yanking him out of his classroom to standing face-to-face didn't feel natural.

"Hi," was all I could think to say, as I wrapped the tiny word inside a deep breath.

"Hi," he replied, his eyes challenging mine.

As he looked at me, I felt momentarily disoriented as words felt cumbersome in my mouth.

"And what do I owe the grand gesture?" he eventually asked.

I will not start the sentence with um.

I will not start the sentence with um.

I will not start the sentence with um.

"Umm," I started the fucking sentence before looking at the bulletin board, as if I was going to find the answer in the Django Reinhardt Jazz Festival poster. I could have offered him an explanation, an excuse, a lie, maybe even an attempt at a joke, but the intensity radiating off my chest felt like a life force that wouldn't allow backpedaling or, my trusty default of self-deprecation.

"You know, you're cute when you're nervous," he finally said, smiling at me with the charm of a movie star.

"Nervous?" I countered.

"It's okay," he said in a breezy tone. "I'm flattered."

"Flattered?" I couldn't mask my discontent at the word before remembering I was talking to a model. "Oh, I forgot," I said, fluttering my eyes. "That's your default emotion."

"No, no." He held out a hand to stop my thoughts from roaming. "Really, that's not what I meant," he said, his expression transitioning from amused to kind. "So, what's up?"

"I guess, I just wanted to apologize for being so standoffish. I haven't been very professional." I smacked my lips in a conclusive manner.

"Professional?" he said with a curious tilt of his head. "Is that what this is?"

"Is that what *what* is?"

With his gaze slightly lowered on me, he bounced his finger back and forth between us. "This."

"This," I repeated, watching as he took a step closer to me.

Standing now inches apart, I wondered if he could hear my heart hammering against my shirt. I shifted my weight, using it as an excuse to also take a step closer, wanting so badly to close the space between us.

"You have more to say, Monsieur Albrecht," he quietly teased.

"I might," I said, taking some, but not all, of the power back, "but I don't want to flatter you anymore than I already have." My glaze flicked upward. "I mean, isn't that your agent's job?"

"For ten percent it is." He looked at me now with fascination. "So, tell me, are you done or what?"

"Done with what?"

"Done being such a queen, so you can ask me out already?"

CHAPTER 18

Carla

Sweat glistened on my upper lip as I sat beneath the unforgiving, bulbed dressing room lights. My cheeks were so red, I felt I should've slathered on sunscreen. Alex was doing my makeup where I had to constantly check her work in the mirror to ensure she wasn't straying from my request for simplicity. But I could barely hear my thoughts over Bez, the lead singer of the Weekend Warriors, singing over his Kings of Leon CD blaring from their dressing room. His voice drunkenly boomed the lyrics of "Holy Roller Novocaine" followed by a crash of glass and an outburst of frustration for not having written the near-perfect rock song.

Alex stood in front of me, her gaze meticulously studying my face. As her eyes moved up, down, and across, she seemed satisfied with her work with her lips puckering in approval. Poking the mascara wand back into its tube, she announced, "And I'm done." She stepped aside proudly. "Whaddya think?"

I took a good look at myself through the graffiti-tagged mirror. I had feared her eyeshadow palette, named I GUESS THAT'S WHY THEY CALL THEM THE BLUES, would be too flashy. But thanks to her blending skills, you'd never guess that I was wearing five shades of blue from a makeup kit named after an Elton John song.

Then, like a crack of thunder, Barbie appeared in the doorway. "Did somebody call for wardrobe?"

In her hands were two shopping bags that she hoisted up triumphantly, as if announcing her arrival. She basked in our excitement at seeing her, seeming perfectly at home backstage as she strode into the room. With the swagger of a rock n' roll cowboy, she wore black leather jeans studded with rhinestones that caught the Hollywood dressing room lights like little stars.

"Wait until you see what I brought," she sang, setting the bags down on a table before standing behind me. Looking at me through the mirror, she gave my hair a few fluffs for volume. "God, you look like Elizabeth Taylor." She then gently tugged at it. "Don't run off and get married now!"

I swatted her hand away playfully. "I won't."

"Well, not yet, at least," she mumbled before turning to the shopping bags. "Now, let's see what we have here."

Alex and I stood by, watching as Barbie began to pull clothes out. Seeing the articles in all their glitter rock glory, I could tell they were obviously hers from the '70s. But before her boob job, like the striped sequin tube top that would have shimmied down to my waist before I even made it to the end of our first song. She handed Alex a shrunken Tab T-shirt, boasting the soda's one calorie. There was leather, some Marabou feathers, more sequins. More of everything that I could never wear including a T-shirt that said KEEP PUSSY EXPENSIVE.

Alex took that one, too.

"Oh, I remember this one," Barbie reminisced, holding up a sparkly piece of fabric. "I wore it at the opening of Rodney's English Disco, and Miss Sable wanted to rip it right off me."

I leaned in for closer inspection, attempting to visualize it as an actual garment, wondering where she put the rest of her body.

"I think I'd have to wear everything in that bag just to cover myself," I quipped.

"That's probably true," Barbie agreed.

I looked at my worn jeans and short-sleeved sweater, thinking they were fine. "I'll just wear this." I looked at both of them. "Seriously."

"Okay," she said, seeming almost ready to give up. "But just answer me this one question and I'll leave you be. Do you want to wear your charity shop duds with jeans that sag at the butt as an artistic form of expression or as a way to hide?"

Looking at her like it wasn't that deep, I explained, "I just don't want people to think that I *think* I'm so great."

"Honey," she said, looking at me like she was about to break some news to me. "You're on stage with a guitar, they already think that."

"I don't want them to," I argued.

"Well, you don't get to decide that."

Alex set aside the T-shirts Barbie gave her, walking closer to me, seeming to want to take a stab at it.

"La, don't you remember when we were kids and how we obsessed over the clothes our favorite bands wore?" I looked at her, unable to dispute the fact. "And how it felt like a continuation of the music, like they had created this world for us to get lost in?"

I thought back to my teenage bedroom walls covered in magazine clippings of my favorite bands, remembering how much I loved the styles. There were the mod haircuts and preppy style of Britpop, the cat eye-shaped glasses and vintage sweaters of indie rock, the ruffles and red lips of girl punk.

"We lived for those details," she reminded me, her words transporting me back to our deep dives into rock fashion, wishing we had more than a Contempo Casuals to shop at.

"Why not have some fun?" she suggested, leaning in closer to examine my eyes. "Besides, I did all that work, so you are not going out there with those jeans that look like you have a diaper stuffed in your butt."

"Look, I get it," I said to them. "I really do, and next time, I'll come prepared with cooler clothes." My gaze then swept over to the sequined loin cloths, knowing there was just no way. "Thanks for thinking of me though."

"Well, let's not toss the baby out just yet," Barbie said. "I *may* have one last trick up my sleeve."

She reached into her seemingly bottomless bag, and, instead of pulling out a *Blonde Ambition*-era coned bra or some Renaissance Festival corset that would push my boobs out like coins in a slot machine, she took out something else entirely. In her hand was a dark blue dress, that she turned forward and back like a game show host. "It used to belong to my old friend, Starla and let me tell you, she looked great in it." She eyed me up and down. "She was small-boned like you."

I rose to my feet and walked towards the dress, thinking we might be on to something. A classic 1960s sheath, it boasted a high neckline she knew I'd appreciate, paired with a matching belt of the same knit fabric. The capped sleeves contributed an air of sophistication, hinting at a time that tastefully revealed skin one body part at a time. It was a vision in vintage simplicity, embodying the departure from the full-skirted housewife dresses of the '50s to the streamlined empowerment of the 1960s working woman. I loved its design, but I also loved the symbolism, which felt like a silent protest of my mom's old-fashioned standards.

"I thought you'd like it," Barbie said sneakily.

Taking it in my hand, I could feel the quality of the expertly cut wool that I already knew would be a nightmare under the lights. As I admired it, one of her sequined tube tops caught my eye, practically winking at me. In that moment, I understood the strategy and locked eyes with Barbie.

"You brought all that other stuff to warm me up into wearing this, didn't you?"

With a knowing grin, she said, "And it worked like a charm."

Pete

As I walked through the loading alley of The Trop, I saw Bez first. Decked in black jeans that looked tattooed onto his malnourished thighs and a T-shirt with more holes than fabric, he had an unlit cigarette dangling from his chapped lips.

Flanked by a chorus line of girls that looked borrowed from an American Apparel ad, they wore one-piece bathing suits as tops.

"Opening act band!" he called out as soon as he noticed me. "What's shakin', Sticks?"

Surprised by the nickname, I walked over to him with my hand extended. "Thanks for having us tonight," I said before acknowledging his entourage. "Hello."

"Hi," they all sort of replied, looking bored by the backstage scene.

Bez looked at my outstretched hand like I had human shit smeared on it. "What the fuck is this?"

"What?" I flipped my hand to see if I did, in fact, have shit on it.

"All of this?" he said, pointing at me as his face begged for an explanation.

"All of what?" I looked down at myself.

"Come on, dude," he groaned like I was fucking with him. "You're not even *possible*."

"I'm not?" I smiled as he continued pointing at me like a restless kid at the zoo. "I came straight from work," I explained, leaving off that I planned to change since I didn't owe him an explanation.

"Yeah, and are you, like, an accountant or some shit like that?" For some reason this made the girls giggle, which I could see fueled his validation as he tried to one-up his own comment. "Or, like, a lawyer or a banker or some shit?"

"Accountant was funnier," I pointed out. "But no, neither. I'm a receptionist."

"A what, dude?!"

"A receptionist at a French language school in Beverly Hills."

"Get the fuck out of here!" His head fell back in laughter, and when he finally came to, he asked, "Isn't that a chick's job?"

I let out a low sigh because, seriously, what fucking year were we in? I was relieved the girls didn't giggle at the clearly sexist comment, with one even calling him rude.

"It's not rude," he snapped. "It's an observation? Like, duh?"

"An outdated one," I felt the need to interject.

"Outdated," he mocked, as if I were speaking in jargon. "Sorry, dude, but the word I think you're looking for is," he cupped his hands around his mouth and howled, "GAY."

For fuck's sake.

He completed the sentiment with exaggerated hand gestures and hip thrusts that seemed more homoerotic than the homophobic burn I supposed he was going for. As I watched him entertain himself, I was taken aback, for sure. I guess hadn't noticed this side of him before because I was too busy tuning his band's instruments. But there I stood with my jaw slightly dropped, which I then snapped shut in fear of inviting another comment from him. The only bright side of this exchange would be the story I'd have for my very gay date with Misha the next day, hopefully doing things with him that would fuel Bez's nightmares.

Or not, I reconsidered, seeing how much he seemed to be enjoying himself.

I contemplated correcting him but valued my sanity more than asserting moral authority on someone too drunk to even get it. An unspoken agreement that we were done with each other had us turning away from each other. As I cracked my neck left and then right, attempting to reset the last few minutes, a familiar voice swooped in.

"Thought I heard a Long Island accent out here."

I turned around to find Alex walking out of the venue, tapping the topside of a pack of cigarettes against her palm. My shoulders relaxed as I stepped toward her.

"Oh, hey," I said, not expecting to sound so relieved.

"Hey, there," she said before her eyes popped over to Bez who was now holding court with the roadies. "I had to interview him today. Charming, huh?"

"A delight," I said, motioning to her cigarettes. "Do I have time to bum one of those?"

"Yeah," she said, plucking out two cigarettes.

"Parliaments?" I eyed the pack as I reached for the lighter in my back pocket. "Those are, like, *the* worst cigarettes."

"I know, they taste like shit, but after a drink, you hardly notice." She leaned forward to let me light her smoke. "But they're dual purpose."

I didn't know what that meant, but at that moment, I didn't care as I leaned against the building's brick wall and took my first drag. Bez's voice faded and my mind quieted in those few seconds to myself. I knew Alex and I had things to talk about, but smoker's etiquette dictated having the first drags in peace. I exhaled, looking up at the final slice of dusk I could see between the two buildings that made it an alley.

"So." I turned to her.

With a low chuckle rife with meaning, she replied, "So…"

I blew out a stream of smoke. "She's pissed, isn't she?"

"About what exactly?" She spoke confrontationally.

"We'll start with me being ridiculously late?"

"That's fine." She sucked in a long drag before releasing it above our heads. "She knows *that's* not your fault."

The natural response here would have been to inquire about her emphasis on the word *that*, but I wasn't ready.

"How's work?" I asked instead, briefly glancing in the direction of Bez's voice now at the other end of the alley. "Besides today's gripping assignment."

"Uninspiring," she said with a bitterness that I could relate to.

"And New York life?"

"Pretentious."

I let out a small laugh because I was sure it was.

"There's the whole highbrow thing that's always been a part of New York, but now it's disguising itself as lowbrow, if that makes sense."

"Highbrow, but fake lowbrow," I recited back to her as I imagined it perfectly. "Move out here." I smirked. "As you can see, we're all pretty lowbrow *lowbrow* here."

"Yeah?" I got her to sincerely smile. "I'll think about it," she clearly joked, sucking in another drag. "I guess I'm just exhausted with the whole money-makin' Manhattan culture of work, work, work, as if that's what defines you."

"Again," I said now with a fuller laugh, "move out here. No one works. And if they do," I pointed to myself, "it's apparently a source of comedy."

She took a step back, giving me a once-over. "I'm liking this whole country club look you got going on here."

"I was actually planning on changing inside." I reached for my tie to loosen it.

"You should keep it," she advised. "You two will match."

Just as I was going to ask what that meant, I noticed her sizing up the rest of me.

"What?"

"I approve." She nodded her head righteously.

"Of?"

"All of it." She waved her hands in front of me before giving my bicep a light squeeze. "California looks good on you. Does a sun-kissed glow and a gym membership come with residency?"

I chuckled before saying, "No gym, but I stay active."

She shot me a conspiratorial glance. "So, I've heard."

I slanted my head at her. "Not like that."

"You said it." She pressed her lips together as if trying to control herself.

"Look," I said. "It's really not what either of you think."

"No?"

"No," I asserted.

"Alright," she partially accepted as she looked directly at me in defense of someone she loved. "Then what is it?"

"A long story that I take full responsibility for fucking up."

"You're going to *have* to do better than that, Albrecht." Her eyes bounced towards the door. "She's not showing it, but she's really hurt and, not to mention, confused."

I closed my eyes momentarily. "I know."

"So?"

"Alex," my eyes shot open, "I tried talking to her, but she won't let me get any words out."

"Can you blame her?"

"No," I said. "I guess I can't."

We stood for a few moments looking away from each other as we smoked while shifting our weight to ease the tension.

"I should probably head in," I gently broke the silence, stepping on my cigarette. "But we'll talk, okay?"

"Okay, Pete." She dropped her arms and forced a smile. "You guys are going to be great out there."

"Thanks," I said, forgetting for a moment why we were all even there. "And even though you're pissed at me, I'm glad you're here."

"Thanks, I am too," she said but I could tell she wasn't satisfied with our exchange as she looked off seeming to grapple with something.

"What is it?" I asked, knowing I'd regret it.

"Can you just tell me one thing?"

I agreed with my eyes as hers shot up seeming to resent having to even entertain what was about to come out of her mouth. "I guess I want to know: why her?"

Confused by the question, I remained expressionless. "Why who?"

"Pete, you know who."

"Oh, right," I said, feigning sudden recollection. "*Her.*"

"Now back to my question." She crossed her arms. "Why?"

"What do you mean, why?"

"Well, what's so special about her?" she asked, her hands outstretched in confusion. "Do you really have a deeper connection with her than you do with Carla?" Alex's jaw then clenched as she muttered, "She's going to kill me for asking you that."

Before I could articulate that no one could ever match what I had with Carla, she cut in, "Like, are you knitting for her too?"

I stared at her, feeling incredulous while thinking she had to be fucking kidding. Knitting? Was this *really* the issue here? I then shook my head feeling vindicated on why I kept my hobby to myself because of dumb shit like this.

"Well," she pressed, "*are* you or aren't you?"

"Knitting for her?" I couldn't help but smirk at how serious she was taking this one detail as if this were the real problem here. "Surely, you're joking."

"Stop buying time."

"Alright, Alex," I said, letting my arms drop in defeat. "I'm not knitting for her, and would you like to know why?"

"Obviously."

I eyed her crossed arms, knowing she'd regret the hard stance.

"I'm not knitting for her because there is no *her*."

I placed a strong emphasis on the word, giving her time to let it sink in. As I stood there, I watched her eyes narrow in focus, appearing to piece *something* together. There was a brief flicker of confusion before more soul searching until they lit up with understanding, signaling we had a winner.

"That's right," I confirmed, answering her unspoken question. "There is no her because Misha isn't a girl."

CHAPTER 19

Carla

"You sure you're going to be okay in those shoes?" Barbie stared at the slingback heels on my feet. "God, you have teeny tiny feet," she remarked. "Maybe *your* name should be Barbie."

Chuckling, I took a few test steps from not having worn heels, well, ever. "I should be okay. Just takes some getting used to," I said, looking around the room, seeing it from my new height. "But I like the view up here."

"Just be careful with all those cables on the stage," she advised as she swooped her hand down to take my drink. "And careful with this." She held the cup to her nose and recoiled like Joni did when she smelled the fresh mint overgrowing in the garden. "No more until after the show, Missy. I'm cutting you off."

"I'm just nervous," I confessed. "I'm not sure I'm going to pull this off." I bit my lower lip thinking about it.

"Well, why not?" She looked at me seriously. "You told me you've been practicing."

"I have, but to tell you the truth, the sound check wasn't all that great. The sound guy was a total dick."

"Ah," she said, giving me a weary look.

"He was talking to me like I was stupid and not listening to *anything* I was saying." I got hot thinking about it again. "I wanted to scream."

Barbie bobbed her head knowingly. "Your first experience with rock sexism," she said with a sigh. "I guess some things will never change."

She saw me eyeing my drink. "But drinking more isn't going to fix that!" She walked to the refreshments table and cracked open a bottle of water. "Here, honey, drink this instead."

I took the bottle just as her phone rang, the vibrating making the tassels on her bag shimmy. "Oh, that must be Kurt," she said, taking it out of her bag. "He's sorry he can't make it tonight. He has to work." She pressed the phone to her ear and shouted her usual greeting to him, "Can you hear me?" As she took the call, she stood guard, positioning herself in front of my drink.

Giving her space, I drifted towards the doorway, pulled by the electricity of pre-show excitement. The air in the hallway was pungent, an acidic mix of cigarette breath, expensive, opium-based perfume and warm backstage sawdust. I walked down the long, dimly lit hallway, passing beautiful people who were there to see and be seen, decked out in rock couture. As I headed towards the back door, I spotted Alex and Pete coming in. I quickened my pace towards them, my social anchor, as I navigated my way through name-dropping conversations about this star or that star –first names only, of course – and who was throwing the afterparty later.

I tried to catch Alex's eyes, then Pete's, but they seemed lost in what looked like a private moment. Alex, who normally noticed and reacted to every detail around her seemed unusually preoccupied, as she walked alongside Pete like… they were friends. But when Bez, who still called me 'Tits,' walked in after them, I understood their alliance, because who knew what gross things he was saying out there? When Pete's eyes finally met mine, they passed through me, as if I were a stranger. But when his eyes snapped back with a spark of recognition, I knew we had found each other.

"Oh, wow," he said, his eyes sweeping over me in awe, seeming overwhelmed by where to place his focus. "I'm sorry I didn't recognize you." Our eyeline was just about at the same level. "You're so tall."

I glanced at my feet and shrugged. "Heels."

"I see that."

As I looked back up at him, I knew I was supposed to be mad at him, and I was—furious, in fact. Yet, I liked the way he looked at me as if noticing me for the first time. His attention lingered on my dress, a grin sneaking onto his lips as I was sure he was also thinking that we now looked like old-school flight attendants in our matching friendly-skies blue. Then, his focus shifted to my freshly cut hair.

"I love it," he softly said. "We can see your face now."

I looked away, making my chin-length barrel curls toss, which must have looked dumb like a shampoo commercial. Realizing this, I quickly pressed my hand against my head to make my hair stop moving. I could see him catch this moment I had with myself as we exchanged smiles. Slowly, I watched the smile fade with his tired eyes telling mine they didn't want to fight that night. I pressed my lips together in agreement with our unspoken pact. It was then I noticed Alex, whose jaw and shoulders were relaxed. Instead of regarding us as romantic adversaries presently at odds, she looked at us like orphan siblings reunited by their parents. Taken aback by her unexpected tenderness, I edged closer to her.

"What's going on?" I asked. "You guys are acting weird."

"Nothing," she said, her voice peaking to a slightly higher octave, which clearly meant *something*.

When she could see I didn't believe her, she forced a chuckle in dismissal. Her eyes then seemed to consult with Pete's, who I swore gave her some sort of signal.

The vodka coursing through my bloodstream emboldened me to insist something was off, my eyes alternating between them. "Where were you guys?"

"Outside," Pete said, while Alex simultaneously added, "Smoking," their words overlapping in an obvious attempt to conceal something.

"Okay," I responded, my tone deliberately sounding unconvinced. It was then that something hard and flat slammed into my shoulder.

"Holy mother of—!" I cried out, pressing my hand against it. "What was that?"

When I turned around, I saw the huffy stage manager I had only spoken to once that day, standing with the clipboard that had whacked my shoulder.

"Sorry," she said, clearly not meaning it. "The Disenchanted?" Her tone was no-frills and direct, implying she'd seen one band, she'd seen them all.

"That's us," Pete and I confirmed in unison.

"Let's go," she instructed, already pivoting towards the stage door. "Your twenty-eight minutes start now."

"Twenty-eight?" Pete questioned, as the two of us tried to keep up with her like nervous assistants. "I thought we had a half hour."

"Well, yeah," she tossed back without breaking her stride. "But you're gonna lose two walking to the stage."

Pete

Thank God for our curtain call was all I could think as I saw Alex trying to resolve our story's third act. After telling her about Misha in the alley, we both agreed that Carla should hear it from me after their weekend together. Now, I wondered if we were going to make it until then.

Following the stage manager, we stampeded through the backstage tunnels as if we were important people, the stage crew guiding our way with flashlights aimed at the floor. As we got closer to the stage door, I could feel the air become thicker with humidity and tension coming from the waiting crowd. Carla and I kept up the crew's pace as we glanced at each other, sharing a nervous kind of energy reserved for a band that hadn't rehearsed since 2001.

"Are you ready?" I asked her as one of the crew guys opened the stage door for us.

"No," she said, lightly out of breath. "How about you?"

I offered her a look in solidarity. "Not at all."

Before stepping out, I peeked at the crowd, surprised to see the floor already packed by the hundreds. I felt like we were getting away with something. I could tell she did too as we exchanged a complicit look like a cashier had undercharged us for something expensive.

"Shall we?" I said with my arm out to guide the way.

I waited as she smoothed her hands down the front of her dress, which, I had to admit, really did look stunning on her even if we now looked conceptualized like a Pan Am Flight Crew decided to start a band. At least my mother would have gotten a kick out of it.

Together, we walked out. The wooden stage floor squeaked under our feet, making it feel like a plank walk. Carla kept her head down, careful not to look out, while the masochist in me looked directly at people with a predisposition to hate us. Skeptical eyes. Folded arms. Lifted chins. And record store clerks, whom I was surprised to see, since the Weekend Warriors seemed a little low rent for their refined tastes. But this was Hollywood. I looked out into their dead eyes following us as we walked across the stage. Decked in our navy blues, I could see the lowered bar of their expectations, as they glared at us, like, who do these assholes think they are?

As I looked at our stage set-up though, I realized Carla wasn't kidding when she told me that the Warriors had given us no room. She managed, however, to get my Gretsch into a tight spot next to a Marshall stack with her guitar and vocal mic positioned directly beside it. So close, in fact, I was afraid my ride cymbal would knock into her elbow during the set. Nonetheless, I walked to my kit, which looked happy to be back on stage, blinking her tangerine sparkles under the bright lights. I settled onto my padded throne and adjusted the seat up a few notches. I took a quick look around my drum area, feeling like I had walked into my childhood bedroom after many years. The squeak of my stool when I shifted to the right was still there. The warm wooden shells still smelled like my parents' basement. And the battered skins looked up at me like war scars from practice sessions and bygone shows.

I grabbed a new pair of sticks and rubbed my thumbs up and down their smooth finish, knowing I'd eventually destroy the poor guys. The crowd continued to stare at us, almost daring us to prove them wrong as I hit the kick two times to signal to her that I was ready. She looked up from the final tuning of her guitar with a shrug conveying she was as ready as she'd ever be.

As I cracked my sticks to count down to our first song, I realized we hadn't bothered to write a set list. She looked back at me, though, with trusting eyes that said we wouldn't need one and that we'd go where the music took us. But when she strummed the first chord on the acoustic, it not only sounded worse than it did in her apartment, but I could barely hear it.

Her eyes widened at mine where this time they said FUCK.

CHAPTER 20

Carla

I didn't know what we were going to do. I had tried to avoid this very thing at sound check and lo and behold, there we were. Standing in the I-told-you-so, my mind raced with panic as I considered the options. I knew we could have gone through the set with the imbalance of sound and be written off as another bad opening band, which I supposed would be a rock n' roll rite of passage because how many terrible ones have we all seen? But we deserved more as I could feel the eyes of the crowd now boring into me. I looked back at Pete, who looked prepared to fix the situation, forcing me to think quick on my high heels.

Behind me was one of the Warriors' electric guitars. A sexy Fender Mustang in Daphne Blue that looked like silk to play. I gestured to Pete to give me a second as I pulled the strap of the acoustic over my head. Only I could feel my fingers trembling as I grabbed the turquoise guitar and slung it around my neck. Feeling the solid wood grounding me and the shiny lacquer in my hand, I leaned into the mic.

"Hey sound guy," I said, my voice slicing through the tension of the near-silent venue. "Can you turn this bad boy up?"

There was no response as I searched into the dark depths of the theater. Every nanosecond that passed, thickened the tension as I squinted into the blinding lights. I tapped the mic to catch the attention of whoever was in the booth and repeated, "Can you turn this up?"

I purposefully avoided looking at Pete, feeling the nerves twist like knives in my stomach at the thought that this might backfire somehow. The idea of switching back to the acoustic, though, was not an option. Straining to see in the dark over the heads of the audience, my eyes eventually adjusted where I could make out the shadows of his arms flailing about in denial of my request. Fueled by a fear of embarrassment, I had no choice but to press on.

"You mean you're not going to turn on this guitar for me?" I asked, my voice dripping in feigned astonishment. This caused a ripple of unease through the crowd as they murmured to each other as my gaze dropped to the front rows. "You hear that? Mr. Sound Guy isn't going to turn this on for me."

"Turn it on, man!" someone called out as the crowd cheered in agreement.

"Turn the thing on!" another voice said. "We want to hear some music!"

"Turn it on! Turn it on!" the crowd began to chant. "Turn it on!"

I suppressed a smirk that tugged at the corner of my lips as Pete then applied a light drum beat to their chants, crafting a rhythmic protest against the sound guy. The energy was electric, charged with suspense. If we used up all our minutes rallying against the sound guy, it would have certainly counted as the theatrical debut Barbie was pushing for, and I didn't even need to wear the tasseled pasties.

"Turn it on! Turn it on!" they continued, their excitement surging with each call. It was then I heard the static buzz pulsing through the guitar, bringing the blue beauty to life and signaling victory.

"I think we have a live one," I joked as I strummed the guitar, the powered-up notes making its way to the back of the room. "Alright, then, let's do this."

I took a second to look at the crowd, firmly on our side, and after thanking them for their help I said, "We're The Disenchanted. Nice to meet you."

Pete

And that was when the magic happened.

Together we ripped through a new arsenal of songs without leaving much room for thoughts or doubts. The thing about these new songs, though, was that they weren't the ones we had written that week. Not even close. The darling riffs and bright, airy texture of the indie pop songs I'd composed to match her lyrics, morphed into a maelstrom of sonic chaos. With the use of the Warriors' pedals and her rage toward me, she transformed the sunny songs reminiscent of a spring day in 1963 into a carnival of sound. If the songs before were on one tab of LSD, the sounds she thundered out were quadruple dosed; reminding me of the time in high school when I puddled my palm with liquid acid that made the Terrapin Station turtles dance off the record sleeve. She delivered frenetic energy and raw emotion, combined with undiscernible lyrics —more like coughs and echoes in cadence with the music.

I responded to her urgency with powerful, driving drums traveling with her into dark and deliberate places. As we careened through twists and turns of sound with lo-fi grit and dissonant chords, she kept me on edge. It was a musical meeting of the minds, creating a synergy that our bullshit rehearsals couldn't touch. This was us exposing our insecurities to total strangers who, at best, wouldn't understand us and, at worst, would dismiss our pain as boring. We kept going, taking the songs off the rails and awakening the beast that was our band. We were so fucking back. Our tension and frustration with each other fueled the set. We played as if we'd never see each other again, but I knew that was far from the case. This was only the beginning of being even more aware of each other than ever before.

Carla

Better than sex.

That's how I would describe the music we were improvising. Although, it was an easy comparison since I hadn't experienced great sex yet. All the scales, chords, and transitions I thought I had forgotten had returned with renewed vigor, guiding the performance. The energy derived purely from the heart and had me tapping into emotions that I had long invalidated. His drums were no longer just the heartbeat but the spine of our music. He provided a framework amidst the melodic noise, driving the music forward with manic intensity, yet keeping it tight with the paradox of chaotic control.

Unpredictable and unforgiving, we wove a tapestry of sound together.

Through my guitar and echoey vocal calls, I declared that my feelings mattered. I could feel him replying to my musical accusations with steady and circular rhythms, giving me space to express myself but hitting with accented off-beats when he didn't necessarily agree. The back-and-forth was visceral, the intensity electric, and the audience forgotten, as we delved into our unresolved issues. It felt incredibly personal, as if we were finally working through some of our problems, with the stage serving as a neutral space, like a couple's therapy session.

Sharing a song is akin to letting any set of ears walk into the dark tunnels of your mind. Every note bore the weight of our relationship landing somewhere between fighting and fucking.

Pete

Closing out the anarchic set in just under twenty-two minutes, I slammed down my final hit on the crash cymbal. Afterwards, I circled around my kit to stand beside her, panting out of breath, feeling out of sorts. As our exchange settled like ashes, the audience looked wrung out in the spin cycle, wondering what the fuck they just saw. They erupted into applause of the newly converted, howling their approval at the insanity they'd just experienced. *Alright,* I thought, catching my breath, my shoulders finally dropping in relief that we had pulled it off. I wiped the back of my hand across my damp hairline, and looked at her, acknowledging the pride and relief on her face. I smiled, feeling closer to her than I had in a long time. Curious for reactions, I scanned the crowd, catching one guy eye his friend with a look of surprise that this no-name band wasn't bad after all. A few girls, who looked younger than us, gazed at Carla with stars in their eyes, and even the hoodie-sweatshirt-wearing record store guys were forced to unfold their arms.

This was when I felt a strong presence from one side of the room. As if an invisible finger was slowly guiding my chin, I followed the sensation to my left, my gaze landing on a familiar face waiting for mine. Suddenly, the crowd of two thousand narrowed to just one as I set my eyes on Misha's. Over the sea of heads, our gazes locked, his pale blues shining just as brightly as they did up close. He smiled at me, looking both impressed and confused as he clapped his hands. The cocktail of emotions apparent on his face revived the shiver down my spine, contradicting it with my sweat. Despite my delight and surprise of seeing him, I couldn't help but think, *oh shit*. Because maybe it wasn't Alex who was going to crack open the third act after all.

CHAPTER 21

Carla

We walked off stage as the Warriors' crew began barreling their gear past us. In the wings were Barbie and Alex with arms outstretched, ready to receive us like we were newborns.

"What the fuck, you guys!" Alex shouted as she yanked me in for a hug so hard I felt like I was going to burst open. "What were those songs?"

"I really don't know," I managed to squeak out. "They just sort of came out."

"Well, it sounded really good." She loosened me from her grip and turned to Pete. "You weren't half bad either."

I checked to see his reaction, wondering if they were still on their long-lost sibling trip and felt reassured when he shot his eyes to the ceiling in response to her snide comment. I turned to Barbie who had a fist planted on her hip.

"Now where in the hell did you learn to do all that?" She looked at me like I'd been keeping a secret. "You told me you haven't played in years!"

"I haven't," I said, not having an explanation even for myself. "I guess I just stopped thinking for a second and decided to go for it."

She nodded with a seasoned look in her eyes. "That's how it happens."

I turned to Pete, wanting his take, knowing this was exactly what he'd envisioned for us. But his expression was unreadable, his eyes blurring again into watercolors that made it impossible to know what he was thinking. Instead of contributing his own recap, he looked past me as if something was pulling him away. When I turned to see what he was looking at, a stage crew guy broke my flow of thought.

"Hey," he intercepted. "We're stacking your gear over at loading door B, and the alley has been cleared so you can pull your van up."

"I got it," Pete quickly volunteered before looking at me. "Can I grab the keys from your bag?"

"Uh, sure," I said before my attention was pulled away by Barbie who was clearly disinterested in band logistics. Alex also had no reaction to Pete assisting the crew as she moved in closer to tighten our circle.

"You know," Barbie said, deftly guiding my arm out of the way of a passing kick drum, "I was watching that crowd out there, and I haven't seen such a reaction to a band's first show since I saw The Runaways at The Whiskey." Barbie scanned our still faces, realizing the reference was lost on us. "The Runaways were teenagers in lingerie!" she clarified hastily, waving her hand around as if dispelling our ignorance. "Why don't you pick up a biography one of these days!"

Alex and I couldn't help but laugh that she was still yelling at us, even backstage.

"But alright, my girlies," Barbie said conclusively, eyeing a crew guy walking toward her. "I'm about to head off."

"You sure?"

"Kurt and I are going to Costco early tomorrow," she explained just as she turned toward the crew guy.

"Ma'am," he said. "Your taxis out back."

"Thank you for calling it for me." She patted his shoulder before turning back to us. "I guess you know your backstage days are over when the road guys are calling you ma'am."

She then took my hand, holding it firmly. "Now you have fun tonight," she advised, her gaze briefly following Pete as he walked by with one of our amps. "And a little word of wisdom from an old glitter gal is to take the night off from your *stuff*." She gave me a look that suggested that I knew what she meant. Her eyes then shifted over to Alex to include her. "And you girls knock on my door this weekend and tell me everything while we water the plants out back."

Alex's face lit up. "I get to come to the famous watering of the plants?"

"Sure," Barbie said, surprised by her enthusiasm. "I'll even have you do some weeding if that's what gets your rocks off." She returned to me. "Be safe and call us if anything should happen."

"I will." I gave her hand a final squeeze in appreciation, knowing this was beyond her duties as a building manager. "Thank you for everything."

"You got it, honey."

Alex and I watched as Barbie made her exit, the crew and backstage crowd parting before her, almost biblically, as if sensing her rock royalty status.

Alex turned to me, her expression shifting from reverential awe to a spark of devilish glee. "Guess it's down to you and me."

I met her gaze with playful suspicion. "It appears so." I raised an eyebrow in piqued curiosity. "What did you have in mind?"

"First, let's swipe some good booze from the Warriors' dressing room."

"Do you think we can do that?"

"We're about to find out." She tugged on my arm. "Come on!"

As she pulled me in the direction of the dressing rooms, I looked back to see Pete racing past security and down the stairs that led to the floor. It would have struck me as odd, him wanting to be packed in with all those people, if I hadn't already figured out where he was going. Or rather, who he was going to. My heart then spasmed as the truth settled in because as it turned out, he *was* an insensitive asshole who invited his new girlfriend to our show.

Pete

I hadn't wished for a superpower since I was ten years old. but that night, if I could possess one, it would have been the ability to freeze time. To have a pause button that would have allowed me to talk to both of them without creating more tension, because I knew every second that passed, Misha would think I was some kind of double-life-leading psychopath. And each second I didn't talk to Carla only drove the irreparable wedge between us. The decision, however, was made when Alex dug her eyes into me, reminding me of our pact to leave it alone for the weekend. I had to remember it was her weekend too, and she probably didn't want to spend it dissecting our bullshit.

Out in the club, I breathed in the air moist with beer breath and sweaty armpits, while the deep bass of Click Track remixes pulsed against my temples. I shouldered my way through the crowd, receiving a few double-takes from people recognizing me as the dude on stage, with some offering encouraging remarks that made me smile. Reaching the bar, I settled into its squared-off corner to scan the faces of each person I passed. With machine-like precision, I logged each detail: dyed black hair; bleached blonde hair; the *John Kerry is my Homeboy* tee the celebrities started wearing. Then another one, and another. After a few more rounds of data entry, no one matched his visual description, making me entertain the idea that I had created a romantic mirage of someone I simply wanted to see. At that point, anything seemed possible. Just when I stopped looking, my wish for a superpower was granted as time felt like it did, indeed, freeze. My eyes locked into his where that feeling of being the only two people in the room returned. My longing for him washed over me, like those cliché movie scenes where a spotlight highlights the romantic interest, and, like "Dreamweaver" starts playing.

Pushing that particular song out of my head, I watched him edge his way around the people who were oblivious to our moment, making me feel sorry for them for not feeling the way I did right then and there. Nothing could eclipse the thrill of running into a crush, which was a mix of panic and exhilaration that I feared would fade with age. At 40, would I still get the butterflies, or would they die off in the winter of my life? At that moment, though, I felt free in the spontaneity of seeing him while also feeling in over my head. I looked at his sun-streaked hair tucked behind his ear, looking so beautifully out of place in the Urban Outfitters crowd. With ease, he got through the crowd and once he was standing in front of me with nowhere to hide my emotions, I found myself saying the first thing that came to mind.

"What are you doing here?"

A look of surprise crossed his face. "Shouldn't I be asking you the same thing?"

Carla

Who were all these people? I asked myself as I sat in our dressing room now crowded with unfamiliar faces. I had chickened out on stealing alcohol from Warriors' dressing room, which left me alone and sipping the last of the warm vodka on an itchy couch that smelled like dandruff. My gaze swept over the room, looking at the perfectly symmetrical faces of people talking over each other. There was the guy claiming he'd been following our band for ages, even mentioning a gig at the Silver Lake Lounge that never happened. Then, a girl, who possibly starred in a show I'd once worked on. Another who kept checking the door for something, or rather, someone. These people were duplicates of each other, united by a longing for something to happen. I took another sip, observing humans validate each other while not actually listening and approving of me by proximity while ignoring me. I looked in my empty cup and put it down on a nearby table.

Gripping the couch's armrest, I pulled myself up and left the room of people who mostly pretended they hadn't seen my band. In the hallway that felt narrower and darker than before, I headed nowhere in particular. Since I lacked Alex's chutzpah to walk into another band's dressing room, I kept walking. Past the loud talkers and models, I figured I'd end where I needed to be.

"You look lost," said a voice behind me.

Startled that someone was watching me, I jumped. When I turned around, I was surprised to find someone who hadn't been a part of the same rotation of people I had seen since four o'clock that afternoon. As I tried to place him in the backstage hierarchy, I noticed his clothes first. Not dressed functionally like the stage crew, nor styled in rock n' roll drag like the Weekend Warriors' entourage. He was too short to be a model, and not bright-eyed and people-pleasing enough to be an actor. There was something almost rustic about him. He had the warmth of Laurel Canyon in the '60s with his full beard, auburn hair and fitted Western-style shirt with pearl snaps down the front.

"Am I right?" he asked, seeming sure of himself.

"What? That I'm lost?" I mirrored his grin. "I might be," I teased, "but not in the literal sense."

"Bullshit," he replied. "Someone whose band tore down the house like that couldn't possibly be lost."

"You saw our show," I stated.

"I did." He looked impressed. "I wasn't expecting an art installation to open for these guys."

He read the bewildered look on my face.

"No?" He slightly turned his head, looking at me from the corner of his eye like I was putting him on. "Come on, those irregular time measures, sudden key changes and then the whole vintage vibe."

I did nothing to hide my annoyance at his neat packaging of my band. "We're actually not that contrived."

He looked at me like I had it all wrong. "There's nothing wrong with a mission statement."

"A what?"

His eyes twinkled, reading my defensive stance. "Come with me," he said with ease, gesturing to the door behind him. "We can watch the show from the mezzanine where you can find insult in everything I say."

I didn't have a quick enough response to get out of joining him, not that I was so sure I wanted one, so I followed him out front. As we threaded through the crowd, I kept my eyes on his shoulders, careful not to catch a glimpse of Pete and his girlfriend I envisioned tucked away somewhere. We pardoned our way through the standing-room-only crowd, where I caught people noticing him. Some wanted him to stop, and many seemed thrilled by the sighting as he politely wished them a good show and kept walking.

Up in the VIP area, there were more people eager to talk to him, but in this case, he wanted to talk to them too. I walked to the edge of the mezzanine, leaning on the banister to look out. The stage below glowed in electric blue, with the silhouettes of their instruments holding court. Then, the house lights dropped, the crowd's roar filling the space, as if compensating for the darkness. "We've Only Just Begun" by the Carpenters played to announce the band's entrance. As they walked out, their shadows teemed well with the '70s FM radio tune, winking at the ironic side of nostalgia with a song you'd hear in a nail salon.

I leaned on the railing, peering down at the crowd to see their faces shining brighter than the stage lights. That look was the magic of rock n' roll. Regardless of the band, there would always be that spark that happened right before a show that made it seem like everything would be okay. The combination of heat rising from the floor, the alcohol spiking our blood levels, and the expectation for greatness created an energy that, if harnessed, could quite possibly power up a small town.

"Helloooo Hollywood!" Bez howled under the gold spotlight shining on him.

He stepped back with his arms out as if receiving the crowd, while pointing at this person or that person to make them feel important. Basking in his own showmanship, he circled the stage like a panther, preying on the front row. After a few more rounds of him revving the crowd up, the scuzz-rock guitars erupted into a catchy riff, accompanied by Bez's full body convulsions and slithering tongues. Though it was more satirical than sexy, I couldn't help but smile. Not because I was particularly rooting for him, but because it reminded me that in the next hour, I had nowhere else to be. All my problems were on hold, which was why I turned to rock music in the first place, as an escape from everything. From the girls who made fun of me at school, from my family who loved me but didn't like me, from never feeling good enough. I didn't want to go into the group therapy Barbie had hinted at, because it was there, I felt safe.

Wrapped in what felt like a blanket of sound, there were the stage lights to feel acknowledged in, yet shadows to disappear in. I realized a life of sticky floors, easy conversation, and drinking without judgment was what I wanted. However, as my eyes refocused on the stage, I realized my dream, however, could've used a slight revision in which it didn't include a lead singer sliding a microphone down his crotch and poking it out of his fly.

Pete

The Weekend Warriors didn't give Misha and I much time for pleasantries or to ease into each other with the guitars thrashing so loudly I could barely hear my own thoughts. The club throbbed in a whirlwind of energy, creating an excitement I didn't think the band deserved.

"What?" I shouted in his ear, which I realized was too loud as he flinched. "Sorry," I mouthed.

He shook his head that it was fine.

"What did you say?" I tried to say as clearly as possible, knowing my face was contorting in an unattractive way from having to shout. He pointed to his ear helplessly to indicate he couldn't hear me, which only mounted our frustration. Trying again, I leaned in closer where my nose accidentally grazed the edge of his ear, shooting a buzz down to my stomach. Misha stepped closer, leaving barely an inch of space between our bodies that I tried not to look down and notice.

"I said we should just wait for the song to end!" he replied, gesturing to the stage.

I nodded in agreement as we turned our focus to Bez, our unfortunate common ground, who was now gyrating his genitals. The first song hit its final note as we quickly turned to each other, our faces hopeful we'd get some conversation in.

"Are you a fan of this band?" I asked, seriously fearing the answer.

"I don't even know who this band is," he said with humorous dismissal. "A friend of mine got tickets but had to bail at the last minute." He looked at me like it was my turn. "What about you? I mean, are these guys your friends?"

The timing couldn't have been worse as we glanced at the stage in time for Bez's pelvic thrusts at what looked directed at teenage girls.

With a tortured look on my face, I said, "We just opened for them."

"So, let me see if I have this straight. Mean language school office administrator by day, rock drummer by night?"

I eyed him with suspicion that he knew my exact title, tipping off that he'd been snooping around about me.

"Something like that," I answered, loving the upper hand before he took it right back.

"But you're so uptight!" He dropped his head back like he couldn't believe it.

I shook my head, smirking in dismissal of the accusation. "I'm really not."

Seeing he wasn't convinced, in amused frustration, I dropped my head on his shoulder to exaggerate my disagreement. I stayed there for a moment as if pained by the whole thing.

Our sudden closeness was then shattered when Bez announced the next song titled, "Just the Tip." Despising my association with the band, I shot my head back up as we turned our attention back to the concert, which felt like the worst anchor ever. Watching Bez's inflated display of masculinity with Misha felt like what I imagined taking a girl to a strip club would be like: awkward as all hell. I knew Misha could handle it, but I couldn't help but feel somehow responsible, like I'd endorsed it since my band had shared the same stage. I wanted nothing more than to go somewhere with him, but I didn't know how to suggest it smoothly in the loud rock club. So, we continued watching the show as I waited for small moments of connection like when our hands would occasionally brush as people squeezed by, or sharing a quick smile, and exchanging wide-eyed shock at something Bez did, like when he announced the next song, "The Pink Stink."

So. Fucking. Gross.

Misha turned to me right as the song ended. "Quick before he starts singing again."

"What's that?" I smiled, incapable of hiding how much I loved that he was dying to talk to me.

"So, I'm not sure if you have band stuff to do or whatever, but I was wondering if you wanted to go somewhere after." His eyes bounced to the stage implying he'd had enough. "Or now?" He stepped closer, this time sliding his hand around my waist that made my entire body melt.

"Now?" I teased, letting myself play with him a little.

"Yes, now," he asserted. "Because I'm dying to know something and I'm not sure I can wait for our date tomorrow."

"And what's that?" I looked at him with eyes weighed down by what I wanted to do with him. "What is it that you're dying to know that simply can't wait?"

Matching my intentions that closed us into a bubble of us, he leaned in and with his breath warm on my ear said, "I'm dying to know if I've been imagining those blow job eyes you've been giving me for the past few weeks."

CHAPTER 22

Carla

The Warriors pounded through their setlist with the finesse of a bar fight. I would have perked up when Bez announced their final song of their encore if he hadn't named it, "Suck Everlasting." *Is nothing sacred?* I thought, repulsed by the sexualization of my favorite teen fantasy novel. Feeling I had filled my quota of air-humping that year, I headed for the VIP bar before it closed.

Leaning my elbows on the bar's polished wood, I eyed the top-shelf options while noticing there wasn't a cash register to be found. Or a bartender, for that matter. Wondering if it was self-serve, I eyed the room in search of a clue, wondering what everyone else had done.

"Oh, God," Alex stammered, walking towards me. "I got stuck talking with the Warriors' manager, who wants to pretty much redact half of the article because Bez comes off like a sexist sleaze."

I looked at her like I wasn't terribly surprised.

"Oh, and FYI, Pete's leaving." She patted her back pocket. "I have the keys to the Volvo."

"So, now we have two vehicles to get home?"

"No, my dear," she said. "I told him it was his turn to deal with the van."

"Oh." I thought about it for a second before looking at her. "Was he with anyone?"

"No," she said, shaking her head. "But now we have wheels, so you can show me what this town is all about."

"I don't even know what this town is all about."

"Well, as much as I had fun pranking your neighbor last night, it's not going to cut it tonight because so far, this place looks like Long Island with a tan." She leveled a penetrating look, knowing she was right. "I want a real Hollywood adventure."

"I've lived here for three years and have yet to have one."

"I'm so shocked," she said flatly.

"Furthermore," I said ignoring her snark, "I don't even know what that means, *a real Hollywood adventure.*"

"We're going to find out."

Over my shoulder, I noticed the guy who'd invited me up. I figured he'd forgotten about me, but when I caught him stealing a glance my way, I liked the feeling of being wrong.

"I saw that," Alex muttered. "Who are you —"

Before she could complete the sentence or look over her shoulder, I firmly placed my hand on her arm.

"Don't look!"

"Why not?" Her expression suggested I had lost my mind. "How old are you?"

"It's just that...." I pleaded as I allowed the sentence to dissolve unfinished.

"I'm going to look."

As stealthily as a person who'd had vodka for dinner could, she looked over her shoulder to trace my gaze before snapping her head back. "Oh, my God. Are you flirting with Ted?"

"Who?" I stole another quick glance. "There's more than one person there, you know."

"Yeah, but only one of them is your type." She looked again and I wanted to freaking kill her. "You might just get your no panties ending this weekend after all."

"Oh, come on."

"La, it's a good thing," she encouraged. "Ted Phillips is nothing to sneeze at."

"Fine," I gave in. "Tell me who he is in a discreet way." I looked at her like my hand was being forced. "You know, out of curiosity."

"Oh, now you want to know?" she ribbed. "Okay, I'll fill you in. He's Ted Phillips from Click Track."

"Okay," I said. "What else?"

"What else?" She looked at me like I was testing her. "Well, the reason any of us are here right now is because of him. You know he started the label out of his kitchen only four years ago."

"Impressive," I said, meaning it while looking again, now reassessing him with his new minted status of an indie rock mogul.

She then leaned back to check me out, as if looking at me in a whole new light. "Who I'm impressed with is you because damn, I didn't think you'd be eye fucking him."

"I am not." I looked to the side, blushing. "He just invited me up here to watch the show."

"Did he now?" She licked her lips as if feasting on the fresh gossip.

"Yes." I tilted my head. "He thinks our band is art rock, or whatever he said to describe it."

From the corner of my eye, I could see him walking towards us.

"I think he's walking over," I whispered sharply. "Act natural."

In a hasty bid to appear nonchalant, I shifted my weight, as my mind scrambled for a suitable topic for him to walk into. I looked at my best friend, though, knowing it was hopeless since we hadn't had a suitable conversation since 1995.

"Hey there," he said as the two of us slowly turned to face him. "Sorry, I got caught up talking to these guys." He motioned behind him.

"It's cool," I said with nonchalance as his eyes flicked over to Alex.

Noticing her, he extended his hand. "I'm Ted."

"Alex." She returned the gesture. "Nice to meet you."

Ted's gaze then shifted to me with an expectant lift of his brows in realization that we hadn't been formally introduced. I stretched my hand out.

"I'm Carla."

"Still Ted."

"Naturally," I replied, my hand still in his as we kept them locked for a second or two longer than his handshake with Alex's.

"So, I was wondering," he said, breaking the moment, now alternating his gaze between Alex and me. "What do you ladies have going on tonight?"

Alex and I contemplated for a few seconds, looking at each other as if considering other offers, which Ted accepted good-naturedly.

"Not sure yet," Alex responded coolly. "Why?"

"Roy G. Biv is having an afterparty and I wanted to know if you were interested."

After a deep breath and nod, making sure to eye Ted with enough contemplation to convey our busy night, we accepted with a breezy *why not?*

"Great," he said, seeming pleased we wanted to come. "Let me just say bye to these guys and we'll head out together?"

He glanced at us both for confirmation. Just as I was about to say we had our own ride, Alex jumped in," Sounds great." She smiled sweetly. "We'll wait right here."

"Awesome," he said. "I'll be right back."

Once he was out of earshot, I turned to Alex. "But we have a car."

"La," she said. "I am not showing up at a big-time producer's party in a used Volvo with squeaky breaks to announce our arrival. Like I said, I want the real Hollywood experience."

I let out a sigh. "Fine, we'll go with him, only if you stop saying that."

"I'll stop saying it when I finally get it and so far so good." She looked over at Ted like he was the key to making it happen.

"Fine," I said in a grounding tone, hoping to bring her down to planet Earth. "But no promises."

"Honey." She linked her arm in mine. "Trust me when I say promises have already been made."

Pete

That night, I had the pleasure of discovering why Los Angeles is the least romantic city in the world. It wasn't the smog. Or the mix-and-match architecture. Or simply because it wasn't Paris. It was the parking. The parking situation was enough to sterilize any hints of romance as Misha and I strategized like teammates to figure out what to do with a van and his station wagon. A 300-point turn later, squeezing the van into his guest parking spot in the underground garage and we were home free.

As I followed Misha through his courtyard apartment complex, I felt overly aware of everything around me. We passed the rows of mailboxes in the dimly lit portico painted palm green as I envisioned him in his California casuals, like flip-flops, gauzy shirts, and whatnot, collecting his mail. The swimming pool in the middle, lighting the way like an otherworldly creature in a sci-fi film, cast reflective waves across our faces as we walked around it.

"You live in a hotel compared to my place," I remarked.

"You're on the cool East Side," he jabbed. "But what we lack in hipster cred, we have in amenities like parking spots and pools."

"If you're into that sort of thing." I winked at him.

I followed him down a small corridor and up a stairwell that smelled of fresh paint. In front of his door was a rickety metal screen, probably dating back to the building's 1940s architecture. When he pulled it open, the weightless frame knocked into his shoulder as he slipped his key into the door.

In his apartment, I breathed in the scent of his hardwood floors mixed with the sweetness of a nearby fig tree. As he turned on the lights, the first thing I noticed was how comfortable his place felt. He had adult furniture that matched, and an oversized coffee table with a few hardcovered books stacked in the middle. I wanted to collect more information, like the titles on his bookshelf and the albums stacked in the CD tower, but there was no time as he was now facing me. Without skipping a beat, he reached for my tie seeming to get straight to the point.

"How long have you been wanting to do that?" I asked, keeping my eye on his hand as he wound my tie around it.

"Since you got mad at me for coming in late and you and I were in that small room together."

"While I was conducting the exam?" I kept my voice low and serious as he took a step back, pulling on the tie to take me with him. "That's not very professional now, is it?"

"No, Monsieur Albrecht," he confessed. "I'd say it's not."

"The school has rules against that kind of conduct," I informed him, letting my backpack slide off my shoulder.

As we edged closer to a nearby wall, I guided his back against it, fully embracing the rigid office administrator role I suspected turned him on. I slid my hand up the wall, effectively cornering him into an intimate space. Looking at him, I ran my thumb across his lower lip before he gently bit it, taking it in his mouth. I watched as he circled his tongue around it, making me wonder what else his tongue could do.

"What do you want tonight?" he whispered, still working his tongue up the side of my thumb.

Watching him take pleasure in something so simple, I smiled, knowing I wanted all of him. I took his other hand and guided it down to let him feel what he was doing to me. Slowly, I slid it up and down over my dress pants, letting him feel how hard he made me. I raised an eyebrow in admission that there was no hiding my attraction to him now. No snarky comment or room for misinterpretation, as I had fully exposed myself to him.

"So?" he prompted me, still wanting an answer as my breathing intensified with each stroke.

With our lips a breath apart, I repeated the question, just barely getting the words out, "What do I want to do tonight?" I said, my eyes beginning to roll back. "I want to have a very long night with you."

CHAPTER 23

Carla

I sat in the front seat of Ted's swanky BMW as we drove to Roy G. Biv's party. In the back, Alex sat with one of Ted's friends who wore blindingly white sneakers and only talked to Ted. As Franz Ferdinand's "Take Me Out" surged from the car speakers, I watched the neighborhood transform from the dense, urban mosaic of Hollywood into the sprawling, manicured landscapes of the fancier part of town. The surplus of street parking was the big tip-off, revealing the area's wealth as Ted veered off the main street. Twisting up and around the winding veins of the Hills, we passed the fake Corinthian columns of palatial Greek palaces and replicas of French chateaux. I recalled Pete critiquing the French ones, branding them architectural Frankensteins for mixing styles from several distinct French regions. He found the blend stylistically cumbersome, "an affront to the French eye" I think was his phrasing. I teased his French eye for being pretentious.

Given we were headed to some big music producer's house, I envisioned it being the one at the end of the cul-de-sac, that resembled a Rubik's Cube. But Ted surprised me when he turned into the driveway of an English Tudor, which made me ponder if it was architecturally accurate or an eyesore to the trained English eye.

"I'm guessing you've never met Damien?" Ted asked as he inched past a valet attendant.

"Who?" I looked at him.

"Damien," he attempted to clarify, but was met with the same puzzled look on my face. He continued up the long driveway, before parking behind a Bentley with the vanity plate reading, HITZ ONLY. "Damien is Roy G. Biv's real name," he explained, pushing the gear into park. "And just a heads-up to try not to take what he says personally."

"Okay," I said, twisting myself in the direction of the back seat to catch Alex's reaction, her face reflecting my cynicism at the warning.

"Well, he's just sort of up his own ass."

I glanced at the Bentley's license plate, which suddenly made sense, making me wonder why stuff like this didn't embarrass people more.

Alex then leaned forward between the two seats. "Just how far up his own ass is he?"

Ted seemed to appreciate the question as a genuine smile crossed his face. "Pretty far up there," he replied with a chuckle that made him look like a teenager.

Alex and I looked at each other from the corner of our eyes, knowing exactly how to handle guys like this.

"Noted," she said.

We walked up the stone path, following the sounds of the new Modest Mouse song playing inside. Everyone except Ted's friend nodded along to the bouncy song as we neared the front door, which Ted swung open like he lived there. Stepping into the round-shaped foyer, we found groups of people whispering among themselves. Their gazes flickered with recognition towards Ted and his friend, while drawing a disinterested blank on Alex and me.

I looked around the place to collect my first impressions when I found my eye drawn upward. The ceiling, I immediately noticed, was wooden. The coffered molding was a deep red, like the color of fox's fur, and seemed like an expensive feature for such a transitional room. The walls, painted in a rich peacock blue, showcased a work of art I knew I was supposed to be impressed with and, beneath it sat a baroque upholstered bench that I was pretty sure no one had ever sat on.

"Theodore," said a guy walking down the hall.

"Damien," Ted greeted the music producer back.

A stout guy, he sported a Sonic Youth T-shirt and the same toothpaste white sneakers as Ted's friend who had already vanished into the party. Damien pulled Ted in for a hug while they exchanged remarks about London and some person's party in Tangier. After releasing Ted, he turned to Alex and me with extended arms now aimed at us, looking like he was ready to receive us.

"Ladies," he said.

Alex and I offered short waves to let him know that we weren't going to hug him.

"New York chicks?" He turned to Ted like we weren't there.

"Chicks?" Alex gave him a long *are-you-kidding-me* stare. "And yeah, we're from New York."

"I knew it." He clapped his hands in self-victory, completely missing the point. He then pointed a finger up like he was about to say something important. "New York is my favorite city to go to, but...." he declared, holding a pause to build anticipation, "but it's also my favorite city to leave!" Throwing his head back at his own joke, he quickly added, "I kid, I kid. I love New York."

Before he could tell us where he was on 9/11, I interjected, "You have a really lovely home."

He looked at me like it was the oddest thing I could have said before returning his focus to Ted.

"Anyway," he said in a more serious tone. "What's this I hear of some no-name, art rock opening band who wiped their asses with the Warriors tonight?" A greedy look dripped down his face as he was about to dig into some inner circle gossip. "Did Bez lose his shit?"

"Too wasted to notice," Ted said to Damien, who fidgeted in the discomfort of being out of the loop. "But yeah," Ted continued, "the opening band was great. Not sure where they've been hiding this whole time, but I definitely want to see more."

His gaze briefly met mine before returning to Damien who was still contemplating. Leaning back with stacked arms, he seemed skeptical of new information he wasn't a part of.

"So, the no-name art rock band came out of thin air?" He shook his head as if not buying it. "But I would've known about them already. I go to Spaceland to check out new bands all the time and I've never heard of," he looked at Ted for assistance, "what was their name again?"

"The Disenchanted," he answered.

"That's right," he recalled, nodding his head. "And I heard they didn't have merch or even a manager to speak of? Where are they from? Mars?"

"They're very mysterious but who knows? They very well might be the next big thing." I could see the teasing glint in Ted's eye, taking evil pleasure at the constipated look on this big-time producer's face. "I told you, man, you should've come."

"Huh," was all he could say to recover from his self-inflicted embarrassment before addressing us again. "Sorry, ladies," he said. "Boring shop talk."

"Boring shop talk?" I made sure to look offended. "How so?"

"Sorry, I forgot I was with feminist New Yorkers here," he cracked another joke, this sexist in the Sonic Youth T-shirt, which made me feel bad for Kim Gordon because you really can't choose your fans.

"Were you at the show tonight?" he asked, as if talking to children.

"We were," we answered together.

"And did you happen to catch the opening band?" I saw his eye creep over to Ted's who looked visibly uncomfortable. "No, no," Damien reassured him, misreading the cautious look on his face. "Crowd reaction is just as important, if not more, than what us industry people think."

"I'd still tread lightly," Ted warned, to which Damien waved him off.

"Anyway," the producer turned back to us, still looking at us like we were simple. "What did you think of the opening band tonight?"

Alex lifted her chin, signaling me to answer the question.

"What did I think?" I took a moment as I thought of the best way to answer such a stupid question. "Well, I may not be the best person to ask."

"And why's that?" Damien pinched his chin, looking at me with the plasticity of a concerned politician. "Not your taste, or you're not really into music?" He held out a sympathetic hand. "Hey, not everyone is. I feel ya."

"No," I said flatly, looking at his hand. "Because I might be a little biased."

The producer pinched his chin again to reflect.

"I see," he considered it. "Because you thought they were cute and that might be shaping your opinion." He looked judiciously at Ted. "Looks sell records, too, so why not?"

"No," I said firmly. "I'm biased because I'm the no-name, art rock band who wiped my ass with the Weekend Warriors."

Pete

Was it still a first kiss if it never had an actual end? I didn't know but as our tongues danced circles around each other, I wondered at what point the first kiss turned into the second, third, and fourth? On his bed, Misha and I made out like teenagers as I registered everything I liked about the moment.

There were his soft, slippery lips moving on mine with my socked foot up running up and down the back of his leg, like we had been in this shape together before. I liked the meaningful way he undid the buttons of my dress shirt like each one counted. Or the way his hand pinned down my wrist above my head, as I surrendered to his control. But what I liked most was knowing I got to do this with him all night.

His hands traveled down my body, shooting electric currents through me, his touch making me feel like I was going to come at any given second. I kissed him harder to distract myself because I wanted to hold off as long as I could. As I opened my mouth wider to take him deeper, I began to feel lightheaded with disbelief that I had this kind of access to his body, where I could kiss it and bite it and suck as I pleased. I wondered what else I could do with it that night.

"So," he said in between a kiss or two. "How do you want to do this?"

This was a question I feared. I had hoped this part would have worked itself out without conversation and we'd just be doing it one way or another. But I knew there was more protocol involved and that Misha, I was learning, was too considerate to assume. With his sweet eyes looking down at me, he softly brushed my hair back, wanting to know what I usually did. A surge of adrenaline immediately raced through me, since I didn't have a prepackaged answer. He kept his expression soft as I fumbled, feeling swept away by my inexperience.

Wrapping my nervous fingers around his, he whispered, "It's okay if you've never done it before."

"How can you tell?" I asked before wincing at the dumb question. "You don't have to answer that."

He gently tapped the tip of his nose against mine. "How about you tell me how you've imagined us?"

I looked up at him. "Do you really want to know?"

"I do."

I continued looking at him, savoring the moment where it felt like we were sharing the same breath, passing it back and forth in the inch of space we left between our lips.

"I imagined you inside me," I revealed. "Fucking me." I then smiled at him. "Can that be arranged?"

He smiled, seeming to appreciate the phrasing. "I think it can."

Our bodies continued getting acquainted, this time using our mouths to explore each other. Moving counterclockwise in his bed, I didn't know up from down as we took our time getting to know one another. As I worked the length of him, tasting his skin inch by inch, I reveled in him watching me. As he ran his thumb across my cheek to feel himself inside of me, my eyes locked onto his that silently said, *of course, you like it when I do this.*

He then took me in his arms to gently guide me on my back. He aligned our bodies in a position more intimate than I had imagined, proving my reality was a much better writer than my daydreams. Looking up at him with drowsy eyes, I felt myself opening up with a sense of trust. I didn't want him to feel indebted to me for being my first. Instead, I wanted to share this closeness, even if it was just for the night.

"You can pull my hair, bite me, scratch me, tell me to stop," his words kissed my ear as he eased on the condom. "I'll do whatever you ask me to."

Summoning my courage for what I already knew was going to be one of the bigger moments in my life, I replied, "I might do all of those things, but I won't tell you to stop."

Carla

We were in an alternate universe, far from studio apartments and parking tickets. As Alex and I explored the house, walking down long hallways, we made random lefts and rights, following the din of party conversation. We entered the main room, which felt like an archeological dig into fame, and since we were nobody, we used our superpowers of invisibility to observe famous people in their natural habitats. Interacting with each other like unicorns in an enchanted forest, we floated by, catching snippets of conversations. A blockbuster leading man, whose billboard we had just passed at Sunset Plaza, talking with a '90s supermodel about pesticides being sprayed on soy products. Two alleged pop star rivals sat together on a pink velvet couch and complained about dancing in rhinestone bodysuits. America's current cinema sweetheart swayed while holding a cocktail glass to a Billy Idol song, while a former cinema sweetheart stole glances of herself in the reflection of an oversized mirror. There were the plastic smiles of industry executives who saw nothing but bags of money in the room. Nameless spouses of famous people who made a statement by marrying a 'normal person' but had so much work done, their faces looked like the villain in *Saw*. The White Sneakers Guy who wouldn't talk to us in Ted's car suddenly learned the art of conversation with one of the Charlie's Angels. The music video dancers no one wanted to dance next to. The wannabes who laughed every time a famous person said something. And us, the onlookers who probably shouldn't have been there in the first place.

Among the carefully crafted faces, I caught Ted casually chatting with a guy I didn't recognize. Our eyes met and he tossed his eyes up, as if to disassociate himself with the glitz I suspected he was secretly into.

Alex and I made our way over to the bar that could've been in a restaurant. The marble top displayed apothecary jars filled with fresh-cut herbs and fruit, making the place smell like a garden. Sitting on velvet stools, we watched the bartender slice open a blood orange and then slap the top-end of a sprig of basil to release its aromas.

Alex turned to me. "So, what do you think?"

"About which part?" I asked as our attention steered to the pop star popping-and-locking to his own song.

"Well, that, for starters," she pointed out, as we tried our best to stifle our laughter, knowing we had cracked open a treasure trove of stories. She continued surveying the room when a former Disney star fell flat drunk on her face before ambling off, thankful that no one important saw her. But we did.

To avoid being pegged as spies in the plastic surgery prom, I buried my face in the crook of her neck to muffle my laughter, feeling my stomach burn a hole from how tight I was holding it in. Just as I was about to ask her if this was what she had in mind for her big Hollywood experience, or whatever she had called it, a humorless voice from behind cut in.

"I see you two are having fun," her voice said.

Slowly, the two of us turned around to see a girl around our age wearing a pink latex bodysuit with lightning-bolt shaped eyebrows, looking at us with daggers. Her teased blond hair towered over us and from the look on Alex's face, she knew who this person was.

"Sorry," I said, knowing we were about to get kicked out for being too loud. "We were just—"

"Your bitch faces don't fool me," she cut me off, placing a hand on her hip.

"Seriously," I said, not wanting to stir trouble, because my best friend and I were still nerds chuckling like we were in our high school cafeteria. "We're just a little out of our element here. We don't mean to be rude."

"Girl," she responded with a sly smirk playing at the corner of her mouth. "I was just fucking with you. This party *is* weird. It's like an acid trip." She gestured towards the pop-and-locker still dancing to his own music. "Case in point."

"Oh, my God," I gasped. "I thought you were going to have us kicked out and since we got a ride here, we'd be screwed walking down that hill."

"I know, you came with Ted," she stated as if fact. "So, word on the street is, you gave the Warriors a run for their money."

"Did we?" I said, blowing off the inflated talk of our show. "It was fun, and nice of Jay to invite us to open."

"He's probably going to get kicked out of the band for that, you know."

"For that?" I turned to Alex and then back to Hot Pink Latex. "That seems excessive."

"It's show business."

Before I could ask more questions, Alex, who was about to burst, jumped in, "Rocktoya, right?"

"That's me," she verified, looking delighted at being recognized especially since "Leo" had just walked by. "But you can call me Roxie."

"This is Carla," she said, placing a hand on my shoulder as I waved. "And I'm Alex who you can blame for bitch face because I'm visiting."

"From back east, I gather?"

"Don't you know it," Alex answered proudly.

"That explains it," she said with a laugh before looking around. "It's usually not this sceney, but the *Kill Bill* 2 premier was tonight, so everyone seems to be out and about, nipped and tucked."

I looked at her like that would explain it as Roxie smiled, seeming at ease that we weren't impressed with premiers and pop stars.

"This is your first time here, right?" she asked us.

We both told her that it was and with a seductive gaze, she said, "Then we have to pop your Roy G. Biv cherries."

She looked around in search of someone. "I'm going to grab your buddy Ted, because I know he'll want to get in on it."

"Get in on what?" I asked, glancing at Alex, who I could see was trying to play it cool.

"You'll see. Everyone has to check out *the room* at one point in their life." She raised her eyebrow. "Think you can handle it?"

"Of course we can," Alex said with the bravado of her Slavic mom that made me smile.

I turned back to Roxie, searching for a hint of what happened in this elusive room, but she wouldn't budge.

"You can't come to Roy G. Biv's and *not* do this," she claimed while continuing to be deliberately vague.

"Alright," Alex agreed. "We'll go to the room, but I have to use the bathroom first."

Before we could wait for permission, Alex dragged me down the hall, where we opened door after door before finding a bathroom.

"What are we being invited to?" I said the second we closed the door.

"Isn't it obvious?" Alex said, unknotting the scarf around her waist and handing it to me. "They want to have an orgy with us." She shimmied her jeans down and sat on the toilet, looking at me. Her glassy eyes seemed to consider it as I immediately rejected the idea.

"No way," I said, my face pulled back in doubt. "Can't be."

At the sound of her pee trickling, she glared at me, challenging me to come up with another reason.

"No." I shook my head wildly, feeling the short strands whip my face. "It's way too…. personal."

Alex tilted her head at me. "Ya think?"

"Why would they want to do that with us?" I searched her face for an explanation. "They don't even know us."

"Beats me," Alex admitted, finally adapting a tone like she too thought it was weird. "Rich, famous people get bored, I guess." She tugged at the toilet paper roll, ripping off her needed squares. "Luckily," she said, bunching it up in her hand. "I have reinforcements." She nodded to the countertop I was leaning against. "Hand me my bag."

I frowned at the fistful of toilet paper she was about to insert between her legs. "Wash your hands first," I instructed, reaching for her bag and looking through it. "What do you need in here? Condoms?"

"No," she said as if that would make absolutely no sense. "Look in the side zipper and take out the baggie."

"The baggie," I mumbled absently. When my eyes landed on what was clearly drugs, I dropped the bag on the counter as if it were contaminated and whipped around to her. "*That's* the reinforcement?" I stretched my eyes open. "Drugs?"

"Drugs?" she repeated, mocking my tone.

"Did you fly with that?" I looked at her like she had lost her mind.

"Of course not." She stood up, wiggling her jeans over her hips. "I got it backstage at the show."

"When?" I looked off, trying to trace back events of the night. "And how?"

"It was easy," she said casually, flushing the toilet. "All I had to do was follow the smell of coke farts."

As I watched her walk to the sink, I waited for her to elaborate but this was Alex, and I knew she wanted to repeat the sentence. Obliging to my best friend's quirks who got pleasure out of shocking me, I said, "I'm sorry, what?"

"All I had to do was follow the smell of coke farts," she repeated, chuckling to herself.

"And then?"

"And then it led me to spotting the person touching their nose, and then blackmailing them," she stopped rinsing her hands to look at me, "just kidding, but from there I asked who had and how much and, voilà, we have party favors."

I looked at the bag again. "What is it?"

"It's just a little coke," she said, sounding blasé as she wiped her hands on a towel. "It's no big deal."

"Isn't this stuff crack?"

"Crack?" Her face became long. "Not unless I cut it with baking soda and cook it."

"Or whatever," I said, dismissing my lack of terminology. "I do know these are hard drugs though."

"Oh, my God. Are you taking a bite out of crime. Is this your war on drugs? Did you learn it from watching me?" She looked off, searching for more Reagan-era anti-drug slogans we were brought up on before I could see she was tapped out.

"I'm being serious." I shifted my weight while looking at her in the mirror.

"I know you are." She laughed. "Come on, I'll show you that it's no big deal."

With reluctance, I watched her handle the tiniest Ziplock baggie I had ever seen as my thoughts drifted to Barbie who I knew didn't have this in mind when she told me to have fun.

Alex, looking at me like I was such a prude, shook her head. "It's not crack!"

"It's a gateway to it."

"Yeah, and so is red wine." She paused in order to make her point. "We're all getting high one way or another. This way is just more fun."

"And more illegal," I added.

"Honey," she said, sounding tired of this conversation. "Everyone does blow."

"Now you sound like a drug addict."

"And you sound like you've watched *Requiem for a Dream* too many times." I made a face that she was right. "Jordan Catalano on smack," she purred, taking a pack of cigarettes out of her bag. "He was still hot."

Noticing it, I stopped her. "I don't think we can smoke in here."

"I'm not." She held one up to show me. "Parliaments are the only cigarettes that have this little indent in the filter here, which is perfect for scooping bumps."

Unimpressed by the innovation, I watched as she began her demonstration. Presenting the paraphernalia like a game show model, she theatrically dipped the butt end of the cigarette into the bag to collect a tiny bit of powder. With care, she snorted it up one nostril.

"See?" she said, sniffling and then swallowing a small gulp.

"How'd you know how to do that?" I watched as she repeated the ceremony on the other nostril.

"You spend enough time in dive bar bathrooms on the Lower East Side, you pick up a thing or two."

"You don't use rolled up dollar bills?"

"If you want hepatitis, you do." She held the cigarette up. "Wanna try?"

I leaned forward to get a better look at the powder, noticing that it was much finer than I had imagined. Instead of the life-destroying poison that 11th grade health class had taught me it was, it looked almost innocent, like freshly fallen snow. It was at that moment, my body felt heavy, and my ankles became weak forcing me to grab onto the counter for balance. I lowered myself onto a padded bench, dropping my head between my knees to gain my bearings. When I came back up, though, the room tipped, making me feel like the marble in my Labyrinth game I had as a kid.

"I think I'm already too drunk," I said, feeling flush.

She sat down beside me, nudging my hip with hers to make room. I inched over and looked at her dangling the tiny baggie in my face. "Well, that's what this is for."

Seeing double, I tried to look at her clearly. "What do you mean?"

"Have some of this," she suggested, gently swinging the baggie side to side as if hypnotizing me. "It'll sober you right up."

"That doesn't even make sense. But if I do this," I said, closing one eye, "I stop seeing double."

"You're going to walk around the whole night with one eye closed?"

"What if I close both?"

"Then you'll miss the whole night."

"That might not be such a bad thing," I groaned, thinking of the orgy we were apparently guests of honor to.

She slapped a hand down on her thigh. "You want to know what I think?"

I turned to her drained, fearing more surprises. "I'm not sure."

"I think you're ready for your slut phase."

My eyes ticked to the side for a second, thinking I hadn't heard correctly. But it was Alex and of course, I'd heard what she said. "I'm sorry, my what?"

"Your slut phase," she repeated like it made total sense. "I'm definitely in mine right now. That way, when I hit my forties I won't have any regrets because I'd have done it all. I won't feel like I missed out on anything because I'll be, well, retired."

"A retired slut?"

She rolled her eyes like I was missing the point and leaned closer, looking at me like an old sister. "Come on, aren't you tired of missing out on things?"

"Like my real Hollywood adventure or whatever?" I glared at her.

"Honey, we're in it, as in right now, so my question is, are you going to live it or sleep through it?"

CHAPTER 24

Pete

Feeling like a whole person, I lay in his arms as his fingertips stroked the small of my back. I touched my lips, swollen and tasting faintly like blood from when I accidentally bit his lower lip. My body throbbed with a blend of slight physical discomfort and euphoria, feeling awakened by the new experience. We caught our breath slowly, my head rising and falling in the rhythm of his heartbeat, our bodies heavy and listless in each other's embrace. I didn't know exactly what he was thinking, only that his touch told me that he liked having me in his arms.

"Can I ask you something?" he asked where I could feel the vibration of his vocal chords through his chest.

"What's that?" I answered. "You're going to finally ask me what my first name is?"

He began to laugh, which made my head bounce up and down on him. "You don't think I know your name, Peter?"

I sat up to look at him, his eyes glowing in the streetlamp light streaming in from the window. Reading the surprised look on my face, he said, "I looked you up on the website."

"You looked me up?"

"You looked me up?" he imitated me. "Of, course I did. I wanted to know who that queen at reception giving me a hard time was."

I rolled my eyes at his assessment of me before I realized the picture he'd seen: the fucking 1-800-MATTRESS shot. Stricken with sudden embarrassment, I buried my face in his chest.

"I can't believe you saw that photo," I bemoaned, my voice muffled against his skin.

"What," he said, his voice hitting a higher pitch, which I knew meant he was lying. "You look cute in it."

"Cute?" I looked at him squarely. "Sweetie," I kept my voice flat, "you already have me in bed, no need to bullshit me now."

He pinched my side, which made me wriggle helplessly as he was getting just the right spot.

"Yeah," he managed to get out, his voice tight from play tackling me, "and I plan to have you again."

"We'll fucking see," I retorted, dodging his attacks before getting ahold of his fighting hand. With agility, I maneuvered myself on top of him with my hand now pressing him down.

"But first," I demanded, "you have to tell me what you were going to ask me."

Out of breath again, our chests lightly heaved in unison as we looked at each other.

"What I wanted to ask," he said slowly, appearing to enjoy the light forcefulness, "is are you hungry?"

I paused for a second, a smirk escaping from my lips. "All that, just to ask me if I was hungry?"

He raised his shoulders like it made perfect sense before giving my bare ass a slight smack. "Come on, Peter," he said, smirking in delight at saying my first name, "let's get you some food."

I followed him out of the room, down the small hallway that linked to a second bedroom as he flicked lights on. In the living room, I saw my backpack on the floor where I'd left it before our first kiss. Looking at it only a few hours later, it already represented the past and the things I didn't know the last time I had it on my shoulder. I hadn't known how long two people could keep their tongues in each other's mouths. I hadn't known that I liked having the back of my knees caressed while having my dick sucked. I hadn't known how bonded I would feel to him when he handed me my glasses just now before getting out of bed. I was someone else the last time that bag was on my shoulders and now I was following him as one of two beings who had shared a moment and were now padding barefoot into the kitchen for a snack. My *before* and *after*.

We stood on the checkered tiled floors of his kitchen as he pulled open the refrigerator door. Inside was a Brita water carafe and next to it about five bottles of Absolut Vodka lined up militantly.

"You really are Russian," I said, impressed at the cultural conviction.

With his arm stretched over the refrigerator door, he peered over it with a steely gaze and simply stated, "No self-respecting Russian would drink Absolut." He reached in to grab one. "This is just water. My neighbor downstairs brings me his empty bottles when he's done." He placed one on the tile countertop beside him. "I like storing filtered water in glass bottles, it's better for you and I refuse to buy bottled."

I could feel myself getting turned on by the sentence itself. "Why don't you buy plastic?" I asked, having to control a potential hard-on from the implication of his words.

"For one, it's overpriced, but do you know how long it takes for one plastic bottle to decompose?"

"Some studies suggest up to 450 years."

"That's right." He seemed delighted but not surprised. "Can you imagine?"

"I try not to," I said, my voice distant and my gaze resolute, as I looked at the first person to ever speak my language back to me.

He shut the fridge, our eyes meeting in mutual acknowledgement, knowing we weren't doing nearly enough.

Reading the spark in my eye, he said, "I figured we had some ideas in common ever since you told me you ride your bike."

"Well, not for a few days, I won't be," I half-joked.

He let out a sympathetic hum, his hand softly grazing my hip, hinting he understood. "I'm sorry," he murmured. "But it gets better, I promise."

I smiled, undeterred by my first time as I felt close to this person. I knew I shouldn't have put as much emotional stock on what could've easily been a one-night thing, but I refused to accept the idea of casual sex as I didn't find anything casual about having another person's body part inside of me. I didn't give a fuck what society dictated.

"I'll be fine." I snapped out of my thought. "But I was wondering if you had something cold and sweet, like a yogurt or something like that."

A sinister look crossed his face. "I might."

He opened the freezer where a puff of vapor steamed up my glasses. Once they cleared, as I had no article of clothing to wipe them clean with, I took our mission seriously. In his freezer with the walls caked in ice, there was a choice of frozen chicken cutlets, ice cream or vodka.

"No Absolut, but this." I grabbed the frosted bottle that felt like ice in my hand. Turning it, I made no attempt to read the label that made its disinterest in the English-speaking market clear.

"Shit," I muttered. "This looks lethal."

"That was a housewarming gift from my dad." He shuddered almost dismissively as he moved things around his freezer.

"I take it you're not close?" I dared asking, testing the limits of our intimacy.

"Well, I don't drink vodka."

Sensing that was all I was going to get, I moved on. "You do eat ice cream though." I made a point to look at his carved abs. "Does your personal trainer know about this addiction?"

"*My* trainer?" He lightly touched my stomach. "What about yours?"

"Please," I retorted, batting his hand away. "This is all cardio."

"I'll say," he said, appearing to like what he saw, which made me blush.

I turned to the freezer, eyeing the mint chocolate chip, mint sorbet, which I didn't even know was a thing, and behind them was Phish Food and Cherry Garcia, which caught my eye. I reached for the two Ben and Jerry's flavors, holding a pint in each hand. "Closet Deadhead?"

He didn't make the connection as the blues of his eyes struck mine. "I like those flavors." He looked at the tops of the cartons. "Why? Are these guys famous ice cream makers?"

"Jerry Garcia and Phish?" I eyed him like he was kidding me. "No, they're not ice cream makers."

"Alright," he acquiesced, opening a drawer to pull out spoons. "Why don't you tell me all about these so-called non-ice cream makers and while we're exploring the wonders of the world, you'll tell me what your tattoo means." His eyes caught mine in acknowledgement that he'd noticed it while undressing me.

I nodded in accord. "Anything else?"

"Yes," he said with a slight twinkle in his eye, "you also can share a favorite story from high school. And not one where you come off cool because I'm sure you have plenty of those. I want a real dork story."

"I'll raise your dorky high school story with you telling me if you wore tracksuits, you know the kinds that swished down the hall."

"After you tell me if you had braces and what freeways you avoid," he one-upped me.

Smiling at him I said, "I guess we're both a little curious about each other."

"I'd say we are."

Carla

The orgy.

The steamy Hollywood orgy.

While there *were* out-of-breath bodies flopping about, Alex and I stood corrected as we were neck-deep in a ball pit the size of my apartment. I hadn't been in one of these since a birthday party at Discovery Zone and while the mechanics were the same, the record producer version featured a built-in Bang and Olufson sound system connected to every song imaginable, a stocked bar we could to swim to if we wanted a drink, and my best friend and an indie electroclash star doing bumps of cocaine off the of side their hand. Otherwise, it was *exactly* like Discovery Zone.

As I tried to float on my back, I caught my reflection in the mirrored ceiling, deciding I was in my freest yet dorkiest version of myself. I swallowed, tasting the drip of Alex's coke slide down my throat, wondering what I was supposed to be feeling. As I felt the balls roll on my back, I daydreamed away, my thoughts racing with ideas when I felt a wave of balls push towards me. I looked over to find Ted making ball pit angels. Or at least trying to.

"I can't stay afloat," he gasped, sinking deeper into the sea of plastic balls.

I extended my arm towards him. "Here!" I called out. "Grab my hand!"

The moment he clasped onto it, a surge of balls pushed against me, dragging me down with him. As I struggled for balance, my stocking-covered feet slipped on the slick surface of the balls like a mouse on a wheel. Full-blown giggling ensued, controlling my entire body as I grasped onto Ted. Just then, Alex put on "Celebrity Skin" by Hole. As its power-chord arena rock opening boomed through the speakers, I continued to grab onto Ted for dear life. The flirting by default felt a little slapstick for my taste, but the lack of available gravity forced us to pile on top of each other like total idiots. The more I tried to tread *balls,* the more I laughed, adding to the absurdity of the entire situation. Finally, he took my hand hauling me like a child to safety to the edge where we paused for a few moments to catch our breath. Across the room, I smiled, watching Alex and Roxie howl the song's lyrics about waking up in their makeup, and has-beens and would've-beens with the song feeling too perfect for us Hollywood outsiders.

Ted turned to me. "Want to know why Damien has this place?"

"Sure, since he doesn't exactly strike me as a ball pit kind of guy."

Ted smiled in agreement. "His main studio," he explained, "is down in the basement but when his artists hold up a project for *ego issues*," he held up finger quotes, "he sends them here." I nodded, imagining it. "Because, really? Who can take themselves seriously in a ball pit?"

"And does it work?"

"It did for me." He flashed a perfect smile. "*Shapes: Volume 2* was nominated for a Grammy, and I owe part of it to a ball pit. Too bad we didn't win because it wouldn't been in my speech."

"There's always the liner notes," I suggested.

"One step ahead of you, it's the cover of the album, hence the title."

I made a guilty face that I probably should've known that, but the way his brown eyes deepened to a rich hot chocolate color told me he found my cluelessness of his hipster fame refreshing.

"And what about you?" he asked.

"What about me?"

"What's next for the band? I noticed you guys don't have a Myspace." He seemed impressed while I tried to keep my expression neutral, concealing my surprise that he had poked around about us in the short time we'd known each other.

"Resisting the wave of the future for art?" he inferred.

I almost confessed that we weren't that well-strategized, but instead, I took a moment to reflect. I looked around the room as Alex and Roxie were now salivating over the naughtiness of "AA XXX" by Peaches. My cheeks blushed, wishing I wasn't sitting next to Ted during a song with lyrics that included *licky*, *sucky* and *fucky fucky*. I decided to focus, though, on his question that he seemed more interested in. *Was* I resisting the wave of the future for art?

"Not really," I answered. "Tonight was just a result, I guess, of a childish hope that I think it's time to finally let go of."

"Then I'd say you're in a band."

"No, it's not even that."

As he waited for a more satisfying response, I gathered my thoughts, wondering how to phrase it tactfully. But this was a guy whom I had overheard say the words *Drew Barrymore* and *lunch* in the same tossed-off sentence, and figured my civilian drama was safe with someone who probably didn't care.

"My bandmate is in love with someone else," I blurted out. "And I don't know what I'm doing with my life, and I know most of my problems are self-inflicted, but my songs are a mix of coming to terms with all of that."

"That's great," he said. "That's like striking artistic gold."

"Gold?" I balked at the idea. "Well, it hurts."

"The best art usually does."

CHAPTER 25

Pete

I didn't have to open my eyes to know that I was alone. Stretching out, feeling his sheets against my skin, my senses picked up the world around me. Through a cracked window came the jingle of the Keys on Van Nuys commercial from a car idling on the street, the clinking of utensils from a neighbor's kitchen and the smell of coffee I'd hoped was coming from his place. I opened my eyes, which stung in protest of daylight as I slipped my glasses on. On the end table was a note for me.

Monsieur,

I'm by the pool. There's coffee in the kitchen and I left a pair of sweats for you on the chair. Help yourself and come out when you're alive, otherwise hang out and I'll be up soon.

xx,

M

Though exhausted, my curiosity about the morning version of him pulled me out of bed. My joints cracked and my backside felt tender, reminding me of our athletic, mostly sleepless night. On a chair by the window, I spotted the sweatpants offering and on the floor lay the clothes I had arrived in. My tie, dress shirt, pants, *et al* lay discarded on the jute rug like an inconvenience.

I walked into his kitchen, pulling the T-shirt I intended to wear for the show over my head. The natural light from the slated glass window cast a warm glow, making me feel at home.

On the counter sat his coffee maker filled to the top and next to it a mug. On it was a printed image of what had to be his first headshot. Long skinny arms hidden under a baggy top, he looked like the gawky little brother of the Abercrombie model I had spent the night contorting my body with. Surrounding the photo were illustrations of film reels and a clapper board, with his full name and contact info boldly displayed. I smiled that he wanted me to see this dorky artifact.

With it in my hand, I headed out to the courtyard imagining him swimming laps, doing poolside yoga, or whatever it was models did on Saturday mornings. I sipped the coffee as I retraced my steps from the night before, passing the tropical plants and bougainvillea, admiring their brighter colors in the daytime. As I approached the pool, instead of hearing splashes of water, I heard the murmur of low conversation. Around a potted palm, I found Misha standing in front of an outdoor table engaging in light conversation while massaging dirt in a flowerpot. His companion was an elderly woman wearing a gold brocade house dress with a matching turban, her hands gently patting the dirt around bright pink flowers in her own pot. I didn't have to be close to detect they weren't speaking English and before I could speculate who this woman was, Misha noticed me.

"Morning," he said, grabbing a dish towel to wipe the dirt off his hands. He turned to the elderly woman's curious eyes as he appeared to explain who I was. It must have been complimentary, because she smiled at me before returning to her flowers.

"This is my neighbor Ina," he said, walking over. "We're planting the summer hibiscus."

I looked at their table, acknowledging the bright flowers sitting among the topsoil massacre.

"Beautiful," I said as I walked towards him, meeting him halfway.

He smiled at me, seeming to study what I looked like in the morning before saying, "You looked like you could use the sleep."

"I did." I held up the mug. "But this is helping even if the mug is out of control."

He smiled at the old photo of himself printed on the side. "I thought you'd appreciate it."

"Oh, I do." I took another sip as my eyes smiled at him over the brim.

"My cousin Sergey made them the first year I decided to give acting a shot. His idea was to leave them at places he knew big time producers and directors went, you know, like cafés on studio lots, thinking I'd get my big break that way." Although I knew nothing about strategies to break into the business, I couldn't help but crinkle my nose because I suspected that wasn't it.

"I know," Misha said, reading my thoughts. "That was when I learned to never listen to my cousin."

He took the mug from my hand, helping himself to a sip. Watching him, I felt a warm sense of contentment at the budding sense of ease we were developing with each other.

"Mikhail," Ina called from the table.

He handed me the mug, walking back to her where I watched them exchange words I couldn't even pretend to understand. As they conversed in their shared language, I felt exactly how I imagined my friends felt coming to my house when I was growing up – standing awkwardly on the outside of someone else's culture. It was then I realized how hard it was to appear natural when you had no idea what was being said around you. When I saw them beginning to tidy up, I walked over to help.

As I gathered scattered grains of dirt, collecting it into the palm of my hand, I turned to Misha. "Mikhail?" I questioned. "Is that your full name?"

"Indeed, it is." He handed me a small pail to drop the dirt into.

"So, you're Mikhail Taylor?"

"Mikhail Sokolov," he gently corrected. "Taylor is my middle name."

I heard the name in my head and smiled. "You sound like a choreographer."

"I hear I move like one, too."

I rolled my eyes, wiping more dirt off my hand. "Was that what that was last night? Dancing?"

He grinned. "At moments."

"Then you're a pretty loud dancer, I'd say."

He swatted me with one of the dish towels, as Ina admired the newly potted plants murmuring comments with clasped hands. Through finger pointing and tone, I inferred Misha offered to finish cleaning up, which she accepted, appearing winded. After bidding farewell to us, she went back to her first-floor apartment, her feet dragging across the stone patio while Misha kept an eye on her.

"She doesn't want me to help," he whispered. "I get it, though. No one wants to feel old."

Once she was safely inside and he heard the door lock, he turned to me. "So, you know, we technically have our first date today."

I raised an eyebrow, looking at him like we had already run a few circles around our first date.

"We can hang out here all day but if you're around tonight, there's party in Hollywood that my scene partner is working the door at."

I was sure my face looked less enthused as I asked, "What kind of party?"

"It's hard to say exactly, but since you mentioned it, do you like dancing?"

Carla

My body jolted awake, the sensation harsh and sudden like a splash of cold water to the face. I opened my eyes to find nothing but darkness, an inky void the felt like outer space but without the stars, constellations or *Moon Safari* by Air. My head throbbed and my heart raced, showing the only signs of life in my imaginary solar system. My mouth searched for saliva, while my skin felt clammy as I patted around for clues. I felt the plush of a comforter and a soft, expensive-feeling blanket. I touched my chest and felt the scalloped lace of my bra, prompting me to inch the covers up. Pawing around in the darkness, I realized I was only in my underwear, my tights conspicuously absent as my mind raced with questions. I reached for a lamp, resulting in a smattering of things falling down. Then I felt a shift in the bed, followed by a man's low groan, prompting me to clamp my hand over my mouth wondering who I was half-naked in bed with. As I looked into nothingness, I asked myself was this it? *Was this my slut phase?*

As I replayed the events of the night before, I recalled the ball pit, the endless glasses of champagne, the bumps of coke that left a gritty residue on my thoughts and then…there was Ted. My eyes widened. *Oh, God, Ted*, I thought as my throat tightened, and my body tensed from not remembering how we got there. Suddenly, his voice cut through the silence, confirming that indeed, my slut phase was unfolding right on schedule. Well, Alex's schedule.

"You up?" he asked, his voice groggy and detached.

"Uh, yeah," I replied, trying to sound just as unaffected. "I'm just trying to find a light to turn on since I guess it's still nighttime." That didn't seem right though. "Wait, what time is it?"

I could hear him moving things around before his cell phone lit up a small corner of his side. "It's eleven o'clock," he said, clearing his throat.

"At night?"

"No," he said, a light chuckle breaking through the dark, "in the morning."

I searched for a window seam to validate his claim but could only see pure darkness as I heard him pull open a drawer, rummaging things around.

"Here it is," he muttered as I heard a button click.

Slowly, the darkness began to lift, allowing light to wash over the room and reveal fancy, French-looking wallpaper. He clicked the tiny remote to stop the blinds from completely rising to the top. With the blankets pulled up to my neck, I took stock of him and immediately noticed that he still had his shirt on. On the floor were his sneakers and nothing that indicated a drunken fit of passion that I was preparing myself to regret. Or defend.

"Ted," I asked carefully.

He appeared amused, his eyes shining in the morning light. "Yes, Carla?"

"This might sound weird but why aren't you naked?"

He smiled curiously at the direct question. "Should I be?"

"Well, why am I?" I peeked again under the covers again. "Well, almost."

"You were hot and in the middle of the night, you demanded I help you take your dress off." He pointed to the corner of the room where it hung on a hanger clutched to an antique armoire. "You were afraid of ripping it."

"Well, it's vintage," I explained.

"I know." He grinned. "You told me."

"Oh, right," I accepted before landing on the next question. "And why am I in bed with you?"

"You passed out on a lounge chair by the pool, and I was afraid you'd sleepwalk into it. So, I brought you up here, but then I worried you'd choke, so I stayed with you."

I looked away in pure mortification before realizing some kind of response was expected of me.

"Oh," I said as if that cleared it all up. "Thank you."

"No problem." He then grabbed his phone beeping on the nightstand. "We've all been there."

"Right," I mumbled, catching a whiff of my breath that tasted like a decomposing animal. Covering my mouth, I felt sticky, longing for a shower to exfoliate the night off my body. But seeing my dress across the room, I wondered how I was going to get to it without giving him a backside view.

"So, hey," he said, his eyes lifting from his phone, completely oblivious to the chitter-chatter in my head.

"What's up?" I was still aiming for casual even with the sheets pulled up to my chin.

"I have to head to the studio now, but what are you and Alex up to tonight?"

I thought about it for a second. "Well, it's her last night in town, so I have to see what she wants to do. Why?"

"Well, if you're up to it, my friends throw this great party in Hollywood called For Tomorrow."

I nodded my head as if I wasn't in my bra with the dirty straps. "Nice."

"Yeah, Binki's spinning tonight, she does mixes of new tracks and the best classics you didn't know you were dying to hear."

"Sounds good."

"I'll put you on the list." He tapped away at his phone, indicating he was doing it right there.

"What kind of party is it?" I asked, knowing Alex would have follow-up questions.

"It's hard to say exactly, but do you like dancing?"

CHAPTER 26

Pete

"Remember the part when I said I *didn't* like dancing?" I said to Misha as I followed him out of the shower.

"Oh, I remember," he replied, not bothering to hide the satisfaction in his voice. "I'll have you know these parties are supposed to be very hip."

"Hip," I repeated as we walked into the bedroom. "You really have to stop selling me on this party."

He turned to his closet while I flopped back onto the unmade bed, stretching my arms over my head. With a towel wrapped around my waist, I lay gazing at the ceiling, reflecting on our day spent doing everything and nothing. Turning my head, I caught his blurry silhouette just as his towel fell to the floor. A smile crept onto my face, knowing that I didn't need to see his body clearly to already know my way around it. My thoughts then wandered back to this party we were going to and chuckled at his fleeting reference to his scene partner working the door. Fuck. If someone had told me before I moved to L.A. that sentences like that would be a part of my social lexicon, I was pretty sure I wouldn't have come.

"What's so funny?" he asked.

I took a moment to gather my thoughts, cautious not to offend his profession with my East Coast snark.

"Nothing."

"Come on," he gently pushed, stepping into a pair of boxer briefs. "Tell me."

"Fine," I relented. "Is this going to be one of those actor's things where there's too much smiling and the word amazing is tossed around?"

Grinning he asked, "Is that what you think happens when actors get together?"

"Is that what I *think* happens?" I repeated the question, propping myself on my elbows. "No. It's what I *know* happens. Thespians can't help it."

"Thespians," he repeated with a theatrical flourish as he reached into a drawer. "Just for that," he said, tossing an item of clothing that landed squarely on my face, "I'm giving you *this* to wear tonight."

I peeled the garment off of my face, reaching for my glasses on his end table. With my eyes back on, I looked down at the bright yellow T-shirt in my hand.

"Riverside Performing Arts Camp?" I shot him an amused look. "You went to theater camp?"

"I did," he confirmed proudly. "And that shirt is one of my most prized possessions. So, take care of it."

Feeling the soft cotton from many washes, I turned it around to read the back. "Bring on the drama?" I looked at him, sharing a flicker of amusement between us. "Babe, do I even want to know about all the dorky shit you did at theater camp?"

"First of all, it's performing arts camp," he corrected me while holding up a finger to take a dramatic pause like someone who went to theater camp would, "and second, it's amazing."

"Yeah?" I looked at him not buying it.

"Yeah," he confirmed, stepping towards me to knock his bare knee into mine. "It's also where I got my first blow job."

"Now if only they put *that* in the brochure."

"No way. It's the best kept secret. Theater kids are some of the horniest kids ever and our parents never suspect a thing. It's genius, really."

"It's theater camp," I reminded him.

"How are you even turning your nose up when you're bi!" he exclaimed matter-of-factly. "You'd be in heaven!" He paused, picturing it. "And quite busy, too."

Surprised by his blunt assessment, I couldn't hide my expression that shifted from amusement to surprise. My mind considered for a moment what this revelation might mean for us, if anything. I looked at him, knowing he could accurately read my face, which I knew then would be both a flaw and a feature of our relationship.

He sat beside me. "Was it supposed to be a secret?"

"Well…no. Of course not, I just didn't think anyone knew."

He gave me a look like I had to be kidding.

"I really didn't," I said with a nervous laugh.

"Sweetie," he said, bumping his shoulder against mine, "the girl in your band?"

I looked at him, my expression perhaps giving away that my relationship with Carla wasn't entirely platonic.

"There's obviously a story there," he aptly stated.

I took a deep breath and slowly nodded my head. "It's complicated," I admitted.

"It looked it."

"And you're okay with it?" I looked at him, needing some reassurance before allowing myself to fall any harder for him.

"What do you mean?" He seemed genuinely confused by the question.

"You don't think that I'm, like, a poser because I'm also into girls?"

He shook his head and laughed. "Only you would ask a question like that."

Seeing though that I was completely serious, he leaned in closer to me. "No, Peter, I don't think that. This is who you are."

And I couldn't argue there.

Carla

I never went away to college, but with Alex and Roxie taking over my place to get ready for the party, it was pretty much how I'd imagined it would be. Like a punk rock dorm room where the Yeah Yeah Yeahs' howled like Saturday night from my stereo, another jug of cheap wine holding court on my kitchen table, and my best friend strutting around with a strapless towel dress. On my bed, I flipped through a tabloid she had picked up at the airport, stopping at an item about the actress Mischa Barton. I briskly turned the page, feeling like the name Misha was following me everywhere I went like a bad rumor. At the foot of my bed, Joni seemed scandalized by all the activity, her eyes darting around, probably wondering when we were all going to leave.

"Um, hello," Roxie called from the kitchen. "Who is *this* hot piece of ass?"

Knowing exactly who she was referring to, my eyes flicked briefly to Alex, before explaining to Roxie that he was the drummer in my band.

"Meow, I wish my drummer was this gorgeous."

"Yeah, he photographs well." I kept my eyes glued to the magazine in an attempt to sever the tail of the conversation.

The effort went unnoticed as she wrapped her head around the doorframe. "You two fucking?"

A few months ago, the phrasing would have made me gasp but my heart felt too tired for dramatics.

"No," I returned the directness in her voice with my own. "He has a new girlfriend."

My eyes shot over to Alex who I noticed wasn't reacting to the conversation and proceeded to follow her as she walked to the bathroom. Sitting in the aftermath of her silence, I admit it caught me off guard because she always had something to say about Pete. But the only response she was willing to provide was the whirring sound of her electric toothbrush.

"Have you met her?" Roxie asked, walking towards me with two glasses of wine.

"Thanks," I said, taking one from her. "And, no, I haven't."

She sat on the bed with me and as we sipped from our glasses, I looked at her noticing how soft her face was when scrubbed clean. The tiny freckles on her nose made her seem more human, contrasting her album titled *MVP*, where the cover's provocative pose of her spread legs suggested what the P stood for. But here, she was just another girl our age who probably knew a thing or two about heartbreak.

"You're avoiding hurt feelings, aren't you?" she asked, licking the sweet wine off her lips.

I forced a smile. "I'm just putting them off for a bit."

"I get it." She sighed. "Making music with guys you're into…well, it's not for the faint of heart."

"No, it's not," I agreed, raising the glass to my lips again to wash away the sting of hurt feelings. The two of us sat in silence, each lost in our own sonic love stories and musical entanglements of our pasts. Then as if struck by an epiphany, Roxie perked up.

"But who cares about this girl, right?" I looked at her unsure if she was referring to my story or hers but went along with it anyway.

"Right!" I said, wondering if I was pulling off the enthusiasm convincingly.

"She's probably just a rebound. One day you and hottie drummer will write your own *Rumours* but, you know, minus 'Go Your Own Way.'"

Before I could continue the empowerment I wasn't so sure I felt, Alex stormed out of the bathroom, pointing her toothbrush at me.

"Are you kidding me?" She looked at me, her face hardened with frustration.

I glanced to the side feeling like I'd missed a beat somwhere. "What do you mean?"

"It's a sincere question, are you fucking kidding me?"

"Again, what do you mean?" I countered.

"I mean, are you really playing the victim here?"

Her words hit me like shock treatment as I looked at Roxie, who mirrored my surprise.

"Please don't look at her for, like, approval," Alex snapped. "This is between you and me."

"What's between you and me?" I glared at her toothbrush, still pointed at me like a tiny pink weapon. "This total meltdown?"

"At least there's feeling and actual emotion in this," she retorted. "I know here in California everyone's supposed to be all chill, but sometimes we need to admit we're actually dodging reality." She looked at the two of us as if we represented the entire state.

"Hey, I'm from Jersey," Roxie interjected.

"And you know where I'm from. So, what's this all about?"

She exhaled sharply, her nostrils flaring, as she looked at me like I was one of the mean girls in high school. Once she was sure I received the message that she was pissed, she stomped back into the bathroom.

"Alex!" I handed Roxie my glass and swung my legs over the bed to follow her. "Seriously, what are you talking about?" I then noticed her empty wine glass sitting on the back of my toilet. "Are you drunk already?"

Her eyes narrowed at me as if I was one to talk. "Not even close," she sneered. "I just don't think you have a right to cry over the situation if you're not even willing to talk to him."

"To who?" I asked, genuinely lost.

"Pete!"

At the mention of his name, my thoughts raced back to seeing the two of them backstage in what looked like an intimate moment, wondering if this was somehow connected. Seeing how upset she was, I convinced myself that it had to be as I took a deep breath in preparation for the hardest thing I'd ever have to ask my best friend.

"Okay," I said, shifting my weight, hating what I was about to ask. "Are you two, like, together or something?"

She recoiled as if I had physically hit her with her jaw dropping in shock. Her beautiful eyes, typically poised and confident now mirrored the pain of loss, hinting that I might have gone too far. With a limp flick of her wrist, she tossed her toothbrush into the sink, her gaze filled with the betrayal that my accusation implied.

"How could you ask me such a thing?" Her voice quivered.

The moment the words escaped my lips, I knew it was a mistake, but I was too desperate for answers, so I remained firm in my questioning.

"Well?"

"Honey," she said, looking at me like I had officially lost the plot. "I think the sun out here is frying your brain cells."

"*My* brain cells?" I pointed to myself. "What about yours? How much coke do you stuff up your nose every weekend?"

"Can we please get some for tonight?" Roxie chimed in from my bed.

"Yes!" Alex shouted as I yelled, "No!" at the same time.

"I really don't want to wake up half-naked next to some Grammy-nominated musician again," I attempted a joke, which looking at Alex's still expression, fell hopelessly flat.

"Wow, Carla, that's *such* a relatable problem," Alex quipped, her tone dripping in sarcasm usually reserved for people we couldn't stand. "Give me a second while I squeeze out a single tear for you."

We remained at a face-off for several long minutes until I could feel common sense begin to creep in. I waited though as I watched her anger reach its peak before slowly deflating like a last breath. I nodded my head thinking this wasn't us as fighting wasn't in our friendship's DNA. Beneath her mask of irritation, I knew were good intentions. We took a few deep breaths as I sat on the toilet seat, and her on the bathtub's edge. As our breathing leveled out, the tension lifted with an unspoken apology that neither of us needed to vocalize.

"La," she said quietly. "You know I love you."

I met her gaze with apologetic eyes. "I know you do," I said. "And I love you."

"Okay then will you please take back what you said about me being with him?" She dug her eyes into mine to express the severity of my implication. "You know I would *never* do that to you."

"I know you wouldn't." I shuddered at myself for even entertaining it.

"We don't do gross things like fight over boys, remember?"

"I know," I said, wincing at my own thoughts. "I don't know what I was thinking. I guess, this whole thing is making me crazy."

"I know it is, which is why you *need* to talk to him," she insisted. "You're imagining the worst. And maybe it's something completely different altogether."

I reached out, our hands meeting over the tiled floor as I gave her a squeeze. "What can I do to fix this?"

She looked at me like I once again had it all wrong.

"You don't have to fix things. I'm not your mother who blames you for her problems. I just think you need to face things and, once you do, you'll be surprised how much lighter you'll feel."

I gripped her hand tighter, signaling that I was really listening. "I promise I'll talk to him tomorrow."

"Good," she sounded reassured. "Because tonight, it's all about us."

"That's right," I vowed. "We're going to go to this party and dance and drink and do it up like it's your last night in town."

"It *is* my last night in town," she pointed out.

I smiled. "I know."

"So, no Pete drama?"

I held up my palm in scout's honor. "No Pete drama."

CHAPTER 27

Pete

Heading to what he termed the *hip* Hollywood party, we sat in Saturday Night traffic in his station wagon, the irony not lost on me. I told him he sounded like someone's dad when he called something hip. He retorted by calling me a drama queen, to which I gladly pointed to my new theatre camp shirt as proof of residence.

"You want to see a real drama queen though?" I threatened, reaching for his CD binder on the floor.

He tightly pulled air through his mouth. "You sure you want to do that?"

"We might as well get it out of the way."

After unzipping it, I flipped the pages, sighing over *American Idol* contestant debut albums, *Greatest Hits* of formerly great artists, and the *Totally 80's* compilation, whose commercial always played during *Beavis and Butthead*. To this day, I can't hear the chorus of "Everybody Wants to Rule the World" without hearing "Caribbean Queen" cutting it off. I chuckled to myself as I continued to turn the pages, revealing more sins of pop music's past. As much as I knew how much I'd enjoy torturing him with say, his Take That CD, I also knew it didn't matter. The old rock snob adage that what someone liked mattered more than what they *were* like didn't check out here.

Because I *did* like him — a model who had a weakness for hippie-themed ice cream, cared more about the environment than his face revealed and planted tropical flowers with elderly neighbors. His music taste was something we could get around, I accepted, just as my eyes landed on Kelly Clarkson's "A Moment Like This." Well, maybe a little playlist intervention wouldn't hurt.

I closed the book and looked at him.

"So, is it over?" he asked, desperate to keep a straight face.

I pretended to mull it over, chewing on my lower lip for effect, before tapping my knuckle on the window. "You might want to pull over here and let me out."

"I figured," he played along before breaking character to grab my leg. "What the hell am I going to do with you?"

"Everything?"

A smile snuck across his face. "I'm working on it."

He made a right onto Hollywood Boulevard, passing The Trop which that night had a sold-out Polka festival. Along the boulevard, instead of pulling into one of the paid parking lots with attendants waving flashlights to usher cars in, Misha pulled into a concrete parking structure of Bally Total Fitness. Slipping his gym membership card into the machine, we parked for free. I caught myself appreciating the ingenuity, discovering at 23, that this was a trait I found attractive in someone.

We arrived at the club, walking past the line of people pretending they didn't want to get in. Bored girls in blue eyeshadow wearing off-the-shoulder Pat Benatar and Blondie T-shirts made up most of the line. But there were also guys sporting black-framed glasses, which I could see from the side weren't prescription. Why anyone would wear fake glasses was beyond me, I thought as I pulled off my very real ones to wipe off a smudge.

As we breezed past the line, the people on it checked to see if we were someone worth craning their necks for. We weren't. We made it to the door where Misha introduced me to the famous scene partner. He went by Jazzy James and had confectionery powder pink hair and wore red patent leather shoes.

"We're at capacity," he said, unfastening the velvet rope for us, which let out a grumble from the people who would've been next. "And I just let in Chloë Sevigny. These people are going to skin me."

Misha and I exchanged bashful looks as we crept past him and the disgruntled line.

"Thanks, JJ," Misha said, reaching back for my hand like I was his boyfriend.

"Have fun, boys," Jazzy James sang out before snapping his head to the line of pissed off people. "If you don't like it, the Saddle Ranch on The Strip is where the new arrivals go!"

We walked down the dark basement steps, my hand still in his as the urgency of "House of Jealous Lovers" thrashed from below. As we got closer to the sound, the air densified with the smell of body odor and cheap booze. Once downstairs, I could only see the people in my direct line of vision of mostly dancing bodies. Every so often a bright flash would go off, burning the image of whatever was in front of me into my cornea for a few seconds. As Misha guided me through the crowd, a girl with a side ponytail and pupils as large as black olives stopped in front of me.

"You'd look cute with this on," she declared, stretching a sweatband over my head before drifting off like it never happened. I immediately reached for it, feeling the terry cloth material pressed against my forehead as I bristled at the idea. Just as I was about to take it off, Misha reached for my hand.

"Keep it," he said, tangling his fingers in mine. "You look like a feisty tennis player."

"You can't be serious."

"I am." He pressed his lips against my ear. "We'll have fun with it later."

With a flirtatious roll of the eyes, I said, "Only for you."

Wearing this ridiculous thing, together we shouldered our way through the crowd to get to the makeshift bar. At the small table tucked away in a corner, stacked with plastic cups and a handle of vodka, I caught Misha smirking at the label where I immediately recognized the look on his face.

"That doesn't mean anything, does it?" I asked.

"No." He chuckled, pointing to it. "These random backward letters aren't even in our alphabet, so not only is this not a word, it's also unpronounceable."

I smiled in recognition, reminding me of when my dad and I would come across incorrectly used or flat-out made-up words in French. Misha and I exchanged a quick, amused glance when a cute bartender in a faded Joy Division T-shirt turned around with eyebrows raised in expectation. "What'll it be, guys?"

"I'm having a Sprite," Misha announced, addressing both the bartender and me. "And you?"

I quickly assessed the selection, seeing they also had a metal tub where beer cans floated like dead bodies in the pool of melted ice. I leaned closer to see it was Pabst Blue Ribbon Light. *Light?* I thought, surprised at the redundancy, since PBR itself was the gold standard in watered-down beer. I weighed my options, knowing the beer was pretty much flavored water, but I also didn't want black market vodka that came in a plastic jug.

"I'll have a Sprite, too."

As the bartender poured the sodas into cups, I leaned into Misha's ear. "So, do you not drink?"

He shook his head.

Sensing my curiosity, he elaborated, "My father drank and even if he's sober now, I figured why start a pointless decline into middle age with stuff I don't even like the taste of."

"But wasn't it your dad who got you vodka as a housewarming gift?"

He pushed out a smile. "That's my father for you."

As the first sip of cold, citrusy soda went down, its brightness tickling my throat, the DJ seamlessly transitioned from The Rapture song into "I Want More" by CAN. I looked at Misha as if the second coming had arrived in a moldy basement club.

"You're kidding me!" I shouted over the music.

He looked at my soda, thinking it was related. "What's wrong?"

"Nothing! Nothing at all!" I placed a hand on my head, feeling like it might just fucking explode. Here I was, in this "hip" Hollywood club, hearing the last song I ever expected they'd play. Yet, there it was, one of my drum heroes, filling the room with his cyclical, even-grooved drumming as if speaking to me, telling me it was okay to have a good time.

"I just love this song!" I cried out.

"I've never heard of it!"

Given his CD collection, it hardly came as a surprise. Nonetheless, I took our sodas and placed them on a nearby ledge to pull him onto the dance floor.

"So, you do dance!" he said, his eyes bright with surprise.

"I do when the music's good!"

Feeling nothing but pure liberation, I reached for him, snaking my arms around his neck. Together, we moved as if the German dance song was meant just for us as the crowd closed in on us, the floor packed with moving bodies. I liked the way our lemon zest breath played with my senses, tickling my nose. The music went from CAN into a track by !!!, further stoking the crowd's enthusiasm before easing smoothly into a Postal Service song. I glanced over at the DJ, her blonde bob moving with the music and felt grateful for her medicinal talent, selecting music that felt therapeutic. Then, in an instant, it felt like the room was going to explode when the sudden, electrifying surge of violins from "Toxic" began. (A Britney Spears song I only knew because of Victoria.) The energy felt so intense, it threatened to shatter the brick walls making me feel like we might get pummeled over. With no space left between us, I could feel his pelvis grind against mine as we moved in ways that, if we continued, would make a mess out of the both of us.

"I know *this* song!" he announced proudly.

I dropped my head onto his shoulder for a moment before looking back at him and smiling. "I'm sure you do."

We danced as a camera flashed every few minutes, momentarily bleaching the scene. The humidity rose, dampening our T-shirts with every beat we moved to. I reached for his arms that I had spent the weekend holding onto in various positions and drew them tighter around my waist. His hands found their way under my shirt, pressing himself even closer to me, causing my eyes to flutter back in surrender. Amidst the sea of bodies, the years of my suppressed desires dissolved into a heady intoxication of freedom. I guided his hands further up my shirt without a care who saw, as we moved together, the friction amplifying the thrill.

In celebration of my newfound freedom, I reached for his face, guiding my lips to his. Kissing him, he tasted like him, which I now knew was warm, a little sweet, and if soft had a flavor, it would be this. Despite our practically bruised lips from endless weekend kisses, the dizziness of our first one returned, now paired with a high that I was his for the night. My grip on his shirt tightened, feeling like I couldn't get close enough to him. At that instant, I craved more.

"Let's go," I said, taking his hand to leave the club.

Carla

We arrived at the unmarked club and nearly gasped when we saw the line. It stretched out of the alley, snaking around Hollywood Boulevard. We trailed behind Roxie as she passed the line of club-goers, with a few heads turning in recognition. At the door loomed an intimidating looking guy with pink hair, clipboard in hand, and chin raised. I braced myself for rejection, recalling scenes in movies when this happened. Even though Ted had put us "on the list", something about saying it out loud felt, well, douchey like the lyrics to a bad pop song. Thankfully, we had Roxie who didn't seem equipped with those fears and stomped as fast as her platformed heels could carry her.

"JJ!" she called out, embracing the door guy like an old friend.

"Hello, my love," he said as they hugged, keeping their arms at a distance to protect their complicated hairstyles.

She then stepped back to admire him, nodding her head in approval. "I see we've gone pink," she said. "Very nice."

He patted his hair proudly before shooting a judgmental glance. "Like two weeks ago." He raised his eyebrows. "Where have you been?"

"I just got back from a quickie East Coast tour," she said with a faux frown. "But I'm home now."

"Well, good, come by tomorrow for tea and gossip." He unclasped the velvet rope and leaned toward her. "These people are going to murder me. I said they were next, and I just let Jenny

Lewis and her little Marc Jacobs bag in and now you." A salacious grin took over his face. "I'm going to have to do, like, ten Hail Marys tonight because I am plain awful."

"You're plain fabulous," Roxie said as she puckered her lips to plant a kiss.

"Have fun, my little foxes," he said to us as Alex and I thanked him in passing.

We walked into a hallway even darker than the alley. It took a moment for my eyes to adjust as we descended the uneven concrete steps, my hand gripping the sticky banister. Each step down brought us closer to what felt like a wall of sound as the rapid pulse of "Such Great Heights" reverberated against my chest. In front of me, Roxie wobbled in her metallic platform boots, while Alex and I patiently kept up in our sneakers.

Before stepping down from the final step, I looked out over the crowd, seeing the tops of heads and bouncing shoulders glow in the heat of the club lights. A bright flash then whitewashed the space, exposing sweaty faces and vibrant clothing bursting into view. We navigated through the crowd, our heads still bobbing to the Postal Service song when suddenly the atmosphere shifted like the arrival of a storm. The unmistakable intro of "Toxic," sliced through the club like lightning, sparking a total frenzy with Alex and Roxie screaming, "Britney!"

The crowd surged like a human tidal wave, dragging us with it, which forced my bag off my shoulder. Immediately, I dropped to the floor to find that the strap had snapped off with my contents spilling out. Alex joined me, helping me swat at the dancing legs and moving ankles to stop them from stepping on my things. In the chaos, we had a girl's butt in our face, a heel that narrowly missed my tube of ChapStick, while another foot cracked Pete's half of the Santa Monica Pier keychains. I didn't want it to feel symbolic and pretended not to notice. Alex respected the significance, though, by quickly gathering the broken pieces and tucking them into my bag's inner pocket.

"It's fine," I shouted over the music. "I'll just throw it away at the bar."

"No," she asserted, closing the zipper for safe keeping. "We'll glue it later."

"Really, it's okay," I said, blowing it off in part of keeping my promise of no Pete drama. I looked at her like it was time for me to move on, but she didn't seem to buy my shrug-off.

"We'll fix it tomorrow," she insisted, taking my hand to help me up. "Now, come on, we're about to miss the best pop song of the century."

When we popped back up, we found Roxie scanning the crowd over our heads as if searching for someone. I looked around partly hoping for Ted but when I didn't see him, I shot her an inquisitive look.

"This might sound weird," she shouted, still squinting in the direction of the stairs. "But I think I just saw the guy in your band."

Alex and I looked around for a second before consulting each other with a look of doubt. Shaking our heads, we told Roxie that it wasn't possible, but she seemed almost offended by our unified certainty on the subject.

"Why not?" she asked.

"It would be too contrived for him here," Alex explained, holding back a chuckle. "Meaning he'd never come to a party like this." When we could see she was still annoyed, Alex placated her, "Okay, what was this guy wearing?"

"A T-shirt," Roxie replied in which we were forced to politely nod our heads because sure, Pete would be wearing one. "And this, like, Richie Tennenbaum tennis sweatband thingy on his forehead."

Both of us knowing Pete didn't do fashion irony, we couldn't help but chuckle while shooting her an apologetic look.

"We're not making fun of you," Alex said as I nodded along. "If anything, we're making fun of him because he's so…. *him*," she explained, waving her hands to imply he was in his own world.

I couldn't help but agree as I looked around, unable to imagine him in a place like this. "It was someone who probably looked like him," I added to our theory. "That's all."

Roxie seemed to have already lost interest in the subject and was now eyeing a cute bartender in a faded Joy Division T-shirt. A Smiths song then came on, rivaling the excitement of Britney as she eyed the bar offerings. Next to me, Alex cooed the lyrics to the saddest dance music to ever exist, throwing her head back like it was feeding her soul. As we swayed to it, I wondered what the weekend would have looked like had she not come out but decided to stop the what-if from planting roots because she was there now.

As the bartender lined up shots that made the air smell like a First Aid kit, I relinquished all inner chatter knowing the only person I needed to be with was with me right now.

Pete

When we got home our exploration deepened in unexpected ways. Just when I thought we'd settled into our roles, Misha took pleasure in reversing them by letting me do to him what he had been doing to me all weekend. Lying on my back, I admired his body as he guided himself up and down on me. With his eyes lost in the pleasure of having me inside of him, I felt like we had invented a new form of intimacy together. I pulled myself up to kiss him, tasting the salt of his skin working my way up to his lips, wanting every part of me inside of him.

"Who knew you were so sweet?" he whispered.

"Shhh." I smiled on his lips. "Don't tell anyone."

"Is it just for me?"

I nodded that it was, taking him deeper into my mouth.

Afterwards, I sat up in bed, the sheets pulled up to my waist. While he prepared peanut butter and jelly with banana sandwiches in the kitchen, I flipped through an odd script I found from a pile on the floor. My eyes followed the highlighted scenes for the part of "Agent Busy Body," which I assumed was his. When he returned, I held up the script.

"You were in a play called *Poo Poo Goes to Hollywood*?"

"I was," he replied, thankfully seeing the humor in my question. "And I got paid for that one too."

"Wait." I dropped the script onto my lap. "You sometimes don't get paid?"

"For plays?" He returned my look of shock, handing me the tray. "You usually *don't* get paid. Well, not for the small ones, which is what we mostly have out here."

"Then why do it?"

"For the love of acting, of course," he said with breathy theatrics.

"Not for the *Respect for Acting*?" I nodded toward the technique book on his dresser, its cover adorned with a woman in various dramatic poses.

"Hey," he warned playfully. "Don't mess with Uta."

Once he settled in next to me, I handed him one of the sandwiches. As we bit into them, we released sounds of satisfaction at the much-needed sustenance. We washed our meal down with chocolate milk, sweet enough that the sugar crunched between my teeth.

After, he set the plates on the floor and stretched onto his side. With his head rested on his bicep, he looked at me with tired, contented eyes. Feeling overwhelmed with tranquility, a sort of peaceful haze of being both nourished and freshly fucked, I realized I hadn't smoked a cigarette in almost twenty-four hours. As we lay there, our naked bodies facing each other, it felt like there was nothing between us. Just our tired selves and the smell of peanut butter on our fingers.

"Tell me something," I said, brushing a stray hair away from his face. "Why are you taking French classes? It doesn't seem like a very fun language to learn as a hobby."

"It's sort of a boring story," he said, flicking his eyes up dismissively.

"I'm not here to be entertained."

His eyes wandered for a moment, as if evaluating the cost of revealing more. A flicker of hesitation crossed his face before his gaze returned to mine, finding reassurance in me.

"Alright." He tucked in closer pulling my leg over his hip. "It's just more of my dad's bullshit." I remained silent, noting the recurring theme. "When I was in junior high, I started taking French—"

"Junior high?" I said, not meaning to cut him off. "I assumed college when you noted you had taken French in school."

"No, I was eleven but for some reason a lot of the basics you seemed to be so impressed with," he raised his eyebrows at me, "I somehow remembered."

"I was not *impressed*."

"You were *so* impressed."

"Anyway, go on with your story." I batted my eyelashes in playful defeat.

"*Anyway*," he continued, "my dad thought French was useless since we live here in SoCal."

"Useless?" I was careful not to make a judgmental face.

"My dad's theory was that I would never need it in the 'real world,'" he tossed a glance my way, "whatever that means. But it was me who had the last laugh when I was sent to Paris for Fashion Week one year, where French seemed *somewhat* useful."

"And it's one of the official languages of the UN," I added, hoping I didn't sound annoying.

"Another thing my father finds useless."

"Oh, wow, okay," I said, getting a better sense of his dad's views.

"I was always his excuse to drink. This was, of course, only a preview for five years later when I really gave him something to drink about..." his voice trailed off as he looked off, appearing to revisit the painful memory. "His theory was—or rather, *is* — that I'm choosing to be gay just to spite him."

I let out a heavy sigh, reminding me of my uncle's disproportionate reaction to my cousin's coming out.

"What about your mom?" I gently probed.

"My mom, bless her, defended me, which he then used as an excuse to leave our family and start a shiny new one up in Santa Barbara. He sobered up and now plays the perfect dad for my half-brothers." He took a deep breath. "So, why am I taking French? To say, "fuck you" to my father."

He fell onto his back as if finishing a sprint. As he stared at the ceiling, I could feel him thinking and decided to let him be until he signaled a return to the conversation.

"I know I now have the benefit of adult logic," he eventually said, still looking up at the ceiling, "but the burden of believing my dad's issues were somehow my fault still haunts me, so I try to live the exact opposite life of my dad."

"That makes sense," I said softly. "If you don't mind me asking, what does he do?"

He looked at me for a moment as if measuring his words. "He's a psychiatrist," he replied with a wry smile even though I knew there was nothing funny about it. "They really do make terrible parents. Well, at least mine did."

Not wanting to offer platitudes or ask questions that didn't add value, I did what felt right and took his hand to gently pull him closer to me. He melted into my arms where I combed my fingers through his hair, as we let ourselves simply breathe together.

"Sorry for the therapy session going on here." He let out a nervous laugh.

I kissed the top of his head. "Talking is good."

I wanted to add that his dad sounded like an asshole and wondered why he even spoke to him, but I had learned from Carla that some families don't know any better than to exist in dysfunction.

"I've made a nice life for myself, though," he said dreamily, relaxing in my touch. "So, I try to look forward instead of back." I could tell he meant it as he took long, satisfied inhalations as if appreciating the moment.

"And what about you?" he whispered. "Have any ghost stories? Or are French-office-administrator-slash-rock-drummers immune to bad memories?"

I chuckled, imagining such a thing. "Do I give you that impression?"

"A little bit," he said softly as he tipped his head up to meet my gaze. "You're just so assured, it seems like nothing could break you."

"Of course I've been broken."

I considered sharing my own story and the ripple effect it had on me. I wanted him included in the select few that I would expose my emotional scars to, but there was someone else I needed to tell first. I owed it to her.

CHAPTER 28

Carla

Despite their efforts, Alex and Roxie didn't score their drugs. Sniffing around the club, their noses twitching like airport hounds, they complained they couldn't smell any "cocaine farts". I felt compelled to remind them that not smelling gas in an enclosed space with the humidity of Palm Springs was *probably* a good thing. It was a bleak day when I was the voice of reason.

When the lights flicked on after the last song, exposing raw, partied-out faces, we decided against looking for an after-party. Roxie said we weren't high enough to want to see daylight with any of these people, to which Alex agreed with the severity of a political take. Instead, we piled into a taxi, heading back to my place to polish off the jug of wine and to cook whatever I had — frozen veggie burgers, scrambled eggs with salsa, and stale tortillas that tasted like paint chips. Laughter echoed through my apartment, prompting my upstairs neighbor to stomp in irritation, which only fueled our teenage giggles even more. The night ended with the three of us packed in my bed, playing a game of "Would You Rather?"

Would I rather never play music again with Pete or drink a poo shake? (With soy milk, Roxie thoughtfully added, in case I was lactose intolerant.)

Would Alex rather go on tour with the Weekend Warriors or marry the Paul Giamatti guy whom she could only communicate with on Craigslist Missed Connections?

Would Roxie rather 69 Roy G. Biv or do a duet with Greenday?

When she confessed she already had 69'd Roy G. Biv, the room went silent as a dark hush settled over us. I dug my nail into my thigh in a desperate bid to choke back laughter that I feared would embarrass her as I simultaneously fought off images of Roy G. Biv's crotch in her face.

"It's okay, guys," her voice cut through the darkness. "You can laugh. He's really fucking gross."

"Oh, thank God," Alex exhaled, and with that release, our laughter burst forth like a breached dam. As I doubled over with a fiery ache in my gut, it set off more foot stomping from my neighbor. The night dwindled down with our laughter petering out, followed by an unfortunate description of the shape of Roy G. Biv's penis before fading into soft murmurs and eventually sleep.

Daylight came with the sound of pounding in what felt like minutes later. Unsure if it was my hangover, my neighbor, or something else, I looked over at Joni on the couch who simply blinked in the direction of the door as if telepathically answering my question.

"Honey!" Barbie's voice sounded frantic. "Open the door!"

I stumbled out of bed, almost tripping over Roxie's boots as I reached for the door. Half-dressed and half-witted, I opened it to find her standing with her hands on her hips and backed up by the Los Angeles Fire Department looking like the cover of a Blondie album.

"The neighbors smell gas!" she bellowed, shooing me aside to let the firefighters in as Joni booked it out the door. I looked around in disbelief, feeling it was a repeat of the night before because how were we still talking about smelling gas?

"Don't just stand there!" she barked. "Open the windows!"

Suddenly realizing what she was saying, panic set in as I bolted across the room to open the windows. In bed, the girls were startled awake with Alex pulling my comforter up to her neck and Roxie blinking around the room in confusion.

"What's going on?" Alex asked, her eyes following the men in full gear charging through my apartment.

"The neighbors smell gas and think it's coming from here," I explained, my voice tense, turning toward the kitchen at the sound of my stove scraping against the floor. "It can't be though, right?" I sought an explanation from the girls, who were clearly still processing the sight of the uniformed men.

"Were you girls cooking last night?" Barbie shouted from the kitchen.

"We were," I called out. "Why?"

"Well, you knuckleheads didn't completely turn off the stove!"

In stunned silence, I turned to Roxie and Alex, wanting to pin the blame on one of them, but I honestly couldn't recall who used it last. As the sound of the firemen's radios cracked with urgency, I braced myself for a lecture as I heard Barbie's heels approaching.

"Who smokes here?" she asked, her voice eerily calm. "I know you do." She pointed to Alex before settling on Roxie. "And what about you, Missy?"

Roxie raised her hand, her guilt evident. "Sometimes."

"I thought so," Barbie said, her gaze sweeping across us like we were suspects in a line-up. "All three of you girls could be dead right now." She then zeroed in on me, reserving the iciest glare. "And you could have killed Joni."

She surveyed the scene: the empty wine jug, the bowl overflowing with cigarette butts, and finally, to our bleary, hungover faces. I bowed my head knowing what she was thinking. She had warned me about this, and there I was, barely dressed, with the fire department in my kitchen, sitting in her silent "I told you so."

"Drinking is fun and games until people start dying," she scolded us, making sure she equally met all three sets of eyes.

We remained silent with shoulders hunched, feeling and looking small. We apologized to Barbie and then the firemen, who reiterated her lecture on how lucky we were. As I escorted them out, Barbie tapped the top of my head. "This is your get out of jail free card. Learn from this."

"I will."